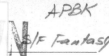
Zombie
Alive

Copyright 2012 Mark Tufo

Discover other titles by Mark Tufo
Visit us at marktufo.com
and http://zombiefallout.blogspot.com/ home of future
webisodes
also, find me on FACEBOOK

Cover Design by http://www.ebooklaunch.com

Dedications:

To my wife who makes all of this possible and still puts up with me! (Even if she didn't like that one scene with the sc…oh wait you guys haven't read that yet…never mind) Honey, I love you, I write it even though I know written words cannot truly express the meaning.

To the men and women that serve our great country, I will always appreciate the sacrifices you perform on a daily basis, a salute to each and every one of you.

To the New York Giants (2012) YES!!!!

To my most awesome of readers, without you folks I am merely someone poking at a keyboard with two fingers if you've ever contacted me you already know how I feel about all of you!

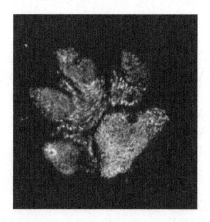

Riley

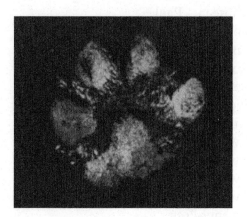

King Henry

Table of Contents

Foreword

Hello Dear Reader,

If you find this journal, let us start with the basics. My name is Michael Talbot; I am/was the owner of the material you now hold in your hand. My life has been one living hell after another since the age of around eighteen when I tripped on some bad mushrooms and cursed to the gods about my lot in life. Since then, I have been relegated to alternate horrific realities. In some I am younger, some I am older, some I live through and some I don't. (I still have a hard time writing down that I have died on no less than three accounts.)

The only constant is that I am aware of what is happening, but the people I encounter along the way are not. Some are threaded throughout my lives and show up constantly, like my soul mate, Tracy, and my best friend, Paul. Some appear in one reality but not another for some reason, like Mrs. Deneaux (thank God for that, at least). Some enemies remain the same, like Durgan, others not so much. I have been hunted down by zombies, aliens, ghosts, and a few other creatures from the depths of a mad god's deranged mind.

I can't imagine that the Big Man has taken any interest. My guess is that I have pissed off one of the lesser gods (imagine that), one of the Greek or Roman deities who have been relegated to paganism since Christianity took hold. I'm not even sure if the true God is aware of my plight; and if he is, why does he not rein his wayward children in?

So I write these journals; mostly to keep my mind from addling and to keep my multiple horrors compartmentalized. So when you feel the need to complain about your lot in life, be careful who is listening and be very specific on what changes you would like to have made.

Each misadventure that I have, in no way reflects on the other. They are not a continuation of any other story. One does not need to read my Zombie Journals to know what happened on Indian Hill or even at The Spirit Clearing, but they should be aware that the main person (me) is always present. I do not know when this god will tire of his plaything...if ever. For me, the nightmare has been going on for decades. For him (or her – it wouldn't be the first female I've pissed off), it may only be seconds. I look forward to one day having a normal life, if such a thing is still possible.

So if you find this and you are a pious person, I would welcome your prayers to whomever you deem a higher authority. Maybe your entreaties will not fall on deaf ears like mine have.

Chapter One

"What now, sister?" Tomas asked.

"We kill Michael Talbot, his family, and his friends and then we rule this world," she said absently as she fingered the locket around her neck.

"You've gotten more than you could have ever asked for, Eliza. Why not just leave him alone?" Tomas asked with chagrin.

"Why, dear brother, are you concerned for him? Do you still carry some vestiges of your humanity? Do not worry…that will fade with time," Eliza said with a sneer, her canines flashing menacingly.

"You have it wrong, Eliza. It is not him I am concerned about, it is us. He has shown over and over that he is unwilling to yield to death."

Eliza struck so fast, Tomas did not have time to defend himself against his sister's slap, and it rocked him on his heels. "He is a pathetic human," Eliza spat. "I will never fear him or any of his kind again! Do you understand me?"

Tomas nodded, dumbfounded.

"You, Tomas, are now the reason that we have something to fear from him. Without our help, he will never die. Once his family dies and is ground into dust, we," Eliza said, pointing to him and to herself, "will become his sole mission in life. He will blame us for every one of their deaths. No, we must kill him while he still has weaknesses walking on this planet. You, Tomas, have prevented Michael Talbot from eking out the rest of his existence in relative peace."

Tomas knew his sister's words for the lie that they

were, but still they stung. "Eliza, break the stone," Tomas said pointing to the blood locket. "We can leave this world like we were supposed to lifetimes ago."

Eliza looked at Tomas long and hard before she began to laugh, much like a wolf laughs at the rabbit before devouring it. Cold, cruel and with no mirth.

"That's rich, Tomas, for a second, I almost believed you. Not that I would have done it, mind you, but I almost believed in your sincerity. How cunningly perfect of you! I break the locket, you rule the world unimpeded."

"I do not want the world, Eliza, I want my sister," Tomas begged.

Eliza's laughter encompassed his soul as he spun on his heel and walked away.

Tomas was about a city block away before the echoes of her laughter faded.

"Tomas," came so clearly in his head, he stopped and looked around for the source.

"Mr. T?" Tomas asked.

"Tommy?" came the question.

"He's in here somewhere, Mr. T, he…I…we're so tired."

Michael's heart sank, hearing the pain in his adopted son's voice. *"Is there anything I can do?"*

"Kill my sister so that I can be released." Tomas could "hear" the gasp from the other end of the connection.

"I never thought I'd hear those words from you, Tommy. Does it work like that? Will all those bitten by her revert back to their former selves, like in the movies?"

"No," Tomas said, shaking his head silently and conveying that gesture to Mike. *"But it will release me to join her."*

Michael got the message. If Eliza were to die, Tomas would join her in the afterlife. *"Where do us soulless ones go, Tomas?"* Michael asked, his fear shining through the words brightly.

"Nowhere near the garden, Mr. T. It is a lonely, dark place we are destined for, but even that is preferable to the hell I walk in now."

"How charming," Eliza said as she approached Tomas. "We will have to talk, Tomas, about your choice of friends. I do not think Mother would approve."

"Eliza, the pleasure I receive when I finally sever your head from your body will only be trumped by the look of shock on your fa…"

And, like an old AT&T operator, Eliza severed the connection, or so she thought.

"I will kill him, Tomas, and you *will* help if I have to drag you kicking and screaming through the blood and guts of the mortals."

"I'll be there, Eliza, but it will only be to witness your demise," Tomas said heatedly.

"We are family, Tomas…you and I. Is this how you would treat one of your own?"

"Mr. T and his family are my true family!" Tomas shot back defiantly.

"Blood!" Eliza said fairly quaking. "Blood is the thickest bond, Tomas. It is something which you share nothing of with that mongrel!"

"I do now, sister. Remember? I bit him."

"You are a fool, Tomas. You jeopardize everything we have and everything we can attain, for what?"

"Love, Eliza, for love, the most basic and strongest of all human emotions."

"Hate, Tomas, hate is a much stronger emotion because it can burn longer, it can span generations. I've watched it spread across borders for no other reason than there were people on the other side of an imaginary line in the dirt. Love lasts for a few years between individuals, hate spans millennia among the populace."

"If that is the case, then let him have his few years of love. There will still be time for hate afterwards."

"You still don't understand. There is no fun in defeating an opponent once everything he has is lost. Much like a fine wine, it can be savored as we pull him apart, piece by piece."

"Hey! I'm still here. I can hear everything you're saying about me and I've got to be honest, I'm not all that pleased," Mike said, trying to inflect some levity in his words.

Tomas could not help but smile, shielding it somewhat from the raging form of his sister.

"How?" Eliza demanded.

"Not sure. I guess it's some sort of party line, looks like we'll be able to stay in touch a lot," Michael said. *"Maybe I'll be able to sing you some lullabies or read you a bedtime story...you seem to get real cranky without enough sleep."*

Tomas had to turn so that his sister could not witness his delight, although the rising and falling of his shoulders was a dead giveaway.

Chapter Two – Mike Journal Entry 1

"You alright, Mike?" BT asked with concern.

"I'm fine. Why? Do I look bad?" I asked him with the same concern. I didn't want to start turning into that pasty-looking version of Tom Cruise in *Interview with a Vampire*. He always looked anemic, although how that was possible after drinking all that iron-rich blood, I'll never know.

"Well, to be honest, you've looked better, but that's not why I'm asking. You were just standing there, and then this shit-eating grin spread across your face. You looked like you had maybe just taken a shit in your pants and you didn't want anyone to know. That sort of thing."

"That's pretty graphic, my friend. I've got an idea."

"Oh no, why do I ask? Why, God?" BT asked as he turned his head up to the heavens.

"What's going on?" Tracy asked. The activity of the last few days was weighing heavily on her shoulders, fearing for her children and now for her husband. Tracy could not gauge if BT were wailing to the heavens or merely jesting for Mike.

"Your husband has an idea," BT said seriously, never pulling his gaze from the clouds that flew by overhead, oblivious to the prayers that drifted through them, seeking a higher purpose.

"Mike, we've gone over this time and time again," Tracy said, placing her hand on BT's side in commiseration.

"I know, I know," I told them. "But this time, it's going to work."

"Heard that before," Gary said from twenty feet across the parking lot of the Big 5 Sporting Goods store they were in the midst of ransacking. Most everything of any value was long gone, but there were a few small caliber rifles and bricks of .22 bullets, some camping gear, a few packs of dehydrated food and, for some abnormal reason, pallets of knee-high socks. It looked like the World Cup was coming to North Carolina soon.

"No, I've got insider information now," I told them.

Tracy's head bowed as she realized I was talking about Eliza. It was one thing to know about her, completely another to be linked to her.

"She's coming for us," I told them.

BT threw his hands to his face. "Shocker!" he exclaimed.

Tracy punched him so hard in the arm, he actually stepped back a few inches.

"Damn, woman! If I could crane my neck far enough down to see you, I'd swat you away like a fly," BT bellowed.

"Hey, this is pretty cool, I'm usually the one in the middle of the shit storm."

"Shut up, Talbot!" BT and Tracy said in unison, and then they high-fived. Well, to be fair, Tracy way high fived and BT went way low, but it was the same thing, sort of.

"Okay, no shit, we all know she's coming. But I know when and how. I think it's time we went on the offensive."

"I'm listening," Brian said, carrying his third load of socks to the car. "What?" he said as he dropped them in the backseat. "I like to have clean feet; it's an Army thing."

"So you gleaned all this info from her?" BT asked, reluctant to use her name.

I nodded, maybe just a little too enthusiastically.

"Close your mouth when you're nodding, Talbot," Tracy said, "You look like the village idiot."

"Any chance she fed you some misinformation?" Brian asked.

"First off, I think she's probably too arrogant for

that," I said. "I think she'd tell us willingly what she planned on doing, probably thinking there was nothing we could do to stop it," I told the growing group. Gary and Justin nodded in agreement. "But no, I'm pretty sure she had no clue I was eavesdropping on her."

"Whew, buddy," BT said, rubbing his hand over the top of his head. "This isn't like solving the puzzle on Wheel of Fortune."

I stopped him there. "BT, don't tell me you watch Wheel of Fortune?"

"What in the hell is wrong with Wheel of Fortune? Vanna White is a goddess."

I shrugged, I had to agree with him there. She might be a few revolutions of the globe past her prime, but who amongst us had never fantasized about her turning our letters on? Okay, poor sexual innuendo, but it gets the point across.

"So you were saying?" Tracy asked BT as she pushed me to wake me from my Vanntasy. (See? That was much better!)

"No offense, buddy," BT said, "but your ideas suck ass."

For the second time in a matter of seconds, I found myself agreeing with BT. "Granted. But I'm sick of running, I want her to re-think her strategy, I want to bleed her this time," I said with anger.

"You are not talking that 'last stand' shit again, are you, Talbot?" Tracy flared. "Because if you are, I will drag your sorry ass out of here by your balls, upside down!"

BT, Gary, Paul, and even MJ, who was not paying us any attention, covered up their privates in a mutual shared sympathy.

Justin nearly split his side laughing. Travis was shaking his head from side to side, in disbelief that he had just heard those words issued from his mother's mouth.

When I felt I could safely remove my hand from my nether regions, I continued, although I have to admit I had turned a slight degree or two away from Tracy, so as not to give her easy reaching access to my cherished jewels. "No, no I promise no John Wayne stuff. I want her to feel some of the trepidation that we do every waking second. I want her to think that maybe her next breath might be her last."

"Mike, vamps don't breathe," Gary said.

"Analogy, brother, just an analogy."

"Gotcha," he said, clicking his tongue and pointing at me with his index finger.

Well, let's get this part out of the way, I thought to myself. "Tracy, I still want you and Meredith and the boys to head back to Ron's. The sooner you can get MJ back there and working on his wonder boxes I keep hearing about, the better; and this gambit should buy us plenty of time."

She looked at me coldly with her battleship-gray eyes. I waited silently for the tempest within to be unleashed. It never came. "You swear to me, Talbot, that this is not one of your do-or-die stunts, and I will do as you ask."

"Really?" I asked incredulously. "I honestly wasn't expecting that."

"The window of opportunity is closing," she said forcefully.

"Yeah, yeah, yeah," I said quickly. "No, it's not any sort of final encounter."

"Then you teach that bitch that messing with the Talbots means you have hell to pay!"

"Sweet," I told her. "Who wants to stay for the fireworks show?" I asked the growing crowd.

"'Bout fucking time," Deneaux replied, clapping her hands together and rubbing them briskly.

"You're in?" I asked her, unconvinced.

"Wouldn't miss it for the world," she told me, dead serious.

"Huh. What a weird friggin' day," I said, shaking my head.

"What do you need and what's the plan?" Brian

asked.

Like the vast majority of my plans, it was long in thought and very short on words. As I write that, it doesn't make much sense. Suffice to say, it basically boils down to an ambush, followed by the death of a bunch of her henchmen. If we're really lucky, Eliza catches one in that tainted melon of hers.

"Mike, as the only black member of this dysfunctional group, I'm truly amazed that I'm still alive. I mean I've watched almost every horror movie ever made, and without fail, if a man of color is in the movie, he dies first. In recent years, however, it has gotten somewhat better. Now, we sometimes make it to second killed, after the ditzy blonde, but I've got to imagine that a brother's life expectancy in any horror setting is generally a couple of hours, at most."

"I agree with your movie assessment, BT, but how does that apply right now?" I asked him.

"Alright, hear me out…so me still being alive bucks that trend, right?" I nodded in agreement. "But damn, Mike, you keep breaking the cardinal sin of all flicks."

"The splitting up, I know, I know. I feel like the idiot that says, 'Yeah I'll go down to the basement alone to check out the breaker box, and I only have this one wooden match to light my way. Oh, and did I mention that we heard suspicious sounds down there only moments earlier?'"

"Yeah, like that, so you know what I'm talking about."

"Sure I do. I'm usually the one asking the characters on the screen what the hell they're thinking."

"Well, what are you thinking?"

"Well, it is dark and the basement does house the breaker box and my match is the extra-long, barbecue-style."

"I wonder if I could catch up to Alex?" BT wondered.

"I want my family out of here, BT. If only I could I'd send them to some lonely outpost on the moon to get away from this crap. Their safety means everything to me. They're the air I breathe, the food I eat, the…"

"I get it. Don't go getting all soft on me."

"Too much information?" I asked him sincerely.

"I'm starting to see under all that Marine Corps veneer. Are you sure it wasn't the Peace Corps? Don't worry, I won't tell anyone."

"I wonder if Alex would come back and get you."

"You think he's alright?" BT asked.

"I don't know, buddy, but he keeps breaking that cardinal rule, too."

"He sure does," BT said as he walked away.

"Paul, are you sure about this?" I asked my best friend for the better part of three decades. Damn! That makes me sound so old. And then the realization of my eternity slammed into my chest. My best friend, with whom I had shared so many experiences, would be a distant memory as I strode through the world, unencumbered by love. Would I bother with humanity at that point? The only reason I still interacted with people now was because of my wife and kids. If she were to be gone, then what? Would God forgive me? Would it even be considered suicide? I had already made my bed when I traded my soul for my family's safety. I was pretty sure I was on the top of God's shit list and I can guarantee that is not anywhere you want to be, just ask the '04 Yankees. They'll tell you the same thing.

But what of Nicole's baby? I would have to stay alive long enough to make sure he or she was able to find their way through this world. And then if he/she had kids, what then? When would I stop? Would I follow them through millennia, much like Tommy had followed his sister? Each passing day would push me that much further away from the inevitable death I was so seeking. Banned from the Garden, the alternative was excruciatingly painful, if only because I had glimpsed the beauty of it all.

"Talbot, we're leaving," Tracy said, stroking my

cheek, and wiping away a tear. "You alright, husband?" she asked tenderly. "You haven't changed your mind on this, right? No Rambo stuff?"

"What?" Gary asked from the entrance to the Big 5.

"Rambo!" Tracy yelled. "Not Gambo!"

"Gotcha," Gary repeated with the tongue clicking and finger pointing gesture.

"I'll be glad if just to get away from his new mannerism," Tracy said, smiling.

"I'll miss you, wife, but I promise this will be only for a couple of days, max."

"She's that close?" she asked. "She's relentless."

"That's one word. Mine would be much more colorful and would end up being all those funny symbols you see in the Sunday comics when Al Capp swears."

"Al Capp? Nobody reads Al Capp anymore, Talbot. What's wrong with you?"

"You'd think you would have figured it out after all these years," I retorted.

"You know you're nuts, right?" she asked me.

"That may be, but what does that say about you for staying with me this long?" I asked her snidely.

"Oh, I plan on publishing a thesis about you when this ride is over," she told me seriously. "I'll be famous, I'll be up for Sainthood."

"Tell God I said hi when you get there," I said in jest, but it's meaning had so much more depth than the way I had originally intended it. Tracy's smile evaporated.

"Oh, Talbot," Tracy said, falling welcomingly into my arms. "What are we going to do with you?" she said, burying her face into my shoulder.

"There's always the rodeo," I told her. It was the first thing that came to my mind.

She wiped a tear from her eye and looked up at me. "You rarely think before you speak, don't you?"

"What? I think I'd be great, those guys that get in the

barrel and everything."

"You know those are rodeo clowns, right?" she was telling me.

"Clowns? I hate clowns. They are the root of all evil in this world," I answered.

"You honestly believe that, don't you?" Tracy said. "There are zombies and vampires roaming this world, but clowns rule as the supreme evil being in your world."

"That's rich," BT said. "You never cease to make me wonder what the hell is wrong with you."

"I thought the phrase was never cease to amaze?" I asked him.

"Nope," he replied dryly.

"Hey, Mike," Paul said, walking away from a very angry spouse. Why the hell he was exposing his flank to a pissed-off wife was beyond me; and they called *me* the crazy one.

"Hey, buddy. Hey, Erin!" I yelled over his shoulder.

She semi-waved, but it looked more like she was flashing me the finger as she turned away.

"I take it you're staying for the extracurricular fun and activities?" I asked him. He nodded in return. "And you told Erin to leave with the advance party?"

"Right on both counts."

"She'll get over it when she sees your smiling face in a couple of days."

"You think?" Paul asked, looking over his shoulder at his wife's back.

"I'm an old pro at this. You'll be fine."

"I haven't gone yet, Talbot," Tracy said from her car door as she loaded an extra clip of ammo. "I can still kick your ass before I go."

I was going to comment on how good someone, who only a few short months ago hated firearms, was now loading a magazine. But then, the reason of why she was so proficient at this new skill struck. I would rather she remained inept than have to deal with this walking abortion we were calling life. I reverted to, "Yes, dear."

Chapter Three – Mike Journal Entry 2

I actually did not feel bad when Tracy, the boys, and the rest left, because I knew what we were doing was right and it felt good. We would finally make a stand…sort of. No more retreating and firing blindly over our shoulders as we ran for our lives. We were taking the fight to her and it gave me goose bumps just thinking about it.

"This is a great set-up," Brian said, coming up to me as I surveyed the highway below us. "Plenty of clear firing lines and ample opportunity for escape."

"You ever killed a human?" I asked without turning.

"I've killed dozens of zombies," he responded.

"I didn't say zombies," I told him, now turning to look him in the eyes.

"What are you talking about, Mike?" he asked with a 'what the hell?' expression.

"I'm asking have you ever killed an air-breathing human with thoughts, feelings and a hope for the future before? In the Army?"

"More times than I'd like to count," he told me solemnly. "Why?" he asked cautiously.

"Well, not that I consider the stupid bastards that hooked up with Eliza to be much above the zombies, but she has at least a hundred or so human sympathizers that help move her horde around and give her nourishment when she runs a little low on fresh stock."

"Are you shitting me, Mike?" Brian said, looking like he was getting a little green around the gills.

"Not at all, and those are the ones I want to target."

"I wasn't sure what to expect with this, but I guess

this wasn't it. I was really kind of expecting a giant mob of zombies to be coming down the highway and we would just let gobs of lead fly."

"Oh, we're still going to let gobs of lead fly, just a different target than you were expecting."

Brian walked away, maybe now regretting his decision to stay behind, but I was glad he was here.

"How much time do we have?" BT asked, sitting on the rear hatch of one of the new trucks Ron had given us. New in years, not in looks.

Ron was going to be pissed. The one he had given me had been blemish-free; this one looked like we took it through an industrial flaying machine, whatever that would entail. Bowling ball-sized divots creased the hood, the moose damage nearly lost. Well, that was one positive.

"Are you putting on new socks?" I asked him, shielding the sun from my eyes.

"Yeah, Brian gave them to me. They're real nice."

"They make socks in your size? I just figured you used old canoe covers."

"Have I told you lately how funny I think you are, Talbot?" BT said, muscling his left sock over his foot, stretching it well beyond its capacity.

"You've got those things stretched so wide, they look like fishnet," Gary said as he walked by to set up a tripod with a spotting scope.

"Two Talbots, half the fun," BT roared.

To answer your question, we've got maybe two days," I told him, turning back to the roadway. I was almost able to see the leading edge of the evil that was coming.

"You know, I love me some good plinking, but don't you think we should maybe up our arsenal a little?" BT asked as he put his shoes on. The image of BT wearing fishnet stockings gave me a smile that I made sure to hide before I turned to talk to him.

"Yeah, the Big 5 didn't pan out quite like I had

hoped. If this one is dry, it's a good chance that everything in this vicinity is pretty much tanked."

"So I hate to ask, but what's your plan?"

"You're not going to like this," I told him honestly.

"Again with the shockers today."

"House to house."

"What! Are you insane, Talbot? Wait don't answer that. I'd rather not know the answer. You know that's a good way for us to get our heads blown off."

"I think it's a wonderful idea," Mrs. Deneaux said. She had been resting in the front seat. "I'm nearly out of cigarettes."

"Great! I'll grab the Camels under a hail of fire!" BT yelled.

"That would be wonderful, dear," Mrs. Deneaux answered him in all seriousness.

"You two deserve each other!" BT said, pointing between Mrs. D and me.

Deneaux winked at me. I was two parts amused and one big part scared shitless.

BT stormed off, digesting my words.

"He's very dramatic for such a large man," Mrs. Deneaux said, looking at his retreating back.

"I thought I was the only one that didn't think before they spoke," I laughed.

She "pahhhed" at me, but she had a merriment in her eyes that I had never seen before from her. Strange times we were living in.

Chapter Four – Mike Journal Entry 3

"Hello occupants of this house!" I shouted. "We are friendly!"

"Very convincing," BT said sarcastically from the front seat of the truck. I didn't want him to come out. Just the sheer size of the guy made him look like hostility incarnate.

"I'm trying to establish a repertoire, BT," I yelled to him.

"Bullshit, I bet you can't spell the word and probably don't even know what it means."

"I most certainly know what it means," (He was right on the spelling part, though.) "You're a pain-in-the-ass," I told him.

"Hurry up and get your ass shot at, will you? I need to get out of this truck. My leg is starting to cramp up on me," BT said.

"Hi, occupants."

"What are you? Junk mail?" Gary asked.

"Really?" I asked my brother, who was standing next to me, looking at the windows to see if any of the drawn shades moved.

"I just think that you could use a more personal touch," he suggested.

"Give it a go," I told him.

"People of Seventeen Georges Road!" he shouted.

"Much better," I told him. He nodded in agreement.

"We are here looking for supplies, only from unoccupied homes. If you are home, please let us know and we will move on to the next house. We do not wish any sort of confrontation. Again, we are only looking for supplies,"

Gary finished.

It sounded reasonable, but would anyone believe us? I wouldn't, I'd be thinking they were looking for people. I'd no sooner open my door for strangers than I would a pack of zombies. This was more dangerous than taking Eliza head-on, yet here we were on both counts.

"I think I saw the shade move," Gary said to me, I think he was full of it, but we turned around and addressed the next house.

"People of Eighteen Georges Road," Gary said.

"How much time did you say we had?" BT asked, stepping out of the truck.

"Oh, will you shut up that racket!" the person from Seventeen Georges Road said. "Been trying to sleep in a little bit and then you band of idiots comes traipsing through the neighborhood. Should have brought one of those stupid ice cream trucks with the music going, too!" he yelled out from his front screen door.

He stepped out and appeared to be in his late fifties, early sixties, plaid pajama bottoms, old brown slippers, and a threadbare terry bathrobe, that had filled more than one moths belly. The perfect picture would have been if he'd had a pipe in his mouth and an over-under shotgun in his hands. Both elements were noticeably missing.

"What do you need!?" he yelled. "The sooner you dolts get what you want, the sooner I hope you'll get out of here."

I was a little dumbfounded. It was not often these days when I got berated. Shot at? Sure. Dressed down? Not so much.

"Damn! I thought Deneaux had crotchety all sewn up. She's got nothing on him," BT said. Then he sheepishly turned around, realizing that Deneaux was only a few feet away. "No offense," he said to her.

"None taken," she said as she stepped from the cab. "We need cigarettes," she yelled right before she began a coughing fit I was sure would dislodge a hot, blackened lung from her thin chest.

"Plenty of those," Crotchety said. "More than I could smoke in this lifetime. Never smoked before, but when I was in that empty convenience store, it seemed like something I wanted to start. Smoked one of them damn things when I got home and realized I couldn't stand them. Didn't really see a need to bring them back."

Mrs. D was already on the move.

"I've got some food, but I'm not in the sharing mood. Plenty of other houses you can get that from."

"Sir, we don't need any of that, we're looking for guns and ammo." I told him.

"What do you need that for?" he asked in all seriousness. I thought he was dead panning a killer joke.

"You're kidding, right?" I asked him when he was still looking at me for an answer.

"I have never carried a gun, so I saw no sense in starting now. And don't get me wrong, I'm not one of those bleeding heart liberals...just always afraid I'd kill myself figuring out how to use them. I have a knife, but I only use that to cut open packages of stuff."

"Wait," Brian said, not believing a word he was hearing. "You're telling us that you've survived all this time not having to shoot or kill anything?"

"Oh, I didn't say that I didn't kill anything. About a week back, had this mean old raccoon trying to get into my basement, threw a brick at him, but he didn't get the message. Took two slugs with the shovel before he finally died."

"You're...you're playing with us, right?" Brian asked, still not believing a word he was hearing.

"I don't know you from Adam, son, and I've never been known to play."

Mrs. Deneaux pushed past the man and into his entryway.

"They're in the cabinet in the kitchen next to the fridge," he told her, pointing back into his house. A few seconds later, I could hear a sound that could only be described as a cow getting its milk-fattened udders caught in multiple mousetraps, it was that unsettling.

"Is that Deneaux?" Gary asked, placing his hands over his ears.

"I guess she found the cigarettes," Crotchety said.

Brian was shaking his head, walking around in small circles. He was mumbling to himself. "No guns! The world is caving in on itself and this crazy old bastard doesn't even have a gun."

"What's wrong with your friend?" Crotchety asked. "He looks like he has distemper."

Deneaux pushed past the old man, her arms stacked high with cartons of varying smokes. She looked like a schoolgirl that just got a fully paid shopping spree to the mall.

"He'll be fine," I said. "Would you happen to know where we could get some guns then? So that we can be on our way."

"You look like you're planning trouble," Crotchety said with scrutinizing speculation. "I don't like trouble. It tends to get people killed."

"Listen, old man!" BT bellowed. "See this man here?" BT said as he placed his hands on my shoulders. "If trouble were the rarest element on the planet, my good friend, Michael Talbot," BT tousled my hair for effect, "would have the entire market cornered."

"Thanks, man. I appreciate that."

"No, this man needs to understand. If trouble were a fine thread, Mike could weave it into a three piece suit."

"I think he gets it."

"No, I've got one more."

"Fine, go ahead."

"If trouble were a drop of water, Mike could fill a

swimming pool."

"Oooh, that was the best one," Gary said.

"Hilarious, guys."

"And you stay with him. Why?" the old man asked.

"Because, for some damn reason, he always finds a way to stay one step ahead of it," BT said proudly.

"One step isn't a lot of cushion, son," Crotchety said.

"I'd be six feet under, if it wasn't for him."

"Understood. Three doors down, dipshit named Greg Hodgkins, Nascar fan and all that implies was shooting through his window for hours it seemed when the zombies first came. That very same night, I heard his screams for help. The more he shot, the more zombies came. Now I'm no genius, but it almost seems that if you leave them alone, they tend to do the same."

"Yeah? We haven't had that kind of luck," I told him.

"No," Gary said over-exaggeratedly as he shook his head.

I looked over to where this great battle had waged, but except for a few splotches on the curb, I didn't see much evidence. "Where are the bodies?"

"We waited a few—" he started.

"We?" I asked.

"Sonny, do you really think I'm stupid enough to answer my door in my sleeping gear without a little back-up?" he asked as he pulled a small walkie-talkie from his pocket. He must have seen the look on my face. "Relax, no one has you in their sights, just yet. We just kind of keep an eye out for each other."

"I completely understand."

"So we waited a few days until any of the zees that could move on their own power left, and then we piled up the rest of them and had a huge bonfire. We gave Greg a proper burial, although I'm not sure he deserved it. He was kind of a prick. You know the type…has two pit bulls and lets them roam the neighborhood. Kids were scared to go out and play."

"Nobody else wants anything?" I asked trying to be as nonchalant as possible as I did a three-sixty trying to ascertain where his 'friends' might be. It was possible he was bluffing, but the situation didn't necessitate me seeing his cards.

"Those of us that are left want for nothing."

"Thank you…" I wasn't sure how to address him.

"Occupant works just fine, and just so we're clear, you're welcome to rummage all you want in his house and no other on this street. Are we clear?"

"Not a problem, thank you for your hospitality." And for once, I meant it, not a note of sarcasm in my voice. I'd like to say I'd help a stranger, but I think I'd be fooling myself.

Deneaux was busy opening multiple cartons of smokes, smelling individual packs as if they were fine wines, while the rest of us walked down to Greg's former abode. Except for a few busted out windows, his home looked in fairly decent shape. Two rusted-out hulks of cars sat on cinderblocks on the side of the driveway.

"Holy shit," BT said, "it's the living embodiment of a cliché."

"Okay, to make this perfect, he'd need to have an old school, giant, television box, but it has to be broken and have a small, thirteen-inch black and white sitting on top. I answered him. "First gun choice bet?" I asked him.

"You're on," BT said, fist-bumping me.

"Dammit," I said as I walked into Greg's den and found myself staring straight at what appeared to be a mammoth, sixty-five-inch flat screen TV mounted to the wall.

"Now I might not be the most intelligent man, but my guess is that isn't thirteen inches. Do you want me to round up a tape measure to make sure?" BT asked, smiling.

"Find the guns, ass," I told him as I went into the

kitchen, where an H&K 9mm sat on the kitchen table. "How do you feel about 9mms?" I shouted to BT. I was thinking this was going to be a treasure trove and I wanted his first dibs selection off the board.

"That is a weapon of choice of the common thug and I want no part of it, especially since I am looking at a fully auto AK with a drum magazine."

I ran out of the kitchen to see what BT was holding. It was a sight. And I would have loved to have gotten it; that was of course until we figured out that that was what Greg had been using before his demise and he had not saved even one last round to take himself out.

"Hard luck," I told BT, smacking his shoulder as we tore apart the house for fifteen minutes, looking for anything to change the gun from its status of dangerous looking paperweight, to killing machine.

"I can still swing this thing," BT said. He was pissed because after that, I came across a riot shotgun, which I laid claim to, plus about a hundred deer shot rounds. Besides the other arms we found, he had an AR, but it looked like he had run over the lower receiver with a tank. There would be no rounds going down range in that thing.

"Not bad, it's a start," Brian said as we loaded the truck.

"I don't care what old Occupant Seventeen said, but that house was ransacked," BT said, still completely irked about his lack of rounds.

"Maybe if you just wave it around aggressively, people will get scared," Gary suggested.

"Talbot, you had better rein your brother in," BT snarled.

"He's my older brother, BT. He isn't going to listen to me."

"Nice pistol," Paul said as I was looking it over, trying to figure out the cocking mechanism, safety and every other moving part. "You should give it to Deneaux."

I looked at him like he had just snorted some weed.

"No, man, I'm not kidding. The lady can shoot the balls off a gnat from across the room," he told me.

"Paul, I love you, man, but I think all those years of drug use finally caught up with you."

"Well, if they caught up with me, they sure as hell snagged you, too."

"Fair enough, but I'm not the one suggesting we give Deneaux one of the few guns we have right now."

"Listen, I know you're a great shot with the rifle, no doubt. But she's unshakeable with the pistol. I watched her, man, she was like the pistol champ of 1908 or some shit."

"1908 huh? What's that make her? Like one hundred and thirty?"

"She could be," Paul said, looking over to the cab. "Doesn't matter, though, she's freaking amazing with that thing."

"Fine. I'll take your crazy ass word for it."

"You are not giving that old bat that pistol are you?" BT challenged me.

"She has to guard her smokes somehow," I told him.

"We had an understanding, you and me, Talbot. I would hang with you, if and only if, you didn't get any fucking nuttier," BT told me.

"I don't remember agreeing to that," I told him. I walked over to the cab of the truck.

Deneaux was barely visible from the dense cloud of smoke she was producing. I rapped on the window with the pistol. "You want this?"

She rolled down the window only far enough to grab the proffered weapon. "H&K P2000 V3 9mm," she said, putting the cigarette she had in her right hand in her mouth so that she could grab the pistol. I just want to note that she already had one in her mouth, which I can only assume she was holding with her left. "Nice weapon," she mouthed around the butts. She pulled the slide back and looked in the chamber. "Clean too, how many rounds?"

"Fifty-ish."

"I'll take it. We done?" she asked, looking up at me. I nodded, but before I could complete the gesture, she rolled her window back up.

"Always a pleasure," I told her. She waved me off and began to load the magazine. "Who wants to drive?" I asked.

"I'd rather run behind the truck now," BT said and he probably would have too if my emergency field surgery on his shot leg hadn't left him with a pronounced limp.

"Hey, you're the immortal," Gary said. "You should probably drive, all that second-hand smoke would be bad for the rest of us."

"You guys suck," I said. We all got back into the truck. I made sure to honk for an extra-long burst as we pulled away from Seventeen Georges Road, I waved enthusiastically for his hospitality. What can I say? I was feeling a little dour. Seventeen gave me the finger as we rolled away. We couldn't keep doing this house-to-house crap. Eventually, we were going to come across someone that didn't want company, and we didn't have the numbers or the arms to get into a firefight from an undefended position.

I was thinking of scrapping the whole idea of punching Eliza in the eye and just racing to catch up with Tracy. I'd rather spend my last few days with her anyway.

"I've got an idea," Brian said from the backseat where the smoke was only minimally better. Gary and BT had thought it a better idea to sit in the truck bed, it was a balmy fifty degrees out and the sun was shining bright.

"I'm listening," I choked out through the curtain of carcinogens.

"If you can find a hardware store, we're going to need some tools."

I drove back by the Big 5. If I remembered correctly, I had seen a Home Depot somewhere in the vicinity. I hadn't really acknowledged it then, as I wasn't planning on building a catapult at the time. "Hey, you're not planning on making a trebuchet, are you?"

"A what?"

"A catapult-looking thingy."

"I should have sat in the back with the other two," Brian complained.

Paul had his sweater up over his nose, and his eyes were bloodshot. "Shit, Deneaux, could you lighten up a little on the cigarettes? I can barely breathe."

"That's the problem with you young ones today, no longevity. You are like all the products of your time, you're not built to last like us old timers are. Probably would have asked for your HR generalist before you landed on the beaches in Normandy. We weren't called the greatest generation for nothing."

I almost put the truck up on two wheels when I realized I was just about to miss the entrance to the giant, big-box hardware store.

"Talbot, you just about made me fall out!" I heard BT yell.

I waved my apology to him, I was beginning to pass out from the oxygen loss. Brian, Paul and I raced to be the first to spill out of the cab. I think Brian won, but it was a virtual three-way tie without replay.

"How much room you got back there?" Paul asked after his coughing fit was through.

"Enough," BT answered in sympathy.

"What are we doing here?" Gary asked.

"Brian has a plan," I told him.

"Okay just so we're clear. All you military types don't think alike, right? I mean when he says he has a plan, it doesn't involve some crazy stuff, right?" BT asked.

"Hell if I know. He didn't tell me. Let's lock and load insofar as we can," I told the group.

Mrs. Deneaux came out and rubbed her half-smoked

butt on the side of the truck so that she could smoke it later. "Oh come on," she said to me when she saw me watching her in amazement. "You've already beaten this truck into submission. Your brother won't even notice this," she said, pointing to the new, black burn mark.

"You have like five thousand cigarettes…why are you saving that one?" Gary asked.

"I plan on smoking every last one of them," she cackled.

"Yeah, and most likely in the next few hours," I answered. "Alright, let's keep our eyes open for any of the squatters." That's what we were calling the zombies in the sleeping packs. "Any of those and we're out of here, no matter if you got what you need or not, Brian."

"Understood," he said, nodding his head tensely.

I went through the door first, feeling totally inadequate with my .22 rifle. I had left the shotgun in the truck. It had some damage and until I could ascertain if it worked, I wasn't going to risk our lives with it. "This sucks," I mumbled.

"You say something, hoss?" Brian asked as he came up on my left flank.

"Just wishing I had something a little more potent than this pea-shooter," I told him.

"Bet that's what you're wife says," he said. He stopped. "Sorry, man, battlefield humor, helps ease the tension."

"Not for me," I said and he laughed. "Wow," I said softly. The store didn't look like it had even opened for business yet. It was virtually picked clean, except for a few scraps of lumber, haphazardly scattered on the floor. "Is this worth it?" I asked Brian.

"Maybe. What I'm looking for wouldn't garner much attention…I wouldn't think."

"Alright, lead on." The five of us stayed in a tight-knit group, keeping eyes on every angle of approach. The stench of death was present, but it was impossible to distinguish if it was from dead people or walking dead people. Funny, but now I was wishing Deneaux was smoking to quench some of the stench.

We started to head down an aisle, but I didn't like the idea of us being this tightly grouped, I was envisioning zombies flooding in from both ends. "Hold on," I told the group. "Let's do some reconnoitering. Gary, could you go up to the end of the aisle and make sure we're not going to meet anyone we wouldn't want to?"

"Is this about that time I told Mom when you snuck out of the house?"

"That was you?" She always told me that she had gotten up in the middle of the night because the dog had barked. "I got grounded for a month because of you?"

"Well what the hell were you thinking, leaving your bedroom window open in November?"

"I needed to get back into the house, didn't I?"

"Well, how would I know you snuck out? Mom was up, getting a glass of water in the kitchen, I told her your bedroom window was open."

"Do you have any idea how much she scared me when I got back in and turned on the light and she was sitting at my desk?"

"Oh, I bet that was pretty scary," Gary said empathizing with me.

"If I was any older, I probably would have had a heart attack."

"If you were any older you wouldn't have had to sneak out."

"Boys," Mrs. Deneaux said, "this is really fascinating, but I have a cigarette with my lip marks on it that I'm dying to get back to."

The thought of anything with Deneaux's lip marks on it gave me the shudders; apparently Gary too, because he went to the end of the aisle without any further delay.

"Nothing up here!" he yelled.

"I thought you said he was in the military?" Brian asked.

"Air Force," I told him.

"Oh yeah," Brian answered. "I remember."

"BT? Can you, Paul, and D stay here close to the front?"

"You got it, Mike, but this place does not feel right. I think we need to get going sooner, rather than later."

"Understood, we'll make this quick."

"What could possibly make such a strapping young man as yourself afraid?" Mrs. Deneaux asked BT.

"You, for starters," he answered, looking over her head for any signs of trouble.

"I'm going outside to finish my cigarette."

"Shit," Brian murmured as we looked in the tool section.

"What are you looking for? I can help," I told him.

"Bolt cutters," he told me almost simultaneously with Gary's words.

"Movement!" Gary shouted.

"I am so sick of zombies," I said aloud, but not really directed to Brian. My next sentence was, though. "You want to hear something sick?" I asked him.

"Not really, I'd like to get the bolt cutters and get the hell out of here."

I ignored his entreaty completely. "I secretly wished something like this would happen. Yeah." I continued when he looked over at me strangely. "I was sick of my boring ass life and my shitty job. It all seemed so pointless back then. I went to work, came home, ate dinner, said about five words to each of my kids, ten to my wife, went to bed, and then did the same thing the very next day. I mean, I don't know if I was exactly thinking of a zombie invasion. A potential alien takeover or perhaps Chinese troops making a beach-head in California would have worked just as well. I don't know. I really didn't care what the calamity was as long as my family was safe and I got out of my rut."

"Couldn't you have maybe hoped to win the lottery?" Brian asked me as he turned over a toolbox laying on the floor.

"Maybe, but that seemed so farfetched."

"More so than the world being overwrought with zombies and aliens?"

I noted that he didn't discuss the Chinese because that was truly a potential threat. Hadn't thought much about China since this crap started, but they must have close to a billion zombies over there by now. That was a mind-boggling number. I shrugged my shoulders.

"Two maybe three somethings coming this way, still can't tell what they are though!" Gary shouted. He was backing down the aisle towards us.

"Probably safe to say if they aren't talking, we know what we're dealing with," Paul answered as he went back to the front door to make sure our avenue of retreat wasn't sealed off.

A shot fired from the top of our aisle.

"Did you get it?" I asked Gary as he came back to us.

"No, I was firing a warning shot."

"Um, Gary, we talked about this. Zombies don't traditionally care about those kinds of things."

"I wasn't sure, I couldn't see them through the aisles. You sure Glenn didn't just maybe drop you out of the ranger station window that day at Blue Hills?"

I got the shivers just thinking about it. "There they are," I said flatly, pointing to three of the mottliest crew of Home Depot workers to ever shamble along. They were a mess--torn, bloodstained clothes, at least two had suffered some sort of gunfire damage. The third, an old man of about eighty, looked like he had a foot and a half in the grave before this started. Surprisingly, the only things that were relatively intact on any of them were their bright orange aprons. "You can ask them if they've seen any bolt cutters," I told Brian.

He looked over to the zombies and then at me. "I wonder if I can still catch up with Alex. He seemed to have his shit together."

"Only if you take Deneaux," I told him as I put my pop gun to my shoulder.

"Fine, I'll stay," he said as he began to look with a little more fervor through the strewn tools.

"Throwing screwdrivers would be more effective," I said prophetically as I pulled the trigger. The lead zombie paused for a fraction of a second as it absorbed the impact and then began its forward progress again. "Are you kidding me?"

"It looks like it wrapped right around its skull," Gary said, looking over my shoulder.

"Do not tell me this is a new version of zombie," I said, eyeing the zombie for any sign of it stopping.

"What do you mean?" Gary asked.

"Could they be growing thicker skulls as protection?"

"That's impossible," Brian said. "That kind of adaptation would take thousands of years. A-HA!" he suddenly exclaimed. "Not the biggest pair, but they'll do."

"That's what she said," I said, just because that's what men do.

"Bathroom humor, Mike? Here? Mom would be so proud."

"Sorry, it's who I am. And anyway, he started it."

"I've got what I need. Let's get out of here," Brian said, holding the bolt cutters up and heading quickly for the exit.

I placed another well-aimed .22 center-mass on the zombie's forehead. His head snapped back a bit, I saw the gleam of white bone that became immediately coated with a brackish gel that looked a lot like congealed blood. The third bullet finally pierced through and he stopped cold. "You planning on shooting?" I asked Gary as my rifle jammed.

"I was going to save my ammo," he told me matter-of-factly. "What's the matter? You're doing fine."

"I have a jam."

"Well, fix it. They're deaders anyway…"

I looked up. The two shamblers on the left had been playing possum and were coming full-tilt. Well, one of them was anyway. The old man was trying to get his giddy-up going, but that passed him by two decades ago.

The first zombie plowed into me. I was barely able to put my rifle up in time to keep him from biting any part of me off. "Shoot him!" I yelled.

"You guys are all entangled. I can't," Gary said in alarm.

"A bunch coming for the doors!" Paul yelled.

The zombie was an inch from my face, his breath was swoon-worthy, but I didn't have the time for my inner diva to make a show. Its hands were making a clutch for the rifle. I simultaneously pushed him away with the rifle and let go. He could have the jammed piece of shit. I rolled to my right, a Philips screwdriver puncturing my side. The smell of the fresh blood got the zombie moving frantically. He let the gun go, his gray filmy eyes fixed on mine. I never took my eyes off him as my hands reached around the tools, looking for something zombie-killing worthy. I was having no luck as I first came across a rubber mallet and then a hacksaw.

"Are you kidding me, God?" I shouted.

And maybe he was, but then he guided me to a short-handled tool of some sort. I couldn't tell what was on the end, but it had heft, and right now, I could deal with some blunt force trauma. The zombie had pulled himself closer, and I rolled onto my left hip and swung whatever the hell I had in my right arm as hard as I could. The safety-coated hand axe shone dully as it arced down and into the side of its head. My arm shivered from the impact, but the zombie seemed momentarily stunned. I kept rearing back and used as much leverage as I could, bringing my body up and slamming down with as much force as I could muster on each subsequent hit. I could hear his skull splinter with the first two hits, and the third finally broke through. My reward was a huge squirt of his creamy insides. I was repulsed as liquefied gray matter spilled forth. My feet were barely able to gain traction as I pushed away from the scene. Small white maggots wriggled around in the goop for a few seconds before becoming still. I might have decided to get a closer look, but Gary took this moment to put a bullet in its head.

"Little late to the dance, aren't you?" I asked him. He put his hand out to help me up.

"Had to get rid of Papa Smurf and you looked like you were alright."

"Kind of fits him, doesn't it?" And it did. The old man had a white beard, was older than most craters, not to mention he had a significant blue hue to him.

"You might want to take the rubber off your axe," Gary said as we moved back down the aisle to the doorway.

I grabbed a screwdriver and pushed the hair and bone-covered material from the blade. "I wish it had a longer handle."

"I wish it fired rounds," Gary added.

"Well, that too."

Paul was keeping the zombies at bay, more from the smoke screen his shots were producing than actually making a dent in their numbers. BT was down to a broom handle and was pushing the closest zombies away with it. He kept sticking it in their faces and sending them skidding backwards. They didn't get the concept of grabbing the stick. Their arms were uselessly outstretched, trying to get a hold of their potential food.

"Mike! This is fun and all," BT said with some effort, "but I really think we should get going." A couple of zombies jostled into the broom handle, dislodging it from BT's hands.

We had a window of escape, but it was starting to

look like one of those fantastic, heavy-metal-doors-coming-to-a-close, Indiana Jones kind of escape.

And then Dirty Fucking Harry saved the day. Well, in this case, I guess it was Harriet. Mrs. Deneaux came in the front door, cigarette in mouth, cloud of smoke encircling her head, and one eye squinted. She took a quick assessment of the situation and flew through her magazine of rounds. Zombie heads whipped back before their bodies followed. Chunks of hairy, matted bone flew through the air. Eleven zombies dropped. What was going to be a narrow escape was now something we could drive a semi through.

"Thank you," I told her breathlessly as we got to the door.

"If I were fifty years older, I'd marry you," Gary said, kissing her on the cheek.

"I knew it!" BT shouted. "All white women are crazy!"

Mrs. Deneaux cackled loudly as we mostly carried her to the truck.

"I told you!" Paul said as we all got back in the truck.

"What happened?" Brian asked.

"Mrs. Deneaux is what happened!" I shouted. "She just might be the baddest-ass person on the planet right now!"

Brian got the truck moving as a stream of zombies came flooding through the door. "Horrible customer service," he remarked as we pulled out of the parking lot.

"Not bad," I told him as I clapped him on the shoulder. My heart rate was finally coming down to something approaching 'galloping horse.' A few more minutes, and maybe I'd get it to 'hummingbird' status.

"Now what?" Gary asked.

"We find a storage locker facility," Brian answered.

"Huh?" I asked.

"Storage lockers, I'm telling you they're gold mines. My cousin does it for a living."

"Does what, exactly?" I asked, not understanding what the hell he was talking about.

"He used to buy abandoned storage lockers and sell the contents for huge bucks."

"Great, but I don't think we really need an old record collection or furniture for that matter," I told him, more than a little pissed that we had all just risked our lives for this half-assed idea.

"No, Mike, he said he always comes across guns when he does these."

"Come on, who sticks guns in a storage locker?" I asked. It sounded like the most insane thing I'd ever heard. Sometimes I hated having my rifles in a safe at my own home because that would delay me getting to them. How much of a pain-in-the-ass would it be to tell the home invaders at your house to hold off while you put your shoes on and drive down to the storage facility to retrieve your weapons. I'm sure they'd be super understanding.

"I don't know. Folks who only want guns for hunting season, or relatives who have passed and the kids stick everything in storage until they can go through it."

"Or a sporting goods store that's gone under," Gary added.

"Maybe we'll find Harry Potter's magic wand, too." I said. "I don't think the risk was worth the return, Brian," I said, more than a little miffed.

"What do we have to lose?" he replied. "We either find something and punch Eliza in the mouth or we don't and scramble to catch up with the others.

"Fair enough," I relented, but I was far from placated. I did not want to go running into the night again with my tail between my legs.

Chapter Five – Mike Journal Entry 4

I found the rows of orange-colored garage doors to be more than a little unsettling. I couldn't put my finger on it – the uniformity? Great. Was I developing a new phobia? Just what I needed. I did not like the fact that it felt like we were in an alleyway with limited avenues for escape, but I had to admit the zombie apocalypse had passed right by this place.

"See? I told you," Brian said excitedly, almost as if he were listening to my thoughts.

"Told him what? All I see are garage doors," BT said. "Mike, this is a waste of time. There are easier ways to go Dumpster diving."

I shrugged my shoulders. "Let's just give it a go. There're no zombies here and little chance there will be. A small reprieve wouldn't be so bad."

BT growled, I don't think he was seeing it the same way as I did.

"Where do we start?" Gary asked me. It was a daunting task; there had to be at least five hundred lockers spread out on this lot.

Brian went over to the one closest to the gate, which we entered through, and with some moderate muscle power, cut through the cheap lock, opened it and looked around. "Zero for one," he said with some enthusiasm. He grabbed his cutters and walked over to the next unit.

I went to see what was in the unit. It looked like whoever had this particular space had been saving newspapers since the mission to the moon. Yellowing, dry, cracked paper stacked floor to ceiling in most places all the way to the rear of the unit.

"Zero for two," Brian said, barely peeking into the second unit.

There was one small, white kitchen trash bag full of oven mitts in this one. "Who the hell does that? Spends what? Thirty, forty bucks a month to store oven mitts?" I could see if they came from maybe a defunct oven mitt store, but these were used. Most had grease or burnt food on them; none of them were pristine, and yes, I checked them all. And no, I didn't touch them, I ripped the bag open and kicked them around, just trying to wrap my head around the person that put these here.

Brian was somewhere around "zero for twenty-two" when he stopped counting.

"Talbot, we've been here for three hours. Surely there's a better way to waste our time. Maybe a museum or something. I'd rather go look at something aesthetically pleasing than rummaging around other people's shit," BT griped.

"Whoa! Got something!" Brian shouted from pretty far down the alleyway.

"Holy crap! When did he get that far from us?" I asked. We would have been able to get there sooner, but we had to skirt around mountains of debris that had been pulled from previous lockers.

Brian came out of the locker, holding two giant rifles.

"What the hell are those?" I asked him.

"Firearms," he said proudly.

"They look like they shoot grenades," Paul said, looking down the barrel.

"Those are pretty useless," Mrs. Deneaux said, coming up to us. "They're smooth bore muzzle loaders, they need black powder, I'd say a .50 cal ball, and have an effective range of about seventy-five yards, at the most. And that drops off significantly, depending on who is shooting the weapon." She finished off looking directly at Paul, who bowed his head. "Plus, even if we had everything we needed, they take close to two minutes to reload."

"Brian, I don't know how much more time we can stay here trying this," I told him.

"There's weapons in here. I know there are," he said with a measure of desperation.

"There probably are, but look at all these lockers! We could spend days here trying to find them," I told him.

"Leave me someone to watch my back. I'll keep looking and you guys can try some stores nearby."

"I'll stay," Mrs. Deneaux said, lighting a cigarette.

I looked over to Brian to see what he thought; it was his back that needed watching. "Sure," he said, shrugging his shoulders.

"Alright, we'll be back in a couple of hours. If something happens here, go back to the Big 5 store."

"Got it," Brian said, already digging into the next locker.

Mrs. Deneaux was sitting on the bumper with her head tilted up, soaking in the sun as much as her lungs soaked in the caustic carcinogens from the cancer sticks.

"Doesn't much look like she's watching anyone's back," BT said as we walked out of the storage facility.

"We've got to get some wheels," Paul said nervously. "I'm too old to run."

"Buddy, remember we played on the high school football team together? There was a reason you were the quarterback and not a running back."

"Not much of a scrambler then?" BT asked Paul.

"You both know what you can do with my ass," Paul stated.

"Paul, to be fair, I watched a few of your games back then. I think you could beat Dan Marino in a foot race," Gary said in all seriousness.

I started laughing. "Wasn't he in the league for like seventeen years?"

"Something like that," Gary answered.

"I think he had about seven yards rushing total for all those years. We probably should make getting a car a priority."

"I like it much better when I'm not the object of ridicule. Should we talk about Mike's first girlfriend?"

"Don't you dare!" I said, spinning on my heel to face him.

Paul threw his hands up in mock surprise.

"Let's just find a car," I said, trying to change the subject.

We had walked about a hundred yards before anyone spoke again.

"So what about her?" BT asked.

"Paul, there're lines in the sand, and once they're crossed, you can't come back." He didn't seem fazed. "Should I bring up—"

Paul cut me off. "Mike, you swore on your word that you wouldn't ever bring that up again."

"We have an understanding then?" I asked him. Paul nodded eagerly.

"Damn! Just when this was getting interesting," BT said, smiling, happy that he had just stirred the hornets' nest.

There were plenty of cars abandoned on the street, most with the keys still in them, but the tanks were drained dry. These people had left in a hurry, not even bothering to shut their cars off. Some unlucky few had been eaten where they sat. Sometimes their bodies were half dragged out, snagged by their seatbelts as they were devoured alive. Some had telltale bullet holes in them and had been wholly left alone from the main predator that now prowled the earth; but the lesser scavengers still had to eat. Birds invariably went for the softer-tissued eyes; just one more reason to hate the flying vermin. Rats, I guessed from the droppings, were mostly concerned with chewing through whatever footwear the people had been wearing so they could get to the feet. The meat-stripped feet and eyeless dead, for some reason, were more disturbing than those that had been stripped clean by the zombies.

Gary was right behind me. He had one hand on my shoulder so that I could guide him as he kept his head pointed heavenward with his eyes closed. His gagging had been non-stop since we had come across this snarl of dead in the center of town. The worst of the smell had long since passed and the bodies began to resemble something more along the lines of human jerky. But it was still no Yankee Candle store out here.

"What the hell happened here?" Paul asked.

"It looks like zombies came and whoever was shooting didn't care where their bullets landed," I said.

Gary took this moment to throw up on my back. "Are you kidding me?" I asked as I immediately handed my rifle to BT so I could take my light jacket off. I swear I could still feel the runny liquid rolling down between my shoulder blades.

"I…I can wipe it off," Gary offered as he bent over to get the jacket I had just dropped.

"Leave it," I told him. And that was right before he heaved all over it again.

"Sorry," he said with a green-tinged smile.

"Is there anything on my shirt?" I asked BT.

"Aw, man," BT said turning me around.

"Don't fuck with me, man. I'm barely functioning right now thinking about this."

"You're fine," BT said, laughing as he gently slid his hand down my back and mirrored the feeling of warm stomach bile.

I jumped away. "Paul?"

"You're fine, man," Paul said, smiling.

"I'll tell them," I said desperately.

"You're fine!" Paul reiterated.

"You sure you don't want this?" Gary said, picking it up by the right sleeve, just about the only part that wasn't coated in his stomach lining.

"You bring that over here and you'll be walking home."

It was a few minutes and maybe a quarter mile later when we came across our first promising mode of transportation. It was an old Chevy Cavalier right at the outskirts of town. Both curbside doors were open and there were some personal belongings stowed in the backseat. A small house with the front door ajar was only a few short feet from the car.

"Looks like they never made it out in time," Paul said with some sadness and regret.

"The keys in the ignition?" I asked Gary, keeping an eye on the doorway like I expected the occupants to come rushing out, demanding to know what was going on.

"No, but there's a box of ammo on the dash."

"That's promising, what caliber?"

".30-30."

"Good hunting round," I said. The door was intimidating. It was a black, gaping wound into a world I didn't feel that I wanted to enter. It was a normal setting, overlaid with the surreal. "Something's not right."

BT did a quick three-sixty. "Nothing around, Mike," he said in all seriousness.

"No it's in there," I said.

"Forget it then, let's move on," he said.

"There's a car, which probably has gas because they were packing it to get the hell out of here and at least one rifle. We need both badly."

"Gary, you're going to stay out here and watch our backs." It felt strange protecting my big brother, but that was exactly what I was doing.

"I'll go in first." I took a big breath and gulped down my fear. "We ready?" I asked BT and Paul.

BT nodded tersely; Paul didn't even acknowledge my question, but he was right on BT's heels as we entered. First, we were in the living room, which was stacked with suitcases and multiple bags that would have never fit into that car, even if there were no passengers. But I could tell by the toys strewn around the house…that would not be the case.

"Who cares about *things* when you're trying to save your life?" BT asked softly. "They probably would have gotten out of here if they weren't trying to save this," BT said disgustedly as he pushed over a George Foreman grill stacked on a couple of the boxes that looked like they were getting ready to take with them.

To be fair, it looked like one of the top-of-the-line models, but I'm not sure when they thought they were going to get a chance to cook a hamburger, or worry about the fat they would end up eating because it wasn't draining down into the little drip pan. Don't get me wrong, there were possessions that I absolutely cherished when the world was still spinning somewhat on a normal axis. But life and the preservation of it top the list. I have yet to come across a *Star Wars* Astromech figurine that could ever replace the love I have for my kids, my wife, or my Henry. But since they were all safe, I did have a pang of remorse that I had not been able to save at least one of the little R2 units I had.

"I see legs," Paul said, moving over to the far side of the room. He was looking down a narrow hallway. "They're not moving," he added as we rushed to his side, rifles at the ready.

"Is that blood?" BT asked, looking over my head.

The hallway was in the shadows and the rug that was down may at one time have been taupe-colored, but years of use had left it something closer to brown and now something stained it even darker by the doorway where the legs were jutting out.

"My guess is yes," I said. A cloying stench clung to the walls of this house; a blinding dose of claustrophobia struck quickly, lingered for long seconds and then began to diminish. "Wow, that sucked," I said. Paul and BT, who had suffered no such attack, looked at me questioningly.

"I'll go," Paul said, trying to bolster his nerve.

"I'll do it. This was my stupid idea."

"Don't let me stop you," BT said.

The five steps it was going to take me to get down the hallway were worse than at Fitzy's house. At least, this time there wasn't any techno music. But maybe that would have helped drown out the sound of my heart trying to blow through my rib cage.

"Talbot?" BT whispered from the end of the hallway.

I threw an A-OK sign over my shoulder although it really meant shit. Something bad happened here, even above and beyond what you might think in this situation. I kicked what I figured were a man's legs judging by the clodhopper boots he (it) was wearing. No movement yet, I waited a few ticks more, making sure this wasn't the newest brand of sleeper we'd been encountering more and more of. I moved in a half step further, my foot coming down on the hardened rug – the blood, barbecue sauce, and ketchup having completely dried. "Keep telling yourself that, Talbot," I said as my foot sunk into the sticky fibers.

I turned the corner into the bedroom, wholly unprepared for what I witnessed. God had died, pure and simple. Dad had blown the left side of his head completely off. It looked so clean, like it was one of the cutaways you used to see at the doctor's office. "Here, kiddies, is what the inside of your brain looks like when you place a high velocity round up and through the soft palate. See the separation in tissue as the bullet travels through the jelly-like material of your thoughts?" But this was just the beginning of the nightmare.

Across the room lay a crib. I said a silent prayer to a silent master, and all I received was a silent response. A small, blue fist reached up, the fingers not yet deft enough to do much more than clench and unclench in an unending struggle to reach a food source it could not attain. I glided across the room like I was on a moving walkway.

"Whaddaya got, buddy?" a nervous Paul asked. I could hear him approaching.

"If you value anything that resembles sleep for the rest of your days on this planet, Paul, do not come any closer," I told him. I would swear I could hear his boots screeching in the carpet in an attempt to halt his forward momentum even faster.

"It's a kid, right?" BT asked. "Aw, man, it has to be a kid. Is the kid dead, Mike? Did the dad eat it? This is horrible. Let's get out of here, man," BT said, very subdued.

The baby, an infant of maybe four or five months, was emaciated. Small bits of one of his parents lay scattered around him, but this thing hadn't eaten anything more than some errant bugs since December. Its eyes, which seemed sallow and sunken, snapped open when it saw me leaning over its small bed. One small tooth poked through the upper gum. It must have latched on for dear life to be able to break through skin on whichever unlucky parent it had gotten a hold of. It began to rock back and forth, trying to get closer to me, strange gurgling noises bubbling forth from its lungs.

"What is that?" BT cried. "The kid is alive?" I could hear BT coming.

"It's not alive," I said flatly, my eyes fixated on the baby's.

"I...heard...him," BT said haltingly. "Oh sweet, sweet Jesus," he finished when he realized what I was in the room with.

A feeling of intense hunger raked across my head, but that was the furthest thing from my mind. *But not the mind of the one you're looking at* my subconscious piped in. *"HUUUUUNNNNNNGGGGGRRRRYYYYYYYYYYYYYYYY!"* it said, latching on to the word I had associated with its feelings. Apparently, it was a two-way street. *"HUNGRY!"* it shrieked over and over. I blew four holes into its head before the echoing in my brain subsided.

BT was in the room within seconds, picking me up under my arms and pulling me out of there.

"It was talking to me," I kept mumbling long after BT had deposited me on the curb outside.

"You alright, brother?" Gary asked, sitting down next to me.

"I don't think I even know what that word means anymore, Gary."

"Bad in there?" he asked earnestly.

I was half a beat away from coming back with a sarcastic, "You think?" But why prove how much of a dick I already am? He was just trying to help.

"Got some guns," BT yelled from somewhere in the house.

I knew in the grand scheme of things that was good news, but it did little to part the veil that I felt had slipped between my eyes and the rest of the world.

Gary got up. "Any ammo?" he yelled.

"Some," Paul yelled out an upstairs window.

"Do you think God is getting me back?" I asked Gary.

"Huh?" he asked, trying to figure out what I was asking. "What would God be trying to get you back for?"

"I'm not sure I've been a great person, Gary."

"We all have things we're not proud of, Mike," he said, turning back towards me.

"Did you ever chase Bible-thumpers off your property?" I asked him.

"Um no, but now I'm intrigued."

"It was a Saturday morning, couldn't have been much past nine a.m. and I had drunk to my liver's content the night before."

"Hung-over then?"

"Understatement. I think I was still drunk."

"Eww, that's rough."

"Tell me about it. Tracy and I had actually gotten into

a good-sized fight the night before, something or other about me being drunk."

"Go figure," Gary said.

"I know, right?!" I responded, thinking he was agreeing with me, (but now that I'm writing this, I think he was actually coming down on her side.) "So I'm in bed, sleeping my drink off when the doorbell rings. I threw my arm over to the other side of the bed, looking for Tracy to answer the door, but she had already left with the kids to do some errands. I figured it might be some of the kids' friends and they would get the message when I didn't answer the door. So I shut my eyes, and not ten seconds later, they rang the doorbell two quick times."

"What were they thinking?" Gary asked.

"I know, right?!" I was still under the impression he was siding with me, but looking at his written response takes on a whole new meaning. "So I'm in bed and thinking the little shits have one more chance at redemption before the wrath of God comes thundering down the stairs and gives them what for. I shut my eyes again against the hurtful rays of the sun, peeking around the shades. Another two blasts on the doorbell."

"Kind of like the bells of Notre Dame."

"Are you giving me shit, Gary?" I honestly asked because he was so dry in his delivery, I couldn't tell. He shook his head vigorously. "But yeah, it kinda was like those bells, my head was splitting, my vision was blurry, I had to piss like a race horse, and my stomach felt like I had drunk a pint of bacon grease after eating chili dogs."

"That doesn't sound too good, Mike." Gary said, starting to look a little green-tinged.

"Sorry, brother." I had to remember Gary did not have the strongest stomach.

Go on, he motioned with one hand; he kept the other up close to his mouth.

So I ripped the door open, my gaze downward,

expecting to yell at some little puissant about bothering grown-ups on their day off. What I got instead were two women and one man."

"Were they selling vacuums?"

"What? What the hell would make you ask that?"

"I once bought a vacuum cleaner from a door-to-door salesman, one of the best vacuums I ever bought."

"It wasn't vacuums. Can I finish my story?" I asked him. But I think I had lost him for a few beats as he thought about his domicile super sucker. "So there they are at my door and this lady with a far-off stare and wild hair starts spouting about how I can survive the end of the world."

"Did you listen? That sounds like some pretty good advice," Gary said, coming back from the reverie of his vacuum experience.

"Who knew Jehovah Witnesses were so prophetic?" I said more as a statement.

"Jehovah's? They're like bedbugs--once you let them in your house, they're damn near impossible to get rid of."

"You sound like you've had personal experience."

"I invited them in for coffee."

"What the hell were you thinking? You just wanted to show them your new vacuum, I bet." Gary bent his head slightly like I had hit the nail on the head. "How did you get rid of them?"

"It was getting late and one of them had to get ready for bed," Gary replied.

"How long were they there?"

"Not very," he said, avoiding the question.

"What does that mean exactly?"

"Fine, Mike," Gary said, getting a little hostile. "They were there for close to twelve hours! I couldn't get them to leave, I even started vacuuming so I didn't have to hear them proselytizing. Did it for so damn long, I thought my arm was going to fall off."

"Well, at least your carpet was clean." What the hell

else could I say?

"It was horrible," Gary rued.

"Well, then maybe you'll appreciate my story. I had no sooner opened the door when crazy lady number one started her spiel, then the second one tried to hand me a Watchtower. If I had had the presence of mind and knew who was at the door, I would have brought a lighter and burned the pamphlet as she held it. I started yelling at them, saying, 'I'm an atheist! Do you want to talk about life free from religion?!' They started to back up. I think the first lady might have actually even begun to cry a little bit, but what really put me on their 'Do not solicit' list was, as they were trying their best to get the hell out of there, I came out of my house and got all up in the man's face. Reeking of booze, I screamed. 'I'm one of the Four Horsemen, motherfucker! And if you don't get the hell out of here, I'm going to 'rapture' your ass!' They started screaming, running as fast as they could to their Ford Taurus."

"Wow! Maybe you'd better hope the Big Man doesn't favor their religion over every other, or you are screwed! And what's with the Ford Taurus? Is that somehow relevant?"

"Not really. I just think that car is the preferred vehicle of religious zealots everywhere."

"Mike, I'm kind of surprised you didn't have a cabin in upstate Montana, all by yourself."

"Would have, if I could have afforded it." I stood up, feeling marginally better. I didn't think God had anything specifically out against me, just mankind in general. Way better. Misery loves company.

Paul and BT were coming out of the house with a small cache of weapons. The pistol from the father's hand was noticeably missing, which was fine with me. There was the 30-30 rifle with a beautiful Leopold scope, another damn .22 and a shotgun. My eyes grew wide, looking at the beauty.

"Twenty-gauge," BT said, deflating my spirits.

Twenty-gauges were a blast to shoot, but anything bigger than a turkey and you'd have to be a foot away to kill it. Might as well be swinging a machete at that point.

"Damn, I was hoping for a little more," I said, picking up the .30-30.

"There's another room upstairs we didn't check," BT said.

"Master bedroom, most likely," Paul added.

"You two both know there'd probably be more guns there, right?" I asked. BT and Paul shared a knowing glance. Of friggin' course, they knew that. "Someone's in the room?"

BT nodded. "My guess would be the mother."

"Yeah? Why would this nightmare have any other kind of conclusion? I'm going in."

"Why?" Gary asked me.

"This family deserves to be together."

"You need a wingman?" BT asked.

"If I'm not out on my own in five, could you maybe pull me out? And I'll take a bottle of Prozac, if you come across any," I said, trying for mirth. I think it came out more like a grumble mixed with a dose of grim determination.

"This isn't necessary," Paul said.

"You're probably right, but if that zombie upstairs is somehow still holding onto a soul, I'd like to think that I'm putting her to peace and they can finally all be together."

"Aren't they already dead?" Gary asked. "They're souls should already be gone."

"I'm not dead," I told Gary. He looked like he just swallowed a grapefruit. "Relax, brother, I'm not mad. You would think not having a soul would be liberating," I said. "I mean free from guilt, what more could a Catholic boy ask for?"

"I would appreciate you not talking like that," Gary said, truly hurt.

"I'm the walking abomination, Gary. I'll talk any

goddamn way I want!" I yelled at him.

"That ought to get you in His good graces," he retorted hotly.

"My bad. Probably not going to make it through the pearly gates now!"

"I'll send you to a neutral corner, Talbot, if you don't shut the hell up. We all know this is a bad situation. You're just making it worse!" BT yelled.

"Which Talbot are you talking about?" Gary asked as an aside.

"The other Talbot-hole!"

"That's what I thought…because he really kind of started it," Gary said.

"Gary!" BT shouted, "You're not making this any better either! You do realize you're his older brother."

"I'm good, I'm sorry," Gary said, composing himself better and quicker than I was able to.

I had left the scene completely to go back into the house. BT or Paul had pulled the father totally into the crib room and shut the door. One more nightmare locked away tight. I looked up the staircase, wondering if salvation might lay up there. I had my doubts. All this talk of lost souls had me thinking as I ascended, about all those people that believed in past lives. Why would God reassign souls? Was there a finite number? But that would only make sense if there were a set number of people on the planet. There were way more people alive in 2010 than in say, Biblical times. And would God go green? I mean with the whole recycling thing? It just didn't make much sense. To believe in reincarnation, you would have to accept one of two things: either only certain people got to get "used" souls or the vast majority of us running around didn't have one. Or maybe there was a third alternative. Maybe the finite number of existing souls was divisible. That could explain why the whole world had become so corrupt and evil. As more of us were born, we each got less and less of God's essence.

Maybe this whole damn zombie-pocalypse was just a way for God to collect back his broken pieces to finally make them whole, something Humpty had never been able to accomplish. But if that were the case, wouldn't those of us still around be feeling "wholer" or "holier"? How many soulless people had I come across since this all happened? How could anyone with any allegiance to the Big Man align himself with Eliza? The new root of all evil. My thoughts were flawed...well, there's something new and unusual. I was at the top of the stairs and I couldn't even begin to remember how I got here.

The master bedroom was at the end of a hallway that wasn't nearly long enough. I figured it was where I wanted to go because, of the three doors up here, it was the only one not open.

I took a deep breath, and before I could engage my legs into moving, I heard Gary down at the bottom of the stairs.

"Wait, brother, I'll come with you," he said, taking the stairs two at a time.

I thanked him. This might singularly be the most difficult thing my brother had done to date and he was doing it for me.

"What are you waiting for?" he asked. "I said I'd come; I didn't say I'd lead."

I snorted, it was a little undignified, but he let it lapse. I could see the shadow play of someone moving in the gap between the door and the floor. Back and forth it moved rhythmically, at least it wasn't banging up against the door, but we'd learn why in a few more seconds.

I slowly turned the doorknob. Gary's rifle barrel was over my shoulder. At least, it was my right shoulder so I wouldn't get hot brass in the face. As I pushed the door in, we both took a step backwards, weapons at the ready. We could hear groaning and moaning and the stink was excruciating, but there was no onward rush of zombies. The door stopped its inward movement about halfway through its cycle.

"I thought you were like super strong now?" Gary asked.

"You're really giving me shit right now?"

He pushed his rifle past my head so that the barrel could be used to open the door the rest of the way.

Mrs. Dead Husband was straining against bonds Mr. Dead Husband must have put in place before he opted out. She was tied to the foot of her bed, which looked to be made of some stout oak. At least, we knew why she wasn't eating us yet. Her hands were almost touching behind her back, she was pulling so tight on her bindings.

"Are those pantyhose tied to her?" Gary asked. "Didn't know the things were so strong."

Her head, which had been resting on her chest as she swayed back and forth, popped up much like her infant's had. Her eyes almost had intelligence to them. They looked predatory, not the mindless glaze of the undead. Her mouth gnashed in anguish at a food that was so close; the similarities to her baby were striking.

And then I crossed the bridge into insanity or at least my world had.

"Do me a wrong, you bringer of evil."

Gary's rifle erupted, but still the zombie's words echoed in my head even as she dropped to the ground, dead.

"Did you hear that, Gary?" I fairly cried.

"Don't know how I would have missed it. Even a .22 is pretty loud in a small room like this," Gary shouted over the ringing in both of our ears.

"Not the shot…the zombie."

"What about it?" Gary asked.

"She spoke."

"No, she didn't."

"She did, as clear as you and I are talking."

"Mike, I wouldn't screw with you on this. She said

nothing and then I blew her head off. What do you think she said?"

My thoughts were in a tailspin. I've always felt that I was a pace or two closer to the edge than most; but at least I could usually recognize the precipice and step back at the appropriate time. Seems like I misjudged and slipped completely over. "She...I mean *it* said something like 'Do wrong, you bringer of evil.'"

Gary had to step out of the room apparently to gather enough clean air to fuel his laughter.

"What the fuck is so funny!?" I yelled, following him out.

"You're telling me that zombie was quoting a Black Sabbath tune? I find that to be funny as hell."

"What?"

"That line, 'Sing me a song you're a singer. Do me a wrong, you're a bringer of evil.' That's from Black Sabbath, I mean not the Ozzy-led band, but the Ronnie James Dio version. Still an awesome song, though."

"Gary, she spoke to me," I said. Gary looked like he was about to brush me off. "So did the baby." That got his attention.

"Part of the new and improved Mike?" he asked.

"I've got to believe when those psychics talked about communing with the dead, this wasn't what they were talking about."

"No wonder why Eliza is so pissed all the time," Gary said, reflecting.

"That doesn't really help."

Gary gathered himself and walked back into the room. "I know, let's see if this little trip was worth it." Gary gave a wide berth to Mrs. Dead Husband and went into the huge walk-in closet. "There's a safe!" Gary said, sticking his head back out.

"Great, maybe we'll see who he willed his gold watch to," I said, looking at the zombie's feet, which were still twitching. It was creeping the hell out of me, but at least she wasn't telling me she wanted some Dr. Scholl's or something.

"Gun safe, Mike." Gary said as if I were Gary Busey. Does that need any further explanation?

"I know, brother, I'm looking at it, too."

BT and Paul had come up the stairs after hearing the rifle shot.

"What's going on?" BT asked, stepping past the dead zombie and further into the room.

"She was—" I started, but Gary cut me off.

"Found a safe!" he said louder than he needed to.

"How big?" Paul asked from the doorway of the now crowded room; especially since none of us wanted to be any closer to Twitchy than we had to be.

"I never noticed them twitching so much. Do they always do this?" BT asked, looking down at her legs.

"It's not like we usually hang around to find out, but I don't think so," I said.

"Do you notice something strange about her head?" Paul asked, leaning a little over the body.

"Besides having a bullet in it?" came BT's wise-ass remark.

Paul was leaning a little closer.

This seemed like one of those moments in a horror movie where something jumps out of somewhere and scares the hell out of all the watchers.

"Something's wrong, man, don't get any closer," I told Paul.

He looked at me questioningly, but he did as I said. "Wait a second. I'll show you." Paul rooted around in the nightstand until he found something he could use. Ended up being a wooden ruler.

"You going all Catholic nun on us?" Gary asked from the entrance to the closet. "You guys heard that I found a gun safe, right?"

"Two seconds," Paul said handing his small rifle to BT. He straddled the dead zombie and extended his hand with the ruler as close as he dared. "Gut check time," he mouthed, unwilling to suck up any air through his mouth. He moved a five-inch section of hair still attached to the shattered skull underneath. It slapped wetly against the top of her head as he turned it over.

"That's gross, Paul. Is there a point to this?" BT asked.

"Look at how thick her skull is. I'm not one hundred percent sure, but I think the average skull is about a quarter-inch thick. Hers is at least double that."

"Can they thicken their skulls?" BT asked, turning to me in alarm.

"Oh yeah, good first choice, BT, I'm the one with all the answers," I told him.

"I don't think she's dead," Paul said. "Damaged, for sure...but not dead. I think by the time the bullet got through this thick-ass skull, it ran out of steam."

"I hate to get all obvious," I said, donning my captain's hat. (Get it?)

BT finished her off. Once the smoke cleared, he spoke. "Any chance she's some sort of anomaly, like a throwback to Cro-Magnon, you know?"

I was trying desperately to remember almost as quickly as I tried to forget how the scene with the baby unfolded. If I wasn't over-thinking this, the baby was still moving after my first shot. I might have completely missed with my second shot, but the third shot hit home and the baby stopped moving. The fourth shot was mostly involuntary. I didn't give a shit though. There was no way I was going back into that room to see if the baby's skull was abnormally thick. Even if that were the case, it could just mean that Mom had passed that defect down to it genetically.

"I don't know for sure, but we're going to have to keep this in mind, going forward. Let's check out this safe and get out of here. The longer we stay, the more I wish we had all just gone to Maine and let the chips fall where they may."

"The safe is open!" Gary said excitedly. "What're the odds of that?"

"Pretty good," Paul said from the far side of the room. He was looking out the window, keeping an eye on the street around us. "They were getting ready to leave and all."

"Makes sense," Gary said, continuing the conversation.

"Brother, just check out what's inside," I told him. I would have smacked him upside the forehead if BT hadn't got past me and was now in my way.

"Damn!" Gary yelled.

"Grenades! Please tell me grenades!" I said, almost jumping up and down like a schoolgirl that found out the captain of the football team liked her.

"Yeah. Joe Homeowner in suburbia North Carolina has a secret stash of grenades. Get a hold of yourself, Talbot," BT said. "Is it grenades?" BT asked Gary softly.

"Rossi Circuit Judge .45/410 revolver rifle!" Gary said as he held it over his head.

"Zombies could have on Kevlar helmets, it wouldn't stop that thing," I said.

"Big gun?" BT asked.

"Shoulder-mounted cannon," Gary finished. "Only twenty rounds, though."

"Those bullets are probably a couple of bucks each, not something you go plinking with," I said.

"No name twelve-gauge and a snub nose .38, decent amount of rounds for each," Gary said as he pulled stuff from the safe and around it.

BT was shuffling it to the larger room. I grabbed a small duffel bag full of clothes and baby toys that was perched on top of the dresser. I spilled the contents onto the bed, careful not to spend too much time thinking about what the things were or who they belonged to. The pacifier, though, almost dropped me to my knees. I went back to the growing pile of bullets and gun-cleaning supplies and began to stuff them into the bag.

"Cats!" Paul said a little louder than I think he intended to.

"Is that some sort of new expletive?" BT asked him when Paul didn't elaborate.

"No," Paul answered, looking at BT questioningly. "There were cats running by."

"Running?" I asked. Paul nodded.

"How many?"

"Ten, twelve maybe."

"Let's get this shit and be gone."

"Not that I want to stay in here any longer than needed, but what's the rush now?" BT asked me.

"Unless Mouser King just opened up around the corner, something has them spooked," I said, grabbing the handles of the duffel bag and standing up.

"I hate it when you're right," Paul said. "Couple of speeders headed this way."

"Well, it's a good bet there's a bunch of their slower brethren behind them and I am not getting stuck in here as my final stand. I hate this house," I added.

"I'm outta here," Gary said, pushing past BT.

"Don't let me get in your way," BT told him.

Gary was already at the foot of the stairs and not turning to respond. I shrugged my shoulders and followed my brother.

The two speeders had blown completely past the house in pursuit of the cats. The twenty shufflers following had just shambled onto our street and seemed to redouble their efforts with quarry in sight.

The zombies were within thirty yards by the time we were all packed and ready to go. Not close enough for any immediate danger, but how close does one really want to get with one's waking nightmare?

"Hey, G, let me see that rifle," BT said as he stepped back out of the car. He carefully placed five shells in the rifle's cylinder.

"BT, make sure it's tight against your shoulder," I told him right before I covered my ears.

BT slightly rocked on his heels as he fired a round. Doesn't sound like much, but it was the first gun I had seen that could even do something as much as that to the big man.

"OOOOOH WEEEEE!" he shouted. "It took three of them down!"

We all looked through the back windshield. Two were completely out for the count and the third one's legs were still moving, but it was only doing circles in the pavement as its head was on the ground in an ever expanding pool of its own jellified blood.

BT was still celebrating when I tugged on his arm that he might want to get back in the car with us so we could go.

I had a flash of panic in my gut, wondering if anyone had deemed it necessary to check and see if the car actually started.

Paul turned the key in the ignition, a slow churning whirring sound quickly became the rapid tick of a dying starter and then it caught. The engine roared to life just as the first of the zombies banged into the rear bumper.

"That was close," Paul said, looking in the rearview mirror at me and the zombies outside.

"Um, dude, it's still close…we haven't left yet," I told him.

"Right," he said as he placed the car in drive.

"How did he end up in the driver's seat?" BT asked as he watched the zombies retreat.

The speeders up ahead turned when they heard us coming. They started running full speed towards us, the smaller cats completely forgotten.

"Run them over!" BT yelled.

"Don't!" I yelled trying to match him in volume. "There's a chance they could stop this car," I said, thinking of Tracy's long-since defunct Jeep Liberty.

"Bullshit!" BT said.

"Okay, how about crash through the windshield? You want one of those things in your lap? Just think where its mouth might end up," I told him.

"Stay away from the zombies!" BT begged.

"Easier said than done, guys. The road is only so big and they're fanning out," Paul said as he slowed the car down.

"Do your best," I told him as I braced for impact.

"Anyone want to switch seats?" Gary asked from up front.

Hitting at least one of the zombies in front looked to be a foregone conclusion. Gary grabbed the bag I had taken from the house and placed it in his lap. Not a one of us thought it wasn't a wise move.

Paul wrenched the wheel quickly to the left and the car shuddered as the lead zombie smashed into the side view mirror. The zombie's tongue left a saliva string down the entire length of Gary's and my windows. I swear I could see the mega germs swimming in that toxic stew now eating through the glass. (Flair for the dramatic? Sure, I'm not above it.)

The car flung back to the right, but it was either too much or too little of an adjustment. I couldn't tell, because I was still transfixed on the zombie spit inches from my face. That was, of course, until the side of my head slammed up against Gary's headrest. The impact, I think, brought the rear tires of the small car off the ground for a fraction of a second. My head was ringing from the smack. I was shaking the cobwebs away, but I didn't think I was doing such a good job when I looked out the windshield. A zombie was halfway up the hood, his outstretched hands latched onto the windshield wipers, and he was trying to pull himself up.

"Get off!" Paul screamed at it.

Gary was frantically hitting buttons on the console. The static-laced radio shot through the speakers, the sound not a welcome addition to the pain blossoming in my head. At some point, Gary turned on the hazard lights, which was actually fitting, and then he found what he had been searching for. The windshield wipers began to sweep back and forth, the added strain of a one hundred and eighty pound zombie snapping them off in its hands. The zombie looked to me to be surprised as it slid back down the hood and thumped under the bottom of the car. The radio was still blaring, the blinkers were still clacking and now the twisted metal from the broken windshield wipers was etching a groove through the windshield. I turned, the first zombie was already up and running, while the one that had perched on our hood looked like its legs were crushed. He was out of the race and the third had already turned and was still entirely too close for comfort.

"Nice driving, Paulie," I said in all seriousness.

His knuckles glowed a brilliant white where they made contact with the steering wheel.

"You alright, buddy?" I asked him.

"Yeah, why wouldn't I be?" he answered a few octaves higher than normal.

"Gary, you think maybe you could take care of the radio and the wipers?" I asked him.

"Sure thing," Gary answered.

If I hadn't known better, I would have sworn they had both found some helium, and had just moments before, been sucking some down. Gary was nearly as high pitched as Paul. But after some initial fumbling, he was still able to shut down the radio and the wipers. Curiously, his hand had hovered over the hazard button and he decided to leave them on. I could deal with the minor clacking, my headache and the possible concussion that I figured was going to ruin my entire day had already faded into obscurity. I could at least thank Tomas for that.

We had driven a few more blocks. The car was pretty quiet as the first of the fat droplets of rain began to fall. Paul, without any conscious thought, turned the non-existent windshield wipers on. I don't think he even noticed the grating sound of metal on glass or that the rain, that was now coming in sheets, was not being pushed from his field of vision.

Luckily, the rainstorm did not last long. By the time we got back to the storage yard, it had dwindled down to something resembling an ant pissing on a flat rock. (Think about that for a second, it'll come.)

"Are those zombies?" BT asked, sticking his head out the window and into the soft spray as the car came to a stop.

It was still difficult to see through the wet, streaked windshield, so we all rolled our windows down to take a better look.

"Better yet, where are Brian and Mrs. D?" I asked.

"I've had better days," Gary intoned.

"That's like comparing whether or not you'd like to get kicked in the nuts or eat an ice cream sandwich," I said to him.

"Ice cream sandwich," Gary said, without even blinking.

"Wise choice," I said as I got out of the car. The zombies immediately started heading towards us.

"Do you hear that?" BT asked as he placed his new rifle on top of the car door frame.

"Sounds like someone is banging on the locker," Paul said.

"Canned zombie?" I asked.

"Hopefully it's Brian and Mrs. Deneaux," BT said as he aimed for the approaching zombies through his steel sights. The rifle blast rocked the car slightly as the lead zombie's head disintegrated. It was the first zombie kill that actually looked like a movie prop. The head looked like someone had stuffed it with some C4 and just blew it up.

"That was disgusting," Paul said, turning away.

Gary was already gagging.

It took me six shots with my .22 before the second zombie stopped. I may have missed a couple because he was running full tilt at us, but I watched the connecting hits. Its head would snap back a little, like it had got caught up momentarily on a small branch, and forward it would keep coming.

By the fifth shot, I could see BT in my peripheral vision. He was wondering if he should finish the thing off. The sixth shot dropped him like a penny dropped from a skyscraper. Its knees just buckled and he went down, no skidding, nothing.

"What the hell is going on?" BT asked, still sighting through the rifle to see if there were any more targets to acquire.

"Zombie 3.0," I said as I went forward to check out the increased banging on the orange steel doors.

"Brian?" I asked directly outside the rattling door.

If he didn't answer, would I have to open the door to see if it was them? Deneaux, I think, I could shoot without too many issues; Brian would be another matter.

"It wasn't my fault," a whiny sounding Mrs. Deneaux said.

"How the hell wasn't it? You fell asleep," Brian said. It sounded like I was interrupting a repetitive argument. "You killed all the zombies?" Brian asked through the doorway.

"How many did you think there were?" I asked him as I pulled up on the handle.

Brian shielded his eyes from the light as he stepped out. Mrs. Deneaux sat in the shadows a few moments more, letting her eyes adjust slowly.

"That's it?" Brian asked, looking at the two prone bodies. "I figured there were dozens," he said, a little embarrassed.

"Wanna start from the beginning?" I asked him.

"I was looking in the lockers and Mrs. Deneaux was supposed to be watching my back."

"I was, but I got tired of your repeated failures," she interjected acerbically.

"You're priceless. No wonder nothing ever took root in that cold, barren womb of yours," Brian shot out.

"If it were you coming out, I would have made sure to wrap the umbilical cord around your neck a few more times," she said, not missing a beat.

"Whoa, whoa!" BT yelled, "How long have you two been locked up?" he said, stepping in between them both.

"You're lucky it was dark in there!" Mrs. Deneaux yelled, "or I would have shot you!"

"That would have been preferable to listening to you drone on or almost die from your carbon monoxide emissions."

"If I could have smoked more in the hopes that it would have suffocated you, I would have!"

"Alright this is all very entertaining, but our day has also been less than stellar," I said.

Brian was about to unleash some new verbal assault on Deneaux, but stopped when he looked around at the four of us and our hangdog expressions.

"Sorry," he said to us, careful to make sure that Deneaux did not believe she was included in that apology.

"Any luck before they came?" I asked.

His bowed head answered before he spoke. "We've been stuck in that shed almost since you left."

"Alright, let's just find someplace relatively safe to hunker down for the night. I think we could all use a break from today's festivities." Nobody argued; at least that was a step in the right direction.

"Got any good ideas about that?" BT asked, "Because I'm a little hesitant about going into other people's homes right now."

"Oh come on, Mike," Gary said as he saw me looking back at the storage space Brian and Mrs. Deneaux had just been liberated from.

"We'll chain up the front gate and we'll post a guard," I said.

"Hopefully, one that doesn't fall asleep while they say they're watching your back," Brian said for good measure, looking across BT at Mrs. Deneaux.

I smiled inwardly as the old crow stuck her tongue out at him.

"Come on. I'm sure there are plenty of blankets," I said.

"Tons of sleeping bags, too," Brian added. "I've found all sorts of camping gear."

"I wish we had some S'mores," Paul said. "Oh that's right, you don't like them, do you, Mike?"

"Isn't that un-American? Not liking S'mores?" BT asked.

"They make his hands sticky," Gary said, adding his two cents.

"Think of how many more germs you can pick up with sticky fingers!" I said, trying to defend my position. If making my opponents laugh was victory, then I had defeated them all.

"Didn't you ever think to lick your fingers off?" Mrs. Deneaux asked.

I shuddered at the thought.

"Wash them off in a stream maybe?" Brian asked, trying to be helpful.

"Ever hear of giardia?" I answered.

"Come on, as a kid you were thinking about a parasite in water that came from the refuse of wildlife?" BT asked.

I nodded. "I read a lot as a kid."

"Poor bastard," he said, smiling. "I'll take first watch. Won't get much sleep thinking about your S'mores issue anyway."

I didn't tell him that since Tomas' bite, I didn't feel like I'd ever need to sleep again and could pretty much take every one's shift without an issue. I decided I'd take the other watches after his. That's what he gets for making fun of me.

Chapter Six – Mike Journal Entry 5

BT finished up his watch. The sun had long since departed. We had a small flashlight going in the corner of the ten by thirty foot-shed, but it did little to shield us from the darkness within. Every time I even contemplated shutting my eyes, images of the infant from earlier today crept in. I should have just let sleeping zombies lie, so to speak. BT raised the door as quietly as he could, which was still as loud as you would expect a metal rolling door would be. Paul and Brian immediately awoke, Deneaux slept on, snoring like a sailor, (which I guess is an unfair comparison to sailors everywhere, because I don't really know what they sound like when they're asleep.)

Paul started to get up. "I've got it, bud," I told him.

"You sure, man?" he asked even as his head was traveling back down to its resting spot.

"Can't sleep anyway. No sense in both of us being up," I said. He grunted something about thanks, in return, or he belched, sounding just about the same.

"Anything?" I asked BT, who was eyeing my bed longingly.

"I think I heard a couple of cars off in the distance and maybe some gunfire, but it was so far away, I can't be sure."

"Thanks, man," I told him. "Enjoy your beauty rest."

"You have any phobias about other men sharing your bed?" he asked.

I didn't answer, I wanted to hold onto some secrets.

"Okay, so I know it's not because I'm black. Is it because I'm a man?" he asked solemnly.

"BT, I don't like my kids in my bed," I told him truthfully.

"You're kidding me, right?"

"Why would I? Like you need some new and improved reason to think I'm nuts?"

BT just shook his head and grabbed the scant bedding remnants not presently being used.

"No retort?" I asked him.

"Talbot, I am so damn tired and I really think I'm beginning to realize the depth of your illness."

Oh, I doubt it, I thought. "BT, seriously, I'll be lucky if sleep comes at all tonight, sleep in that bed (I couldn't, as hard as I tried, say it was "my bed".)

"You're cool with that?" he asked. "You're not going to try and slip in there with me later tonight, are you? I mean Tracy did leave today."

Was that just today? Seemed like a sanity ago.

"I think I'll be able to restrain myself," I told him.

"Even with this pretty face?" he asked, smiling as he got down onto the sleeping bag. "You're alright with this?" he asked as he placed his head on my pillow. "Because you look like you're regretting your decision."

"I'll be fine," I told him as I tried to shut the door more quietly than he had opened it, with far less success.

The night had a distinct chill to it. I could register that fact, but I felt slightly removed from it. I was comfortable and I had the feeling, I could be running around naked or wearing seven different layers and I would feel the same. And for some damn reason, Pop-Tarts kept leaking into my thoughts, which was disturbing, but still better than splattered, baby zombie brain. (Unless, of course, we were talking about cherry-flavored Pop-Tarts because that might be the singular, most disgusting thing left on the planet.)

I walked the entire perimeter of the storage facility. But after thinking about it, I don't think I ever looked out beyond the chain link fence. My head had been down and I was deep in thought or shallow in disregard. Either one works just fine, but I was paying absolutely no heed to the outside world. I could have walked into the waiting arms of a zombie and not realized it until he or she had bitten me.

My next lap I vowed to pay more attention, but I didn't make it halfway around before I began to daze out again. It really does suck having the attention span of a coconut-laden swallow (whoever picks this journal up may or may not get that reference; it will be a slightly better world if you do). I started to think about life, a normal life, mortgage, taxes, death, pretty much everything that I would never experience again. How the hell is it possible that I'm now missing any one of those things? And then I kept circling back to arriving at Ron's and seeing Tracy and the kids again. Was Nicole showing yet? And what the hell is in Ron's false floorboards in his closet? After kissing my wife and hugging my kids that would be my utmost priority. I was going to have to be careful, though, I wouldn't doubt it if he had a security system in place.

I would have completely missed the zombie pressed up against the fence if he hadn't spoken.

"Eat," it repeated over and over in my head.

"Why don't you kiss my ass," I told it back. It actually stopped for a beat or two, processing where that info had come from. I would bet the thing in front of me hadn't had a real thought in its head since it became infected.

I had established that we could talk, but would it listen? "Dance, fucker," I said aloud. It licked its lips. Okay...zero for one, Talbot. *What the hell are you trying to prove?* I asked myself. Okay, so if I'm asking myself the question, what are the odds I'm going to know the answer? Not aloud, gotta get into its head. *Dance, fucker!* I screamed in my thoughts. I wouldn't bet any substantial amount of money on this, but I would swear it picked up its right leg and dropped it back down. Maybe he couldn't dance. It used to be a white guy, after all.

"Where the hell is a black zombie when you need one? I really shouldn't be left unsupervised for too long," I said aloud and started to laugh.

I had effectively blocked the zombie's repeating message, otherwise I would have just shot him in the forehead and ended this whole experiment. I was already a little antsy that I was this close to one of them and hadn't dispatched it. I was pacing a few yards up and back trying to decide what, if anything, my being able to hear zombies could do to help us. Re-Pete (I named him that because of how he was following my every move; it seemed fitting) kept following, albeit a second or two behind, as whatever was left of his mind caught up and sent the appropriate message.

I walked to the left, Re-Pete followed. I turned and came back to the right, so did Re-Pete, his eyes never leaving mine. Re-Pete was starting to freak me out a little bit, *STAY!* I said in my most authoritative 'in head' voice. As I turned to go back to the left. The only part of Re-Pete that followed were his eyes. I was looking over my shoulder the entire time, wondering when he was going to follow, but he never did. I did my complete small circuit and he never moved.

"Well, that's interesting." I said, scratching my head.

On your knees! I screamed in my thoughts, convinced I was going to give myself an aneurysm. Re-Pete dropped to his knees like a choirboy promised a new bike. (You can go anywhere you want with that, I'm not getting any more descriptive.) His knees slammed hard into the pavement. I heard what sounded like his patella on his left leg cracking in two. Normally, I'd cringe, but the sense of power welling up in me was invigorating and I was thrilled I had hindered him in some way.

Was the next thing I wanted to try possible? *DIE!* I shouted over and over. I was concentrating so hard, my body began to sway back and forth. Sweat was cascading down my forehead. Re-Pete was looking at me like I had lost my mind.

"Talbot?"

My thoughts were snapped; how did Re-Pete know my name? I bent lower to look into its eyes.

"Mike!" An alarmed voice came from behind me. "What are you doing?" I heard heavy footfalls coming up fast. I was physically moved from my spot like a child might move his GI Joe, quickly and without regard for personal comfort.

"You alright, man?" BT asked me as he kept running. We were a good thirty yards away from the fence before he finally put me down. "Are you bit or scratched?" BT asked, trying his best to look me over.

I peered around him at Re-Pete who had gotten back up on his feet. "Well, he didn't die?"

"What?" BT asked in alarm. "Who didn't die?"

"Re-Pete," I told him like he should know exactly what I was talking about.

"Mike, what's going on? Is Eliza here? Is she in your head? Are you bit?" He kept rapid-firing questions at me.

I was still suffering from the mild after-effects from the disconnection with Re-Pete. I guess that's what you could call it. Wonderful! I wonder if they have any medications for postpartum depression resulting from the lost contact between man and zombie. It could open up a whole new market for the pharmaceutical companies.

"Mike! I'm about to slap the shit out of you if you don't start talking to me!" BT roared in my face.

I wasn't quite ready to come back to this semblance of reality, but when BT says he's going to slap the shit out of you, you tend to listen. "Don't you dare!" I said, finally taking my eyes from Re-Pete. "I'm fine," I was able to grunt out.

"I don't know if it's the moonlight or what, but you don't look fine."

I waved dismissively at his words. "Follow me," I told him as I walked past him and back to an eager looking Re-Pete who now only had eyes for the bigger, beefier BT. "I knew you'd leave me at the first opportunity," I told Re-Pete as I approached.

"Huh?" BT asked. "I'm right here, man. Are you sure you're alright?"

"I was talking to Re-Pete," I told BT.

"That's hilarious," BT said without a hint of humor.

"I'm serious, first he wanted to eat me and now he'd rather eat you, but to be fair, I'm sure once he was done with you, he'd want to eat me again. He's non-discriminatory that way."

"I knew it had to happen sooner or later," BT stated flatly. "I mean it really was just a matter of time. The problem now is how do I tell Tracy?"

"What are you talking about?" I asked him.

"You going crazy, that's what I'm talking about. I mean everyone knew you were already precariously perched on the ledge even before the zombies came. That you held out this long has amazed most of us."

"You do know I'm standing right here, right?"

"Sure physically you are, but mentally you're gone, man," BT said. "I'll miss you. I count you among one of my best friends."

"BT, I'm not insane," I said. He merely tapped the top of my head like I was six years old and I had said something cute.

"Come here, BT," I told him, approaching closer to Re-Pete.

"Don't you get too close to him. There are some medications that you can take that, aside from some excessive drooling, will almost make you normal. There's no cure for zombie. Tracy will skin me alive if I bring back an insane zombie."

"All this time, I thought zombies were already insane."

"Come on, Mike, let's get the rest and we'll just head back to Maine. Maybe there's still a part of you that can be salvaged. A small part, sure, but some is better than none."

"BT, shut up and watch."

I said aloud, "On your knees," at the same time as I thought it. Pretty talented right?!

Re-Pete didn't disappoint. He instantly once again fell to his knees. This time his already cracked patella completely shattered with a loud snapping noise.

BT had finally shut up and was looking back and forth from me to Re-Pete. "That's not some sort of trick is it?"

"Yeah, I was using finger snacks as a training aid," I said sarcastically.

"Coincidence then?" he asked, still not quite believing what he was witnessing.

"Get up," I told and thought. Re-Pete stood with some difficulty and was favoring his left leg, but stood he did. "Turn around." Re-Pete did; he was now facing away from us.

BT's nose was almost pressed up against the fence. "You know, this is fucking amazing," BT said, not turning back towards me. Now he turned. "How many do you think you could do this to?"

"No clue, I didn't know I could do this until a few minutes ago."

"Is it hard?"

"I have to concentrate, but it's no more difficult than listening to you talk."

"Funny," BT said turning back to Re-Pete. "Can you make him hurt himself?"

"I don't think directly. I tried to make Re-Pete kill himself."

"Repeat?"

"Re-Pete, P…E…T…E." I said spelling the name. BT was looking at me funny. "He was following me around…I thought the name seemed fitting."

BT looked at me like he wasn't completely convinced

I hadn't stepped over the edge. "Then what about indirectly?"

"Well, I think he shattered his knee the way he's been dropping to them, but I don't know if he's incapacitated."

"Is there a certain distance you have to be from them?"

I shrugged I had no clue. "He stopped listening to me when you pulled me away, but I don't really know from what point he stopped or if it was because I lost concentration while you were jiggling me around like Jell-O."

"Well, walk away. Let's see what happens."

"I'd rather just put a bullet in its head; he's really starting to reek."

"We'll get to that, but we have got to test the limitation of this. We might never get another opportunity like this.

"Yeah, that'd be a shame," I told him, turning to walk away.

"You're still concentrating, right?" BT asked to my retreating back.

"Yes I'm still concentrating, Mrs. Weinstedder."

"What?"

"Nothing, just my old algebra teacher."

"So somehow this whole scene reminded you of an old math teacher? Who did the wiring in your head? Because you should get your deposit back."

"BT what—"

"Stop!" he yelled. "Re-Pete here looks like he's about to break free."

I turned to watch. Re-Pete was slightly swaying from side to side. I took one step backwards, the swaying increased.

"Go one more," BT said, swinging his visage back to Re-Pete.

I did and Ree turned around to face us. I won't say he had a look of confusion on his face, wondering what had happened, first because the light wasn't good enough to see that minute of a facial detail from this distance; and secondly, I don't think zombies have any facial expression beyond perpetual snarl.

"He looks angry," BT said.

"Angrier than normal?" I asked BT as I came closer.

He shrugged his shoulders in answer. We were both up by the fence. Ree was trying unsuccessfully to get his hands through the chain link.

"He really does have a funk about him, doesn't he?" BT asked. "Do you want to try and kill him?"

"I'm having some issues here, BT."

"I'd like to say 'So what else is new' but that almost seems cliché now. That's no human," BT said pointing to Ree. "And it's debatable if that thing is even technically alive, but for the sake of argument, let's say it is. It is still trying to kill us."

"I know all this. I really do, I just feel like a cat playing with a mouse. It seems much more humane to put a bullet in its head than mess with it for our amusement."

"I don't see anything funny here, Talbot, do you?" BT asked with some heat in his voice.

Step back and then get on your knees, I commanded my puppet. He complied immediately.

BT turned to watch and see what Ree would end up doing.

Smash your head against the ground! I yelled in my head, showing the motion I wanted him to take.

Ree was mannequin-still; he did not move.

"What's going on?" BT asked, switching his view back between Ree and me. I was almost swaying as much as Ree had been earlier.

"He won't do it," I said, blowing out a large exhalation of air.

"Are you trying hard enough?"

"BT, I just about gave myself an aneurysm. I don't think I could concentrate any harder."

"I bet you got a D in that algebra class," BT said, placing a bullet in Re-Pete's head as he struggled to get up, his damaged knee finally locking the joint in place. Ree fell over with a solid thud.

"I failed it."

BT snorted. "How far you think you were, fifty, sixty feet?"

"Not much more than that."

"Could you do that with multiple zombies?"

I could hear Gary yelling, asking if everything was alright in the distance.

"We're fine!" BT yelled, moving away from the spreading pool of blood by his feet.

"How far are we away from our locker?" I asked BT.

"A ways," he answered.

"How did you find me?" I asked him suspiciously. "And better yet, why?"

"Mike," BT started, "you've gone through a lot in the last few days."

"Keeping tabs on me, man?" I asked, more than a little hurt.

BT didn't dance around the bush. "Yeah, actually I am. Do you blame me?"

I was a second or two away from flashing into anger and then it dissipated like fog in a hot summer sun. "You know, fundamentally, I'm still the exact same person I was. You know that, right?" I asked him, seemingly for his approval.

"I hope so, Mike. Because I can't imagine doing this shit with anyone but that crazy bastard."

"What's going on?" Gary asked, somewhat out of breath. He took in the whole scene quickly. One dead zombie, me with a slightly wilted look and BT very standoffish. "Everything cool?"

"I hope so, I really do," BT said, walking back towards the locker.

"Mike?" Gary asked.

"BT isn't all that enamored with my upgrades," I said, walking over to the fence to see if I could figure out if Re-Pete had a thicker skull.

"Anything I should be concerned about?" Gary asked, coming up to my side.

"Not yet, brother."

"How much time we got until Eliza comes?"

"Tomorrow."

"Do you think we'll need more weapons?"

"I've got a little surprise of my own set up. We should have plenty of guns for what I want to do.

"What about the zombie?"

"He's dead now," I said, walking back towards the shed. I could not see anything more in the dark.

Paul met me about halfway back. "Hey, buddy, do you need any help?" he asked still fumbling with his pants.

"It looks like you're the one that needs a hand. Now, I'm not offering, I'm just saying."

"Go figure, I find a camp potty, toilet paper, a small flashlight and some damn comic books. The night couldn't be any quieter and I find the perfect spot to take care of some personal business."

"Sorry, man, but you should know better by now," I said. I felt for Paul I truly did. Women don't really get it, but a man's time on the throne is one of relaxation, a time when he can let go, both literally and figuratively. Not bathroom humor, just fact.

"I'm going to see if the office is open. Maybe there's actually a door to the bathroom there."

"Be careful, my friend."

He waved a hand at me. I hoped it wasn't the one he had been using for other needs earlier.

Mrs. Deneaux was sitting outside in a plastic lawn chair, smoking a cigarette, I couldn't tell if she was asleep or not. The fluid motions she made when extracting the smoke from her lips and flicking the ash was a much-practiced maneuver. It was her own small dance of death.

Mrs. Deneaux magically produced a half-empty pack and one cigarette leapt out at me. I took it much like a drowning man would take a glass of water, or an apple from a serpent. You decide.

Gary had grabbed my shoulder and gave me a brotherly squeeze as he went back into the storage unit. Brian walked by, stopping only long enough to tell me he would take over the patrol. I thanked him as Deneaux lit my smoke.

"BT doesn't trust you," she said after a few peaceful moments. She wasn't looking at me, but rather up at the sky and the blazing stars.

"And you?" I asked, taking a heavy intake of smoke, also marveling at the sight above us.

"All I know is that if you turn me into a vampire and I'm stuck in this old wrinkled body forever, I will make sure to never leave your side. I'm no longer a Miss Stewart."

I started laughing. "I'll keep that in mind; and who is Miss Stewart?"

"It's of no concern now. So how are things, Michael?" she said. At some point, she had stopped looking at the stars and her eyes sparked brightly as they focused intently on me.

"That's quite a gaze you've got going on there," I said, trying to deflect some of that attention.

"It is not every day that someone has their soul stripped from their body. I have also given mine up, but I fear I will have to atone for it a lot sooner than you, I expect."

My mouth opened to ask her what she had done, but she cut me off at the pass.

"It is not something I wish to discuss. Perhaps I will write it down in a journal. I see you scribbling in that thing all the time. I would love to know what you think of me."

"No you wouldn't," I said.

Now it was her turn to laugh. "No, perhaps I

wouldn't. Do you lead us to salvation, Michael?" she asked in all seriousness. "Is that even possible?"

"To be honest, Mrs. Deneaux…"

"Vivian."

"Vivian," I said. Her name felt like I was swirling broken glass around in my mouth as I tried to say it. "I'm just trying to make it through tomorrow."

Her gaze shifted back to the heavens. We actually enjoyed an easy silence for a few moments before she stood up. "I'm going to get a few more hours of sleep. I believe that we will make it through tomorrow," she said, heading back into the shed.

And then what? I wanted to say, but I wished her a good night and I meant it. I stayed there, looking at the stars swirling overhead until the morning sun began to bathe my face in its presence.

"You out here all night?" BT asked, stretching his arms wide.

"I guess so. I think I might have discovered a new planet."

"Okay, so it's early and now I'm not truly sure if this is sarcasm or are you telling the truth?"

"He's full of shit," Gary said, coming up from behind. "So what's on the agenda today?"

"Is Brian back?" I asked, I hadn't seen him since he had taken over patrol duty and how long ago was that? Four or five hours at least.

"He's not in there. Probably couldn't handle Mrs. Deneaux's snoring," Paul said.

"Vivian," I corrected.

"Who the hell is Vivian?" Paul asked.

"That's Deneaux."

"What are you talking about?" he asked, rubbing his eyes.

"Mrs. Deneaux's first name is Vivian," I clarified.

"Okay, but what's that got to do with Brian?" Paul

asked.

"Nothing."

"Maybe we should worry less about Vivian and more about Brian," BT said forcefully. "He could be hurt, and you two are worried about someone's first name."

"Who's hurt?" Mrs. Deneaux asked, coming up from behind BT.

"Nobody we hope," I said, "But Brian hasn't come back from patrol."

Mrs. Deneaux immediately went back into the shed and began to put on all her clothes as well as strapping on her pistol.

"Good idea," Gary said. "No guarantee we'll be coming back."

Within five minutes, we had all our meager supplies and mini arsenal of weaponry ready to go.

"Okay, once around silently. Hopefully, he's just holed up somewhere, getting some shuteye. If we don't find him and the perimeter looks safe enough, we'll call out for him. Sound good?" I asked.

I got terse nods in reply. We all knew this wasn't good. Most folks don't stray too far when a zombie apocalypse is going on and Brian knew enough to come back to the shed to get relief if he was tired. He wouldn't just fail to let his guard down. We walked for a few minutes, but the only noise were the sounds of zippers striking rifles or an occasional boot scuff. Conversation was non-existent.

"Mike?" BT said, softly coming up to my side. I stopped. "Isn't this where we met Re-Pete?"

I looked around. It was still a storage facility, and everything looked pretty much the damn same, but I would bet money that this was the exact spot, with one notable exception. Ree was missing, not the blood spot he had left behind, but his body was most assuredly not present and accounted for.

"What's the matter?" Paul asked, sensing the new

tension.

"Our zombie buddy has gone missing," I said as I scanned the lot.

"How is that possible?" Gary asked, walking over to the fence.

"Mike, he was dead," BT said. "I saw the exit wound out the back of his skull."

"Please don't tell me that now they're adapting so they don't die from a head shot," Paul sobbed. "Could they?"

"No, he was dead," I said flatly.

"How can you be so sure?" Paul asked, working himself up into a fervor. "I mean, so far, they've become fast, they can hibernate when there isn't enough food, and apparently, they can thicken their skulls to try to preserve themselves. Wouldn't it make sense from a purely zombie evolutionary trait to alter the one and only way that you can die?"

"We'd be fucked," I said. "But Ree was dead."

"Who is fucking Ree, Mike? And how can you be so damn sure?!" Paul was yelling now.

"I named the zombie and I know he was dead because I lost contact with him."

Paul was just looking at me with a shocked expression on his face, not grasping what I had just told him.

"It's the zombie whisperer!" Mrs. Deneaux cackled, lighting a cigarette.

"It's a pity those things haven't given you throat cancer yet," BT said.

She held up her middle finger like it was a makeup compact while with her other hand she would dab her extended middle finger on it and pretend to apply base to her face.

"That's actually pretty funny," Gary said.

"Wait! You can talk to zombies now?! When the hell were you going to let the rest of us know?" Paul said with spittle flying from his lips.

"Relax, Paul," BT said, placing his arm across Paul's chest. "He just found out last night."

Paul might have calmed down, but it was marginal at best. His temper went from something like eating a habanero pepper to rubbing jalapenos in your eyes; neither one is a great suggestion.

"What did this zombie have to say?" Mrs. Deneaux asked, leaning up against the closest shed.

"It revolved mostly around him being hungry," I said.

"That's rich," she laughed. "A hungry zombie! Who would have ever thought it?"

"What good does that do us?" Paul asked.

"That in itself…not much," I said.

"But…" BT prompted when I hesitated with the rest of what we had discovered.

"But I can… with limitations now… I made Re-Pete do what I told him to."

"Are you guys pulling my leg? Are there hidden cameras or some shit? Can you make them go away? Better yet, can you tell their hearts to stop beating? If they even still do?"

"Well, I could tell a few maybe to leave, but once they got thirty or forty yards away, they'd turn back around. And it seems that I can't make them directly hurt themselves."

"Almost like they have a failsafe switch?" Gary asked.

"I guess," I told him.

"Could you lead them to a precipice and have them walk off?" Gary asked, thinking of differing scenarios that would lead to a mass demise in zombies.

"Kind of like a zombie Pied Piper," Deneaux said.

Gary shrugged his shoulders. "Yeah, pretty much like that."

"Like lemmings?" BT asked. "That would be interesting."

"Right now, you guys know as much as I do," I told them.

Thankfully, Brian shifted the focus, being under Paul's watchful eye was starting to grate on my nerves. "Hey guys," a slightly disheveled Brian said, rounding a corner.

"We've been looking for you," Gary said.

"Sorry, I know I was on patrol, but there was nothing happening and I felt compelled to keep looking for guns. It's like a quest now."

"Did you move the zombie?" I asked him.

"Why would I do that? I was busy looking in lockers. Did you say how much time we have until our dinner guests arrive?" he asked.

"We've got about four hours," I told the group. The range of emotions went from 'Holy Shit! I'm scared' to 'About time' and whatever else can happen with five other people. I was more on the 'Scared Shitless' side.

"Should we look for more guns?" Gary asked as we all looked down on our less-than-adequate-looking ensemble of weaponry.

My head was going up and down in the universal language of yes, but my vote was a no. "It's too dangerous."

"We have enough time. I can go through a few more lockers," Brian said.

Yeah we could also play a rousing game of Monopoly for all the good that would do, I thought. I told him it sounded like a good idea, though. I wanted to do what every soldier did before going into battle, eat. For some reason, the only thing that keeps you from the thought of dying or killing is eating. We had pulled out packets and packets of dried goods from the camping lockers. Beef jerky, here I come.

Paul and BT went with Brian. Mrs. Deneaux, Gary, and I went through the dried packets, looking for the best stuff from which to make a decent lunch.

"Split pea and ham soup!" Mrs. Deneaux shouted triumphantly, holding the packet up to the sun like she had just reared the newborn king.

"You're kidding, right?" I asked her. "I'd rather eat the packet it came in."

"Who is insane enough to not like ham?" Mrs. Deneaux asked, looking sidelong at me.

Gary was pointing his index finger at me on the sly, thinking that I couldn't see him.

"I can see you, brother," I told him as he pulled his finger back quickly.

The weapons-of-mass-destruction-seeking team came back a couple of hours later with about as much luck finding anything, as the US had been a few years previous.

"We got some swords," Brian said, putting three sharp-edged blades on the ground.

"They any good?" I asked, picking one up. I'd seen some that would fall apart from the impact with a watermelon and others with a blade so dull they couldn't cut a fart.

"They're actually pretty good," BT said. "I think they're Japanese World War II officer swords."

I hefted the blade. It definitely had a deadly enough feel to it. "I plan on being a little closer to the action. Do you mind if I borrow one of these?" I asked them.

"Me too," Gary said, "Where he goes, I do too."

BT just plain grabbed the third. "So what's the plan?"

"You'd think you'd know better," Gary said.

I laid the entire thing out in all its lack of glory. Without rocket launchers, a battalion of soldiers, and an air strike, this would be far from the killing blow I would have chosen. This was more of a gesture, a giving of the middle finger, if you will, in the face of overwhelming odds.

"This isn't going to do much more than piss her off," Brian said.

"Exactly," I told him. "Pissed off opponents tend to make mistakes."

Brian nodded his head in agreement. "Makes sense, in

a suicidal kind of way."

"Have you met Mike?" BT asked.

Gary nodded in commiseration. I punched him in the arm. "I'll tell Dad when we get back," he said, rubbing the tender spot.

I hope you will, I thought, because that would mean we made it there.

Chapter Seven – Mike Journal Entry 6

Eliza was late or early (and gone), or she had taken a different route, or she had laid a trap for us, realizing what I was going to do. These three very different scenarios kept playing out in my head, each vying for its own time in the spotlight. I could deal with her being late or even the trap. Those two scenarios at least meant we were still in the game.

If she had passed while we were messing with Re-Pete, then every second we wasted here put my family in more danger. Another route could potentially be as bad, but as long as we were running parallel to her, and not hours behind, I could deal with that also. That crawling sensation kept worming its way up my back that Re-Pete had been some sort of diversion and she was laughing as she barreled down the highway. The wondering was a nightmare. I was seconds away from pulling the whole plug when I noticed the slightest sway to a young sapling – it was not windy.

"Everybody down!" I yelled.

Ten seconds went by, twenty seconds, I think we were closing in on a minute and still nothing. I was beginning to feel a little foolish…and now that nagging itching sensation was coming back. *Screw it.* I was ready to go. Gary reached out and put his hand on my shoulder when he sensed that I might be getting ready to move. How I let the sound of that caravan slip by my senses, I had no clue.

"Thanks," I told Gary.

"You always were a little impulsive," he told me.

BT was on my left side, looking intently at the rolling nightmare coming our way. His grip tightened on his rifle. Fat beads of sweat rolled off his forehead.

Mark Tufo

"You good, big man?" I asked him.

"Right as rain," he answered without ever taking his eyes off the lead truck. "You think she's in that first one?"

"Maybe before that invasion on Camp Custer when I almost killed her. She might be an arrogant bitch…but she's also a self-preservationist."

"Too bad," BT said.

The three of us were down in a culvert on the side of the road. It was almost steep enough that we were just about standing where we lay. Two tandem-trailer semis thundered past. Following them was what appeared to be an endless chain of troop transports and more tractor-trailers.

"Looks like Eliza's playing for keeps," Gary said, sticking his head over the embankment slightly.

"When has that ever NOT been the case?" BT asked.

I can't say that I had ever seen BT quite as nervous as he was now, and I was picking up on it, which in turn made me more nervous. Gary seemed blissfully ignorant of it all.

"Sure would be nice to get a hold of one of those troop transports," Gary said.

"I vote for just making it through the day," I told him.

"I second that," BT said, sticking his hand up slightly.

We could hear gunshots up ahead of us. Paul, Bryan, and Mrs. Deneaux were holding up their end and we were getting close to seeing what we could do about holding our own.

It was long seconds before the entire rolling army knew that it was under attack, but the lead tandem-trailer truck lying on its side kind of put a damper on their forward progress. The screeching metal as the truck slid sideways down the highway grated on my fillings, the vibrations hurting my teeth. I was thankful I did not have a steel plate in my head; it would have probably scrambled my brains more than they already were. The large truck had finally come to a stop. Sporadic fire was being returned as some of Eliza's human sympathizers started to realize they were being shot at and that the lead driver had not simply had an accident.

Eliza was close; I could sense the waves of cruelty emanating from her like ripples in a pond. I'm sure I could have followed the signal back to its source, but then she would have known I was here.

We could hear multiple truck doors opening and men scrambling to get into a defensive posture. Boot falls fell no more than five feet from where our heads were. A troop transport truck almost at the edge of my abilities was parked with the engine running; it was full of zombies.

"Anything?" BT asked, gripping his rifle so tightly, I thought he was going to fuse the metal with the wood.

Now it was my turn to sweat. "It's full of zombies. They're just sitting in there."

"They're very well behaved," Gary said. Not sure why; it was most likely nerves.

"Mike, these guys are getting close. It's only going to take one of them to look over and we're screwed," BT said.

"Cool, so I wasn't already feeling enough pressure; that oughta help," I told BT. I was doing my best to not cause a self-induced brain bleeder.

A hastily thrown cigarette butt flew by the left side of Gary's face. I thought he was going to start coughing from the smoke. Gary, in his entire life had never smoked, not one normal cigarette and not one of those funny, little left-handed ones that I had enjoyed so many of in my youth. Who am I kidding? I still enjoyed them from time to time in these latter years, especially at Widespread Panic shows.

Gary was turning blue in a desperate bid to keep himself from coughing. I grabbed the cigarette and chucked it further down the slope we were standing on.

"Talbot," BT said with no small measure of alarm.

We could hear men talking. The gunfire from our band had stopped. They had done their part and left before becoming outmanned and outgunned. Eliza's men were about to fan out and find whoever had attacked.

I turned my thoughts back to the zombies, who were still waiting patiently in the truck. "Eliza's got them under her control," I told the group.

"We gotta go, Mike," BT said, gripping my shoulder. "We might be able to make it to the tree line before they see us.

"Doubtful," Gary said.

"Okay, she's not communicating with them now, or she would have found me meddling about," I said aloud, but mostly for myself.

"Mike, it's now or never," BT said, flipping his safety off; Gary did the same.

"Okay, so she sent them an order and kind of tied it off. Does that make sense?" I was still only talking to myself. "It's almost like a repeating message and she just has it on loop."

"You should maybe pull the plug on that machine," Gary said as he got himself into a proper shooting position.

"No power cord," I said, intensifying my concentration. I'm still uncertain as to how this is done, though. Can you really 'think' harder? I find just thinking about thinking leads me astray. "More like a rope or a cord." We were seconds away from capture and/or death or vice versa. My senses were so heightened, I could hear individual pebbles as they were crushed under the boot heels of the troops approaching. "I found the knot!" I said excitedly.

"Weeks! I heard something over by the side of the road!" one of the men shouted.

"Time to die," BT said, though whether it was about the man that shouted or for us, he did not clarify.

I felt sort of sorry that the last thing that man saw on this planet was most likely the biggest man he had ever encountered popping up from the side of the road with a rifle.

"Got it!" I shouted triumphantly just as BT's rifle shuddered from the gas release of two bullets. Weeks' friend caught the first round in the side of his neck; blood pumped out as the man tried in vain to staunch the flow.

A small piece of hell broke out that day as BT's rifle kept jumping from the expended rounds. He was screaming a war cry. I watched in horror, almost *Matrix*-like, as return fire began to pass him by, coming dangerously close. I was convinced I was going to watch my best friend die in slow motion. And then the real fun began. Shouts of alarm, pain and terror began to ring out all around us as "freed" zombies began to pour from the troop transport.

Speeders had come to our aid. As Eliza's men had begun to coalesce on us, the speeders had attacked from behind. They were relentless as they chewed on anything within reach. Shots fired wildly as the men turned to face their new threat. BT was still screaming and firing. I had to get up from my hiding spot to drag him down. Okay, to be fair, nobody really drags BT anywhere. He sort of let me. Watching people, even the enemy, being eaten is not something to be witnessed.

"Don't kill them all, BT, or the speeders will be looking for another food source, and I know I can beat you in a footrace," I told him.

"That's alright. I know I'm faster than your brother," BT said, smiling.

"That's not cool, not cool at all," Gary said. "Can we maybe go now?" he asked as the screams intensified.

We ran parallel to the road, making sure to stay deep in our culvert. Now that I had found Eliza's string and knew exactly where it was, pulling it open was fairly easy. I was like a kid that had just discovered an unlocked candy store. Sounds incredible at first until you're elbow-deep in salt-water taffy and three pounds of licorice are already inside your stomach. Oh and don't forget about the dozen or so sugar sticks you've already eaten. I was sort of drunk with the power of it, not yet realizing how much more danger I was putting us in. Apparently, Eliza wasn't fond of the slower-ambling shufflers we'd all come to know and love.

She was much more interested in the devastation that could be wrought from their faster, more mobile brethren.

Zombies were dropping out of trucks like blood from a pierced hemophiliac. (Think about that for a second.) Problem was, there were way more zombies than food. Some zombies had been shot or simply ran out of room on the roadway or were simply pushed out of the way, they began to find themselves in our culvert. Some were far beyond making a go at us, others were not.

"Company," Gary said, looking over his shoulder. He had run up into my back and almost through it.

"You'd better pick up the pace," I told BT, turning back to see what Gary was looking at.

"You sure I'm the slowest?" Gary asked, jockeying for position on my side.

"Gary, I'd trip you if you weren't," I told him.

He stopped to look at my expression. I'm not sure if he was happy with the answer he divined. He began to push ahead of BT.

"What the hell?" BT said loudly.

I started firing. I was well beyond the point of caring if we were discovered or not. Besides, Eliza's men were doing all they could to merely survive right now. They were in full scale battle mode, whereas we were just a minor skirmish in comparison.

BT took an immediate left, heading straight for the tree line. The zombies had heard the cacophony and started to come into our ditch, further up, effectively cutting off our escape that way. A quick glance to the left had me wondering which avenue would be better, thorns the size of small rhino horns, glistened wetly, each looking big enough to bleed all of us dry or the zombies. Good thing BT was cutting the path first!

I was vaguely aware that some of the trucks were starting up and pulling away. Some of Eliza's henchmen would survive the day, but most, I felt, had met the end they so well deserved.

I almost fell over BT as he slid down like a baseball player going for a triple on a ball that was a double at best. Gary was way ahead of me on the curve with this one. He was on his hands and knees, crawling underneath the worst of the brambles. A zombie stepped on Gary's ankle in an attempt to get at him, and if not for getting hung up in the stickers, it would have succeeded. The zombie kept trying to power its way through and was only rewarded with more piercings. I got down and began to scramble for all I was worth. The top of my hoodie got snagged on a branch and I was hung up like dirty laundry. A zombie grabbed onto the bottom part of my leg and was coming in for a bite when I screamed for him to *STOP!*

I turned to look at it and see if I had any effect on him. The intensity of my yell forced blood to pour from its nose. Its eyes glazed over for a fraction of a second and then it just stopped. It didn't move. I would have liked to maybe kick it in the head four or five hundred times, but I wanted to get out of there quickly. More zombies were coming and I wasn't sure if I could do the same to them. I snapped off the branch I was affixed to and went deeper into the tangle.

BT had pretty much uprooted the fauna as he went through. You could have driven a Geo Metro through the hole he left. The only problem with his passage was that it left an avenue for the zombies to follow. Once we all made it through the ten or so feet of thorns and into the woods proper, I stopped to get an idea of our pursuit. Zombies were haplessly stuck in the path that Gary and I had forged, but zombies were already halfway through BT's gap.

"Should have been a little more careful about that," BT said.

"You think?" I asked him.

Gary killed the first two zombies coming through, sealing the hole for the moment.

Zombies began to fan out. Some would be stuck

hopefully forever; others were beginning to find inroads toward us.

"We've got to get going," I said, pretty much needlessly.

"I thought Justin was the one with the flair for the obvious?" BT asked.

"He had to get it from somewhere," Gary added.

I was going to tell them these rifles would be useless in the dense copse of trees, but refer back to the "obvious" banter. Zombies were already in the woods behind us, and were approaching as rapidly as the vegetation would allow.

"BT, go!" I said, smacking him on the shoulder. "Gary, you get behind him. I'll try to make them stop."

The gunfire from the roadway had become sporadic and then had abruptly ended. The food was doing what food was supposed to do, either getting eaten or fleeing. As the menu became slim pickings up top, more and more began to find their way down the embankment and joined in the pursuit of us.

I thought I might have possibly heard a woman scream. Eliza in frustration was my hope, but we were being hunted vigorously and we did not have time to gloat.

"Zombies in front," BT said breathlessly. His trailblazing was beginning to take its toll. He turned left into somehow thicker foliage.

"This is horseshit," I said as a third branch smacked off the side of my face. We would be leaving a blood trail Henry could follow. (I'm implying that bulldogs do not make good bloodhounds.)

Gary stopped for a second to take two well-aimed shots at zombies that made an angle of approach, which would have put them dangerously close to snagging BT.

BT pressed harder; he looked to be hung up. He quickly shucked off his jacket and kept pressing. He popped through a particularly dense bramble to emerge on the other side. Somehow, zombies had beaten him to the punch. We were nearly encircled and barely had enough room to pivot around and find open firing lanes.

"Stop, BT!" I yelled. "We make our stand here."

"Not quite the Alamo," he said with resignation, placing more rounds in his rifle.

"Any chance you can make them go away?" Gary asked, shoving rounds into his magazine.

"Yeah, one at a time, and as soon as I move to the next one, the previous one will come back," I told him.

"Not very effective," he told me honestly and without malice; he was merely stating his feelings.

"Mike, now would be a most awesome time for one of your last-ditch efforts," BT said between expended rounds.

The noose was tightening quickly around our necks. The sun was nearly at high noon, the preacher had said his final words, the hangman's hand was on the trip lever and the townsfolk were staring wide-eyed, fearful to blink, lest they miss something.

A zombie flew in from our right, a tree root making it fall at the last moment. It latched on with its teeth to BT's pants, below his knee. The zombie's hands scrambled to seek purchase. BT quickly turned the butt of the gun and slammed it into the side of the zombie's face. The impact dislodged the majority of its teeth from its head. Its nasal cavity had completely been pushed in from BT's second head strike. It fell to the ground in a heap of crushed bone and leaking brain.

"That would have been a good one to tell go away," Gary said to me.

"Thanks for that," I muttered.

The trees and bushes, which moments earlier were preventing our escape, were now the only things keeping the zombies from completely overwhelming our meager defenses. As much of an impediment as they were to us, they were double that for the zombies, who were nearly oblivious to them as they tried to get at us. I watched as at least two zombies lost an eye when finger-thick branches pressed into their eye sockets. One had popped its left eye completely free from its orbital socket; the other had impaled the branch into her eye, yet neither one of them stopped trying to get to us.

Something niggled in my mind. I placed my hand on Gary's back. "Stop shooting," I told him barely above a whisper.

"BT, quiet!" I said a little louder.

A zombie launched at Gary, and as if a Pit bull on a short leash, it wrenched back in mid-flight. "That you?" Gary asked, wide-eyed.

I shook my head in the negative and placed my index finger to my lips.

One zombie not more than a foot from BT's face took one long mournful look at the meal it was foregoing and headed back the way it had come.

"Eliza?" BT asked, wiping the sweat from his brow.

"Tommy," I said quietly.

"Tomas you mean?" Gary asked, correcting me.

I didn't know the reason for the name change, if it meant anything at all. It, however, felt right calling the presence in my mind Tommy.

"That was pretty fortuitous," BT said.

"Almost too much," I said.

"You think he was helping us?" BT asked.

"It sure seems that way. Let's get out of here before his big sister figures out what's going on."

"Back to the obvious, but I completely agree," BT said.

It was another twenty minutes until we were finally able to push through the small woods and into the neighborhood beyond. I almost wanted to kiss the pavement when we got to it, but who knows what someone had on their tires when they drove over this spot. I shuddered thinking about my lips coming into contact with whatever it was. It could have been skunk road kill, for all I knew.

"Something wrong?" BT asked. "You've gone all pale. You've got that look like you just touched a shopping cart without a sani-wipe."

"Damn, BT! How long have you known me?"

"Long enough. Let's get back to the rest."

"I'm glad we're out of the woods, so to speak," Gary said, "but I hate feeling this exposed."

Lower income housing dominated our left side; most looking vacated. Some looked like a war zone and others looked expectant, like they were waiting for a savior or a meal. Zombies would be trapped inside some of them, as would regular people, clutched in the vise-like grip of fear. People who would rather starve to death than brave anything on the outside. The meek would not inherit this world. They would die as they had lived, alone and in the shadows. We, the bold, would either die in a blaze of glory or triumph grandly over evil. Can you tell I was feeling slightly magnanimous over our victory? Already forgetting our near disastrous retreat. That's how I survive. If I remembered every close call, I'd be huddled in a bomb shelter. Thank God for short-term memory loss. See? All those years of smoking marijuana did have a higher purpose beyond getting high!

Zombies started coming out from backyards; it was one congealed mass of excrement and blood.

"All the noise must have disturbed a hive," BT said. "We've got to get off the street."

"See how easy it is to become Captain Obvious?" I told him. He didn't see the humor, and to be honest, neither did I.

Options were limited. The majority involved the deaders, but a fair portion were not. We would have a difficult time outrunning them. I had no desire to go into a house for fear of the inhabitants, whether dead, alive or a state in between.

"Which house looks the best?" BT asked, popping off

a few rounds for good measure.

"Any of them have a moat?" I asked.

"Or a gun turret?" Gary asked.

"Right," BT said. "What more was I really expecting?" he asked himself. He charged for the closest house.

I hoped the damn door was unlocked because, if he had to cave it in to gain entry, that meant the zombies would be able to follow us. BT's flight triggered something in the speeders. They veered off from the main group and began to angle towards him.

"Let's go, Gary, or we're going to be cut off!" I yelled to his back. Gary had already figured this problem out and passed me by before I could finish my sentence.

BT, with his rush of adrenaline, ripped the screen door clean off its hinges. I was too scared to even comment on him affecting the resale value. A bullet hole ripped through the front door, and had to have been an eighth of an inch from BT's head, max. The splintering of wood forced BT to turn away. He looked back towards me, wondering where the shot had come from. I was frantically pointing to the next house. The shot had come from inside; someone did not desire to entertain guests.

BT had already jumped down off the steps when the next shot rang out. As the echo from the shot died down, all that was left was my heavy breathing and the combined footfalls of BT, Gary, me, and the zombies that pursued us. The next house had a security screen door that was locked tight. I didn't spare it a second thought as I jumped down the stairs. BT had passed me up and was heading for the next house in line. Gary was rapidly falling behind and in extreme danger of being overtaken. I was stuck; I didn't have enough bullets or the right firing angle to do him much good. My heart lurched as Gary chanced a look over his shoulder and stumbled ever so slightly, giving the zombies more ground.

Gary had a three-foot lead on the closest zombie.

Either BT got into the next house, or I would have to go back and tell my father I had lost his son. "God, I could use a little help right now."

The security screen of the house I had just tried swung open." Get your ass in here!" a woman screamed at me.

BT was heading to the fifth house when he heard the woman. Gary was running towards me. I swung my head back and forth. Gary might just make it, but no way BT could get back though.

BT saw my dilemma. "Get your ass in there, Talbot! I'll figure something out!" he shouted, still running.

"Listen!" the woman shouted at me. "I didn't make it this long to die with my front door open. Either get your ass in here or get eaten on someone else's lawn!"

I spared one more look at BT, who was on to the next house. "Godspeed, BT," I said softly before running back up the stairs and inside. The woman didn't spare me a second glance as she waited for Gary to get there. "He's not going to make it," she said, more to herself than to me. "Your friend is not going to make it," she said, getting ready to pull the door shut.

"He's my brother," I told her, placing my rifle against the doorjamb to hold the rifle steady, and more importantly, to keep her from shutting the door too early. I had a shot, but it was a shitty one. There was about a three-inch window between Gary's head and the closest zombie's head. As long as Gary didn't do any bobbing and weaving, I should be fine. At least, that's what I kept telling myself as I applied slow, steady, even pressure to the trigger. The rifle went off before I was ready. I watched in alarm as a tuft of Gary's hair blew back from the force of the bullet. His trailing zombie fell, taking with it some of the closer ones in pursuit.

Gary's hands were still pumping as he fought for more speed. I saw the glistening of red welling up from the side of his head as he hit the bottom step. He jumped, launching past me and the stunned woman, collapsing on her living room floor. Blood pumped from the wound on his head. "I've been shot," he said right before passing out.

The woman slammed the door shut, or at least, tried to as my rifle was still in the way. "How the hell have you made it this long?" she asked as she pulled my barrel in, quickly slamming the door and reengaging the lock.

"I get that a lot," I told her as she moved me inside so she could shut the heavy, steel front door. I admired her security. If I had half this set-up, I would still be in Colorado riding the apocalypse out in relative style. That was a pipe dream, but a dream nonetheless.

"Josh! Get the first aid kit!" the lady yelled up the stairs.

A kid of about twelve or thirteen came running down carrying an oversized white case with a large red cross on it.

I expected at any moment for her husband to come down the stairs also. When that didn't happen immediately, I began to wonder if this lady and her son had opened up their door to strangers. I would remember to ask her later, after she finished making my brother stop bleeding on her carpet.

"There's a lot of blood, Mom," Josh told her. "He didn't get bit, did he?" the boy asked in alarm.

"No, the one over there shot him," the lady said as she cleaned the wound.

"Why, mister? Why did you shoot him?" Josh asked me.

"He's my brother," I tried to say in explanation.

"If I had a brother, I wouldn't shoot him," Josh told me.

"Wait, no. I didn't shoot him because he's my brother. I was trying to save him."

"By shooting him? Mom, didn't Uncle Dave tell you not to open the door for the crazy people?" Josh admonished his mother.

The woman looked up at me. "Are you crazy?" she

asked, still wiping blood and placing gauze in the wound to staunch the blood.

How did I answer that? More than a fair amount of people, especially recently, had called me crazy. I did the prudent thing, I stayed silent.

"Wonderful," the woman said sarcastically, wrapping tape around Gary's head. "Your brother will be fine, unless of course you're not quite through with him yet."

"Why do I keep running across comedians?" I asked her.

"Come on, put your rifle down and help me get him onto the couch," she told me.

"What about the zombies?" I asked her, not yet quite willing to yield my only means of defense.

"They can't get in," Josh told me. "The only way things can get in here is if we let them in," he said pointedly looking straight at his mother.

"They needed help," she told him quickly.

By the time we settled Gary down into the couch, he looked to be more comfortably asleep than anything else.

"He'll be fine," she said, sticking out her still bloody appendage. "My name is Mary, Mary Hilop."

I looked in horror at the proffered hand. "Um, your hand is soaking with blood."

She pulled it back slightly to look. "There's like three dots, and it's your brother's blood anyway."

"I don't know where he's been," I told her.

"Oh, for Christ's sakes," she said, heading into the kitchen and turning on the faucet.

"You're not worried about contaminated water?" I asked her in all seriousness.

"It's well water, and are you going to make me regret my decision to let you in?"

"My name is Mike Talbot, and that's my brother Gary," I told her. "And why did you let us in? You don't know what kind of people we are."

She stood for a long time with her hands under the water. (And, I'll happily admit, she was using liberal amounts of dish soap.) I think she was deciding what she did or did not want to tell me. She finally turned the faucet off and turned to face me. "This morning I was saying my prayers, like I do every day. You know knees on the bedroom floor, hands on top of the bed, and I was just getting up when I heard an answer back." She looked me straight in the eye, wondering if I was going to think she was nuts.

I didn't so much as flinch. That was far from the craziest thing that had happened to me, and I'm just talking about today.

When she realized I wasn't going to try and have her committed, she continued. "The voice said I should help those as I would want them to help me. And when I saw you and the other two running from the zombies out there, I put Josh and myself in your places and thought what would I want someone to do…so I opened the door."

"That was very brave of you," I told her, meaning it.

"Did I do the right thing?" she asked me.

"Well, I think so. You saved my brother's and my lives."

"But were you worthy to be saved?" came her next question.

"My brother is," I told her flatly. She left it at that, and I silently thanked her.

"What of the other man?" she asked.

"BT, his name is BT and he's quite possibly the best friend I have ever had. We've traded saving each other's lives so many times, I'm not even one hundred percent sure who is in the lead, although I suspect it is me. I have got to go and try and find him."

"Not for a few days," Mary said, turning back to the kitchen window. She stood on her tiptoes and pulled the shade to the side. "The zees will stay out here for a few days before they go to wherever they go or some other hapless idiot starts running down the street and then it starts all over again."

I'm pretty sure she just called me a 'hapless idiot.' I've been called worse, but it still stung.

"When they first came, they were out there for a couple of months."

"You never had a breach?"

She turned back to me. "No, my ex-husband ended up being a paranoid delusional. He spent more on the security of this house than the actual worth of this place."

I'm a paranoid delusional, but my house fell in the first few days. What I wouldn't have done to have talked to her ex beforehand. "Where is Mr. Hilop?"

That was a pretty personal question, and I was still some guy she had just let into her home. I thought she might lie and say sleeping upstairs, but she came out with the truth. "It ended up being his sickness that got the best of him. He was convinced that the zees would be able to get through the back basement window and he went to the hardware store to fix that problem and get some supplies for my son's hobby, he'd do anything for him. That was three months ago. I'm figuring he's not coming back, although Josh is still holding out hope."

"Food isn't an issue?" I asked.

"You heard the part where I said he was delusional?"

"Gotcha," I told her. "So…you said a couple of days?" I asked, coming up to look through the barred window.

"Yeah, they go somewhere and only come out when someone rings the dinner bell."

"They go into a stasis," I said as I quickly pulled the shade back into place. Three zombies were fighting over some sort of scraps and I had no desire to discern what it was. "They all pile up into this giant mass of decayed flesh and stink and sort of hibernate. Our best guess is that food is becoming scarce and this is a way for them to extend their lives, such as they are."

"They're cognizant?" Mary asked incredulously. "They have thought beyond hunger?"

"It's some sort of parasite, so it has a survival instinct, but beyond that…" I shrugged my shoulders.

"How long have you been on the run?" Mary asked.

I got a faraway look in my eyes. "Since the beginning," I told her.

I know she wanted to press me for more information. She and her son had ridden out the entire storm in the relative safety of this house. Luckily, Gary saved me.

"I can't see!" he screamed from the living room.

Josh had pulled down all the blackout blinds when the zombies had returned. Besides a few strategically placed emergency candles, the house was as dark as the inside of a coffin.

"You're fine, Gary," I said. "Shit!" I yelled as I slammed my shin into a table leg.

"Mike? Mike? Is that you? It's so cold and dark where I am. I can't see you, brother. I've been shot in the head and I think it's the end for me. Mom, is that you?"

"No, my name is Mary," Mary said, getting to his side quicker than I could. Being familiar with the house, she was able to navigate through it more rapidly.

"Mary? Such a beautiful name. Are you my guiding angel?" Gary said dramatically, maybe a little too much.

Mary produced a small flashlight and checked Gary's wound and his pupils, and then turned to me. "Is he prone to histrionics?"

"You tell me," I replied.

"You know that your wound is not much more than a scratch, right?" she asked Gary.

"Are you sure? Because I see the light," Gary said.

"It's a Ray-O-Vac penlight," Mary told him.

"Oh," Gary said, sitting up. "Then I'm fine. Mike, you know I'm going to have to tell Dad that you shot me."

"I figured as much. Good to see you vertical, my brother."

"Are we in a safe house?" he asked.

I nodded my answer. For someone who a second ago couldn't see anything, he did have a fast response.

"What about BT and the rest?" he asked, getting more comfortable.

"Josh, could you please get me some water and aspirins?" Mary asked her son.

Josh had been at the far end of the room, almost completely obscured in the shadows. I thought I might have detected the glint of a weapon. I couldn't fault him that. In fact, it was quite the opposite, I thought it was admirable that he remained vigilant over us, protecting his mother and his homestead.

"I don't know about any of them. BT was too far down the street to turn and make it back. And I haven't heard anything from the rest."

"The rest?" Mary asked as she gave the glass of water and tablets to Gary.

The ham made a great show of effort in reaching out to get the meds.

"We were with another three people besides the big man you saw."

"What were you doing?" Mary asked, helping Gary more when she realized he was having a difficult time. He was completely soaking it up. Even Josh from across the room could tell he was over-exaggerating. The only one who was missing it was Mary.

"Payback," I told her vaguely.

"Against who? The zombies? But you just said they don't really have any feelings beyond survival," Mary said as she checked Gary's forehead for a temperature. "You feel a little warm."

"Yes, I do," Gary said as he slouched in his seat like sitting up straight was now the most difficult thing in the world.

"Oh, you poor baby," I told Gary. "I hope you're going to be alright."

"He's been shot in the head!" Mary shot back at me vehemently. "And you did it! Maybe you should be a little nicer to your brother!"

Gary was smiling over Mary's shoulder at me; I could tell by the flash of his white teeth. "Yeah...nicer," Gary said weakly, slouching even further into the couch cushion.

"I've got to find BT," I told Mary.

"Unless you've got a machinegun on you somewhere, you're not going to get past the zees," Josh said.

"Any chance you got one?" I asked.

"Even if I did, mister, I wouldn't be giving it to you," he told me.

"Fair enough. Do you have anything you could spare?" I asked.

Mary was shaking her head from side to side. "Greg took his rifle and a pistol with him when he went. The only reason he left behind the pistol Josh has is because he had no bullets for it."

"Mom!" Josh said hotly. "Why would you tell them that?!" He stormed out of the room.

"I don't think he's convinced yet about your intentions. You'll have to forgive him. He has a lot of Greg in him."

"That's probably a good thing these days," I told her.

"Didn't help Greg out much," she said.

"But you two are safe," I told her. There was an awkward silence as Mary thought that through. Gary saved the day with a soft moan.

"Oh, you poor baby," Mary said, stroking the side of his face.

"My ass," I said.

"What was that?" Gary asked with strain in his voice.

"Mary, do you mind if I walk around the house,

looking for a way around the zombies?"

"You won't, but feel free."

"Thank you," I told her.

She had already forgotten I was still in the room as she turned back to Gary's ministrations.

I did a complete circuit of the house. In typical zombie fashion, we were surrounded. It wasn't thousands, maybe a hundred or so. My OCD half-thought about counting, but the asses wouldn't stay still long enough for me to get an accurate tally. One would go, two would come, a few would just run endless circles around the house until I started to recognize them and I had counted them more than once. With two full magazines, I might be able to cut a path through; but then what? Most of these zombies were speeders, and I was no track star.

I walked up the stairs to see how disappointed I could get with an aerial view. I had just pulled the shade to the side when Josh spoke.

"I've kept her safe all this time while we've been waiting for my dad to come home."

I don't know what stopped me... Divine intervention? A brain? My conscience? I don't know, but I had just about turned and said 'You know he's not coming home, right?' If Tracy had been here, she would have smacked me just for thinking it; and somehow she would have been able to tell. I was stuck. I had been so intent on flat out telling him the truth, I couldn't think of a viable alternative. I came out with the lame, "That's nice."

He gave me a look I'd become all too familiar with seeing.

"How long are you going to stay?" he asked. I'm not sure if it was because he wanted us gone, or it took the burden of protecting his mother off his shoulders.

"Just long enough until there's a way through the zombies and I can get back to my friends."

"What about your brother? He's going to need time to

heal."

"Him? He's faking."

"I thought so. He's not a very good actor."

I laughed. "Your mom is buying it."

He stopped to think about that for a minute. "That's alright. It gives her a chance to stop worrying about me."

"You're a smart kid." He was probably on to something. Mary, on some level, probably knew Gary was hamming it up, but it was a diversion from the nightmare outside.

"Yeah, I usually like to build radio-controlled cars, but guarding this house is a full time job," he sighed heavily.

"Can I see them?" I asked. We've all established that I'm just a larger version of a kid so I wanted to see them; and the word 'diversion' was now stuck in my head.

The kid's room was crammed with at least a dozen different vehicles that I could see. There was a lunar module with six wheels, a tank that fired projectiles, some racing cars and other sets that were in various states of repair or disrepair.

"I'm still working on this one," Josh said, picking up what looked like a waste basket on wheels. "My dad went out to get me some parts for this. He had come over to work on it with me and then the zombies had come."

"What's it going to be?"

"A half scale R2-D2."

"No way? That's awesome. You have some incredible stuff here."

Josh sat down heavily on his bed. "I haven't touched any of them since he left. He didn't come back and he was out getting stuff for me."

Man, I hate the serious talks. I sat down next to him. "Listen, Josh…I'm a father, too."

He looked up at me with 'Really?' written all over his face.

"There's nothing I wouldn't do for my kids, from

giving up my life all the way to seeing a smile flash across their lips. You're dad went out trying to do just that. You can't blame yourself for his actions. It was something he wanted to do."

"Thanks, mister. You seem like you'd make a good dad."

"Thanks, kid. Now if you could just tell my wife that, I'd really appreciate it. Can you show me how a few of these work?"

Josh's face lit up. He was back in his element, tinkering with the small machines. We spent a few hours going through his wheeled assembly. It was nice to forget for a while what lingered mere feet away outside.

Mary finally had to come up and get us for dinner. Her first two shouts had fallen on deaf ears as we recreated the chase scene from Mad Max.

Mary had made us a simple meal of beef stew and corn, but it was warm and we were safe. I said a silent prayer for my family and friends before I sat down. I noticed only two settings at the table – one for Josh and one for me. "I'm sorry we're late. Did you guys already eat?" I asked from the kitchen.

"No," Mary said. "Your brother is still in a lot of pain, so I set up a tray for him out here and then it didn't seem quite right that he had to eat alone, so I'm staying with him."

Josh rolled his eyes as he sat down. I snorted out a laugh.

"What's so funny?" Mary asked a little peevishly.

"Ah, nothing," I said, trying to stall for a more acceptable answer. "Josh had just told me a funny joke before we came downstairs."

"Josh, it had better not be that one you heard at school!" Mary yelled from the living room.

"Thanks," Josh mouthed.

"Better you than me," I said quietly.

"What are you two whispering about in there?" Gary moaned. "The noise is hurting me."

"You two stop it or I'll make you eat upstairs!" Mary yelled.

Funny, Gary didn't seem to complain about her volume and she was right next to him. And actually, going back upstairs sounded like fun. Josh's myriad of radio-controlled vehicles was a good diversion from the cold hard truth. 'Diversion.' There it was again. The word kept popping up in my head inadvertently; maybe I should actually pay it some heed. I was three spoonfuls into my stew when I looked over to the wastebasket. Gary's blood-soaked shirt and a bunch of bandages dominated what I could see.

"Hey, Josh, can your cars go faster than a person?"

"Yeah, why? You want to race? Because I will SO kick your ass." He said the last word softly so his mom wouldn't hear. But she was entirely too busy cooing over my malingering brother to know anything about what we were doing.

"What's the range on the transmitter?" I asked him, an idea beginning to formulate in my head.

"If you're talking inside, it would be the whole house."

"What about outside?"

"A football field, I guess. I don't usually let them get out of sight, though."

"Do you have one you wouldn't mind not seeing again?"

"No," he answered quickly and decisively. "Why?" he asked hesitantly.

"I've got an idea," I said, my gaze still focused on the trash.

"Oh, kid, don't listen to any of his plans," Gary said. He was leaning up against the entrance to the kitchen. Mary was helping him stay propped up.

"I told him not to get up," Mary said, exasperated.

"But he just wouldn't listen. He's a stubborn one."

I noticed that her eyes seemed to shine a bit as she talked. Looks like someone has a crush and someone else is eating it up in a big way. I was about to give him silent kudos until he spoke.

"I had Mary help me get up, because when I heard how quiet you two were in here, I knew it meant you were thinking about something. You have to be careful, Josh, my brother's 'plans' usually don't work out so well."

"Don't you have an injury to pretend about?" I asked him.

"You shot him in the head!" Mary exclaimed.

"It's alright, Mary," Gary said calmly. "Now do you see what I've had to put up with?"

"You poor baby. Here, let me help get you back to the couch, or would you be more comfortable in a bed? I'm sure Josh will give you his."

"Mom!" Josh yelled.

"The couch is fine," Gary moaned.

"Oh brother," I said as both a euphemism and a commentary on his acting skills.

"But I'd love to hear Mike's plan before I do," Gary said, smiling to me when Mary turned to scowl at me for delaying his return to a horizontal position.

"Mom, Gary is smiling," Josh said, pointing over his mom's shoulder.

"It's a grimace," Gary said as Mary turned back to face him.

Mary turned back to hear me out and Gary took his index and middle finger and pointed at his eyes, then at Josh as if to tell him, I've got my eyes on you.

"Mom?!" Josh wailed.

"That's enough, young man, I want to hear what Gary's brother has to say."

At least, I knew where I was on the pecking order. I'd gone from 'Mike' to 'Gary's sibling.' "I've got to find my friend," I started. Mary was about to protest. "I know there's no way out right now, but I can't wait two or three days until they clear out. He might need our—"

"Gary's not going anywhere in this condition!" Mary stated with a tone that said it was not open for discussion.

"Okay, *my* help," I clarified, Mary nodded in ascension. "I would like Josh…" I knew I was treading on thin ice here. She would kick me out in a heartbeat if she thought I was putting her son even remotely in danger. I figured it best to continue my dialog and quickly. "With Josh's permission, of course." Mary's stance was telling me that whatever hare-brained scheme I was coming up with, it wasn't Josh's decision to make. "No, nothing like that," I said, putting my hands up. "I don't need Josh."

The kid instantly looked like he deflated.

Mary appeared a little heartbroken at the sight of her son.

"See? What did I tell you about his 'plans?'" Gary said.

"Wait a second. I need Josh, but not in any way that exposes him to the zombies. I need his skills and a radio-controlled car…if he'll do it."

Go on, Mary motioned with her hand.

I laid the rest of it out there. Josh was immediately on board; he seemed actually pretty excited about it. Mary took a few minutes longer, trying to think of any way in which this exposed her son to anything close to danger, but she finally placed her stamp of approval on it.

"I'm going with you," Gary said.

"In your condition?" I asked him. "I think not."

Mary nodded with my words.

"You made your bed, brother, now you need to lie in it," I said cryptically.

I pushed away from the table, placing my dishes in the sink. I thanked Mary for the meal. I would have normally waited for the morning to launch my ingenious idea, but the moon was nearly full and there were no clouds. It was a fairly bright night and I wanted to get BT back into the fold as soon as possible. The big guy was probably scared to death without me.

Gary found me about an hour later. I was in a small sitting room on the south side of the house. I was alternating between staring out the window at the zombies that periodically walked by, and stretching out my muscles for the endeavor they were about to undertake.

"You sure about this, brother?" he asked me.

"Of course not," I told him.

"I'm serious," he said.

"So am I," I answered.

"What about back-up?" he asked.

"I appreciate it, Gary, I really do. Listen I'm no track star and that goes double for you. I won't get to BT if I'm looking back for you." Gary looked down. "And hey, if something happens to me, would this be the worst place in the world to wrap up the remainder of your days?"

"You've always been like a younger brother to me," Gary said.

"Kiss my ass," I told him.

"You be careful."

"I will…I always am."

Gary snorted. "Now I know you're lying, because you're insulting my intelligence."

"Go find Mary. Maybe she has some tea that can help you with that."

Gary left and I was once again alone with my thoughts. I finished stretching quickly because no one should be exposed to my thoughts for too long.

I was as ready as I was ever going to be when I came out of that room. My head, however, was still clouded with doubt for what I was about to do. Why did everything always seem like a good idea right up until launch time? Then it seemed just about the craziest thing ever.

"Mom? Any words of wisdom?" I asked, looking to the heavens.

I could picture her saying, "What the hell are you thinking?" What response would I have to that? Thinking had never been my forte. There were a multitude of reasons why I did not build rockets when the world was slightly more normal.

"The car won't flip?" I asked Josh.

He looked at me like I should leave that up to the pros.

"What are you eating?" I asked, looking at his sandwich. It smelled really good, but it looked like warmed-over vomit.

"A peanut butter and maple oatmeal sandwich," he said between big bites. He was busy adjusting something on the chassis.

"Oatmeal?" I asked. Josh never looked up.

"He loves it," Mary said, shrugging her shoulders.

"So this won't flip?" I asked again, not wanting to look at his train wreck of a sandwich anymore.

Oatmeal leaked from the sides of the bread as he stared up at me. "Have you been listening to me at all?" he asked testily.

"His wife says that a lot," Gary said from the couch.

I turned to flip him the finger, but Mary was boring holes in me, so I thought better of the gesture. It ended up being a half-hearted wave, which he returned eagerly.

"It can't flip over because there is no top or bottom. I designed it that way so if it went over a bump and flipped over it would never get stuck."

"That's awesome," I said, picking up his engineering marvel, which was basically just four oversized tires attached to a chassis. "Have you ever gotten it stuck?" I asked, turning the machine over. He didn't immediately answer, and I moved the machine so I could get a better look at the boy. "Josh?"

"Well not stuck, really," he hemmed and hawed.

"Feel free to keep going," I urged.

"Well, I've had some problems with this wheel," he said, grabbing what was at this moment the front left, but at some point could be the front right, back left and/or back right. Yeah, it didn't make much sense to me at the time either. In my world, front was front, rear was rear.

"Um…so what kind of problems?" My idea's value was beginning to plummet.

"You really shouldn't badger the kid," Gary said.

"Badger the kid? Hey I know I get accused of not thinking before I speak all the time, but this isn't our entry into the county fair where the worst that can happen is a last place finish."

"Honey, what's wrong with your car?" Mary asked him.

Josh took an extra squishy bite of his sandwich, and sticky oatmeal plopped to the floor. I would imagine this was a stalling technique. I'd employed that method many times myself with varying degrees of results. He gulped down his bite. "Sometimes this wheel gets stuck," he said, looking up at my eyes and then his mother's.

"How often does it get stuck?" I asked.

"More than it used to."

Not much of an answer, I thought as I ran my hands through my hair in the traditional "I'm screwed" way.

"Mike, you can't still be thinking of doing this?" Gary asked, rising up from the couch.

"I don't have a good feeling about BT, Gary. I can't explain it, but I really think he needs my help."

Gary looked at me funny. "BT needs your help?" he finally came out, asking the obvious question. "Are you sure this isn't just your overactive imagination or your senseless need to put yourself in danger or is it just a way to commit suicide by zombie?!" Gary said heatedly.

"Well don't hold back, brother! Tell me what you're

really thinking."

"You're upsetting him!" Mary came to Gary's defense.

I didn't see it that way, looked way more like he was doing the disturbing.

"Mike, ever since we left Maine, you have done everything in your power to put us in as much danger as possible. It seems like you go out of your way to find the worst situation, then you head right for it, like you just can't wait to see a new and unusual way to die."

"I don't remember forcing you to leave Maine, Gary," I said forcefully.

"Someone had to watch your back," he said, advancing a step on me.

"You do realize, Gary, that we are in the midst of a zombie apocalypse, right? And that we are no longer on the top of the food chain. Going out for smokes can now be a life or death situation."

"You know I don't smoke and neither do you, but you'd probably pick up the habit just to see if you could get them."

Gary was pretty worked up. I hadn't seen him this angry since they cancelled *Battle of the Network Stars* sometime back in the late seventies. "Gary, I'm not doing this out of some ill-conceived way to commit suicide. My family…my friends are in trouble, I could never, I would never leave them or their fates up to the whim of a crazy bitch vampire."

"No swearing in my house," Mary said loudly. Then she stopped to look at me when she processed the rest of the sentence. "Crazy bitch vampire?"

"Mom, no swearing," Josh echoed his mother in a much-practiced routine.

"Like *Dracula* vampires?" Mary asked hesitantly.

"Worse," Gary said, still with heat in his voice.

"What? He's not joking?" Mary asked as she sat

down heavily, nearly missing the edge of the couch. Gary caught her under her armpit to keep her from hitting the ground.

"Her name's Eliza and she's got this thing for Mike," Gary said as Mary settled deeper into the couch, trying to hide herself from the advancing shadows in her mind.

"And you came into my house!" Mary shouted, rising quickly from her perch. "How dare you!" she said, shaking with rage.

"You opened the door to us," I told her.

"I wouldn't have had I known!" she shouted.

"I'm sorry. I really didn't have the time to give you our bio when we were trying to save our lives," I told her.

"Cool, you know a vampire?" Josh asked, surprised.

"It's not nearly as cool as you might think," I told him.

"Does she sparkle?" he asked.

"Why would she sparkle?" I asked Josh. I was clearly confused.

"You wouldn't understand the reference," Gary interjected with no further explanation.

"Can we forget about all this sparkly shit!" Mary shouted.

"Mom!" Josh yelled.

"Sorry, Josh. Mommy's a little stressed-out at the moment. Where is this vampire now?" Mary asked, swinging back and forth between Gary and myself, searching for a truthful answer.

"Well, I mean she could be anywhere by now," Gary said.

"Where was she the last time you saw her?" Mary asked, trying to extract the information like a stubborn impacted tooth.

"Well, what's your definition of 'saw'?" I asked her, trying to get the heat off Gary.

"I swear, I'll throw you both out right now if I don't

get a straight answer!"

"What about my head wound?" Gary asked with alarm.

"Oh for Christ's sakes! I've cut myself worse shaving my legs!" Mary shouted.

"Eww…gross, Mom! Why would you shave your legs?" Josh asked, clearly turning the shade of green I had when I saw him eating his sandwich earlier.

"I'll bet your legs don't bleed as much as my head," Gary said as he absently touched his wound.

"I'll ask you one more time, Mike, and then you and your brother will be hitting the streets," Mary said seriously. "Whether or not you 'saw' (in finger quotes) this Eliza, where was her last known spot?"

"I-95," I told her.

"I-95 goes up the entire East Coast. Could you please be a little more specific?" Mary said, heading towards the front door.

"Well, if you were to open that door you're heading for and look across the street, past the small copse of woods, you would basically run into her last known whereabouts," I told her.

I could tell that opening the door had suddenly lost some of its luster. Zombies were a nightmare that many people had not been able to wrap their minds around and had paid the ultimate price for that disconnect. Vampires…well, basically the same path, but you had to go a lot deeper into the woods, so to speak.

"Did Mike tell you he was a half-vamp?" Gary said, still fingering the bandages.

"What?" Mary said, almost falling over herself to get away from me.

"You're not helping, Gary. How hard did that bullet hit?"

"Way cool!" Josh said, coming to get a better look at the circus attraction.

"Stay away from him!" Mary shouted, but I didn't know if she was talking to him or me.

"Do you drink blood?" Josh asked excitedly. He may have heeded his mother's words and stopped his advance, but his curiosity was unbridled.

"No, but I've got this thing for Pop-Tarts now," I told him honestly.

"He has a psychic link to Eliza," Gary added absently.

I thought Mary was going to faint. "Gary, feel free to shut the hell up whenever you want," I told him.

"What? She has a right to know."

"Does your friend out there turn into like Bigfoot or something?" Josh asked. "I mean, because I saw him running down the street and he was HUGE!" Josh said, spreading his hands as far apart as he could.

"No, but that would be cool," I told Josh.

"Yeah, it really would be," he agreed, nodding as he answered.

"Does she know you're here?" Mary asked cautiously. She kept eyeing the door anxiously as if she expected her to bust through at any moment.

"No," I answered.

"How can you be so sure?" Mary asked.

"Things would be way worse," Gary said. "I really only have a scratch?" he asked her.

"Oh, honey," Mary said, reverting back to her caregiver status. "But it really is a nasty looking scratch."

I don't know if she was a trooper and had assimilated the information and was dealing with it, or she just chose to push it down deeper into her psyche. Not my call, but whatever gets you through the day can't be all bad.

"Can we still go on with the plan?" I asked Mary. She seemed to have lost herself in Gary's wound. "I'll take that as a yes," I said to Josh.

"I would," he agreed with me.

"You think it's better to drag this behind rather than tie it to the top?" I asked Josh for maybe the third time.

"Even for an adult, you don't listen well," he admonished me. "I'll tell you once again, this car has no top or bottom to tie anything onto. If it were to flip, it would get stuck on the clothes, like a turtle."

"That makes sense," I told him.

"That's what you said the first two times I told you," he said.

"Hey, cut me some slack, kid, I'm the one running with the zombies. I'm a little nervous."

"I guess I would be, too," he answered, thinking about it.

"Gary, I know your head is probably still aching, and you might be woozy and everything, but do you think you could lay down some covering fire if I were to say, trip over something?"

Gary was fighting back a comment. I could see the machinations behind his eyes working frantically, but apparently higher reasoning or a higher purpose took over. "I don't think this is a good idea, Mike, but I'll always have your back," he said, getting up, even with Mary's disapproving stare.

Nodding my thanks to him, I stuffed Gary's bandages and bloody shirt into a laundry bag, secured the top, and then tied a nylon rope from the neck of the bag to a strut on Josh's car.

I opened a window and immediately regretted my decision. The smell that assailed us was hideous – the sour stench of death. Josh hurled his peanut butter and oatmeal sandwich. It looked pretty much the same coming up as it had going down. I would not be adding that to my list of foods to try.

"You going to be alright?" I asked him as I lowered the car by the laundry bag rope to the ground.

I could hear Gary gagging in the background; Josh

started back up. "Great," I muttered, "dueling gaggers." My support system was not looking up to task.

Mary saved the day. "You two are going to ruin my carpet!" she yelled, getting up to clean Josh's internal spillings.

A zombie startled the crap out of me as he smacked into the bars. It had come dangerously close to stepping on the car. More zombies were coming to investigate the din and they weren't generally too concerned with foot placement.

"Josh, you have to get that car out of here or they're gonna bust it," I said. That seemed to get him. The smell was one thing, but losing one of his remote-controlled cars was another.

The zombie was eyeing us hungrily (pun intended). It was tough to say if intelligence burned behind its opaque eyes, but this was no clodhopping brain chaser either. Josh gulped loudly as he looked straight at the zombie.

"Umm, I have to get closer to the window so I can see the car," Josh told me as he turned his large remote on.

"Cover your ears," I told him.

Mary was coming back from the kitchen with her cleaning supplies. "Don't you dare!" she screamed just as the report from my rifle rang out.

"COOL!" Josh yelled, taking his hands away from around his ears.

The zombie had fallen mostly straight back, but its left arm was resting on top of the car.

"No shooting in the house!" Mary yelled.

"I'll keep that in mind the next time," I told her honestly. Zombies were within a couple of feet of the window. "Josh, now or never, buddy."

I'll give him credit. He mustered up all his courage and stepped up to the window. And then nothing, I saw him moving buttons back and forth and side to side and we could hear the car trying to do something, but the zombie had it pinned.

"I think I can get it free," Josh said excitedly, up until the point a zombie woman cracked it in half. Josh looked more crushed than the car that was now getting ground into the dirt.

I quickly undid the knot on the small laundry bag and shut the window, drawing the shades and pulling the curtains shut.

"Well, that didn't work," I said, going into the kitchen, I sat down heavily in a chair.

"Josh, honey, are you alright?" Mary said, putting her cleaning supplies down to grab her son in a bear hug.

Josh wept a little, but he tried his best to hide it from us all.

"It was a gift from his father," Mary said over his head to me.

I can't even begin to convey how big of an ass I felt like at this point. If you've read all of my journals, you know I have a penchant for saying or doing the wrong thing at the ultimate wrong time, but this one? This one took the cake.

"What…what am I going to do if…if Da…Dad comes home with the parts for it now?" Josh sobbed into his mother's arms.

"Josh, he'd understand. You were trying to do something good for someone else. You guys would rebuild it, that's all, honey," Mary said. She seemed to have correctly punched all the right buttons. Josh pulled back from her arms, wiping his tears away.

"I've got another car, Mr. Talbot, if you want to try again that is," he said to me.

"I would, Josh. My friend is out there and I'd like to find him."

"I understand, because if I knew where my dad was, I'd try to find him, too," Josh said, wiping his nose and extricating himself from Mary's arms. "I'll be right back," he said, heading back upstairs.

Mary let out a half sob, half gasp. "I'm watching him

grow up right before my eyes. Sometimes, he'll always be my sweet six-year-old, and then sometimes like now, I can see the man that he is becoming."

Gary finished cleaning up the carpet as Josh rummaged around in his room.

Josh came down the stairs with what looked like the monster truck version of a radio-controlled vehicle.

"Oh, honey, are you sure?" Mary asked, placing her hand to her chest. "That was a Christmas present."

"Mom, Hugo is the best chance Mr. Talbot has of getting to his friend."

I gathered that Hugo was the name of the truck. "Josh, I don't know how this is going to turn out."

"He never does," Gary added for good measure, coming back from the kitchen.

"I thought the peanut gallery was closed?" I said hotly.

"Boys," Mary said, playing referee.

"It's alright, Mr. Talbot. Maybe if you find your friend, then you could go and maybe find my dad."

I looked over at Mary. I would be lying if I said anything but the truth of where I thought his father was.

"I know that look," Josh said. "You don't think my dad is alive. But he has to be! He wouldn't have just left us, not now."

"Josh, I will promise you this, if I can get to my friend and get back, I will go check out where you think your dad went."

"Electronix Emporium," Josh said quickly, now beaming. "No fooling? You'll go check?"

"He's a lot of things and many of them not good, Josh, but a liar isn't one of them," Gary said.

"Gotta love a good, back-handed compliment," I told my brother.

He nodded his head in appreciation.

We moved to a different window on the same side of

the house, one where we hoped there would be less zombies. We were right, but then we encountered our next situation – Hugo would not fit through the bars.

"It's almost like it wasn't meant to happen," Gary said. "Like a sign, a bunch of signs."

"Since when did you become a fortune teller?" I asked him sarcastically.

"Since my fortune got tied up in yours," he answered quickly.

"As good a time as any, I suppose," I told him.

"It's only going to fit out the door," Josh said, slamming the window down before we attracted any more visitors.

"I'd rather not open any doors," Mary said.

"How were you planning on letting me out?" I asked.

"Hadn't thought that far," Mary said as realization dawned on her that she really hadn't gotten that far.

"See what happens when you're around him for too long?" Gary asked sympathetically.

"Is that like his vampire psychic powers warping our mortal minds?" Josh asked expectantly.

"No, he's always had this effect on people," Gary said dryly.

Josh looked a little bummed that it wasn't a supernatural cause that made those around me go crazy.

"Back door for the car, front door for me?" I asked the household.

"No," Mary said without hesitation. "I will not have both of my doors opened simultaneously. You don't even know if this will work. We put the car out, Josh sends it on its way and we see if they follow."

I didn't like the plan. At absolute best, the car had a hundred-yard range with Josh's controller and then it would just stop. I needed a bunch of zombies to go and check this thing out and in a relatively small amount of time before the car hit its max threshold for signal catching. I should have given the kid way more credit. He had a trick or two up his sleeve to give me the time I needed.

"How we looking?" I asked Gary and Josh, who were peeking out a window adjacent to the door.

"There's a few milling around, but if you don't stop to wash your hands or anything, you should be fine," Gary said.

"You're on fire tonight," I told him.

He grinned back.

"You ready, Josh?" I asked.

He spun the wheels on the truck I was holding in response. The torque and the shock almost made me drop the thing. This time, I had secured the small bag of bait on the top of the car, careful to make sure that nothing hung down that could get hooked up in the wheels.

"This sucks," I said right before pulling the door open. Zombie heads swiveled to the noise, food recognition dawning on their eyes as they began to forge ahead. I started to fumble with the security door, which was, I guess, out of my skill set because I couldn't get the damn thing open. Mary rushed to my aid, undoing the lock and pushing the door open. I looked at her in gratitude.

"Put the damn car down!" she shouted at me, never taking her eyes off the advancing horde.

Josh already had the wheels turning as I placed it on the ground. The car shot from my hand as it made contact with the hard surface. A zombie slammed the door into my hand. I was sure I felt a couple of bones shatter as Mary wrenched me on my back, pulling me in. She quickly locked the screen door, and I scrambled out of the way as she hurriedly shut the front door.

My hand was already turning that bluish shade of pain and internal bleeding.

"You righty or lefty?" Mary asked, holding my hand.

"Righty," I told her, "but I shoot leftie."

Her face sank a little as she held my rapidly swelling

left hand.

"I'll be fine," I told her. "I have wonderful recuperative powers."

She looked at me funny; I did not feel the need to elaborate.

"Mike, your hand is broken," she said, pushing her finger into the bluest part as if to prove her point.

"Yup," I winced.

"Hey, they're following it!" Josh stated exuberantly.

I figured I only had seconds before the car had traveled its furthest radio-receiving distance and then they'd turn their attention back to me.

"Wish me luck," I said as I once again opened the front door.

Hand Slammer was gone this time and I had, at least, learned something from Mary as I got the security door opened much more easily. I looked immediately to my right, expecting to see Hugo rapidly approaching maximum distance. All I saw were zombies who were heading towards the side of the house. I ducked my head back in, Josh and Gary had shifted to another window. The kid was brilliant. Instead of just taking the car and heading for maximum distance, he was dodging and weaving it through the zombies, thereby giving me way more time to get the hell out of here.

"Go," Mary said, her eyes wide with fear – partly because I had the front door to her house open and partly because I wasn't moving yet.

I jumped down the three steps and started running in the direction I had last seen BT heading. As soon as I hit my stride, I began to doubt the validity of my entire plan. I'm all for 'alone time' and the need for it; but somehow, during a zombie-pocalypse doesn't seem like the right time. Should I shout? There weren't tons of zombies out, but I also didn't want to change that status. By my reckoning, one zombie is one too many.

I skipped Mary's neighbor's house and, as I approached the next, I began to wonder if BT had perhaps traveled through a backyard or two and maybe got on to another street. I mean, what then? He knew where we were, but I had no clue where he was. Why don't I think this shit out before I act?

I could hear Josh's car off in the distance, but for some reason, that distance was getting closer.

Chapter Eight

"That's awesome, Josh, they're all following it," Gary said excitedly.

Josh did not immediately answer as sweat began to form on his head. "I've lost control!" he shouted. "I think the batteries in the remote are dead."

"Shouldn't the car just stop?" Mary asked.

"No," Josh said in resignation. "I put the car on 'auto' so that it would keep running when it was out of range."

"Well, that's alright then, isn't it, honey? We'll get you another one," Mary said, leaning up against the front door as if she thought it might open without her there to stop it.

"Which way did Mike go?" Gary asked, moving from the window on the side of the house to one of the sidelights by the front door.

"Left," Mary answered.

"Figured as much," Gary said as his eyes tracked Hugo heading left.

"Shit," Josh said.

Mary did not correct him, not this time. If ever there was a time and a place to use an expletive, this was it.

Hugo was heading down the street towards Mike like a heat-seeking missile.

Chapter Nine – Mike Journal Entry 7

"Shit," I said, watching Hugo head my way. "I bet Gary's working the damn thing."

Hugo was cool; the two dozen speeders trying their best to catch him were not.

"Here we go again," I said as I began to run. Couldn't I get déjà vu, at like Oktoberfest, while I was sampling different beers? Because that would be so much better.

I started running down the sidewalk. Hugo was about dead center on the street. I don't know about you, but I'd never had much luck with RC cars. Usually I crashed them into something or they broke consistently, but not good old Hugo! Nope. He was running straight and true, right down the bloody center (English slip) of the road. He was looking like he could do it all night long. What was even way better was that the damn street we were on did not have a curve in its foreseeable future. The one and only thing I had going for me at the moment was that the zombies were completely focused on the truck and its bloody contents (not an English slip, actual stuff it was hauling).

I had a few options. First, keep running in the same direction. Hugo would pass me up shortly and I would become victim to those old zombie posters. You know the ones, "I don't have to be fastest, only faster than you!" Hugo would zip away and the zombies would turn to me for solace and food. I might be able to keep one or two at bay, but I did not understand my powers well enough or even know if it were possible to do much more than that.

Second, I could cut across a yard and start searching elsewhere, but here we come back to the needle-in-a-haystack analogy, although with the size of BT, it's more like a cop's nightstick than a needle, which in reality, shouldn't be all that hard to find in one haystack. Or third, I could hide behind a bush against the house I was next to. I didn't like the idea of not moving, especially if even one zombie was looking my way when it happened. But it might work, I'd just let them run on by. I thought through all of these scenarios in a flash, and was already diving into a small mulberry bush as I was thinking it. Hugo was almost even with me by the time I was able to turn and feel that I was completely concealed from the road. The zombies were a good twenty yards trailing, but they didn't look like they planned on stopping. My upper torso was completely under the bush, but the bottom-most branches were still a good six inches above my back, and my legs were uncovered. This, all of a sudden, felt like not such a great maneuver. If a zombie saw me and headed this way, it would be all I could do to extricate myself from my hidey-hole and get up to full speed.

"Dumb, dumb," I said softly as the zombies approached. Then I heard the unmistakable sound of the crunching of plastic, and the high-pitched whining of spinning tires upturned. *Are you shitting me?* Hugo took this most inopportune of times to flip. I stuck my head out an inch – two at the max – to see what happened. I was done in by a fucking pothole! How damn ironic is that? The very job I had been doing before the zombies came, and my equivalents down in North Carolina couldn't do their part to make our streets a safer place to drive on.

The zombies pounced on the truck. The wheels stopped spinning as Hugo's life came to an abrupt end. Gary's shirt was shredded in the feeding frenzy, bandages and swabs flying like chaff in World War II. Zombies sprang up as they realized they had been duped. Well, maybe they didn't figure that part out; they just knew they weren't eating anything with substance and now they were on active search mode again. I pulled my head in slowly, not wanting to give my spot away. The moonlight felt like it was shining bright enough to rival a morning sun. Sure, no clouds when you want them, unlike that time back in 1978 when I was trying to watch the lunar eclipse. Oh yeah! They were all over the place then. Stayed up all effin' night, didn't see a damn thing except for clouds. I told God that he should probably stick to his day job and leave the ironic comedy to the professionals.

"Awesome," I whispered, putting my head down for a second. Had to be at least thirty zombies just milling about, no more than thirty to forty feet from where I hid. They didn't go back to Mary's house, which would have been a blessing. They just milled around, like stoners in their parents' basement. They just didn't know what to do with themselves. I'd been one of them, so I knew this could possibly go on all night. I guess zombies were a lot like stoners; neither did much in the way of action until food was involved. At least I would be able to keep myself amused.

I would have to do something before daybreak. I was entirely too exposed like this. I decided I was not going to wait until the very end to do something. Normally, I'd wait until the sun was beginning to peek up over a nearby rooftop. I was sick of close calls when it was time to move. I slowly inched further back and closer to the foundation of the house I was hiding next to. The loud snap when my rifle sling caught a branch above my head, snapping the dry appendage in two, did not go unnoticed. I stopped moving completely. I mean, except of course, for my heart which was banging so hard it was popping my chest off the ground by a good six or eight inches. (Yes, yes, it's my flair for the dramatic, I was scared. You have thirty or so zombies stop everything they're doing and more or less look in your direction and let me know how you hold up.)

I didn't even want to breathe, but when your heart is slamming away and your adrenaline is juicing the works, it just isn't possible. I let a small exhalation of air go. *GOD, ARE YOU KIDDING ME?!* I screamed in my head. The night was just cool enough that I could see my breath as it lazily swirled past my face. Might as well have been crashing cymbals together. A couple of zombies had honed in on the movement of coiled, cooled air, but as of yet had not made any direct connection between it and a food source. I had to imagine that they would come check it out. What the hell else were they going to do? I'm sure they weren't worried about missing an ice cream social or something.

A few of the inquisitive zombies started to slowly make their way over towards my location. I was gradually inching my way back even further so that I could stand and make a run for it. I was tempted to head back towards Mary's, but I wasn't sure if I'd make it, or more likely, if she'd even open the door. Oh, I'm sure she'd make a good show of it for Gary. But I could almost picture her fingers fumbling with the lock on the security door (yes, the same one she had already twice proved how adept she was with) as zombies began to chew on my flesh. And then she'd have this small, devious smile that would flash across her features right before she shut the front door.

I wasn't even going to attempt that avenue. Mothers are entirely too protective of their offspring…and now that she knew who and what I was? Yeah, better to not try that at all.

The problem at hand was that the three amigos kept advancing on my spot, not with any determined reason yet, but that was only a matter of time. I thought about sending them off one by one, but then I would definitely be giving my position away. If the rest of the troop joined in the fray, I would not be able to divert my attention to each of them in turn quickly enough to repel them.

"Piss, shit, and vinegar," I muttered. Pretty archaic curse words, but it seemed like the right thing to say. I must have been channeling an old man, because I don't remember ever using or hearing that particular combo of words in that fashion…ever. My feet were up against the house, I wasn't going any further back, next thing for me was to rise and run.

"Did it crash?" I heard Josh's voice from up the street.

"There's a bunch of zombies in the road, but I don't see your truck…or Mike for that matter," Gary answered.

Every last zombie turned to the voices. I was completely forgotten as the zombies went from ambling to full throttle in mere moments. It might not have been the cavalry to the rescue, but the outcome was just as effective.

"We should probably get back inside," Gary told Josh.

My smart-ass comment would have been, "Do you think?" But right now, all I wanted to do was a small jig. I wanted to, but I wouldn't. There was still a good chance that somebody alive and breathing would be in one of these houses and they would never be able to unsee that. I didn't want to put anybody through any more stress than they had already been. There's a few things in this life we should never be exposed to, one is my dancing; another would be anyone picking their nose and eating it; and third would be zombies. Anyone still alive who had already seen two of those, I would not heap any more misery on.

The zombies were racing down the street. I could hear Mary urging the boys in and then the resounding thuds of both doors being shut. I once again felt alone and scared. Man, I just can't seem to get my shit together. Two seconds ago, I was praying for this and now that I've got it, I don't know what to do with it. Time to find my friend. I didn't have a shred of proof, nor any type of psychic link to him, but I just couldn't shake the feeling that BT was in trouble. I stayed as close to the houses as I could. Hating every time I had to run across a side yard to get to the next dwelling. I was figuring I was in more danger of catching a round from a homeowner at this point while I was in the open.

I had traveled another two houses when I started to see signs of a struggle. This was no CSI crime scene where I needed a magnifying glass and special chemicals. The headless zombie kind of gave it away, followed by a second and a third. I was passing the front of the house and the zombie bodies were beginning to stack up. My heart or maybe my stomach or just plain both were struggling to find room in my throat. On the right side of the house, I could see a six-foot privacy fence. The gate was gone or buried under even more zombie bodies. It was impossible to not step on a zombie as I made my way through the constricted area. I now heard the distinctive sound of metal on metal. The repeated click was nerve-wracking. I pictured all sorts of travesties, but nothing could live up to the truth. I turned into the backyard, thankful that the space opened up and I could stop stepping on bodies. Twenty to thirty zombies lay strewn about, some with bullet holes, most with caved-in skulls, some with sliced off arms and decapitated heads.

The metallic sound got louder. I approached cautiously. The sound was coming from behind a large home-heating propane tank. I thought (hoped) it was merely the wind pushing something against the large drum – a great theory, mind you, if there had been any breeze at all. The air was as still as death. *Great analogy, Talbot,* I berated myself.

I gave a wide berth to the tank as I approached. I saw large legs first, splayed out on the ground. I moved quickly around to see BT leaning up against the tank, his revolver planted firmly under his jaw, I didn't move fast enough as the hammer came down on an expended round. He pulled the trigger again, the metallic click sending me flying to pull the gun from him.

BT barely registered my existence as I pulled the gun from his hand. He looked up at me with a tear-soaked face.

"I've been bit, Mike," BT sobbed.

Chapter Ten – Paul, Brian, and Deneaux

"Mrs. D, I really think you should take more cover," Brian said as he hid behind some strategically placed road debris.

The overpass they were on appeared to be the perfect place for their ambush. There was no access to the highway on this road, and by the time anyone traversed the steep grade to get to them, they would be long gone. That was the theory anyway.

"Nonsense, I am no spring chicken. I'm not getting on the ground like a savage."

Paul shrugged his shoulders at Brian as if to say, 'I don't know what the hell she's talking about.'

Mrs. Deneaux had searched four backyards before she found a lawn chair that she liked. Brian had carried the piece of furniture here for her. He would have left it behind if he hadn't thought she was nearly his equivalent with the firearms. He thought Paul was a loyal and brave friend, but when it came to shooting, Paul was best left to the job of spotter.

Mrs. Deneaux was sound asleep, head lolled to the side and half a burnt cigarette hanging out of her mouth when the earth begin to tremble.

"You feel that?" she asked, awakening with a start.

"No, what's up?" Paul asked.

"Nothing. Must be gas," she said, laughing.

"Wonderful," Paul answered, moving slightly away.

"No, I felt it too," Brian said, looking up over their barricade.

"You must be ripping them," Paul said to Mrs.

Deneaux. "Whoa! I felt that." Paul looked down the roadway. "You see anything?"

Brian placed his binoculars up to his eyes and held them steady. "Nothing yet," he said calmly, but his true rampaging emotions were threatening to rip through his imposed demeanor.

Mrs. Deneaux flipped her rifle's safety off and rested the barrel on top of the guardrail. Her heart cracked off some rust as it beat a little quicker. She had led a decent life, not fulfilling and not overly happy, but it was her life and she was not in any rush to give it back to her maker. Besides that, she had some serious sins she still had to atone for. She wasn't convinced there was an underworld – who needed to believe in that when evil is present all around, every day. But she was not one to test her luck either. If there was a Hades, he would have to wait just like everyone else to get his due. She put her index finger in her mouth and stuck it in the air to find the prevailing breeze.

"Does that really work?" Paul asked.

"Watch and learn," she said, placing her eye to the scope.

"Here they come." Brian pointed down the roadway as he pulled his binoculars down.

"How can we be sure it's them?" Paul asked.

"Well, first will be the smell, and then the underlying sense of evil that will pervade everything...and then the old standby, your friend said they'd be coming this way and in this form," Mrs. Deneaux said, never taking her gaze from her aperture.

"Okay, so there's that," Paul said.

"This a little much for you, bud?" Brian said, egging Paul on a bit.

"You do get that I was a manager at FedEx before this shit happened, right? I didn't go off and play Army boy for a few years. I've played paint ball maybe three times my entire life and the only gun in my house belonged to my wife.

So excuse me if I'm a little fucking nervous that we're about to get into a firefight with an enemy that probably outnumbers us a thousand to one," Paul said heatedly.

"Quit your bitching," Mrs. Deneaux said, looking up. "Most of them won't even have a weapon," she cackled, referring to the zombies that were being carried in the trucks.

Brian snorted. "Sorry, man," he said when Paul directed a glare at him. "I was just trying to gauge your combat readiness."

"He didn't do so well," Mrs. Deneaux said. "They're in range." She steadied her eye back down on the scope. "You give the word, Brian, and the driver of the first truck is a dead man."

Brian shivered at the iciness with which she delivered those words. Killing a man was not an easy task. She, however, sounded practiced at the event. "I want you to be able to tell if he's a genteel before you shoot."

Mrs. Deneaux laughed.

"I don't get it," Paul said.

The trucks rumbled closer.

"God, there's so many of them," Paul said.

The driver of the lead truck saw a glint of light from above. As he looked to see what was reflecting, he thought he saw a small wisp of smoke, followed immediately by a warm, stinging sensation in the center of his chest. His heart stopped beating from the ruptured aorta long before his brain caught up with the fact that he was dead. The truck jerked to the right and then immediately back to the left, the G-forces pulling the cab free from the trailer. The cab went off the embankment to the left, smashing into a tree with the tortured sound of twisting metal and breaking glass. The trailer's front dropped onto the pavement. Sparks shot back forty feet as metal grated noisily on the roadway.

The trailer may have come to a peaceful stop had not the truck behind it plowed ferociously into its rear end. The troop transport's rear tires came off the ground as it slammed into the tractor-trailer, spilling the undead contents all over the roadway. Zombies that weren't immediately liquefied from the accident got up and looked around. The small group atop the overpass was left to wonder why the zombies didn't do anything except stand in place, almost like they were awaiting direction. But those questions would have to wait to be answered as Eliza's live men got out and began to search for the threat.

Mrs. Deneaux, smoothly pulled her bolt action back and then forward, placing another round in the chamber. The driver of the third truck had stopped in enough time to avoid the collision and had just stepped out of the cab when Mrs. Deneaux sheered his arm off above the elbow.

Paul, who now had the binoculars, told her that the driver was not dead.

"I did it on purpose, sweetie," Mrs. Deneaux said almost kindly. "I was hoping that maybe the sight of blood and someone screaming and running around like a headless chicken would get the zombies moving. Doesn't seem to have worked." She pulled the bolt back and pushed it forward again.

Brian once again got that chill up his spine. *She's either mad as a hatter, or insane. Neither is a very good prospect.*

Brian started to shoot, not nearly with the precision or icy coolness with which Mrs. D dispatched of the enemy, but it was effective all the same.

"Might be time to get going," Paul said as he saw troops rallying. "It looks like they know where we are and they're getting ready to fight back."

As if on cue, shots began to pepper their location.

"Good enough warning for me," Brian shifted to get his things together, ready to leave post-haste. The round that hit him smashed through his collarbone and exited his abdomen. He immediately rolled on to his back. "Fuck! I didn't think it would hurt that bad!" he said as his breathing became rapid.

"What would?" Paul turned, beginning to rise with his rucksack. "Damn," was all Paul managed to say as he looked down on Brian and a blossom of blood spread from Brian's shoulder to his stomach.

"Bad?" Mrs. Deneaux asked, as she realized they weren't leaving quite yet. She dropped her magazine and started to put more rounds in it. "I'll keep shooting. You need to get pressure on his wound."

Brian was breathing heavily, straining the air through clenched teeth. "It feels like someone has dragged a branding iron across my chest," he hissed. "And I can't move my left arm."

Paul gingerly opened Brian's light jacket and pulled his shirt up. The sharp intake of air was all the information Brian needed.

"It's bad?" Brian asked.

"Brian, everything's bad to me. Remember me saying I was a manager at a FedEx? Worst thing I ever had to deal with were cardboard cuts," Paul told him as he took an extra shirt from his backpack and placed it over Brian's exit wound. "It looks like your collarbone is pretty busted up and the bullet grazed across your chest. That's why it's burning; and then it went in and out of your stomach."

"Gained twenty-five pounds since I've been out of the Army. Most of it is gone now, but if I had stayed in shape, the bullet would have missed," Brian said, still in pain, but realizing he might not be quite dead.

"That extra weight might have saved your life, at least the sexual part," Paul told him.

"What are you talking about?" Brian asked as he repositioned himself.

"Look at the direction that bullet was heading," Paul said as he got some bandages and tape.

Brian looked down to his left, past the busted collarbone, at the scrape that went to the right of his left nipple to where the bullet entered into his stomach and came out right below the navel. "Oh shit! That was close," Brian said, placing his right hand on his still present male equipment.

"I'd take a scar on my midsection any day of the week," Paul commented, doing his best to place a field dressing on the wound so they could get out of there.

Mrs. Deneaux was still rhythmically shooting, but their location was under heavy fire. Mrs. Deneaux's lawn chair had already suffered two grievous wounds. The only thing saving her life was how thin she was.

"Well, that helps," she said as she lifted her head from the scope.

The shooting had stopped on both sides, but the screaming intensified from the highway below.

"What's going on?" Brian asked.

"I think Mr. Talbot has held up his end of the agreement," Mrs. Deneaux said as she gleefully clapped her hands.

Paul got into a crouch to look over the guardrail.

"Oh, I think you could do the Electric Slide and no one would take any notice of you," Mrs. Deneaux said as she stood to get a better vantage point of the slaughter down below.

Paul was perfectly happy with his vantage point. "The zombies are attacking Eliza's people." He pumped his fist.

"I think now would be a good time to get gone," Brian said, pulling his water bottle over.

"Let me get a sling on your arm first." Mrs. Deneaux placed her rifle down and assessed Brian for the first time.

Brian was none too pleased with her gaze. He could tell she was sizing up his mobility, and if he were left wanting, she would not have any problem leaving him behind. *She's a dangerous one*, he thought. But he said nothing as she did a reasonably good facsimile of a sling with an old t-shirt.

"Not bad," Brian said as he stood up slowly. Blood rushed out of his head, sending him into a brief, but intense bout of vertigo.

"You alright?" Mrs. Deneaux asked, and it almost sounded like she cared.

"Fine," Brian answered as he steadied himself on the back of her lawn chair. He prayed that its compromised integrity would sustain his weight for just a little while longer. If he plunged to the ground now and passed out, he was certain he'd find himself alone on the bridge when he awoke. Blood slowly pushed its way back up and into his head; the dizziness passed.

If Mrs. Deneaux hadn't been so busy assessing Brian, she might not have missed a chance to end the entire conflict. Paul decided to seize the day as he grabbed Mrs. Deneaux's rifle. He stood completely upright. A slight breeze was blowing left to right as he placed the crosshairs of the Winchester .30-30 on Eliza's breast.

Brian and Mrs. Deneaux turned as Paul fired.

"I hit her!" Paul screamed.

"Who?" Brian asked, swallowing down some bile that had swirled up from his gut.

"Eliza! I hit Eliza!" Paul shouted, almost dropping the rifle off the railing.

Mrs. Deneaux grabbed it before he could. She started looking through the scope for any signs that the vamp was dead. "I don't see anything. How far away was she?" she asked.

Paul started counting off trucks. "Nine or ten back," he said proudly.

"That's about a three hundred yard shot," Brian said, finally able to move without the threat of falling.

"Did you compensate for bullet drop?" Mrs. Deneaux asked, moving the scope further out to look for Eliza.

"Bullet what?" Paul asked. His previous high beginning to sink.

"At that distance, the bullet could drop about ten inches roughly," Brian said.

"If you were aiming for her skull, that could still have done her some damage. Might have hit her in the chest."

Paul's head sank." I was aiming for her chest, figured I had a better chance of hitting that."

"Gut shot the bitch," Mrs. Deneaux laughed. "Bet that hurt."

Brian thought her laugh sounded very much like what drowning babies crying would. "We should really get out of here now. I can't imagine that anything good can happen from pissing Eliza off."

***

Eliza had been so intent on finding out why her zombies had turned and what she needed to do to rein them back in, she had not been anticipating an outside threat.

"This is Talbot's doing! I can smell the stench of him all over this!" Eliza spat.

"I think it would be best if we left him his small corner of the world, Eliza," Tomas said, smiling as he walked with his sister.

"You did this!" she said vehemently, spinning on her heel to confront him. "Without your help, that animal Durgan would have killed him and we could be out exploring vast new ways to torment the world. I will not be bested by a mere man."

"He is no longer merely a man, sister," Tomas reminded.

"No, thanks to you."

Tomas shrugged at the jibe. "He has struck you hard, Eliza. Most of your humans are either dead or have fled. I beg you one last time, leave him be."

"Never!" she screamed as she stepped out from behind a truck and smack dab in front of a speeding bullet.

Her midsection punched in from the projectile as her upper torso bent over. Tomas grabbed her before she could fall and pulled her back behind cover.

"It is not a fatal blow," Tomas said, inspecting the wound.

The zombies around the siblings did not advance, but they had stopped what they were doing and were now watching them intently.

Eliza sat in her brother's arms for a while longer. The searing pain was something she had not experienced since her human youth when a gang of Huns had trapped her in an old barn and beat and used her for three days before they tired of her. For the first time in half a millennia, Eliza doubted her intentions. "Why won't he die, Tomas?" Eliza begged.

"It is for something you have forgotten about, Eliza: family. He fights for the lives of his family. He knows no stronger bond."

"Then that is the bond we must break," Eliza said as she stood up. The bullet had worked its way out of her skin and the wound was nearly healed.

"Did you hear nothing I said?" Tomas fairly cried.

"I heard everything you said. If we kill Talbot's family, he will follow closely behind."

"Not until he exacts his fair measure of revenge. He will not strike out if we do not corner him."

"Maybe that would have been the truth at one time, brother. No, we must strike while he is at his weakest, while he still has family to use as leverage and while he is still learning the powers that you bestowed upon him. You sealed his fate when you bit him."

There was nothing he could do to sway her from this course, and when the final showdown did come, on whose side would he fall? He still hadn't made up his mind.

The cries of her humans had nearly died out. A few trucks could be heard pulling away and zombies were spread out everywhere hunting for food, including the ones that had stopped for a moment, checking out Eliza to see if she would be coming up on the menu.

"We should leave here, Eliza, in case he has any other surprises in store for us."

This time, Eliza made sure to keep under cover and concealment behind the remaining trucks as she herded her zombies back in. And on that highway was where she would leave them, two thousand zombies, through the coming winters and summers. Those zombies would sway forever, as leaves fell, as rain poured, as sun soaked them, tied to Eliza's last order to stand still.

"You're just going to leave them here?" Eliza's first-in-command asked, as he swung the command truck around.

"I fear that a couple of the zombies looked at her with a less than flattering stare," Tomas told the man.

The man wouldn't miss them. It was tough to feel sorry for the creatures that tore his wife apart in front of his very eyes as she fell from the ladder they were climbing to get up their apartment's fire escape. He had thought about just letting go and joining her, but he wasn't brave enough for that. Not brave enough to die and not brave enough to live. Eliza had come across him a week later, still huddled in the far corner of his apartment, covered in his own filth, too scared to even cross his own living room to get some water.

She had promised him a chance to strike back at those responsible for his wife's death. Dean had never been a God-fearing man, but he knew the devil when he came across it, and the only thing missing on Eliza were the horns. It wasn't that he believed her words, it was what he knew she would do to him if he didn't join her. A coward is led. He felt this was his punishment for not dying with his wife. He had seen and done more acts of brutality, cruelty, and evil in the last few months than any person should ever be exposed to, and all in the name of Eliza. He knew his wife was looking down on him, frowning, and that he would never see her again.

There was no place in Heaven for the likes of him, not anymore. Maybe at one time, he had the whole meek thing going for him, now he was certain he was damned. If he had not thought that, he would have killed himself months ago, but he was afraid of meeting whatever it was that had spawned Eliza. So, afraid of this eventual meeting, he had begged first Eliza and then Tomas to bite him. Eliza had laughed cruelly at him when his request came.

"You would give up your soul so willingly?" she asked, flashing her lengthened canines.

"More than anything, mistress," he had groveled before her.

"You disgust me," Eliza told him. "The only way I would bite your pathetic neck would be to drain you dry…to watch you shrivel like an exposed worm in the mid-July sun."

"Please, mistress! Have I not served you well?"

"Do not think I am fooled. You serve for preservation, not loyalty."

Dean withdrew; was he that easy to read?

"I can see by your reaction that I know your heart," she said. "Do you not wish to once again see this wife you were wailing about when I found you?"

Dean sniffed, wiping his nose clean, nodding his head vigorously.

"But you know now that there is no place for you in your God's Heaven, don't you?"

Dean nodded again.

"You think I'm cruel?" Eliza said through thin lips. "How about your master that banishes His children from his garden because they merely thirsted for knowledge! Or floods an entire world because of acts from a few that He finds depraved. Or allows the undead to walk among His creations, devouring them because they went too far with the knowledge they had obtained? That sounds cruel to me!" she yelled. "How about letting a man's wife be allowed into His

Heaven, but deny the husband entry!" she said as she picked Dean up by a finger placed under his jaw.

The pain was excruciating as his entire body's weight was suspended by his jaw. Eliza's finger had broken through skin and was threatening to come up underneath his tongue. He yearned for death at that moment, to be free from the pain she was inflicting on him. He cared not what happened to his eternal soul as she paraded him around like that for a few moments more. When she finally pulled her finger away, he crashed to the ground, staying there many moments longer, until Eliza beckoned him like nothing had happened at all.

"How far, mistress?" Dean asked as he drove away from the scene of carnage.

"Until I snap your neck or tell you to stop," Eliza said, staring straight through the windshield.

And from the mood she was in, Dean fully expected the neck snapping to be the outcome.

***

Paul, Brian, and Mrs. Deneaux worked themselves off the bridge long before Eliza had made her departure and were making as good a progress as they could. Brian was slowed considerably by his injury, but it wasn't like Mrs. Deneaux was blazing any trails.

"Get in the woods," Paul urged. "I hear someone coming."

"Is it Mike?" Brian asked, hoping that was the case.

"Possible," Paul stated as he ushered the small group along. "But there were also a bunch of people running for their lives from that raid."

Mrs. Deneaux had just entered into the underbrush as three heavily armed men rounded a corner on the road up ahead. One of the men was holding his side like he had the mother of all stitches from running.

"Hold up," one of the men said. "I thought I saw

something." He was pointing to where Paul and the others were now hiding.

All three had assault rifles. *This will be a small scuffle*, Paul thought as he tried to get his rifle ready with as minimal movement as possible.

"Whassa matter, Vinnie?" one man asked the cohort who was holding his side.

"I cut myself getting down off the truck," Vinnie said.

The man who asked the question brought his rifle up to Vinnie's head. "Lemme see the cut, Vin," he asked.

"Come on, Lenny. I cut myself. Get that gun outta my face!" Vinnie yelled.

"What are you two hollering about?" the leader said, turning to face the other two men.

"Vinnie says he's cut," Lenny said.

The leader turned his gun on Vinnie. "You know the deal, Vinnie. Let's see it."

"It barely got me," Vinnie cried. "It's more like a nip."

Vinnie collapsed to the ground as Lenny shot him through the back of the head.

The leader butt-stroked Lenny. "You fucking mook! You got blood and brains all over me!" he yelled at Lenny's prone body.

Lenny's face was swelling rapidly; broken blood vessels began to turn purple and blue. Lenny turned his gun on the leader. "You ever do that shit again, Sam, I'll blow your fucking head off."

"I hope you give me more warning than you did Vinnie," Sam laughed as he reached a hand down to help Lenny up.

"I was really hoping they were going to shoot each other," Brian whispered to Paul. Paul nodded in agreement.

"If nothing else, it looks like they forgot about us," Paul answered.

Sam bent down and picked up the gun Vinnie would

no longer be using. They walked past the hidden trio, more interested in what potentially lay behind, than to the sides.

"They're heading towards our truck," Brian said.

"Should I shoot them?" Mrs. Deneaux asked.

"No," Brian said, "you won't be fast enough with that bolt-action, and I can't even hold my rifle." He left unsaid Paul's marksmanship skills or lack thereof.

"We're screwed if they take our truck," Paul said.

"Yeah, we're also screwed if they shoot us," Brian said.

"Maybe Mike is already back at the truck," Paul said hopefully.

Brian was in the midst of standing when Mrs. Deneaux's claw-like hand gripped his bad shoulder. He nearly swooned from the pain, but it had the desired effect as he fell hard to the ground. Brian was about to let loose a litany of choice swear words as a small tribe of seven speeders ran by.

"Fucking Grand Central Station," Paul cursed, making sure the zombies were well past.

They could all hear the roar of an engine start up ahead.

"Well that settles that," Brian said. "We need to get another ride."

"This is all jacked now!" Paul said with some alarm. He was beginning to break down. Brian had seen it numerous times in combat. Some people just don't deal well with accumulating stress.

"I sure could use a cigarette," Mrs. Deneaux said.

"How is Mike going to find us?" Paul asked, his voice rising over the sound of the oncoming truck.

Shots began to ring out, a large thud was immediately followed by the screeching of tires and the sound of a large heavy object hitting an immoveable tree.

"Should we check on it?" Paul looked to Brian.

"Busted truck, seven zombies, two armed

hostiles…don't see the upside, Paul."

"We can't stay here," Mrs. Deneaux said wisely. "That noise is going to bring more of one or the other or both. And as much as I enjoy both of your company while we lay here in the grass, I would rather be sitting in a car with a warm cigarette in my hand."

"I can't believe they just took our ride," Paul said angrily.

"I bet that's not the worst thing they've done today," Brian said, getting up gingerly, his shoulder aching.

He could feel a flush coming on his cheeks and knew that he was going to need antibiotics soon to fight off any infection the bullet may have allowed to enter in to his body. The closest bottle was in the truck that now sounded like Sarajevo, and not the good Olympics one, but rather the war-torn one of a few years later. He thought to possibly wait for the outcome of the battle and then finish off the survivors – no matter of what variety – and grab what he needed. But more speeders ran by as the three refugees melted deeper in to the woods.

For an hour they followed the road, but always remained hidden in the brush. The way was slow going, but the chance of being seen was minimal.

Brian finally brought them to a halt as exhaustion began to set in.

Brian was making a decent showing of going slowly to allow time for Mrs. Deneaux to keep up, but the evidence of Brian's burgeoning infection was on his face. His complexion had paled considerably and sweat dripped from his features, though the weather or the exertion didn't merit it.

"You look worse than I feel," Mrs. Deneaux said as she sat on a small stump.

"Holy shit," Paul said, finally taking notice of his walking partner. "Let me see your wound."

"I'm fine," Brian said, swaying slightly in a non-existent breeze.

Paul cautiously pulled Brian's shirt up; deep red lines radiated out from the entry wound in Brian's stomach. "We need to get you some meds," Paul said.

"How could he be sick so fast?" Mrs. Deneaux asked.

"What do you mean? He got shot," Paul said with some heat.

"I understand that, but he shouldn't already be showing these signs of infection. It takes at least one or two days to get those symptoms. Something else is going on here."

Paul stepped back, Brian's shirt fell back in place. Brian felt like decisions were being made regarding him, but fever was beginning to cloud his judgment and all he wanted to do right now was lay down.

"Sergeant Wamsley reporting for duty," Brian said as he went to the ground, mostly under his own power. Paul placed his head on a small patch of moss.

"He's burning up. We need to get him some help," Paul said.

"I think it's too late," Mrs. Deneaux said coolly, finally getting to light her smoke.

"What are you saying?"

"You can't really be that dense, can you? I really would have thought Michael would have a better screening method for his friends."

"I'll pretend I didn't hear that, and you'll explain to me what I'm apparently missing."

"He's dying, and fast, from the looks of it," she said, taking a large drag off her cigarette.

"We just need to get him some pills and he'll be fine."

"Nothing short of a medical team and a blood transfusion are going to save him now, but I'll allow you your fantasy."

"You'll *allow* me? How fucking considerate!" Paul

shouted.

"I'm wondering if he's turning into a zombie," Mrs. Deneaux pondered, completely ignoring Paul's outburst.

Paul couldn't help himself, he moved from his protective stance next to Brian to one in which he had a better angle to see if any change had taken place.

"I see that you think that, too," Deneaux laughed.

"I didn't, until you said it. We need to go get him something to help," Paul said, fear fighting bile to be the first to root itself firmly in his throat.

"We? I think not. I'll only slow you down and someone should stay here to keep watch over him," Deneaux said, pointing to the prone figure of Brian with her cigarette holding finger.

Paul doubted her sincerity on the whole 'keeping watch' part, but she was slower than a three-legged tortoise racing in molasses when it came to walking through the woods. "I'm not even sure where we are," Paul said with some rising alarm. The thought of going out on his own was not sitting well. Paul looked all around, the trees suddenly looking very constricting.

"You can wait a few more hours until he dies. Then we can leave here together, dearie," Deneaux said, completely catching Paul's anxiety attack.

Paul trudged out of the woods and onto the roadway, trying his best to gauge their location. It would do no good to get what he needed only to find out he didn't know his way back.

Paul heard Mrs. Deneaux cycle a round into her rifle. He fully expected to hear the shot ring out as she 'took care' of Brian's illness. *And would that be so bad?* he thought. *Mrs. D was probably right, he was already a dead man.* "And now I'm risking my life for him," Paul muttered, stopping his forward progress. "He'd do the same for me. I think," he said, going again.

"Twit," Mrs. Deneaux said as she watched Paul's

conscience at work. "He's as dead as this one," she said as she casually kept the rifle pointed at Brian's head.

She wasn't overly concerned with her future survival. She was a survivor, always had been and she saw no reason why that would change now. She would give Paul two or three hours at the most to get what he needed and get back. If he wasn't here, she was going to seek out a more hospitable location to spend the night and the next morning she would resume her search for Michael. Nothing ensured her continued existence more than staying with the penultimate survivor.

The only flaw she saw in Michael was his commitment to others, although that would work in her favor this time because he would not leave until he had the rest of his raiding party with him.

Brian stirred restlessly in his fever-soaked dreams, Mrs. Deneaux pushed his shirt up to watch the ever advancing infection as it branched to his heart. Once it got there, nothing could save him, except a priest and that would only be his everlasting soul.

Paul felt completely exposed as he walked down the road. He looked longingly to the brush-covered street sides, but time was of the utmost importance. He hesitated. *Who would know if I turned around now? I could tell Deneaux I didn't find anything. She'd suspect and I'd know,* he thought, chastising himself.

Paul had started walking again when he got a creeping sensation at the back of his neck. It was that same feeling he got so long ago at the gas station when that man had begun to approach him, when this whole thing had originally started. He had ignored that feeling then and almost fell into a trap. "I'm going to be pissed if I turn around and there's nothing there, I'm just scaring myself," he said aloud much like people who enter a dark basement whistle so as to abate their fear.

At first, what he saw just didn't register. Luckily, his

lower reasoning abilities of survival kicked in. Two speeders, a large male and an even larger female, were bearing down on him. Paul involuntarily cried out as he began his own sprint. Cognitive thought slowly came back as Paul tried to do some basic calculations in his head. *Had to have at least a couple of hundred yards head start on them, should I turn around and look? No I'll lose time.* He could swear on more than one occasion, he could feel fingernails narrowly miss his neck and he would put on another short burst of speed.

He had gone less than a quarter mile and knew his time of running was rapidly coming to a close. "Can't...keep...this...up!" He huffed. He stole a quick glance over his shoulder, hoping the zombies had stopped their pursuit. No such luck, the lead zombie dressed in tattered camouflage gear was, at the most, twenty feet away.

I'm screwed, Paul thought. *Okay, okay.* His mind going into overdrive. *What would Talbot do?* Even in the dire situation, he smiled a little at the comparison to the popular *'What Would Jesus Do?'* slogan. Paul held his rifle up to his face, not sure what he was looking for, or if he'd even be able to tell as the firearm swayed violently back and forth in his field of vision. *I think I see red. Does that mean the safety is on or off? How many bullets do I have? What are the odds I could hit him with the rifle over my shoulder? About as good as you stopping and aiming.* He swore he heard Mike say that last part.

Paul planted his left leg to turn and make a shot, the force of his forward momentum causing his ankle to roll. He fell and spun hard from the pain. Camo man had not broken stride as Paul rolled over two complete times. Tears had already welled up in Paul's eyes as the Camo man lunged for him. Paul pulled the trigger of his rifle. He couldn't have placed the shot any better if he had put the rifle on a gun stand and fired it off. The bullet struck Camo man squarely in the forehead. The zombie's forward progress halted immediately as brackish, gray-green matter leaked out the entry hole, and the smell of sulfur-laden, stagnant water assailed his nostrils. Paul's triumph was short-lived as the Amazonian woman who had been struggling to keep up was now gaining by leaps and bounds on the prostrate Paul.

Paul sat up to get a better shot, the pain in his ankle throbbing with every beat of his heart, which at this moment, meant it was pretty much a continuous pain. "Gotcha now, bitch!" Paul screamed as his well-placed shot slammed the woman in her calf. Her immeasurable bulk crashed to the ground as the bottom half of her right leg snapped in two.

The zombie woman landed on her face and some of her teeth broke out as she made hard contact with the ground. As she rose, Paul noticed white jagged pieces of her shattered incisors poking through her bottom lip like shards of glass used on top of rock walls. She looked in sorry shape, but yet she rose. Paul sat there, watching her in stunned silence as she got to her feet. Her knee-high skirt did little to hide the hideous sight Paul was gazing at. The zombie advanced slowly, her left foot landing normally on her sneaker-clad appendage, her right foot and a full six inches of her lower leg folded away at a ninety degree angle as it came down. Paul could hear the bones in her leg as she cut through her calf muscles and made contact with the pavement. The sound was mind-numbingly sickening. It sounded like a wet fish being slapped down on a marble table; Paul was mesmerized with the horror of it. The zombie cared little for the irreparable damage she was committing as she approached. Blood spurted from the veins and arteries in her leg as she ripped through the tender vessels.

Paul pulled up his rifle, realizing at this distance even he would have a hard time missing. He pulled the trigger, or more correctly 'tried' to pull the trigger. He was not even rewarded with the satisfaction of a dry fire. He tried the trigger again, nothing. He turned the rifle over – an expended brass cartridge was lodged half in and half out of his rifle. Paul pulled back repeatedly on his bolt, the piece would not move and Stumpy was gaining.

Paul turned over and used his gun as a makeshift cane to prop himself up. He thought sourly that this would be the time it shot, while it was firmly entrenched in his armpit. *How many horror movies have I seen like this?* Paul asked himself as he limped away, the injured zombie nearly on his heels. His ankle was swelling. He could feel it testing out the boundaries of the boot he was wearing. If he took it off now, he'd be lucky if he could get a sock to stretch over it.

Paul nearly spilled a second time as he paused to look over his shoulder. Stumpy was losing ground and height as she continually splintered the bone in her calf. *A little while longer and she'll be down to her knee*, Paul thought. *Would she keep trying to walk with an exaggerated swaying gait? Or would she drop to her knees and come after him that way?* Paul really didn't want to wait, fearful that at any moment, he would run into another zombie, and with no other weapons than an unwieldy club, he wisely decided that confrontation would not be in his best interests.

It was another two hundred yards before Stumpy fell over. Paul heard the thud and possibly a low soft moan, of that he was not sure. The zombie opted for the crawling mode of transportation. Paul was relieved; the savage pain in his ankle was impeding his forward progress. He could slow his pace down now, he was in much less danger from her now than he had been moments earlier, but he was still a long way away from safe.

When Paul pulled his gaze from his traveling companion, he realized that he was on the fringes of a residential area. The house on his immediate left had been abandoned long before the zombies had come. Signs warning of danger and to not trespass were displayed prominently on the front door. It looked to Paul like the only thing holding the house up was force of habit.

The house on the right did not look much better, but as of yet, had not been officially condemned. He thought about going into that house, but it looked eerily similar to a house that a young couple had gotten trapped in, in some zombie movie Mike had made him watch. Paul was under the impression that if a movie didn't star Charles Bronson, it wasn't much worth watching. He had suffered through it to appease Mike, but mostly because Tracy had made some unbelievably good *queso* dipping sauce and he had brought with him a near insatiable case of the munchies.

He limped further down the road. The next house on his left looked like it could stop half the Mexican Army. And if they couldn't get in, what would be his odds?

"I'm going to the next one," Paul said as he turned to look at his pursuer. Her arms and hands were bloodied, but yet she still came. "It'd be awesome if you'd stop," Paul told her, but she paid him no heed.

The next house had some promise, scary promise, but promise all the same. The front door was intact; however, it was wide open. That was not a common sight these days. "Well," Paul reasoned, "whatever got in at least had a way out." That reasoning held sway with a zombie, but if humans had ransacked it, little of any value would be left for Paul to use. "At this point all I want is a chair and two aspirins. That would be just about the best thing I could think of right now. Twenty-four Mapledog Lane it is," Paul said as he made way for the door. Stumpy changed her course to match Paul. "I'll get us some tea ready," Paul told her.

The house was pitched in darkness; Paul expected no less. He did a quick scan of the entry room and then immediately opened up the drawn shades to let in some much needed diffused curtain light. Dried blood coated the far wall and even abundantly dotted the ceiling. Bits of matter, the origin of which he cared not to dwell upon, littered the small throw rug and wood floor.

Paul looked out the door. His traveling companion was still making her way towards him, but was still an extremely safe distance off. Paul still felt a powerful urge to shut the door though and try his best to put her out of his mind. But he feared that a much more mobile threat might still be lurking in the household and he wanted to be able to get out as soon as possible. Against his better judgment, he left the front door open.

"You make sure to ring the bell before you come in!" he shouted at the zombie.

She did not either confirm or deny her intention.

Paul kept his rifle out in front of him as he went from room to room. At this point, it was no more than an early detection system as the barrel would strike something first, but as a weapon, it was almost useless. He wouldn't even be able to get a good full extension on his swing in these tight quarters. The house was a disaster, but from the looks of it, not by looters. A battle had been waged here, the chunks of fingers and bits of bone scattered around led him to rightly believe that the zombies had come out victorious in this round. Animals had done a fair amount of damage also, getting to anything in a carton or box, Paul laughed a little as he stepped on a small pile of Sugar Smacks.

"I guess even raccoons have enough sense to stay away from that stuff," he said to the empty room. As he got past the kitchen and further into the house, the smell of disuse became prevalent. It wasn't the overwhelming stink of the dead or the undead, just stagnant water, mold, mildew and old food. He never thought he would be thankful for those odors. Blood was the dominant color as he entered into the aptly named dining room.

"This must have been the last stand," he said reverently. A small candelabrum was on the ground with matted, bloody hair stuck to the bottom. "About as good a weapon as my own," he said as he made sure to step around it. The copious amount of blood on the floor was strewn with footprints and animal tracks. Some were hand-like, paw prints of raccoons, but the more disturbing were the various sized prints of dogs. Paul had a healthy fear of dogs since he had been bitten as a youth. But they all looked old; human, zombie and animal alike. The blood had dried long ago and it appeared that nothing currently shared the house with him.

He did one more run-through of the entire first floor of the ranch. Thankful that the small home did not have a second floor. He locked the basement door on the first pass by. He blamed his sprained ankle and the pain it would cause to go downstairs on his decision to lock the door, but mostly he was just afraid of going down there. The basement from his vantage point on the top of the stairs, did not appear to have any ambient lighting coming in and he couldn't see the point in stumbling around in the dark looking for anything, especially when he didn't know what was down there, if anything worthwhile.

Paul went into the bathroom. The medicine cabinet was opened, but surprisingly it looked like everything was still there. He pulled down a bottle of aspirin and immediately gulped down three of them, sticking the rest of the bottle in his pocket. Stomach pills, flu medicine, cough syrup, and hemorrhoid cream. Most of it was standard fare, and everything but the cream ended up in his pockets.

"Come on, everyone has unused meds somewhere," he said. Paul shut the mirror on the cabinet, completely confident that he would suffer the same fate as every horror movie ever produced in the last fifty years. Something would be behind him as the mirror shut. His heart almost stopped when he realized the cliché he was performing. "Not enough scary shit going on, I've got to see if I can drum up a few more quarts of adrenaline." Nothing was there, but his fear wasn't quite abated. He knew that you could not see the reflections of vampires. He turned as quickly as his injured ankle would allow, it was not fast enough. Whatever had been behind him was now gone, even if it was all only in his imagination.

"No more mirrors," he said, chiding himself. "Kitchen cabinet or nightstand?"

Paul headed for the master bedroom in the small two-bedroom house. The first thing that struck him was how neat the room was, even the bed was made. "Who makes their bed in a zombie invasion?" Paul wished Mike were here to share this moment. They'd definitely get a good laugh over it.

Paul shuffled over to the nightstand. A molded-over mug of coffee stood alongside a lamp as the only inhabitants on the top of the small nightstand. Paul pulled out a book called *Indian Hill* by Mark Tufo that looked to be about half read, judging by the bookmark. "Doesn't look like they'll ever finish that," he said as he tossed the book onto the bed.

"Bingo!" Paul said excitedly as he grabbed four prescription bottles. The first was full of thumb tacks. "Okay that's not going to work," he said, tossing it beside the discarded book. The second was Xanax. He knew it was for anti-anxiety and didn't know how it was going to help in this present situation, but he stuck it in his pocket. *The whole world is one giant anxiety now*, he thought. The third contained painkillers. He opened up the bottle and shook them out in his hand. "Eight, that should be enough," he said as he popped two in his mouth.

"Perfect!" he yelled sarcastically as he shook the lone pill around in the bottle labeled Amoxicillin. It was the right drug but the wrong quantity. "I do not want to do this shit all day," he complained. He quickly went into the kitchen. Besides a lot of canned goods, there was nothing there that would do him any good in his present situation. He grabbed a small screwdriver he had seen in one of the drawers and sat down at the table to see if he could get the jam in his rifle out. "Might have been a good idea to do this first," he said. He then moved his chair when he realized he had his back to the front door. Paul had just finished prying out the jammed cartridge when the first effects of the painkillers began to take effect. "Now that's what I'm talking about," he said as he stood, testing out his new not-caringness on his injured ankle, for that's all that painkillers truly do, they numb the mind, not the injury.

Paul debated heading back to Brian with the one antibiotic or setting out again to look for more. Would one pill do anything? Or would it be akin to pissing on a forest fire? He decided to keep looking. It would take him too long to hobble back to them and then out again, and that's if he didn't need to take a nap somewhere in the meantime. Paul was deep into the effects of his prescription meds as he stepped out of the house. His first footfall out of the house landed squarely in Stumpy's mouth. Paul toppled over as the zombie bit down hard on the toe of his boot. Paul was halfway to meeting the pavement before his lagging mind was able to catch up to the situation. He was thankful that it was not his injured ankle in the zombie's mouth, but that was about it for the pros as his face raced to meet her injured leg.

His mouth opened in the exclamatory 'O' shape as he got a face full of zombie calf. He knew without a doubt you got the zombie virus from being bitten. *What are the repercussions from the other way around?* he thought as he tasted her vileness upon his lips. Paul twisted around and over, as did Stumpy. She had a good hold of his boot top and was not going to yield her prize.

"Fucking bitch!" Paul yelled as he brought his right foot down on the top of her head.

He immediately regretted his decision, three more pain pills would not have been able to mask the intense pain his ankle brought from the jolting contact with her skull. Pain was his all-consuming thought as he swayed from side to side on the ground. Stumpy stayed with him, move for move. As the pain level came to a manageable point, he tried to crawl away, but the zombie was having no part of it. Her mouth had not left his boot as she tried to gnash her way through the heavy material, her arms had come up and she wrapped her hands around the bottom of his leg. *Death by crawler*, Paul thought, *Mike's going to love this.*

The rifle! The idea ripped into his thoughts. *But I*

can't even swing it like this. Paul whined in response to himself. Even Paul's psyche was let down by his inability to reason together a workable escape plan.

"Oh yeah, I fixed the jam!" Paul said with elation.

Paul's subconscious did a small, sarcastic jig in celebration. It would be tough to miss from this distance even for Paul, but whether from lack of judgment or impeded painkiller judgment, Paul did not take into account what was on the other side of Stumpy's head, namely his boot. He placed the barrel on her skull and fired. The relief of having Stumpy fall to the side was immediately replaced by the pain in his foot where he had just lodged his bullet.

"Are you fucking kidding me!" he spat.

Paul rolled violently from side to side, not caring that half his movement brought him into contact with the newly departed Stumpy. "So much for Saturday night dancing!" he shouted at the top of his lungs. The endorphins released from the volume helped to diminish the pain, but not nearly enough. Paul finally looked down at his foot. Blood was pumping out from the bullet hole in the top of his boot at an alarming rate. *I always thought if I died from a self-inflicted gunshot wound, it would be something a little further north,* he thought as he crawled back over to the front door so that he could sit on the stoop and access how much damage he really had incurred.

As he pulled himself up, he reached into his pocket and immediately downed another two painkillers. He debated waiting for them to take effect before doing what needed to be done, but thought better of it because he could possibly bleed out before that happened. Paul undid the laces, feeling strangely detached as he did so. The boot came off without a hitch; it was the sock that was proving difficult. Not that it was stuck to anything, but rather he just didn't want to see what lay hidden beneath it.

"Ours is not to question why, but rather to do or to die. Why the hell am I quoting Tennyson?" Paul asked himself as he looked down on his blood-soaked sock.

His next question to himself paralyzed him with fear. *I just shot myself with a bullet that went through a zombie.* Paul ripped the sock off, the webbing between his second and third toe had a nice round hole blown right through it. *No bones, that's good.* Paul couldn't figure out how he was going to get up and on which leg he could stand. He opted to crawl on his hands and knees to the fridge. The only thing reasonably viable in there were the cans of diet Sprite.

"Can't hurt any more than it does now," he said, grabbing four of the cans. He moved over to the kitchen chair and opened the cans, dumping the entire contents on his injured foot, hoping that it would somehow disinfect the wound.

"Does aspartame have any antiseptic qualities?" Paul asked his wound. It wept some foamy pinkish fluid onto the floor in response. "Doesn't look like a wound that would be my undoing."

Paul was stuck in indecision. He was effectively hobbled with a right sprained ankle and a left foot with a bullet wound in it. A rifle with exactly two rounds, no antibiotics and enough pain pills that he might not even feel a bullet to the brain if he went down that road.

"Whoa where'd that come from?" he asked the air. "Fuck! I'd probably miss." And then he started laughing; he almost choked, he was laughing so hard. "Okay, what are my options? I can try to get back to Deneaux and let her know what happened." He dwelled on that for a second. "No good, she'd shoot me as soon as I said I was infected. I could try to find Mike. He'd at least wait until I changed over before he shot me. No, I'm not doing that either. Plan C." Paul gimped over to the front door, shut it securely, locked it tight and sat back at the kitchen table. "Hell, if I'm going to turn into a zombie, I'm doing it with some style." He took one more painkiller, rationing the rest for later that night.

Chapter Eleven – Ron's

Travis had pulled up a recliner and fallen asleep by Ron's shortwave radio. Tracy put down her cup of coffee to drape a small blanket around her son.

"You should get some sleep, too," Ron said, coming into the room.

Tracy grabbed her mug of coffee and walked to the other end of the room so as not to disturb her son.

"They should have called in by now," she said, staring out the large picture window at the pond which was just beginning to reflect the morning light.

Ron was all ready to pull out the standard responses. Maybe the radio is broken (likely possibility, knowing his brother's penchant for breaking things), or maybe the batteries have died (possible, but not probable; Ron gave them enough batteries to last a year even if Mike had left the damn thing on all day, every day), or they were making such good time, they didn't think to let anyone else know (also another possibility, considering Mike's 'what-me-worry?' attitude). But he was not so selfish as to not let his loved ones know what was happening. Ron didn't even go with the standard, "Everything will be alright." The lie died on his lips before he could say it.

Ron sat down at the living room table, looking at the same view as Tracy, occasionally remembering to drink his rapidly cooling coffee.

"Anything?" Travis asked, looking over at his mother and uncle.

A small terse shake of Tracy's head was all the answer he needed.

"Any more of that?" A stretching and yawning Cindy asked.

Tracy was pretty sure Cindy and Travis had arm wrestled for the right to sleep in the chair by the radio the night before. Cindy looked like she may have paced the entire night away.

"I'll go get you some," Ron said as he got up to head into the kitchen.

"He…they have to be alright," Cindy said, hugging herself.

"How's Perla doing?" Tracy asked, wanting to avoid that conversation completely.

"Someday she'll be alright, but not today," Cindy answered, now realizing that maybe she didn't want to dwell on the fate of her fiancé just yet either. "The view is beautiful," Cindy told Ron as he handed her a cup of coffee.

"Thank you," Ron said. "If you guys need anything, please let me know. I'd like to get to work as soon as possible before it gets dark."

Work involved designing, and building all viable means of defense of the Talbot stronghold. Ron wasn't a betting man, but he was fairly certain Mike would be back and he would be coming in hot. Meaning every zombie and vampire for a thousand mile radius would be in chase. That was Mike; he never got himself halfway into trouble, he always made sure to be fully wedged tightly in its grip, and he planned on being as properly prepared as possible.

"Hi, Perla." Cindy said as she wrapped her arms around her friend.

"Anything?" Perla asked.

Only the resulting silence answered her.

"I'm going to help Uncle Ron," Travis said, removing the small blanket.

"Be careful, hon. Your dad used to tell me all sorts of horror stories about your uncle and that machine he's using."

"The back hoe?" Travis asked.

"Yeah, that thing. Just be careful."

Travis looked like he wanted to tell his mother that there were way worse things to be afraid of. But now that he thought about it, being around his uncle using a fifteen-ton machine had its own inherent dangers.

***

Ron was fueling the machine and getting ready to check the hydraulics when Travis came out to the garage to meet him.

"You need any help?" Travis asked.

Ron actually preferred to work alone because he didn't have the greatest track record running the big vehicle. There were enough houses with their siding missing to attest to that. But he could tell his nephew needed to keep busy doing something.

"Sure, I can't get into the tree line with this beast and I need some holes dug about yay big," Ron said, roughly showing a box about a foot deep by a foot across.

"What are they for?"

"Explosives."

"Sweet," Travis said as he went over to the wall and grabbed a pick and a shovel off the pegboard. "I should have stayed with them," Travis said to his uncle, his back still to him.

"They're just late calling in. You don't know if anything is wrong," Ron answered his nephew. It sounded flat even as he said it.

"I'm faster than any of them…I'm as good a shot as my dad. I could have kept them out of trouble," Travis sighed, turning to face his uncle, his teenage features strained from the stress.

"Alright, I'm not going to lie, ever since your dad was a kid, he found some of the most unusual ways to get into trouble. It's like he has a trouble-homing beacon on so it knows where to go. But somehow he always comes out smelling sweeter than when he went in. Now, I don't know what kind of mess he's gotten himself into this time, but there's no reason at all to think he's not going to pull out of it like he always does." Ron's words seemed to have a measurable effect on Travis. "Come on, we've got a lot of work to do before they get back." Ron wrapped his arm around Travis' shoulder and showed him exactly where to start digging.

***

"Hi, Tony, how you doing?" Tracy asked. She was sitting at the table with the radio.

"I wish they'd hurry up and get back," he said, sitting down next to her. "This not knowing is horrible. If I was twenty years younger, I'd be out there looking for them."

"I saw you on that on-ramp. I think you could handle yourself just fine."

His eyes twinkled at her as he flashed a smile and grabbed her hand. "How have you put up with him so long?" Tony asked, half kidding, but also half serious. "That kid has more kinks and quirks than piping done by the Three Stooges."

"That's a pretty old reference, Tony, and I never liked that show growing up."

"Butch…I mean Mike and I," Tony started with a faraway look in his eye, "used to sit and watch it every Saturday morning. I'd seen them all, years before as a kid, but it was a way for the two of us to be together to do some bonding. I'd always wished that I had spent more time with my children as they were growing up, but Mike got the least time of any of them. Maybe that's not such a bad thing now that I think about it." And then he smiled.

"Well, at least I know where he gets his humor from. They'll be back, Tony."

"You're that sure?" Tony asked, looking her in the eyes.

"I am," she answered. "Do you want me to get you some more coffee?" Tracy asked, getting up so as not to give away her illusion of holding it together.

"I would," Tony said, handing her his cup.

As Tracy was leaving the room, she turned to answer her father-in-law. "In spite of every flaw that man possesses, and there are more than I care to count, he is a wonderful father and husband with whom I cannot imagine spending the rest of my time here on earth without. That is why I have put up with him and why I know he will be back."

Tears welled up in Tony's eyes.

"I'll be right back with the coffee," Tracy said, giving Tony some time to collect himself.

Chapter Twelve – Mike Journal Entry 8

"Oh fuck!" was the first thing out of my mouth. In retrospect, I wish I had thought of something better. My best friend had just been dealt a death sentence, and the most profound thing I could think to say was an expletive. My English teacher was going to slap me upside the head if she ever found out. And then I followed that initial bad opening statement with one almost equally as lame. "Are you sure?"

BT rolled up his sleeve. A neat half-moon wound on his forearm wept blood. "And before you go asking if what bit me was a zombie, you can match the wound up to that one's mouth," BT said, pointing to a zombie that lay close to his legs.

I wanted to tell him that most likely wasn't going to happen. The zombie in question appeared to have every skeletal feature in its face and skull crushed, but even still, it was easy to see that it was indeed a zombie and not some random urbanite, gone cannibal. I sat down heavily next to BT. "How long ago?"

BT looked over at me. "Couple of hours, I think, lost track of time after I pulled that trigger for the thousandth time. I was really hoping to avoid the part where *you* blow my head off."

"Wait…what? I can't do that, BT!" I exclaimed, getting back on my feet.

"Listen, pencil-neck, you are not going to let me become a zombie. I will purposefully hunt you and you alone until I eat your skinny ass."

"Great, you can join Eliza." I meant it as a jest, but as the reality of that statement hit, we both became silent for a moment. I tightened my grip on my rifle.

"You have to, Mike. I won't hold it against you. I'll talk to you when you get upstairs."

We both stopped talking.

"This really is going to be an awkward conversation," I said to BT, referring to his statement about running into me on the streets of Heaven.

"He has to let you in, doesn't he?" BT asked. "I mean you've done so much good."

"That's just it, BT, there's nothing for him to let in. Whatever corporeal part of me I housed is gone, and that, my friend, was my golden ticket. Without it, I'm just another bag of bones."

"I would have brought more beer if I'd known we were going to have a party," BT said.

'What?' my stare asked.

"You know, the whole pity party thing."

"Not hilarious. Come on, get up," I said, extending my hand.

"Wouldn't it just be easier if you shot me where I sit?" BT asked.

"Come on, man, let's just see if there's anything we can do. Maybe the wound wasn't deep enough to transfer the parasite. The house I just left…the lady living there is a nurse."

"Mike, you're stalling."

"No shit!" I yelled at him. "How much of a rush do you think I'm in to put a bullet in my friend?"

"Okay, fair enough," BT said as he got up. "You think a nurse in North Carolina is going to have any kind of answer for me?"

I didn't reply. I didn't think the Dalai Lama himself had an answer, but it bought me some time. Within a few minutes, we were within sight of Mary's home. Some of her dinner guests had departed, but not enough of them. I'd say a good fifteen to twenty were still hanging around for some leftovers or maybe a doggie bag.

"How we going to get by them? I've got ten rounds," I told BT.

"I'm fully loaded," BT answered.

"You're holding a bat."

"Yup. It hasn't ran out of ammo yet."

"Where's your sword?"

"It got stuck," he answered.

I had no desire to know how it had become so imbedded in its victim that not even BT could dislodge it.

"No way, BT. We'll figure out something else."

"By the time you think of something else, I'll be nibbling on your innards. Yo, zombies, I've got something for you!" BT yelled, standing up from our hiding spot behind a small bush.

"I hate close combat, BT."

"Don't get anywhere near my swing…homie don't play that," BT said with a wild glare in his eyes.

***

"Mom! Mom! I see the big man again and Mike!" Josh shouted from his mother's bedroom window. He had been keeping a watch out ever since his play partner had left.

Mary and Gary came running in from the kitchen.

"My God, he's huge!" Mary exclaimed.

"What the hell is he doing?" Gary asked, watching as BT roared and brought his bat up. Gary turned slightly to his left and saw zombies running straight for BT. "They'll kill him." And then Gary watched in alarm as Mike stepped up next to BT. Gary ran out of the room into the living room to grab his rifle.

Mary was too enthralled in the scene before her to notice the departure.

"Mom, what are they doing?" Josh turned to look up at his mother.

"You should stop watching," she said robotically, but she made no move to shield him from the view.

***

The first zombie reached BT and met a blissful exit from this world courtesy of a Louisville Slugger, the preferred choice of zombie slayers nationwide. The zombie's skull conformed to wrap itself around the bat – crushed bone giving way to hard wood. I don't know how I saw it, but the force of the contact was so hard, I watched the zombie's dental fillings fly from its mouth. There were seven of them, apparently somebody liked their sweets.

BT had pulled the bat back and was swinging again before the first zombie could find its final resting place. It was those damn twitching legs that I think about a lot when I'm awake in the middle of the night. BT's next swing caught zombie number two square in the mouth; and the shattering of its teeth made me cringe. The third zombie that made it to BT was a young woman, and BT didn't hesitate a beat as he brought the meat of the bat down on the top of her skull. The sheer force of the contact brought her to her knees, her brain ruptured around the intrusive object.

"Any time you want to join in is fine with me," BT growled through heavy breaths.

"Right," I said, bringing my gun up. There was just something so visceral, so raw, so fluid in BT's motions as he killed the zombies. It was like he was doing a Tai Chi demonstration.

"Mike, my bat cracked. You should probably start doing something," BT's arms rippled as he shattered another head like an eggshell.

He had taken out six zombies before I fired my first shot. I wasn't thinking about it then, but on some level, I realized that I had about a five-foot, zombie-free bubble around me. I just wasn't under attack. I started picking off zombies, four out of five fell from my cartridges. Now the fun would really begin as I had to reload the magazine. The barrel of BT's bat whistled past my head.

"Ooh! Sorry about that," he said as he thrust the wooden-sharded handle into a zombie's eye socket.

I was three rounds into my reloading procedure when shots began to ring out.

"Been waiting for some help!" BT yelled as he roundhouse-punched a zombie in the temple. It hadn't died, but it did drop to the ground, dazed. The rest of BT's bat was lodged in the neck of a zombie that was desperately trying to pull the foreign object out.

Now that BT had stopped using the bat, I got closer to him so that we could defend each other better. I popped the magazine into the rifle and got ready to acquire a target.

"What the hell?" I asked.

"They stopped attacking," BT said.

Eight of the ugliest zombies walking the planet were just staring at us. They saw food, but something was holding them at bay. I more than half expected to see Eliza or Tomas walk out from one of the nearby houses.

"What are they doing?" Gary yelled from across two front yards.

A zombie looked to the new sound and immediately began chasing Gary down.

"Oh shit," he said, not wanting to shoot because of his angle to the zombies and then us beyond. "I'll see you in the house!" Gary yelled as he retreated back to safety.

"I do not want to die, Talbot," a heaving-chested BT said to me as we watched the zombies chase after Gary.

"You just took on eighteen zombies with a wooden stick, I'd say your actions speak differently."

"No, just because I'm pissed off shouldn't be construed as a suicidal gesture."

"I'll keep that in mind. Let's see if Mary can do anything for you."

I know BT wanted to tell me we were wasting everyone's time thinking a nurse in a North Carolina suburb had the only known cure for the virus that was systematically taking out mankind. But when you are thrown a lifeline, it matters not that it is made from smoke. We are hard-wired for hope, plain and simple.

"What was up with the zombies?" BT asked as we walked back to Mary's.

"Damned if I know," I said as I took two shots. Two more zombies went down, but that still left half a dozen. The remaining zombies did not even look in our direction as we approached. They were too busy sniffing around the front door – probably picking up on the stink of Gary's grievous injury.

"Is your brother alright? I saw a bandage around his head."

"I shot him. I was saving his life!" I added when BT stopped to look at me.

"How much time you think I have left?" BT asked as we walked into Mary's front yard. The zombies still didn't care about us, but they were exactly where we needed to be.

BT doubled over as painful spasms racked through his abdomen. *Less than I hoped,* I answered him, but only in my thoughts. I rubbed the man's back as he bent over; I noted that my hand was almost level with my ear as I did so. I didn't know what to do. I was exposing everyone to a zombie if I brought him into Mary's home and there wasn't anything I could do for him anyway. It was a pipe-dream to think that Mary could either. I'm sure one of the topics she might have brought up while we were in her house was how she had developed this incredible cure for the zombie disease and had been waiting for some nice men to come and help her disseminate the medicine. Yeah, you would think that would be the conversation starter.

I could not shoot my friend. The alternative was to leave him out here to fully become what was already happening. My hand immediately fell away as BT dropped to his knees and blood flowed freely from his nose while his head sagged down. His chest was covered in snot and blood from the discharge.

"Oh, my dear God," I said as I placed the barrel of my rifle against the side of his head.

"Please do it," he begged. "I'd do it for you."

Chapter Thirteen – Paul

Paul had found two emergency candles in a kitchen drawer next to the oven. The drawer was too close to the heat source as they had semi melted out of shape. Paul had to cut the bottoms off to enable the misshapen candles the ability to stand on their own. Even then, he had to let some wax drip onto the tabletop to make them stick.

Paul decided that he did not have eight hours left like the wrapper on the candle bragged about, and he lit both of them. The small room was almost entirely lit up. Paul popped one more pain killer. The wound in his foot was completely forgotten as he gazed deeply into the fire of the two light sources. He was certain he had discovered the meaning of life in those flames. It was a pity he did not have a notepad to write down his findings.

"I wonder what it will feel like?" Paul had turned around and was having a conversation with his cast shadow.

"I bet it hurts," he said, as his shadow mate nodded in agreement or it could have been the flicker of the flame.

Paul was mesmerized as his dark companion picked up a gun and held it to its own head.

"I know that's what I have to do," Paul said as he scratched behind his ear with the long-necked lighter he had used to light the candles. "But I'm afraid." The shadow man put down the gun at the same time Paul's itch was sated.

"I'm not really religious, but I've always heard that suicide is instant damnation. Would God make an exception, you think?"

The shadow shrugged its shoulders in indecision just as Paul shivered.

"You sure don't talk much," Paul said, turning back towards the light.

"I should leave Erin a note. Yeah, and how am I going to get it to her? Well, that's not really the point, is it?"

"Man, I am messed up. I would swear there were two candles on that table." Paul snorted as he realized there were. "My mouth is so dry, I sure could go for a beer." Paul took a swig of the diet Sprite and almost threw it up when he realized it wasn't the beer he had been hoping for.

"Hey that's pretty good," he decided.

"Mike, I could sure use your help right about now!"

***

"Mike, I could sure use your help right about now!" A much younger and somewhat skinnier version of Paul echoed his older self. Paul was pinned tight in his smoldering car, the steering column nearly crushing his sternum. The thickening smoke was making vision difficult, but it was not so dense that he could not tell what happened to his missing shotgun seat passenger. That and the hole in the windshield left little doubt.

I need to check on him, Paul thought. *Where's Dennis?* Paul's mind raced, trying to locate their third friend who had also gone to the *Cheech and Chong* Drive-In festival. Paul could not turn his neck far enough to look into the back seat of his 1970 Buick Century and determine the fate of his friend.

"Help!" Paul thought he shouted, but the weight on his chest and the choking smoke might have seriously hampered any volume. Someone must have heard it as the passenger door opened and Mike peered in.

"Paulie, you alright?"

"Yah, except for the broken ribs and potential barbecuing, I'm doing dandy," Paul wheezed.

"Paul, I'm going to get Dennis out first," Mike said.

Paul figured Dennis was either not quite as stuck as him or in worse shape, so either way, it made sense that Mike would try to get him out first. Paul, however, was not looking forward to burning alive. He had read once that it was the most painful way to die; although, whoever had done the study and who were the test subjects he wasn't sure.

"Dude, just hurry! Barb's (Paul's mother) gonna be pissed if I ruin this new shirt she bought me." Paul tried to laugh at his poor attempt at humor, but it came out more as a grunt.

"Dude, save your strength. I'm going to need your help when I get to that steering wheel," Mike said, lifting his broken arm up with some difficulty.

"I didn't know you were double-jointed." Paul swooned a little at the sight of the broken, bent appendage, but would later remember it as smoke inhalation poisoning.

Paul sat for time un-recordable as the heat in the car began to turn up. The back door opened and Paul could crane far enough to see Mike climbing into the backseat. Mike's heavy grunting dominated all. It was even louder than the crackle of vinyl seating on fire. When Paul heard the heavy thudding off to his left, he figured Mike had extracted Dennis.

Paul watched a line of flame traveling closer and closer, as if seeking him out. "Umm, Mike, it's my turn, buddy," Paul said, pissed at himself that he was letting fear put a quaver in his voice, but he'd take that over frying in his car any day.

"Mike?" Paul asked. No answer. "Dennis? Guys? Come on, man, what the fuck?" Paul pressed up against the steering column, but his fractured ribs prevented him from giving the thrust he needed to escape his fiery prison.

Paul turned to his left as far as he could. He could just see two sets of legs on the ground. Mike must have passed out. "Mike! Wake up! Mike! Help!" His crying out was as much for his rescue as for his friend's. He thought that Mike and possibly Dennis were suffering from more grievous injuries than he knew.

Paul started to make his peace with God, and was doing fine just up until he caught on fire and then all bets were off. "Talbot! Get up!" Paul screamed in a last ditch effort to get some assistance.

Paul finally heard some rustling on the ground. "Thank you, God," he whispered.

Paul turned as Mike stuck his head back in the car door. "Paul, I just want to get him clear."

Paul understood the necessity of the act, but he wanted to be clear of the burn zone, too. Self-preservation is a powerful instinct. It's not called friend-preservation for a reason. "Hurry up," Paul ground out. Mike did not hear it as he was already dragging their friend to safety.

"Paul, I'm going to need your help," Mike said as he climbed back into the car, quickly slapping out the flames that had crawled onto Paul's leg.

"Mike, I don't have much left." Paul was mad with himself that he felt defeated, but the smoke, fire, and pain in his chest were quickly draining him of fight and life.

"Bud, use whatever you got, because we either both get out of here, or we're both going to be on the school lunch menu tomorrow."

Paul didn't think this was the right time for a joke, if that was even what it was, but it had the desired effect.

"Fuck that," Paul croaked, thanking anyone that would listen that he hadn't started coughing when he pulled in a particularly nasty influx of polluted smoke. *Although we'd probably be the tastiest things they've had in a few years,* Paul thought. He wanted to tell his friend the joke, but the pain was too intense and he didn't think he could afford to inhale any more noxious gases.

"When I say three."

What about three? Paul thought. Consciousness was becoming as elusive as a Vaseline-coated eel.

"Three!" Mike said.

Where was one and two? Paul wondered.

Air seemed to rush into Paul's lungs as Mike pushed up on the steering column, and lucid thought came back in a hurry. Paul began to fight back for the life that Death was in such a hurry to get its greedy hands on. The steering column moved by minute fractions of an inch. What made the rescue attempt even more infuriating was that, as the column moved up, so did Paul's compressed chest. For all their straining, it did not appear that they were making any headway. Death had parked its ass on top of the steering wheel, its sightless eyes peering deeply into Paul's face. Paul could just see its silhouette and the light that shone through it and beyond it.

"I'm not ready for you," Paul told Death.

"Most aren't," it answered back.

Paul hadn't been expecting a response. Now he knew how close he truly was, and with every last ounce he had left, he pushed up.

"Dude, this isn't going to feel good."

"What?" Paul asked, not sure who he was asking the question to, and why Death would hurt him?

And then blissful sweet air! Paul's chest heaved with the glory of it. The cold of the night was exhilarating on his heated skin. Paul glanced over and back to the car. Death was becoming a phantom shadow once again. Paul let loose a scream that Jamie Lee Curtis would have been proud of as Mike dragged him further away from the pops and cracks of his car while it went through its death throes. Paul looked one more time into the car before he passed out. Death flared brightly for a moment and then was gone.

"Did you see that?" Paul asked, but Mike was looking in the other direction and Paul had the feeling he might have already blacked out.

When he awoke three hours later in the hospital, he was hooked up to a variety of machines, each with its own distinctive trills and beeps. Mike was asleep in the bed next to him and Dennis was nowhere in sight.

"Mike? You awake?" Paul asked, barely above a whisper. His chest hurt, but it wasn't the all-consuming pain that it had been in the car.

"Dude, they gave me Diadlin. If I open my eyes, the room spins like a top on a playing record," Mike said.

"Is it any good?" Paul asked.

"It's unreal, I've tripped with less intensity."

"Where's Dennis?" Paul asked, concerned that possibly their friend hadn't made it.

"I think he went to get some potato chips."

"Huh?"

"He's fine. Got a knot on his head…that's about it. I think he's going home tomorrow."

"What about you?"

"Compound fracture on my left arm, no baseball for me this spring. But if they keep giving me this shit, I won't really care."

"Dude, I'm sorry," Paul said, almost crying.

"For what? It was an accident."

"It wouldn't have happened if I wasn't so fucked up."

"Nobody died, man."

"We would have, if not for you."

"I guess that makes me a hero," Mike said. Paul knew he was kidding; but kidding or not, it was the truth.

"I guess it does."

"Dude, you're embarrassing me, and you need to be quiet for a while. I think I've found a way to move things with my mind."

"Are you shitting me?"

"Nope, try it, man. You're on the same shit as I am."

The remainder of the night went quietly as Paul and Mike tried to move things around their room with mind control. It was an unsuccessful experiment, but thoroughly enjoyed by both.

***

Paul was still staring deeply at the candle; half of it had burned. "Four hours, I can't have too much time left. I sure wish I could get on WebMD and see what the symptoms were so I'd know when to take myself out...to the disco!" He laughed. "Okay let me run down everything I'm feeling. My right ankle twinges and my left foot burns a little, my eyes feel like someone is hanging barbells on them, my mouth tastes like dry cotton and...that's about it. No fever, no craving for brains. Can the virus not survive outside the host? Come on, how long would it have taken the bullet to go from its head to my foot? That can't be it. Was the bullet too hot for the virus to survive?" Hope, which was at an all-time low in Paul, surged. "It's a pathogen right? How hot was the bullet? It's got to be some absurdly high temperature, right? Maybe it cooked it! I friggin' might be alright." Paul thought about getting up and doing a jig, but even in his painkiller-addled mind, he knew that to be the bad idea that it sounded like.

Chapter Fourteen – Mike Journal Entry 9

"What are you doing, Mike?" Gary shouted from a window he had just opened.

"He's been bit," I said. At this point, I was full on crying.

I watched as Gary's head dropped. The zombies who had previously been at the front door began to quickly move to the sound of Gary's voice. I was just so sick of it all. The pressure of everything was taking its toll. My friend was dying because of some stupid idea I had of giving Eliza a black eye. Even if I had succeeded in killing the bitch, it wouldn't have been worth the price of my friend.

"What are you going to do?" Gary asked. He was obscured by the zombies, but his words were not.

Just stop!! I screamed in my head. The zombies by the window didn't move away, but they did stop jostling in their ever-earnest need to eat us.

"Wow, that was weird," Josh said, I guess from behind Gary. "They look like they're frozen."

"Mike, what's going on?" Gary asked, but I barely heard it as I looked over to BT whose spasms had stopped. He wiped his lip, and then began to stand up. I looked up into his eyes as he got to his full stature.

"You alright?" I asked him, fearful of his answer.

"I'm not sure," he answered. "The pain stopped."

"Stopped? That's the word you'd use to describe what happened?" I asked him, a glimmer of hope beginning to flower.

"I guess. I can't think of a better way to describe it. One second, I was in such intense pain, I couldn't think, and the next I wasn't. What's going on?" he asked. Then he looked at the grin which I think was spreading across my face.

"I think I've gone two up on the lifesaving competition," I told him.

Horror showed in his eyes. "No way!" he sputtered out. "I just killed fifteen zombies with a damn baseball bat! I think I just saved your ass, right then! At worst, making us even."

I didn't have the heart to tell him that I was never really in danger. The closest I came to getting hurt was when part of his bat almost hit me. "Fine, I'll give you that one, although I might lodge a formal protest."

"What's going on, Mike?" BT asked, picking up on my now good mood. It was hard not to. I had just been holding a gun to his head and now I was smiling like it was Christmas day and I was seven years old.

"I'll explain it to you when we get in the house. Come on, my friend."

Within a few moments, we were at the door having a rather heated, one-way discussion with Mary. She was doing most of the yelling and we were doing most of the listening.

"Was he bit?" she asked for maybe the umpteenth time.

"Well...technically, yes," I answered her in kind.

"Well then, didn't I already tell you that you cannot bring him in?" Her pitch elevated each time she asked the question in the hopes that it would finally register with us on some level.

"His name is BT," I told her.

"Don't!" she yelled even louder. I can't imagine how it must have echoed in that small house. She was making my ears ring and I was on the other side of a thick steel door. "I do not want to know what his name was."

"I'm telling you, I've stopped it. He won't become a zombie now."

"Holy shit!" she yelled. "Do you see that?"

BT and I looked around, thinking there must be some new threat.

"I think I just saw a fat pig flying!" she continued.

"Hilarious, Mary. I'm telling you he isn't in any imminent danger of turning into a zombie."

"Imminent?" BT asked quietly.

I shushed him with my hand. "I'll explain later."

"Imminent?" he asked again.

"Gary, could you please tell her?" I asked my brother through the door.

"Tell her what, Mike? I wouldn't even know what to say, and besides...this is her house."

"Come on, Captain Fix-It, tell me how you stopped a virus once again with your mind control," Mary was taunting me with a sneer in her voice.

"Did you see the zombies by your bedroom window?" I asked her.

"She's nodding her head," Josh said for his silent mother.

"Why do you think they just stopped attacking?" I asked, trying a different avenue.

"They're just asleep or something. Zombies sleeping doesn't mean that you've learned how to cure people from a zombie bite," she said.

"I never said anything about a cure," I told her.

"I'm not cured?" BT asked quietly.

"Mary, please, I need to get his wound cleaned out and a quiet place to think about this."

"Why don't you just fix his germs along with the virus, or whatever the hell it is?"

"Mary, I'm not a doctor."

"But yet, you've somehow managed to stop zombieism."

There was that sneer again; it was infuriating. "It's not like that. I told you, I was given some sort of link to them

188

and I have some moderate control, if they are nearby."

"How nearby?" BT asked. "I mean, do I have to go into the bathroom with you now?" BT asked, looking completely mortified.

"I shouldn't have even let you in! You jeopardized my entire family."

She was right; anyone around me was in more trouble just for being in proximity. I couldn't argue that point.

"What if I can guarantee you that I can control a zombie if it is around me?" I asked, but Mary didn't respond.

"She's listening," Josh said.

"Meet me back by the bedroom window."

"What are you going to do?" Gary asked.

"Just hand me some rounds through the windows," I told him.

The six zombies were right where I had left them. Gary dropped the rounds out the window, not wanting to expose any part of himself, I couldn't blame him.

I loaded my rifle up. "You guys might want to cover your ears and turn away." Nobody immediately moved to do either of those things until I placed a round dead center in the forehead of the closest zombie. Mary was shouting something, but I couldn't hear anything, at least not until the fifth zombie fell, leaving one zombie standing.

"...does that prove?" she was yelling.

"Huh?" I asked. My ears were ringing. I had not felt anything from dropping those five zombies. I was wondering if it was due to the loss of my soul or the callousness of the world we now lived in. Both reasons sucked. I didn't see one being much better than the other.

"What does that prove? You killed five sleeping zombies. Aren't you the Great White Hunter?" she said with contempt.

I didn't answer her because it would have been laced with expletives and I didn't feel like going down that road. Looking back, I wish we had just gotten Gary and gone to a different house.

I handed BT my rifle.

"Now what?" he asked. He had, apparently, not gotten the memo.

I was staring intently at the zombie. Its frozen state evaporated as its hunger lust came back into its eyes. BT immediately brought the rifle up.

"Hold on," I told him; the zombie did a quick scan of those around him.

"Mike, this really has a feeling of one of those things that sounds way better on paper," Gary said.

The zombie didn't seem very interested in me, but BT looked pretty good from the way the zombie was licking its lips.

"That's disgusting," BT said, holding the rifle up; the barrel was almost touching its forehead. "Mike, I have absolutely no idea what you're up to, but I'd really like to."

"See how he's keeping it from attacking?" Josh told his mother. The kid was pleading for my case. His mother harrumphed.

With some effort, I was able to pull the zombie's attention away from BT to myself, but it kept looking over at BT, hoping he wasn't going to leave.

"People don't get it. I'm always telling them the dark meat is sweeter," BT said.

"There is no way you just said that in this situation," I said, trying to keep all my attention focused on the zombie.

"Why'd you kill all the other zombies?" Josh asked.

"Because I wouldn't have gotten them all to listen," I answered him. I could feel the temperature of my body begin to rise as I worked in overdrive to try out an experiment I wasn't even certain would work.

"If you're all focused on this one," BT asked, "am I going to be alright?"

"You'll be fine, I have enough concentration to work on this zombie and keep your virus at bay, but if people keep asking me questions, my strength is going to get a little diluted."

"Mike! Come on, brother! What are you doing?" Gary asked.

"Zip it, man!" BT said, taking one hand off the rifle and pointing a huge finger in Gary's direction.

I think it was the first time I had ever seen BT raise his voice to Gary, but I guess when you have the threat of becoming a zombie hanging over your head, all bets are off.

The zombie jerkily moved closer to me. It was like trying to force magnets of the same polarization together. The zombie really did not want anything to do with me. I kept reeling him in closer. My eyes were watering from the stink of it. Its gray, vein-lined face was less than six inches from mine. It finally stopped trying to find BT and its eyes locked onto mine. Its mouth opened up. It ran its gore-encrusted tongue over the shards of its remaining teeth. This one looked like it had eaten a bag of marbles; blood welled up from where its tongue made contact.

I cocked my head to the side, giving it a large area of my neck to peruse.

"What the hell?" Mary moaned, "I would have never let you in if I had known you were clinically insane. Make him stop!" Mary said to Gary.

"BT told me to zip it," Gary mumbled.

The zombie eyed my neck greedily, and its mouth opened even wider. I didn't think that was possible. It leaned in closer. A thick liquid dropped from its mouth and onto my neck. I was going to go with it being drool, not that that was much better, but it was worlds better than the other myriad fluids it could have been.

The zombie slowly eased its way in, the blood throbbing through my neck was too much. I might not be its favorite thing on the menu, but I was hot and it was hungry. I was holding the zombie a quarter inch from my neck. The strain in my mind and my body was beginning to wear me down. I could feel the heat of decay from its mouth on my neck. If I moved a fraction of an inch, it would bite, and then it licked my neck. Half vamp, former Marine, father of three, none of that mattered; my stomach threatened to completely turn itself inside out. I pulled away.

"Kill it," I moaned to BT.

BT waited until all the noise from his shot went quiet. "What were you trying to prove?" he asked.

"That I can control them. That what is inside of you has stopped its advance – that's what I am trying to prove."

"That proves nothing," Mary said defiantly. "I'm not letting either of you in here with my son and me."

My head dragged even lower. I had expended a lot of energy with the useless test and I had a slow, steady trickle being sent to BT. I could hear rustling inside the house.

"What are you doing, Gary?" Josh asked.

"If they can't come in, little man, then I have to go out," Gary told him.

"Wait," Mary said. "Are you sure? You could spend some time here, with us," she added a little pleadingly.

"You guys have been great hosts, but that's my brother and his friend," Gary said.

BT and I looked at each other as Gary said "*his* friend."

"I guess he didn't like your 'zip it' comment," I laughed.

BT shrugged.

"But they're dangerous," Mary yammered.

Gary stole a quick glance out the window, looking at us to maybe see if we had sprouted wings or maybe horns. "They don't look any more dangerous than they usually do," he said, pulling away from the window.

Mary looked out the window, I think to her, we had sprouted those things. "How can you say that? One is part vampire and the other is part zombie! What could possibly be more dangerous?"

"Mike's plans," Gary shot out without missing a beat.

"I heard that," I told him.

"Sorry, it was the first thing out of my mouth. I didn't even need to think about it."

"Mom, we can't leave them out there."

"We most certainly can," she answered him.

"She's right, Josh. You guys don't really know us and you certainly don't owe us anything. Could you please just send out a few first aid supplies with Gary so I can field dress my friend's wound?" I asked Mary.

"I'll do it," Mary agreed.

I didn't know at the time she was talking about cleaning the wound herself, not just sending the stuff out.

We walked over to the front door, I expected to be greeted by Gary. Mary was looking around the front screen security door; and when she was satisfied there were no other boogey men besides BT and me present, she motioned for us to come in.

"You sure?" I asked her.

"No, so get in before I change my mind."

BT brushed past me. Mary almost got her neck stuck craning it high enough to look at BT's face this close.

BT sat calmly as Mary scrubbed, cleaned and disinfected his bite and a dozen or so other various scrapes and bruises.

"You don't take very good care of yourself," Mary chided him.

BT was in the middle of eating a beef stroganoff MRE packet. He didn't really know what to say to her comment, so he just kept eating, but he did send me a knowing glance like 'What the hell is she talking about? Doesn't she know there's a zombie apocalypse going on right now?' Or it might have just been indigestion. I'm not sure. I wasn't paying him so much attention as I was one of the things inside of him.

"Man, it's creeping me out the way you're looking at

me, and I'm trying to eat, too," BT said.

"Sorry, man, I'm just—"

"I don't want to know," he said, cutting me off as he dug deeper into his foil food packet.

I could link with what I'd come to know as the Hugh-Mann's, according to my great-grandfather's research. I read most of his findings while someone else had been driving. Contrary to popular belief, I can read; it's writing that most seem to think I have a problem with. I could sense them and they were dormant for the moment, kind of like the stasis we had seen from other zombies, but if BT was to stray more than thirty feet or more, or I lost concentration, then any influence I had would be gone and the process would continue. Right now, I could keep him from becoming a zombie, but if he were to turn, there would be nothing I could do. That would be the point of no return.

Mary had seemed particularly nervous when she first started working on BT, but the more she got into the routine of her profession, the more she loosened up. And there was just something about the big man. If you were not on the opposing side, he made you feel safe.

"Is Mike still looking at me?" BT asked as he dived into a tuna casserole packet.

Mary looked up from a cut on his leg she was actually stitching up. "Yes," she answered, turning back towards her work.

"This food would be much more pleasurable if you weren't looking at me, man," BT said, never looking up. "And you too, little man."

Josh was sitting at the table and looking at BT, slack-jawed. "Are you a wrestler?" Josh asked.

"Josh, that's rude!" Mary said. BT 'umphed' as she pulled a stitch too tight. "Sorry."

BT nodded curtly.

"Competitive ballet dancer," I told Josh.

"What?" BT and Josh both looked at me. Gary just

shook his head as he came in from the living room.

"Sorry, it popped in my head."

"It's still all clear out there," Gary said.

"We've got plenty of moonlight. When BT is all fixed up, we should probably get going," I said. "Although the sun will be coming up soon," I added as the sky to the east was already beginning to lighten up.

Mary's shoulders slumped. We might not be her primary choice for guests, but we were company, and at least one of us was comforting to her.

"I sure wish we could go with you guys," Josh said. "But if my dad came home, and we weren't here, he wouldn't know what to do."

"Are you sure you won't spend the night and get a fresh start in the morning?" Mary asked.

"There are three more of us out there, I have no idea where they are or if anything has happened to them, and they'll only wait so long if they're already at the rendezvous point. On top of that, I'm really late checking in with my other brother. If I don't check in with him soon, he might get a crazy idea to launch a rescue," I said.

"Alright, let me just finish cleaning BT up," Mary said, standing so she could go into the other room and get some more supplies. I had a sneaking suspicion that she was going to drag this out as long as possible. She might even scratch him a few more times so she'd have something else to put some Bacitracin on. I was going to keep an eye on her. BT wasn't going to notice shit if she kept stuffing different MREs in front of his face.

"How many of those things you going to chow down?" I asked him.

"Don't bother me while I'm eating, man," BT growled, placing one arm protectively around his newest packet, which looked like pork and beans or something equally as unappetizing.

And just like that it hit me. I thought back to Eliza's

caravan and the zombies under Eliza's control. She wasn't actively directing them to sit and behave. She had given them an earlier command and had somehow tied it off like those damn, infuriating bread ties. You know the ones; you can never figure out which way they are tied. You spin them to the left for a few turns before you realize that it isn't getting any looser, so you do the other way, and for some physics-bending reason, you get the same result. I can't even begin to tell you how many loaves of bread I have just ripped the plastic sleeve on. You want to talk about pissing my wife off? Alright, enough of a divergence.

I knew it was possible to tie commands off; I just wasn't sure how to do it. I felt like I was five again and my dad was telling me to tie my shoe. Sure, he had showed me like fifteen times previous, but it might as well have been advanced geometry. I wonder if Eliza would be so kind as to give me a lesson. And then the second dawning came to my mind.

Tomas? I reached out tentatively. I felt like I had enough control that I could communicate with him and him alone, but I wasn't completely sure.

My sister is extremely angry with you, Michael, Tomas answered.

So she's not dead?

What do you want? Tomas said wearily, or maybe warily.

BT is in trouble. Now I panicked. How much information did I want to give him (or them)? Stupid, stupid, I should have not brought his name up. *Forget it, nothing,* I said, just about to close the connection.

Michael, it was obviously important enough that you felt the need to seek me out.

"Dammit!"

"What?" Gary asked.

"Did I say that out loud?"

"I don't want to know," Gary said, walking out of the

room.

BT's been infected. I laid it all out there; he was no worse off than he had been a moment before.

There was no response from Tomas for long seconds, and then I heard what could only be described as a sigh. *I'm sorry for your loss.* When I hesitated, Tomas spoke. *"There is nothing I can do to help him."*

I actually think you might be able to.

Even if I could, I do not understand why you think that I would be willing to help you.

Cut the shit, Tomas! Tommy, George, whatever the hell you want to call yourself now. You are not so far removed from that boy I knew, the one that I adopted as one of my own. Eliza is not evil because she has no soul. Eliza is evil in spite of that. You helped me on that rooftop and you know it, no matter how you are trying to justify it to yourself or your bitchster. You could have let me and all the rest of us die up there. I'm telling you now, BT will die without your help! Don't do what you think you're supposed to do, or definitely not what your sister would want you to do, do what is right! I shouted internally.

How is saving BT so that he can try and destroy us doing what is right? he asked.

He had a valid point from his angle. Just because I thought it was right didn't mean everyone else would. Damn semantics.

Listen, we can go round and round, but here's the deal: BT has been bit. I have halted the advance of the virus, but I do not know how to hold it off indefinitely.

There was a bigger pause than when I had told him about BT's infection. I thought maybe I had not made myself clear enough.

After more long moments of silence, he responded. *Eliza grows suspicious and is even now attempting to see what I am doing. We do not have much time. You will have to give me access to him.*

I wasn't so sure about this, I just wanted a 'how to'. Once he had his fingers inside BT, so to speak, he could do something irreversible.

Michael, I can sense your indecision. You're right. I could have let you all die on that rooftop. What purpose would it serve to now undo that? I'm running out of time, Michael.

Dammit.

"What the hell is that?!" BT yelled in exclamation.

"It's just a little hydrogen peroxide," Mary answered. "The same stuff I've been using this whole time."

"No, in me! Something's in me," he said, standing in alarm.

"Josh, get out of here!" Mary yelled. "He's turning into a zombie!"

"I am?" BT asked with alarm.

"Hold on!" I yelled, coming in late to the party. I had been so intent on watching what Tomas was doing, I was unaware of my physical surroundings. Gary was moments away from putting a bullet in BT.

"Mike! What's going on?" BT asked, looking like he was getting ready to jump out of his own skin.

"I asked for some help," I told him.

"What kind of help...and *who* specifically?" he asked with a very large note of concern.

"I asked Tomas for some help."

"Tomas, as in Eliza's brother Tomas?" Mary asked Gary.

Gary shrugged his shoulders. "I told her everything. You guys were gone for a long time."

"Yes, that Tomas," I said, answering her question.

"Mike, don't you think you should have maybe asked me before you let the enemy in?"

"Tomas is here?" Josh asked, running to the front window. "I don't see anyone."

"Did you ever stop to think that he could really do

some damage?" BT asked. He was more than a little pissed off.

"I took a risk. It was a calculated risk," I told him.

"With my life!" he yelled, bringing his fist down on the table. Mary jumped as if she were startled, but it could have been that the shock wave from the table had caused her to raise up off the floor.

"There were not many options, my friend," I told him.

"Don't pull that 'my friend' shit with me!" he roared.

I hadn't seen him this mad in a long time, if ever.

"He's inside me!" he said thumping his fist against his chest.

It's done, Tomas intoned. *Do not contact me again.*

We'll see, I answered him, but he was already gone.

"You don't get it, BT, I had to ask for his help. I couldn't hold them off indefinitely. While I'm thinking about it or while I'm conscious, it's easy enough to keep telling the parasites to stay put. But I have no idea what happens if I sleep. And I love you, my friend, but I don't always want to be within shouting distance. Do you?" I asked throwing it back at him.

"Well...not really," he answered, a small measure of anger dropping off.

"I guess I'd never have to worry about running out of toilet paper," I told him.

"What are you talking about?" Gary asked.

"Because BT will always be around and if Mike runs out, BT will be able to hear him. Have you not been listening to the conversation?" Josh asked.

"So am I supposed to shoot him, Mike?" Gary asked me.

"I think he's fine now."

"How would you know that?" BT asked me suspiciously.

"Tomas is gone," I told him.

"So how would you know if I'm good or not?" BT

asked once again, threatening me with his finger.

I didn't answer. I was hoping against all odds he would just drop it.

"Are you saying you can get in me too?!" His temper was beginning to flare again. "So what? I'm like a 7-Eleven? Always open?" BT was pacing around Mary's small kitchen. He was running his hand across his head. "I don't like this shit, Mike. Sorry, kid," BT said to Josh. "I think I'd rather have Eliza rooting around in there. At least, I'd know what she was up to. You scare the shit out of me, man."

"So you can like mind-control him?" Josh asked, making his arms move like a robot.

"Really?" Gary asked, "Because there's a few things I'd really love to see him do."

"Nobody is making me do anything I don't want to do, right?" BT asked, threatening to come over and smash my skull if I didn't give him an immediate answer that completely meshed with his.

"I can't control him," I told Josh.

"Damn right, I'm uncontrollable," BT said, crossing his arms.

"Okay, rebel, calm down, so I can finish cleaning you up," Mary said. "We're out of immediate danger, yes?" Mary asked, looking over towards me.

I nodded my answer, hoping that BT hadn't picked it up. No such luck.

"What am I thinking now?" BT asked me.

"You're thinking about how you'd like to pop my head off my bony body," I told him.

He bounced up like a spring-loaded toy. "He can read my damn thoughts!" he yelled.

"Relax," Mary laughed. "Even I could have read your thoughts about that."

BT seemed to settle down as he finally sat. "How would you feel if you had a crazy Talbot running around in your head?" he asked her.

"Just so we're clear," Gary said, "he's talking about Mike and not me."

BT looked defeated or maybe just tired. I couldn't really blame him either way. I couldn't even begin to think about what he'd been through the last few hours.

"Mary, when he's all cleaned up, could you find him a place to get some rest? If you don't mind, I'd like for us to spend another night."

She nodded, gratefully. I think she really liked having some company, someone who could take the pressure off her constant vigilance.

"What about the others?" Gary asked.

"They're on their own for the moment."

Chapter Fifteen – Mrs. Deneaux

Night was rapidly approaching. Mrs. Deneaux had removed Brian's jacket, justifying her actions by saying that he was burning up and that she was chilled.

"He would have offered it to me himself, if he were awake," she wrongfully assumed as she peeled the coat from his fever-racked body. The lines from his gut wound had grown a deeper crimson, almost violet red, and were now mere inches away from his heart.

"I knew he wouldn't make it," Mrs. Deneaux laughed as she realized she had just summed up the fate of both of the travelers she was with. Her plan was to wait out the night on the off chance that the twit, Paul, had found some medicine and had not become a casualty himself. When he didn't show by morning, which she just knew would be the case, she would walk out and either find Michael or her own mode of transportation.

Mrs. Deneaux had no illusions. She had only survived this long because of the charity of others or at the very least, the indifference of them. She knew Brian was a lost cause, as was Paul, even if he showed up in the nick of time with medicine. Brian was in no shape to protect anyone, and to her, it seemed that Paul had survived along similar lines as her own, by the grace of others.

The night almost passed by uneventfully. She heard something going on maybe two or three streets over, but who and what it was were not discernible. She felt as if she had slept, but she couldn't remember. Mostly she had stared at Brian and smoked cigarettes. With the moon still high in the sky, she found herself in the same spot and in the same position she had been when she had initially fallen asleep.

She had a small mountain of butts by her side, her exhaled smoke nearly obscuring her vision as she scanned the woods around her.

"Zombie," she said, standing up and crushing her latest butt into the ground. She exhaled the blue-gray smoke. The zombie hadn't quite locked onto their position.

"Must have smelled the smoke. My husband always said these would be the death of me. I can't imagine he thought in this fashion, though." Mrs. Deneaux looked quickly down at Brian. He was on his own. She would not be able to move him and where to, anyway?

Mrs. Deneaux moved away from the small clearing and her smoldering pile of ash, to hide behind a fairly thick bush. The zombie was coming up on her left. If it kept its present course, it would run into her before getting to the clearing.

Mrs. Deneaux picked up a small stone. "No sense in both of us dying," she said as she threw the rock at Brian. It landed a few inches from his face. He took no notice as he slept.

"Dammit," she said, taking a peek from behind her cover. She picked up the only other thing within arm's reach, a thick branch – it was about a foot long and six or seven inches around. She hurt her shoulder throwing it as hard as she could. Whether divine intervention or the luck of the devil, the branch struck Brian in the right cheek. His moans of surprise and pain changed the zombie's angle of pursuit.

Brian stirred slightly, a red mark blooming on his face as he opened his eyes. Pain, confusion, and recognition registered on his face as he looked straight across the clearing and could only see the eyes of a hiding Mrs. Deneaux. He tried to pull himself up, but completely lacked the energy.

"What is going on?" he scratched out of his fire-seared throat. Mrs. Deneaux held up her index finger to her lips. Brian could hear someone approaching. His initial hope was that it was Paul, but it made no sense that Deneaux would be hiding from him. *Maybe she wanted to play a prank*, he thought, but nobody in their right mind played those kinds of pranks anymore. You were more likely to end up with a bullet wound than a laugh.

Zombie or other people, not very likely to be a wild animal, at least not here. Brian's vision focused on a stick that was no more than a few inches from his face. He felt and then realized the source of his initial pain, which caused him to awaken.

"Bitch," he said just as the zombie plowed through the opening and lunged straight for his head.

Brian fought for his life harder than Mrs. Deneaux could have imagined. More than once, she thought that Wamsley had gained the advantage and that she would have to shoot him, lest he came after her when he was done. The zombie had finally landed a knock-out punch when it bit the same cheek she had prophetically hit with the stick.

She left her hiding spot amidst the screams of Brian and the moans of the zombie as it ate its meal. "That was close," she said, staying in a half-crouch until she was far enough away that she felt comfortable rising up.

Mrs. Deneaux looked around; there were no other zombies in the vicinity. She felt no regret when she realized she could have just shot the one that ate Brian. In hindsight she could have, but the prudent path had been the one she had taken. By not firing a shot, she had preserved her own life while also not alerting any other zombies in the area to her whereabouts. And just because she could not see any, did not necessarily mean that there weren't any around.

"I should have never killed that two-timing bastard of a husband," Mrs. Deneaux said as she hefted Brian's rifle onto her shoulder. "That wasn't the first time he had cheated on me and it wouldn't have been the last. If I had just ignored it like I had all the others, I could be on the Riviera. They would never have allowed the undead in there, much too exclusive." She laughed at her own joke.

Mrs. Deneaux found herself walking down the center of the roadway. She knew this might not be the best approach, but she was above skulking around on other people's lawns.

Chapter Sixteen

Paul took one more painkiller that night, not because he was in any abundance of pain, but primarily because if he were to awaken as a zombie, he would be pissed with himself for not having done so. Moonlight streamed through the kitchen window as Paul picked his drool-laced face off the table. The candles were close to burning out. Paul's legs ached as he shook the plastic bottle, which he was still clutching.

"One lone pill to rule them all," he coughed out as he popped the top and took the remaining tablet elixir. "Breakfast of champions," he said as he downed his warm diet Sprite. "Yuck! That doesn't taste nearly as good as it had earlier. So now what?" he said to the empty bottle. "I've got to get back to Brian and the other one."

Just thinking about her gave him a headache. The approaching light of day was not bringing with it the promise that all those motivational posters talked about. He was effectively hobbled, one of his friends was dying from infection, and three others were missing. He had no means of transportation, and in reality, didn't actually know how to get to Ron's. Sure, he'd been there before, but he wasn't driving and they were always smoking or drinking while they were heading up there. It wasn't like he could pick up a phone and call anyone. The more he thought about it, the more he couldn't remember having ever been so alone.

He got up to look for some more pills or at least an accelerant, maybe some Jack or SoCo. He sat back down quickly. "Maybe I'll just wait until this kicks in a little," he said as his ankle seemed to be high on the pain priority list today. He was deeply immersed in his distress when he heard shots. "Damn, that sounds like it's right out front," he said, shuffling away from the table to the window next to the front door.

"Deneaux?" Paul was having a tough time putting all the images in front of him into a cognitive state. There was Mrs. Deneaux, looking like a skinny, old, female Rambo; rifle slung over her shoulder, giant, oversized pistol in her hands, zombies running at her from up the street. Paul craned his neck, but the wood from the windowpane prevented him from getting a better look. It took him much longer than it should have to realize that he should open the door to get a better look…and to help. His head was as fuzzy as a schoolgirl on her second beer.

Paul pulled the door open, loudly cursing at himself as he dragged the door over the top of his shot foot. "Motherfucker!" he screamed. A fresh stream of blood spewed out as the bandage and wet scab was neatly pulled off.

Mrs. Deneaux looked over quickly. Paul was standing in the doorway to the house immediately to her left. He was swearing about something, but she had no idea what and no time to figure it out. She started to make her way over towards him. "You need to cover me!" she shouted.

Paul looked up, red veins criss-crossing his eyes so much, it was almost a solid color. "What?" he asked, finally focusing, the anger and pain welled in his features.

"You need to shoot, shithead!" Deneaux yelled.

"Where's my gun?" Paul asked, more to himself than to her, but she heard him.

Deneaux was certain if she wasn't so pressed for time and bullets, she would have shot him dead for being so damn useless.

Paul scrambled around. His rifle was on the sofa. He didn't remember putting it there, but he couldn't pin it on anyone else moving it, so at some point he must have, although for the life of him, he couldn't remember when.

He got back to the doorway. Deneaux was holding her own, but she had put her pistol away and was now using the rifle. Paul's first shot knee-capped the closest zombie to her. Effective, but far from a kill shot.

It did, however, give Mrs. Deneaux the opening she needed. Paul noted that the old crone moved with some serious step when she needed to. "Keep firing!" she intoned. "You're about as useless as a reformed alcoholic at a wine tasting."

Paul started shooting again, but his mind could not race to catch up with her dig.

Mrs. Deneaux pushed past him. Zombies were racing across the lawn trying to get to her. "Shut the damn door!" she said, leaning up against the wall.

Paul was stoned, but not that far gone, and the door was closed before her words had completely finished.

"Haven't had that much interest in these old bones in a long while," Mrs. Deneaux said as she smiled, her tobacco-stained teeth shining dully.

Paul thought he heard one of her cheek muscles groan from the effort of the foreign maneuver. "Where's Brian?"

Paul noted that she paused a half a beat too long before she answered, which was only a side to side shaking of her head.

"What happened to you?" she said, pointing down to his foot, which was now sautéing in a small stew of his own blood.

"Hunting accident," he answered, as he made sure the door was locked. Paul moved away from it as the first of the zombies made contact with the screen door beyond. He shuffled over to the couch and sat down.

Mrs. Deneaux sat in the closer chair. She kept peeking out the living room window until one of the zombies saw her and ran through a small bush to press his face up against the screen. She quickly pulled the shade down, plunging the room into an uncomfortable darkness.

"What happened to him?" Paul wanted clarification. When she answered that they had been ambushed by some zombies and he had gotten eaten defending her, he didn't completely believe the story, but some part of him was relieved that he had not succumbed to the infection. Paul would have felt directly responsible for Brian's demise if that had been the case. If he hadn't shot himself, he might have been able to get some antibiotics.

What Paul wasn't factoring into the equation was if he had not gotten hurt, he might have found some medicine and actually been back hours earlier to help defend their encampment. Every time his mind wandered into the realm of different possibilities, he kept reining it in so that it would not stray too far.

"Now what?" Paul asked.

"Do you have any more of what you've been drinking?"

Paul shook his head in the negative.

"We wait. Do they have any food? I'm starving," Mrs. Deneaux said, heading for the kitchen.

Paul did not answer her as she walked by and began to open cabinets up.

"Talbot always said God had a hell of twisted sense of humor," Paul mumbled.

Paul could hear Deneaux rummaging around for some utensils and a can opener.

"Cold soup will have to do," she said.

"I hope you don't get botulism. That can wreak havoc on someone your age," Paul said it softly, but with no other noise in the house the acoustics were actually pretty nice.

"Maybe you should try it first," Deneaux said as she slurped in a large swallow of Italian Wedding soup.

Paul got back in and leaned against the entrance to the kitchen. Deneaux summarily ignored him as she kept slurping the soup.

"Alright, so we both know, you just fed me a big heaping of bullshit. Why don't you be straight with me now?"

Deneaux looked up from her spoon, her eyes cold and calculating. "What exactly are you talking about?" The creepy smile came back.

"Brian. What really happened to him?"

"I told you. Zombies got him."

Paul kept looking at her, trying to somehow divine the answer, but Deneaux was a practiced and skilled liar. It would take much more than his amateurish attempt to get her to confess to anything.

"I think that's only part of the story and I don't believe or trust you. You can tell me. There isn't a court or even a jury left to convict you."

"Once I feel like confessing, you'll be the first to know," she said resuming her slurping.

"Suit yourself," he said.

Paul grabbed his meager medical supplies from the table and went back to the couch. He re-wrapped his foot, which was on fire and took three aspirins for his splitting headache. He put his head down on the cushion and fell asleep to the sweet serenading of Deneaux's slurps.

When he woke up, seemingly minutes later, the room was as black as Deneaux's heart. He sat up quickly, not quite able to remember where he was or in what state of danger he might be finding himself.

"Good nap?" Deneaux asked without feeling.

Paul looked to where her voice emanated. Eyes darker than the room they sat in stared back at him.

"What's going on?" Paul sat up quickly, reaching for his rifle.

"You looking for this?" she said, ratcheting a round into the chamber.

Paul's heart sank as his blood pressure soared.

"Relax, you look like a rabbit trapped in a fox den. I

was just keeping watch on the zombies outside and you're the only one of us with any ammo left. Is that crawler on the steps the one that did you in?"

"Did me in?"

"The bite on your foot."

"It's not a bite," Paul said, starting to rise.

"Do not get up," she said coolly.

Paul didn't. "She bit my boot, not my foot," he said, trying to explain.

"Then what's all the blood about?" she asked.

"I did not get bit!" Paul said heatedly.

"What really happened?"

"I told you!"

"You told me nothing. What if I were to say that I did not believe you or trust you?"

Paul fumed.

"Come, come, Mr. Ginson, turnabout is fair play."

"What are you planning on doing?"

"Why, whatever I please. You yourself said there isn't even a jury to convict me."

"I know what I said," Paul replied angrily.

"Yes, Michael, they both died trying to save me," Deneaux's words were laced with syrup. "And he'd believe me because he'd have to. What's the alternative? That an old crone like me killed two strapping young men? Huh? Who would believe that?"

"Mike's smart, he'd suspect you were lying."

"Suspect away, you can't try someone on suspicion," she laughed. "I should know."

"So you're just going to shoot me in cold blood, is that it?"

"I had rather hoped to wait until you turned into a zombie, but if you keep trying to get off that couch, I will have to put you down like a cur."

"I'm telling you for the fiftieth time, I did not get bit!"

"Keep your voice down, or your friends will come back."

It took Paul a moment to realize what she had said. "The zombies are gone?"

"Yes, your back-up left while the virus was spreading around inside of you. Obviously, because you were not worth eating anymore."

So what does that say about you, you fucking battle-axe? Paul thought, but wisely kept to himself.

"Listen, Deneaux, I did not get bit. I shot myself, okay? I fucking shot myself."

"Oh, that's rich," she laughed. "Sad, if true, but rich. Worthy of a hearty laugh, I'll make sure to do one over your shallow grave."

Paul hastily pulled his bandage off.

"Easy," Deneaux said from across the room. "Don't go getting any ideas, I didn't say 'bright' because I have yet to see you have one, and I didn't think you were getting ready to buck that trend."

"Look at my damn foot! Does that look like a bite?!" Paul was nearly shrieking.

A high intensity flashlight blasted Paul in the face. His headache, which had been on the decline, came back with a vengeance. "You did that on purpose," he said, shielding his eyes from the handheld sun.

"Of course I did. Hold your foot up."

Paul sat back on the couch and put his foot in the air. Deneaux stared long and hard at the wound. It was long minutes before she spoke.

"It's amazing you've survived this long."

"So you believe me now?" Paul asked.

"I do."

"Can I have my gun back?"

"I think I'll hold onto it for a while longer. At least we know you'll be safer."

"You're a—"

"Careful, the number one cause of accidental shootings is careful aim."

Paul wasn't entirely sure what that meant, but she was holding the gun. "I'm getting some food." Paul stood up.

"There are more candles on the table," she told him before she opened the shade a bit to get a look out into the night.

All the people left on the planet and I get stuck with her, I had more fun by myself last night. The more he thought about that, the truer it rang. Of course, he had been with half a bottle of pain pills. "Should have saved those for tonight. Might have actually made her worthwhile company."

"What are you going on about in there?" Deneaux asked.

"Just wondered what this peanut butter would taste like on some bread," Paul said as he ate the thick, rich goodness off a tablespoon. It was the small things that hit the hardest. Paul thought the last time he had fresh bread was the day of the apocalypse. He had gone to a Subway and gotten a six-inch meatball sub. "Should have gotten the damn foot-long," he said wistfully, popping another spoonful into his mouth.

"Bitch, where are you!" Paul heard from outside the house.

Deneaux was standing up by the window now, her half a smoke hanging from her lip. One word emanated resoundingly from her mouth, "Shit."

"What's going on?" Paul said, coming up beside her. He could not help but notice that her aroma of smoke would offend an ashtray.

"It's Brian."

"Brian? You said zombies got him," Paul said as he got a closer look out the window. The person ambling down the roadway looked somewhat like their traveling companion, but the abundance of blood on his face and clothing made identification almost impossible.

He did not look so much like he was on death's door as possibly he had passed over the threshold; and when he realized he had not quite finished his business back in the mortal world, he had come back a step to do so.

"I've seen zombies that look better than him," Paul added, a little frightened.

"Bitch!" Brian yelled again. "I know what you did, well I got the best of him, you friggin' hag! He couldn't kill me!" Brian yelled, thumping his chest as the blood welled up in his mouth.

Paul made a move to open the door.

"Don't you dare!" Deneaux said as she leveled the rifle on him.

"What the hell is the matter with you? What did you do?" Paul asked in alarm.

"He's a dead man. Look at him."

"What is he talking about, Deneaux? You said zombies got him and that he was dead."

"Zombies did get him. Can you not see that?" she said defensively.

"He doesn't look dead."

"He's a dead man walking," she added flippantly.

"I'm going to help him," Paul said, reaching for the door handle.

"You open that door and you'll be joining him."

"Fuck you, Deneaux, I'd rather be with a person that's about to become a zombie than with you anyway." Paul walked out the door, Brian was still a good fifty feet down the road but immediately saw Paul.

"Paul?" Brian asked, blood and sweat stinging his eyes and making it difficult to see.

"Hey, Brian," Paul said, walking cautiously towards him, not sure if he should be expecting a bullet in his back for his trouble. "Are you alright?"

"Do I fucking look alright?" he asked heatedly, blood spilling from his nose and ears.

"No…you don't, man, I'm sorry."

"That bitch set me up," Brian continued without any prompts from Paul. "I was sleeping and zombies must have been coming or some shit, but she throws a stick at me to wake me up. I look over and she's hiding behind this small bush, and I'm thinking what is this crazy bitch doing? At first, I thought maybe I had just woken up and caught her taking a piss, but to take a piss, you have to be human!" he yelled the last word. "And I'm not convinced of that. She threw the stick, hoping that I would make a noise or that the noise of the stick hitting the ground would cause the zombie to attack me. It was on me before I could even sit up."

Paul couldn't imagine the horror; the guy was burning up with a fever, probably had the strength of a newborn kitten and a zombie comes and attacks. Guilt began to heft on his shoulders that he had not at least gone back to stand guard duty. He had spent the night getting stoned, staring at candles. Brian was beyond antibiotics at this point, Paul could count at least two bites on Brian's face alone.

"I need to kill her," Brian pleaded.

Paul pointed to the house he had just come from.

Deneaux threw the cigarette she had finished onto the floor, grounding it out with her foot. "Son of a bitch," she said calmly as she lit another coffin nail.

Brian started walking towards the house. Paul stayed where he was. He wanted to go, but he had only one boot on and no weapon.

"I really need to think things out before I do them," he said as he watched Brian approach the house.

Brian was halfway up the drive when he dropped onto his knees. Crippling stomach cramps hunched him over as his body expelled everything in his stomach. Ropy strings of blood and vomit hung from his chin as he stood back up.

Brian stood still in the driveway for a second longer; he then turned around to look at Paul.

"Fuck me," Paul mumbled. He wasn't going

anywhere fast and now Brian wasn't Brian anymore. Paul got into a reasonable facsimile of a fighting stance.

Brian started running full tilt. "I love you, Erin," Paul said as Brian halved the distance. Bone, blood and brain sprayed across Paul's face as Brian's body, sans the head skidded past. Paul had yet to move from his fighting stance.

"You look like chum for sharks, you should get in here," Deneaux said from the porch of the small house, her rifle still smoking from the shot she had taken.

The shock of the event took a while to wear off. It was more the sounds of the dead in the distance that got him moving. It was still a fifty-fifty debate on whether or not to go back into that house or just keep wandering down the road. "I still need my boot," he said, heading towards the house.

"What do you think you know?" Deneaux asked Paul as he walked over the threshold to the house.

Paul noted that she had lit another cigarette and was sitting on the couch, the rifle draped across her lap.

"I know Brian turned into a zombie and you saved my life by killing him."

"That's all you need to remember," she said, taking a large drag from her smoke. He also noted that she had not so much as a quiver in her hand as she did so.

"You're one cool customer, aren't you?"

"How do you mean?" she asked as she exhaled her smoke.

"All I'm saying is you put a bullet into the brain of one of our traveling companions and you look as calm as if you were watching *Lawrence Welk* reruns."

"Oh, I loved him."

"Brian?"

"*Lawrence Welk*, you twit. That was before television began to cater to the masses and we ended up with drivel like *Charlie's Angels*."

Paul didn't see the reason to argue the merits of TV,

but anything with Farrah Fawcett fueling his young hormones was okay with him.

"What about Brian?"

"What about him? He was a zombie. Should I have allowed him to eat you? Would that make you feel better?"

"No, and thank you for saving my life, but I find your lack of compassion somewhat startling."

"I killed a zombie like I've killed a dozen times before. I feel the same as if I killed a pheasant, maybe less. At least we ate those."

"I guess I don't understand it."

"Tell me what should I feel?" Deneaux asked coolly taking another drag. "Should I go tell my therapist about my touchy-feely feelings, about how I'm all broken up about Brian's death? It is a survival-of-the-fittest world out there and he succumbed and now he's dead…it's as simple as that."

Paul didn't think it was quite that simple, but she held the gun and he didn't think she'd have any problem using it on him. "I'm just coming over to get my shoe."

Mrs. Deneaux tensed her hands on the rifle. "Let's not have any accidents."

Paul couldn't help himself. "Is that what you're calling what happened to Brian?"

"I don't know what you think you know, but I saw him get bit by a zombie. I didn't stick around to see the ending to an event I already knew the conclusion of."

Paul bent down to grab his shoe. Deneaux was mostly showing indifference, but Paul knew it was an act. And then she struck deeply and cruelly.

"Maybe if you weren't so busy being inept and shooting yourself, you would have been able to get back and prevent the whole thing." Her cold eyes remained on his the whole time.

"You really are a bitch," he told her, but her words cut deep. He had been feeling exactly that, but to have them spoken from someone else, even someone he couldn't stand, hurt.

The fight was out of Paul and she knew it, she focused her attention away and to somewhere deep within her own dark thoughts.

"I'm going to try and find Mike."

"Not with this rifle," she told him.

"It's mine, Deneaux."

"It *was*, but it belongs in the hands of someone who knows how to use it."

"Whatever. Keep it, I hope you shoot yourself with it," Paul said angrily.

"Oh, sweetie, I'm not you." Deneaux laughed as Paul pulled the front door shut behind him.

He hobbled to the driveway, sprained ankle, shot foot and no weapon, but he liked his odds more now than he did inside the house.

Chapter Seventeen – Mike Journal Entry 10

As worked up as BT was, he still fell asleep rather easily. His legs were hanging off the large couch, but he didn't seem to mind too much. I had gone outside to pull the dead zombies around Mary's house away. I was moving the last disgusting wretch away when Gary showed up beside me.

"Need some help?" he asked.

"How long you been watching?" I asked.

"About half an hour."

"Nice. I think I can finish this off on my own."

"Did you hear that?" Gary asked as the body I was schlepping was making excessively loud squishy noises. I did not dwell on what could be causing it.

I stood up straight, I wanted to cup my ear to get a better grasp on any incoming sound, but I'd be damned if I was bringing my gloves anywhere near my head.

"I didn't hear anything. What was it?"

"Gunshot."

"Just one?"

"That's all I heard, but it was impossible to hear much beyond your bellyaching about moving these zombies."

"You could have helped."

"Could have."

"Fine, smart-ass, any idea which direction the shot came from?"

"Best guess is back that way," Gary said, pointing to the side and back of Mary's backyard.

"You think it's Paul and them?" I asked, hoping,

although how would he know?

"My guess is probably. Haven't heard much of anything since we pulled into this town...and now a gunshot."

"I'm going to check it out." I had made the decision there and then.

"Well, let me get some stuff."

"I didn't mean to volunteer you, too."

"That's alright. I feel like doing something."

"Helping me move all these zombies would have been helpful."

"Probably would have," Gary said as he headed back to the house to go and grab a few supplies.

I dropped the gloves on top of the last zombie I moved. I swear I could feel microbes crawling around on top of my skin, looking for a particularly large pore to gain access into my system so that they could wreak their havoc. Nothing short of a bath in bleach was going to make me feel any better.

"You alright?" Gary asked, coming back a few moments later.

He handed me a bottle of liquid, anti-bacterial hand soap. I contemplated kissing him.

"I'm with you if you want to go, but are you so sure this is a good idea?" Gary asked.

I knew what he meant, we were low on ammo, it was approaching nighttime, and we weren't really sure what we were walking towards. "Nothing else going on."

"That's the spirit," he said sarcastically. "Why did BT think staying with you was a good idea?"

"Beats me. Let's go and be careful."

"Did you really think you needed to add that last part? Were you afraid I might start singing or something?"

"Sorry, it's just something I added with the kids all the time, it's second nature, kind of like saying 'bless you' when someone sneezes."

"It's nothing like that," Gary said huffily. "It was commonly believed in the middle ages that when a person sneezed that they could potentially let a demon into their body and corrupt their soul, that was why people responded with God bless you. It would keep the demons from taking hold inside."

"Okay," I answered confusedly. Gary still looked peeved. "You still believe in the demons part?" I asked him cautiously.

"It was rooted in some truth!" he said heatedly.

"Okay, okay, I'm sorry. Can we go check the noise out now?"

"Just make sure you say God bless you and not just bless you or you are not conveying the true meaning of the message. That shit really infuriates me."

"And yet I'm labeled as the crazy one. I demand a recount."

"Just go. I told Josh I'd read him a story when we got back."

"He's a good kid," I said absently.

"So is his mom," Gary said.

"A good kid?" I asked, turning to face him as we came to the end of Mary's backyard.

"I meant good person."

"Oh no, you're falling in love. I've seen that look before. We've known them less than two days."

"The heart cares not for such trivial matters as time."

"Gary, her ex-husband could still be alive…and even if he is zombie chow, he's only been gone a few months."

"Time is less significant now, Mike. Nobody's planning their summer vacations anymore, they're planning out how to get their next meal or where the safest place to sleep is. Nobody gives a shit about the Monday morning commute anymore. It's all about the basest of all human instincts."

"Sex?" I asked.

"Survival," he corrected. "Could you please get your thoughts to a loftier perch?"

"But our survival depends on sex, procreation."

"What possessed Mom to have a fifth kid?" Gary asked the heavens. "How can you take something so beautiful as love and debase it?"

"You're like the sister I never had," I told him. "You can cook AND you have feelings."

"Feel this," he said as he smacked me upside the head.

"Can we maybe get going again?" I asked as I rubbed my head. "You even hit like a girl."

We crossed through Mary's neighbor to the back and then through their yard and onto the street.

"It was further away," Gary said as I turned to him.

"Man, it's quiet," I said, turning back around. "I wish we could hear gunshots. At least, we'd know where to go."

"Or where to avoid," Gary added more prudently.

"Or that," I said to him, not really agreeing.

Chapter Eighteen

Paul slowly moved down the roadway, constantly weighing his decision. More than once he had stopped and pondered going back.

"How dangerous is she really?" Paul asked himself on more than one occasion. "She saved my life. But she shot Brian and somehow got him bitten. She's a snake that lies in the grass, waiting to strike her unsuspecting victims." That was usually enough to get him moving.

Mrs. Deneaux was not worried in the least about her secret getting out. *Paul was a dead man stumbling*, she thought. She even allowed herself a laugh at her pun. Still, she was not fond of loose ends. More than once, they had come back in her long and storied life to add some disruption to her plans. She reasoned with herself that she was down to four rounds and why waste one on him when the zombies or something equally as deadly would save her the much-needed bullet. "A ferocious hamster could take him out right now." She laughed again, and long-buried, stale lung smoke ventured out her nose as she chortled.

Chapter Nineteen – Mike Journal Entry 11

"It couldn't have been much further than this," Gary said as we came to our fifth street.

"You know the way back?" I asked, just now thinking about that small fact.

"I've been leaving bread crumbs," he answered quickly.

"Okay, Hansel."

"Don't worry, I know the way."

"I was more concerned with me. If we have to run, I want to know which way to go, because you obviously won't be able to keep up."

"I guess you'd just better not leave me behind this time."

We had been walking up the road, my guess would have been in a northerly direction, but that would have been merely a guess. I always feel like whichever direction I'm walking is north. When we saw a bloody body in the road, Gary grabbed my shoulder to keep me from getting closer.

"That's probably what I heard," Gary whispered.

My heart was sinking, the clothing looked familiar. We were edging closer, keeping a close lookout for the shooter.

Gary had stopped his forward progress.

"What's up?" I asked him softly, looking around. We were both in crouched positions, trying to make ourselves as small a target as possible. But we were in the middle of the road, so we were pretty much fair game if someone were so inclined.

"I think that's Brian," Gary said, trying to suppress

some gagging.

"I think you're right. Stay here and cover my back."

Gary nodded, his mouth closed tightly.

I moved closer, trying to get into as small a ball of humanity as possible. I could see the bullet's entry into the base of the skull. I dreaded what I had to do next. I mean the body had, I think, the same clothes on as Brian, but I wasn't completely sure. It's just not something I pay all that much attention to. I placed my boot under his left hip and kept my rifle aimed at his head. I then turned the body over. The left side of Brian's face was missing, the only way I knew it was Brian was because the right side was in remarkably good shape.

"Fuck," I said. It really seemed like the only fitting thing to say.

"Is that him?" Gary asked from his vantage point.

I nodded.

"Shit," he said.

I agreed wholeheartedly.

When I could tear my gaze away from his destroyed face, I began to take in other details. The one remaining eye was opaque and his skin was gray. Yes, I knew he was dead, but there was a difference to the skin tone of the dead and the undead. I had been around enough of both to unfortunately become a resident expert.

"He was a zombie," I told Gary as I came back to where he was standing.

"Shit," Was all Gary had to say again. I'm thinking that if he said more, he would have to keep his mouth open, and any longer, and more than words would come out.

I wondered what happened to Paul and Deneaux. "How the hell am I going to tell Cindy this?"

"We're still not out of the woods ourselves; you might not have to," was Gary's dour reply. He was not accepting this new wrinkle very well and far be it for me to blame him.

"Michael?" I heard from further up the road.

"Deneaux?" I asked as Gary turned around.

He pointed to a lady standing on a porch step about three houses up.

"Is Paul with you?" I asked as I approached.

I could see her head shaking as I got closer.

"What happened?" I asked as I got to her.

She related her story about how Brian was shot during the initial ambush and that Paul had left them to go get antibiotics. While they were waiting, they had been attacked by zombies, Brian had been bitten and she had run for her life. She had not seen Paul since she had found this house. She had been staring out the window when Brian had come. She had called to him, but when she realized he was a zombie, she had shot him.

***

Her story had holes and the house she was in just about screamed 'liar', but I couldn't figure out why and I didn't want to yet call her on it.

"Big fan of peanut butter?" I asked her innocently as Gary and she sat at the kitchen table. I was walking around looking at the counter.

She was playing the part of a grieving woman, but it did not fit the true Deneaux I had come to know and loathe.

"I can't really stand it, gets stuck in my bridge work," she said as she turned to look at me, holding the near empty peanut butter jar and oversized spoon. "Previous occupant," she said without missing a beat, turning back to Gary.

The spoon was still wet with the saliva of the previous occupant. She was spinning a web and I was willing to let her until she wrapped herself up in it and choked.

I could see the necessity of shooting Brian. He was no longer human, but if she had called to him like she said, she would have had to shoot him in the face, not the back of the head. Why lie about that part? It made no sense.

"You haven't seen Paul since he left to get the meds?" I asked her again.

"Really, Michael, how often do I need to keep explaining myself? If you weren't going to listen the first three times, maybe you should have just saved us both some time and told me that," she said, never turning to face me. She was holding Gary's hands for comfort.

Something reeked here and it wasn't even a zombie.

"Gary, will you help Mrs. Deneaux get her stuff and then we'll head back to Mary's?"

"Sure. What are you going to do?" he asked.

"I want to do a quick once-over through the house and see if there is anything worth grabbing."

"We should just get going," Mrs. Deneaux said. "There have been zombies around all night. We might not get away from here if we stay much longer."

Gary looked over to me. "I'll risk it," I told her.

For the briefest of seconds…she sneered at me. If I had blinked, I would have missed it.

I went through the house. It had been ransacked. Someone had been here before, but there wasn't anything to substantiate whether it was Paul or Deneaux; and besides a few hypo-allergenic pillows, there really wasn't anything we could use.

"Isn't this Paul's rifle?" Gary asked as he handed her the rifle and we got ready to leave.

"He gave it to me when he went to look for the medicine," she said as she grabbed the gun.

I couldn't help myself. "Bullshit! He left giving you his only means of defense?"

"I offered him my pistol. He said he was more apt to hurt himself than anyone else," she said.

"Let's go," I said, not wanting to question her anymore. Now we both knew I had my suspicions about her. The question was, what was she going to do about it?

Gary led the way, Deneaux in the middle, and me at the end, more to keep an eye on her than anything else.

We saw one band of five speeding zombies, which we did not engage; we stayed hidden behind a motor home. They were running at a full sprint, in the opposite direction from which we had come. They very much looked like they had dinner reservations and they were running late, I saw absolutely no reason to alter their dining plans.

Within twenty minutes, we were back at Mary's stoop, once again arguing with her over whether or not she should let us in.

It was actually a good showing from Deneaux that got the door open.

"Oh dear, I feel rather faint," she said as she began to fan herself with her hand. "I haven't eaten in days and I've just been so scared," she said, shivering.

She was actually quite good at the grandmother card, although I'm almost completely sure nothing could have survived in that frozen womb of hers to be born, hatched perhaps, but not born.

"You poor thing! Come on in," Mary said, opening the door and ushering the woman in. "What kind of savages are you two that you would make her carry this heavy rifle?" Mary said, grabbing the gun from an unwilling Deneaux's hands. I suddenly felt much safer.

Josh, who had been watching from the kitchen, went upstairs when he saw Deneaux come in. I knew the kid was smart; this just proved me right. Deneaux made a great show of sitting down heavily on one of Mary's chairs.

"Oh, you poor thing! Let me get you some food," Mary said, retreating to her pantry.

"He's here?" Deneaux asked, pointing to the slumbering BT.

"Does that somehow interfere with your plans?" I asked.

"Relax, Michael. I was merely asking a question,"

Deneaux said, smiling, I think happy that she was making me so upset.

"Listen, I know you're covering something up, and if I find out that something happened to my friend because of you, I'll leave you on the side of the road. Do you believe me?" I told her, now standing over her, my finger pointing directly at her face.

"Oh, I do believe you would, but I've already told you, I have not seen your precious friend since he left us."

"What's going on?" Mary asked as she came back with a tray, an MRE and some utensils.

I walked away, heading up to where Josh had safely retreated.

"Just a misunderstanding," Mrs. Deneaux said, warmly thanking Mary for the food.

I heard Gary ask Mary how BT had been and her reply that he had slept the whole time, before I made it to the top of the stairs.

"She's fucking scary," Josh said, peeking his head out of his bedroom.

"Yes, she is, and I don't think you're supposed to be swearing."

"I'd rather face that Eliza lady than her."

I thought about it for a second. "No, you wouldn't. Close, but no, you wouldn't."

Chapter Twenty

"Mike, where the hell are you?" Paul asked as he hunched down by some trashcans. He had heard something moments earlier and nearly wet his pants when an angry raccoon came out from a row of hedges to claim its trash barrels.

"Sorry, fella. These yours?" Paul asked as he grunted to get away from the large animal. A rabies bite from the raccoon would be just as fatal…and more painful than a zombie bite. Paul backed away carefully, making sure the animal did not crazily charge him. He fell over a long-unclaimed bag of trash. The smell of old diapers and moldy cabbage assailed his nostrils.

"Couldn't be an old florist shop. No, had to be a damn daycare or something," Paul said as he began to stand up. His eye caught something moving on his peripheral, but it was not the raccoon. The animal had taken off, sensing a greater predator than Paul in the neighborhood. *It sucks not being on top of the food chain anymore,* Paul thought as he looked past the trashcans to five rapidly approaching zombies.

He knew if he so much as clenched his asshole, he would wrinkle the trash bag under him and the zombies would come his way. He wasn't yet sure that they hadn't already seen him.

The zombies passed by less than twenty feet away. Paul relaxed somewhat as they began to head off. The small release in tension caused his arm to slip, pushing his elbow down onto a soda can. Paul held his breath as the can popped. He could still hear the zombies' footfalls heading away and felt like he had dodged a bullet until he craned his head to find the best way to get up and saw one lone zombie staring straight at him. Its head tilted like a dog's does when it's trying to figure out what it is looking at.

The zombie started to approach. The blending-in-with-garbage trick was not going to work anymore. Paul thought about turning to run, but right now, he wouldn't be able to out distance a deader. He once again adopted the pose of the fighter as he got on his tender feet. "What are the chances that another bullet saves my ass?" Paul asked the heavens as the zombie ran towards him.

The heavens weren't listening as the zombie ran straight into Paul's fist. Paul was sure he had broken at least one knuckle on the zombie's skull. The shot on the eye of the zombie may not have put a man on his ass, but it should have at least dazed him. It had no effect whatsoever on the zombie. The zombie fell on top of Paul as they both went down onto the stinking pile of refuse. The bag exploded, sending leaking diapers everywhere.

Snapping teeth came within the width of a fingernail from shearing Paul's fingers off. Paul felt the slime of the film that coated the zombie's un-brushed teeth. Paul placed both hands on the zombie's shoulders and pushed away as the zombie attempted to draw closer. When the zombie realized it could not reach Paul's face, it began to turn from arm to arm, looking for a place to seek purchase. Paul had to keep alternating his hand placement in an effort to stay one step ahead of the zombie's teeth. Already his arms were beginning to tire; he did not know how long he could play Hide-The-Flesh-From-The-Zombie before his arms gave out.

No one is going to save me this time, he thought.

Paul shoved his hips upward, gaining some distance from the zombie as he brought his knee up in what could only be described as a ball-busting maneuver. The zombie did not so much as flinch from the contact. Thick tendrils of drool and liquefied plaque hung from the zombie's mouth, dangerously close to Paul's face, Paul kept blowing out great puffs of air in a futile hope to keep the mouth offal from striking him. The smell of the old, wet, moldy diapers competed with the zombie for odor of the decade. Paul was having difficulty getting in enough clean air to work with.

Paul was trying to scramble from under the zombie, but his feet kept sliding in rubbish. *Had a newly axed girlfriend once tell me I was going to die in a pile of shit. I can't imagine she meant this*, Paul thought. *Or maybe she did.*

The zombie was fairly predictable in its approach. After nine or ten times through the cycle, Paul got an idea. As the zombie reached for Paul's left arm, he pulled it away. The zombie would make a slight attempt for Paul's face and then move to the right side. Paul moved his right arm quicker than the zombie was expecting, then he thrust up with his left hip. The death-tangled duo rolled to the right, precariously balancing on their right side until momentum brought Paul on top.

"How about I eat you, motherfucker?!" Paul screamed. Paul made a feint to bite the zombie's arm. Once again, the zombie could not have cared less as it still tried to bite at Paul's hands, but it now did not have as much range in motion. Paul still had no clue as to what to do. He did not want to release his grip. He was afraid he might slip in the piles of garbage as he turned to run and then they'd be doing this dance all over again. Paul did the only option that was available to him as the zombie went for Paul's right hand. With his left, Paul grabbed as much trash as he could, becoming utterly dismayed when his hand went through decomposing diaper.

He began to shove as much refuse into the zombie's eager mouth as he could. The zombie, at first greedily took the offering and then began to fight against the force-fed meal. Paul had already let go and was halfway to getting up. The zombie was still struggling with a Pamper lodged in its throat. Paul's nightmare nearly came to fruition as he slid on a cliché. *No way! A banana peel? Are you kidding me?* But banana peels were much more slippery in cartoons. Paul was quickly on terra firma and shuffling for all his life to the doorstep closest to him. Locked door, crazy resident, home full of zombies or just pissed off squirrels, Paul was placing all his marbles into this bag; there were no other options. He could not make it to another house and he'd much rather see the zombie coming than get brought down from behind like a gazelle on the Serengeti.

Paul's ankle groaned as he climbed the first step. All he had going for him was forward momentum, he brought his foot down and brought up his left. That was no bargain, as his foot wound broke open from the flexion of the move. Blood was seeping through his boot at an alarming rate. Paul had no time to take notice as he reached the top of the third step and got onto the landing. His zombie friend had finally got its feet under it and was now ready to continue its pursuit.

Paul reached out to grab the storm door, his hands slick with an unidentifiable, or at least, unwilling to identify, substance. His hand slid off as effectively as if the handle had been Vaseline-coated. Which brought him to a distant memory with Mike. (See Paul-A-Sode at the end of this journal.)

***

Paul couldn't understand why he got the "warm and fuzzies" when he thought about the past with Mike. *Maybe I'm just expressing my feminine side*, he thought as he once again struggled with the door, hoping that he could marshal up more masculine traits at the moment and force the door open.

Paul was able to pull the door open just as the zombie made it onto the landing with him. Paul squeezed between the storm door and the front door. The zombie was intent on making a "Paul Panini" as it pressed up against the storm door with all of its murderous intent. Paul was staring eye to eye with the monster, his nose skewed at an angle from the pressure being applied to him. Shredded bits of used diapers spilled from the mouth of the zombie. Paul could not imagine anything much grosser except maybe walking in on his parents making love, but he wasn't even gonna go there.

Paul reached behind him with his left hand for the doorknob, while with his right arm he tried to keep the zombie from pressing him into the grain of the front door. His hand, at first, could find no purchase, but as he frantically moved his hand back and forth across the handle and more detritus fell off, he finally made a friction-full attempt. His heart leapt as the handle turned and quickly plummeted when he felt himself falling inwards. Paul was able to pull his shot foot up over the front step and into the house. He was not so lucky with the other as the zombie pressed its attack and wedged Paul's ankle between the storm door and the step.

The fulcrum that was Paul's weight as it fell backward was easily enough leverage to apply the needed amount of pressure to snap the bottom part of his leg. His foot now dangled at a useless ninety degree angle from the rest of his prone body. Paul's screams of pain reverberated in the house. He began to hyperventilate as he was having difficulty catching his breath. The pain was a fire that burned all rational thought from his mind. The zombie kept forcing the door against Paul's useless leg. It was like adding a fresh dose of salt on a newly whelped whipping welt each time the zombie forced the door on his leg.

Paul instinctually kicked out with his "good" leg, barely even able to register the slight spike in pain when the wound made contact with the storm door. The blow had the desired effect as it pushed the zombie away from the door. Paul was able to drag his broken leg in through the opening, crying anew as the splintered bones came back in contact with their newly departed brethren and his leg was once again in the straight position on the foyer floor.

Glass from the storm door shattered as the zombie crashed back into it. The zombie was trying to reach its hands in. Paul screamed as he placed his hands down on broken glass. He pushed back and, with a bloody hand, he slammed the front door. The leading edge of the front door clipped his broken leg as it swung shut. The pain was too intense for Paul, his body shut down in an attempt to keep him from going into shock. Paul laid there with his shredded hands, broken leg, sprained ankle and a bullet wound, his body fighting to restore some order. Paul could not and did not notice the small shadows that crossed his path, as he lay helpless.

Chapter Twenty-One – Mike Journal Entry 12

It was hours later when Mary finally called Josh downstairs to eat, and I thought it would be a little weird if I stayed upstairs and played with his Legos by myself. As it was, it had been a brief, enjoyable respite from the horrors of the last few months. We created all sorts of alternate worlds with the plastic building blocks. Every last one of them did not contain a zombie, not a one.

The table was set with a meal consisting of an MRE and was as presentable as possible, considering the nature of the product being used. I pulled out a chair to sit with the rest of the dinner attendees when Mary spoke.

"That chair isn't for you," she said disdainfully.

"Okay," I said furrowing my eyebrows. "Who is it for then?"

"BT," she said as she tore a cheese packet with her teeth.

"You know he's still asleep, right? I just passed him on the way in here and he's snoring so loud, it sounds like he's clearing a forest."

"The fact remains that it is his seat," she repeated.

"Okay." My eyebrows still furrowed. I was missing something, but I had not a clue as to what.

Mrs. Deneaux was at the head of the table and was looking directly at me. She was smiling as she forked in a large portion of military surplus ham steak.

"Can I eat?" I asked Mary.

"You've worn out your welcome," she said, looking at me with a piercing stare.

"Mom?!" Josh rang out. "What's wrong with you?"

"Hush, honey. Eat your dinner."

Josh stood up and began to walk away from the table. "I'll eat when he does."

"You'll sit down and do what I say, young man!" she yelled. "What have you said to him?" She turned venomous on me.

"We were building spaceships with Legos," I said, backing up. "The only thing I said to him was how cool his ship had come out, and once or twice I asked him for a certain piece. What the hell is going on? I don't know you well enough to illicit this response. I mean, sure if you spent the time to really get to know me, I'd be able to do this to you on a fairly routine basis." I was shooting for humor, but ended up with a self-inflicted wound. She stared back flatly at me.

"We'll be leaving tomorrow," I told her.

"We are?" Gary asked, I noticed he had not stopped eating his meal. I wanted to thank him for his solidarity.

"You can't!" Josh cried.

"What about BT? Is he ready to go?" Gary asked around a mouthful of something that resembled meat. "And Paul? We still need to find him."

It was quicker than a cobra strike and could have been as lethal, the look that Deneaux shot at Gary.

My brain was tossing all this info together in the washing machine of my mind, but no matter how much spin I put on it, it still kept coming out dirty and stained. Deneaux had planted bad seeds about me in Mary's head. Deneaux wanted us kicked out of here, but why? My mind began to spin faster, not just out of here, meaning this house, but also out of here, meaning this city. She was covering something up and all that it could be was Paul. Brian was a dead zombie. How he became a zombie could be debated and how he was shot was up for question also, but the fact remained he had been a zombie and Deneaux had every right to dispatch of him. *Clinical word* I told my brain as I thought of my former ally in survival.

"Two days," I told Mary, but her head was shaking in the negative. "I need two days. Tomorrow we will go out all day, looking for my friend." Deneaux's fork hesitated for a split second as it traveled to her pursed, shriveled lips.

She put her full fork down on her Chinette plate.

"Really, Michael, you just told her that we would be leaving tomorrow. I do not think it is fair to her that you should put her and her son in this much danger."

"Thank you, Vivian," Mary said, reaching out and clasping Deneaux's claw, I mean, hand.

I looked at Deneaux with my '*I know what you're trying to do*' gaze. She merely smiled.

"Fine, tomorrow it is," I told Mary. Deneaux's smile grew further, I was afraid her paper thin skin was going to tear as it stretched beyond its limits. "We'll move to your neighbor's house." Deneaux's smile evaporated.

Mary shot from her seat. "You can't!"

"Sure I can. Who do you think you are to tell me where I can set up my base of operations?"

"That's too close!" she yelled again.

"I've got one friend who is missing and another that hasn't awakened in hours. And you've seen the size of him. How far do you think I can carry him? I'm not going very far until I get both issues resolved," I said to Mary as much as I did Deneaux.

Mary plopped down in her seat, cupping her head in her hands. "Two days and you promise you'll go?"

"I'll leave this house and your general vicinity, yes," I told her.

"That'll have to do," she answered solemnly.

"Yes," Josh said, pumping his fist.

"Can I eat now?"

"Not at the table," she said without removing her head from her hands.

That was fine with me. If I wasn't with my immediate

family, I preferred to eat alone. I didn't generally like people enough to break bread with them and make idle chit chat about things I didn't give a crap about; and don't get me started if I came across signs of uncleanliness on their utensils or dishes. It was best to not go down a road lined with potholes, when holding such a fragile, glass-wrapped psyche like my own.

I grabbed BT's MRE off the table before she could object and headed into the living room. Josh was immediately on my heels. Mary had not stopped him, probably hadn't pulled her head up yet to take note. BT slumbered on as I tore open the near nuclear-proof plastic wrapping.

I don't know how many of you have ever had dealings with MREs, but if you've survived this long, then you, my friend, are a survivalist and EVERY survivalist has at one time or another had an MRE, whether from the military or an Army/Navy surplus store. (You know those places that were located in the worst parts of every town and the guy behind the counter looks suspiciously at every customer like they could be the feds come to get his secret cache of hand grenades and rocket launchers in the back room.)

If, on the off chance that you have somehow made it this far without one, I will relate a short story. When I was in Marine Corps boot camp, eating was one of the only events that any recruit could sort of look forward to. I say "sort of" because we generally were not allowed to finish any meal. I can, without even thinking about it, honestly tell you that I threw more food away during my three and a half months of boot camp than I actually ate.

When we went to the dining halls, it was all I could do to shovel as much food into my mouth before the DIs would start barking at us to get back outside and in military formation. The times we spent out in the field without access to a dining hall, however, were times of depravation and starvation. The DIs would put a box of MREs out in a field, usually somewhere in the neighborhood of one hundred or so yards away, and then tell us that we had five minutes to eat. So, we would race out to the box and tear into it, which in itself takes a little to get through. Removing the metal banding straps without tools was always a good time to see who would bleed first, then as the piñata of meals fell to the ground, it was a scramble to grab a meal. There was not the luxury of choosing one particular meal over another. Did I tell you this one little tidbit? There are twelve meals in an MRE case and we had two boxes. There were thirty Marine recruits in my platoon, easy enough math. You think people fighting for a stupid, sold-out, hot toy during Christmas are fierce? Tell a starving Marine you just took the last meal.

Looking back on it, the ones that didn't get the meal were probably better off. I can't tell you how many fingernails I tore, trying to tear through the five mm gauge, sealed-by-a-glue-fanatic bags. Ripping with teeth was perhaps marginally better, chipped tooth, bleeding fingers, to-MAY-toe, to-MAH-toe, just give me my fucking food! Alright, so let's see where we are. Sprint to box, five guys trying desperately to crack boxes open, ensuing fight for insufficient meals as they spill to the dirt, check so far. So now you have battled and won a meal and are hiding your kill from your fellow predators. You have successfully torn through the hard exterior carcass to get at the 'meat and potatoes' so to speak. It doesn't matter much whether it is wombat or porcupine meat, you're going to eat it.

By this point, three of the five allotted minutes have been used up, and now for the topper. Apparently, Marine DIs do not make much money because they cannot afford watches that keep particularly good time. I would finally be at a point where I could rip open the food's foil container and squeeze food down my gullet (forget the plastic utensils, forget chewing, this was all about sustenance) when the DIs would start screaming at us to assemble. Now some of you may not have ever joined the services. That is fine; we all walk our own path in life, some of you may have chosen the Army, or were maybe a little smarter and went to the Navy or, quite possibly, you were a genius and joined the Air Force. But I was in the Marines. When your DI screamed at you to be somewhere…you did it, no questions asked.

The gut-crippling clutches of hunger were far outweighed by the prospect of suffering the wrath of a DI who felt you had wronged him. Some of you sneakier souls are thinking, don't those camis have dozens of pockets? Yes, they do. Then why not shove your uneaten food in those and eat them later? Any former Marines want to answer this one? Because, my dear reader, DIs know about pockets and they know about what lengths a desperate starving recruit will go to. You would be treated less harshly in the real world if you had just killed a cop and his partner caught you first and was alone with you for a half hour before his back up got there.

Some of you may scoff at that analogy, I had to stand at the position of attention while the recruit next to me suffered the wrath of two DIs for trying to heist a jelly packet that he had shoved down his trousers. By the time they were done with him, well let's just say that the jelly packet would have been the only thing he would have been able to eat.

***

I ended up with a beef stew MRE packet. Think Dinty Moore, but gross. The fat congealed at the top of the packet was the thickest part of the whole meal, including the mystery meat. I ate everything, I was famished. I looked over to BT, who was still sleeping. It left me wondering if getting Tomas into the mix was a good call or not. I had no viable alternative, but still it nagged at me; knowledge is power and now Tomas had some. Life was already precarious. Why I felt the need to keep digging holes around the lip of the precipice was beyond me.

I could hear Deneaux in the next room trying to comfort Mary. It was like listening to a snake tell its prey that everything would be alright. Sure, for the snake it would be. I was staring so hard at BT, I wasn't even looking at him anymore, if that makes any sense. I never noticed when his eyes opened.

"You scare me sometimes," BT said, his vocal chords sounding coarse and dry.

I quickly pulled my thousand-yard stare back in. "Yeah, well you do that to me all the time."

"So we're here a few more days?" he asked as he pulled himself up to a sitting position.

"What'd you hear?" I asked him.

"Enough to know that you must have stomped all over Deneaux's prized azaleas. She does not like you."

"It's more than that, I agree she's not a fan, but there's something more. Do you have enough strength to head upstairs?" BT nodded. "I figure the old bat has ears like one."

Josh laughed.

"Josh is everything all right in there?" Mary called.

"You really shouldn't let him get too much influence from Michael. He sets bad examples," Deneaux chirped into Mary's ear.

"Tell me again why you decided to come with us?" I asked, before she could respond, I continued on. "Or better yet, why did I allow you to come with us?"

I could hear her over-exaggerated heavy sigh from where I was.

"Mom, I'm fine, we're going to play with my Legos again," Josh said, winking to me.

"Be careful," Mary said.

"From the Legos?" Josh asked, completely confused.

"You know what I mean," she answered.

Josh shrugged his shoulders and mouthed, "No, I don't" to me.

"I do," I soundlessly worded to him and then waved him to go upstairs.

BT followed, the big man was moving slowly and had to take a break halfway up the stairs.

"You alright?" I asked him from the top of the stairs.

"I didn't know you cared," he said a little more heatedly than perhaps he meant to, as he apologized when he got up to me. "I'm sorry, man, I feel like I've got the flu, without all the phlegm."

"Gross," Josh said. "Come on," he said, pushing the door to his room open.

BT almost crashed into a rendition of a B-1 bomber as he headed straight for the bed to plop down on it. Josh's bed creaked and groaned from a pressure it had not been designed to bear. Josh and I stared for a few seconds waiting for the resultant collapse.

BT, getting wind of what we were doing, spoke. "It'll hold," he growled, and as if intimidated by his words, the bed did as it was told.

"Can I stay?" Josh asked. "I know you guys came up here to talk and get away from the women, but I'm a man too, so I should be here."

"It's your house, my man," BT said. "I don't see why not."

I was more inclined to send him packing for a few minutes, but I don't think he was going to do any heart to heart talking with Deneaux anytime soon.

"What's going on, Mike?" BT asked. "I caught some of her conversation with Mary, but I kept drifting in and out. All I could really tell is that she wants to get out of here as quick as possible."

"It's nothing concrete, BT, but she's trying to cover her tracks." I related the story of finding Brian and how he was facing away AFTER she had called him, and how she now was in possession of Paul's rifle. I also mentioned how she had said she was alone, but the house she was staying in provided clues to the contrary. "It's nothing but a suspicion, but she did something she's trying to cover up and she wants us to leave the scene of the crime before we turn up any evidence."

"Brian's dead," BT said wiping his hand down his face. "Man, I almost don't want to go back to your brother's and see what this does to Cindy."

"I cannot leave here until I know about Paul. There's no way I could look Erin in the face and tell her that I have absolutely no clue what happened to her husband and my best friend."

"So Brian was a zombie? Why lie about anything to do with that then?" BT asked confused. "Could the bullet have spun him around or anything?"

I looked over to Josh before I replied. "Exit wound was on his face."

"Gross," Josh said, I agreed implicitly.

"She's acting so shifty, even more so than usual. I don't have a good feeling about Paul." I hitched a little. *I'm still mostly human*, I thought, *I'm still entitled to have feelings*. "I've known him for thirty years. I owe it to him at the very least to find out what happened."

"You've got to prepare yourself for the real possibility that he is no longer with us," BT said tenderly.

"I know that, man, I do. With a rifle, Paul wasn't a huge threat; well without…" I didn't, I couldn't finish the damn sentence.

"I'd like to head out with you in the morning," BT said. "Help look for him."

"Me too," Josh threw in before I could even tell BT no.

"No, on both counts."

"You gonna stop me?" BT said, trying to rise up off the bed and use his height advantage as a mitigating factor.

"BT, Josh could stop you right now."

Josh looked over at me like maybe I shouldn't be

throwing him under the bus quite like that.

"Dammit, Mike! I'm as weak as you right now," BT said, cursing. "I can barely move."

I didn't rise to his bait, I did think about putting him in a headlock though, just because I thought I could probably take him. But merely to gaze upon the man is to feel intimidation. "You sure you never played in the NFL?"

"Why? Because I'm big and I'm black?" BT said with some force.

I thought about it. "Well, yeah."

He laughed. "Played some college ball, had some pro scouts interested. It never went any further."

And he dropped it, I don't know if there was no more to add or he didn't want to talk about it.

"What time are we leaving tomorrow?" Josh asked.

"No way, kiddo," I told him. "Your mom, if given the chance, would throw me out into the street in front of a convoy."

"A what?" Josh asked.

"A bunch of trucks," BT clarified. "And he's right. It's too dangerous out there for you."

"I'm almost twelve," Josh said, making it sound as authoritative as possible.

"Yeah, and I'm sure you're going to want to make thirteen," I told him. And then reality with its ugly iron fist hit me with an uppercut. What is the rest of his life really going to encompass? Eventually, they are going to run out of food and they will have to leave their relatively safe haven and neither seemed to have the skills to scavenge in a hostile world. Basically, they were living on borrowed time.

That didn't mean I was taking him with me on a learning expedition, but I still felt for the kid and his mother. Her ex-husband, his father, was gone (*much like Paul*, crept in. I squashed it heavily, but the thought kept peeking from around the edges) and he wasn't coming back. How many 'families' were there still out there like this? Isolated, each its own island of remoteness. There could still be a salvageable community in this city, but they would never be able to become cohesive. There was no communication, no ability to seek others out. The populace would be too fearful to create bonds anyway. There might be a few brave souls like Mary that would open a door to a stranger, but she was in the minority. We were just as lucky she hadn't shot us instead.

Between zombies and criminally opportunistic humans, the world was merely a shell. The day of humans as the dominant species on the planet was coming to close and it was just as violently dangerous and deadly as the great comet strike that took out the dinosaurs two hundred million years ago. There would be a few viable communities still intact, places like Little Turtle or Easter Evans School, but as the zombies' resources became fewer and fewer, they would seek these last food zones out relentlessly. Nothing would be able to withstand that type of onslaught.

Ultimately, the zombies and Eliza would have won, but what was the prize? She would rule a planet of mindless eating machines. I can't imagine she had thought this out completely. She gets off on the power she holds over people and the fear she instills in their hearts. Zombies didn't care, at all, they eat. And make no mistake, we would be just like every other extinct species on the planet, gone and for good. Seen any Tasmanian wolves lately? Maybe a dodo bird or two? There is no species regeneration. And Eliza and Tomas would hardly qualify as Adam and Eve.

Would she live long enough to see another sentient being rise from the ashes of our deaths? Would dolphins come ashore and finally take their rightful place as caretakers of the land? Would zombies give anything a chance to get a foothold? They ate everything. They were worse than locusts. They stripped the land clean of every type of animal. Looks like it was going to be the age of plants. I hope Eliza likes roses.

I had spent the last few seconds mulling over my dark

thoughts when Josh interrupted me. Maybe the kid had an idea what he was in for. "I will make it to thirteen. I miss my dad, but I know he's not coming back. I don't tell my mom that because she needs to believe that I think he is. I need to see what it is like out there. We won't be able to stay here forever, no matter what my mom says. Sometimes I think that she just doesn't want to think about it. I think about it every day. We've got maybe six months of food and three months of bottled water, so what time are we leaving?"

"You're a realist, Josh, and I can appreciate that," I told him, and that was the honest truth. "But you're not my kid and the danger out there, it's real. This isn't a training exercise. I would no sooner put you in any needless danger than I would any of my own."

Mary had at some point come up the stairs and had been at Josh's doorway while I spoke to him. She grudgingly nodded at me for what I said to him, but she still didn't want him to be with me. The kid might have been thinking about going out at some point while he was with his mother, but he had never before voiced it. So again, something else was my fault by default.

"Come on, Josh. It's time for bed," Mary said, grabbing her son by the shoulders, steering him towards his bed.

It didn't seem that late to me, but that wasn't what this was about anyway. I took one longing look at the Legos I wanted to play with and headed downstairs, making sure that BT led the way. If he fell down the stairs behind me, I'd be crushed.

Mary came down a few minutes later. "I'd appreciate if you didn't put any wild thoughts in my son's head," she said hotly.

"Those 'wild thoughts'," I told her with air quotes and everything, "came from the mouth of your son without any prompting from me."

"He doesn't understand what is going on!" she yelled

and then brought her voice down to that inside yelling tone, cognizant of the fact that she had just put her offspring to bed.

"I think you underestimate him. He understands, probably even more so than you. He knows that his father isn't coming back, he understands that you have a finite supply of food and water and more importantly, he understands that as the man of the family, he is wholly unprepared to defend the both of you. I'm not arguing in the least to take him with me, Mary. I'm just telling you what is going through the boy's head. He's growing up fast because he has to. Just because last year he might have been playing with Pokémon cards and plastic dinosaurs doesn't mean he can't comprehend the danger around him now."

Mary sat down hard. I thought for sure she was going to miss the couch completely, again. As it was, she had to put her hand on the armrest to keep her ass from going to the ground. After she had situated herself properly, she brought her wet hand to her face. "What the hell is this?" she said, showing her hand to me.

What the fuck? I thought. It's not like I took a piss on her couch while she wasn't looking.

BT raised his hand like he was in the second grade. "I tend to drool a little, when I sleep sometimes," he finished, adding the qualifier.

"Gross," Mary said, heading for the kitchen to wash her hand off.

"Thanks, man," I said to BT. "That took the heat off for a minute."

"She'll be back," he said as we heard the water running in the next room.

"Wow, she's pissed," Gary said, coming into the room with us. He was talking, but looking at the wrapper to the granola bar he was eating. "These are fantastic, I've never heard of them," Gary said around a mouthful of nuts. (I'm not sure exactly about the contents he was chewing on, I just wanted to write that). "I'd sleep with one eye open, nope maybe both eyes, one for Deneaux and one for Mary. It really is kind of funny how you bring out the worst in the females around you."

"Ah, brother, the one constant I have in life, no matter how far I fall, someone in my family will be there to kick me where I lay."

He smiled.

"Touching," Deneaux said sarcastically. "What time are we leaving in the morning."

"We?" I asked her.

"I want to find him as much as you do," she said falsely.

"You don't lie as well as you think you do," I told her. "And you're staying here."

Her facial expression nearly matched Mary's from a few moments previous. Deneaux left, heading to the opposite side of the house where there was a sitting room and a large chair. I could only hope that she would get sucked into the oversized cushions and teleported to an alternate reality, one where old crones were stoned for being witches. I think Salem may have had it right.

"Why would you let her know you're suspicious? I'd rather tell a pit viper I was highly allergic to its venom and I didn't have an antidote," BT said.

"No way," Gary said. "I'm calling your bluff."

"Let it go, BT," I said as BT turned to Gary. "He knows not what he says. And I want her to know because if she had anything to do with Paul getting hurt, I'll kill her and she knows it. She'll get desperate and even the devil can make mistakes."

"So you're going to leave her behind with me? Thanks, I don't remember when I ended up on your shit list."

"Luck of the draw."

"Wonderful."

"Maybe you can try to keep her away from Mary. The

more Deneaux talks, the more poison she spills into Mary's Kool-Aid," I said.

"What does that even mean, Mike?" Gary turned to me.

"You know. Kool-Aid," I said, not clarifying a thing.

"I have no idea what he means, do you, BT?" Gary asked.

BT shrugged. "I understand about half of what he says and of that only twenty-five percent makes sense."

"You guys should take it on the road. I'm saying that Mary's Kool-Aid is her business and that Deneaux is spreading lies about us, well, me specifically."

"I know what you're saying. I was making sure that you did, too," Gary said.

"Should we take shifts?" BT asked, eyeing his couch hungrily.

"I'll take first watch," I told them, my gut was telling me something was not quite right with the night. Odds were it was the road kill meat MRE, but it had been a while since I'd felt lucky and I'd rather be awake and alert for whatever came down the road.

Nothing happened while I stared out that window, yet the unease in me did not abate, but rather grew. I kept waiting for something, I occasionally even checked on the softly snoring Deneaux to see if she was trying to sneak up behind me and plant a knife in my neck. I could swear on more than one occasion, I felt the icy, cold tip break skin. Only once, did she scare the hell out of me when, on one of my many circuits around the house, her black eyes were staring at me through the gloomy night. She must have had a lot of enemies in her day; she was sleeping with her eyes open. This I knew because her snoring had not stopped. She looked like a cold, calculating reptile like that and I more than half expected her to strike from that chair. I'd take Durgan any day. He wasn't smart enough in life to do anything but come straight at you. Deneaux seemed to have mastered the fine art of subterfuge. There wasn't an angle she probably hadn't exploited at one time or another, and I was wholly convinced, up to and including murder.

I returned to my chair, I had the jitters. My legs were bouncing up and down, restless leg syndrome, my ass, this was a full on epidemic. I won't swear on a stack of Bibles that it was three am (mostly because I was afraid the Bibles would burst into flame), but it seemed that the witching hour had come to fruition and then the dread of death washed over me and was gone.

"Shit!" BT yelled, sitting up. He turned to me. "Was that Paul?"

My head dropped as I nodded.

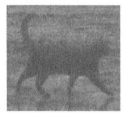

Chapter Twenty-Two

Paul was foggy as he began to pull from the slumber. Something darted by his face. The swish of a tail under his nose would have tickled if not for the fact that the pain from his broken leg blotted every other sensation into near muteness. All of his other injuries combined were little more than dots in the rearview mirror of the semi-tractor trailer that was his broken leg. Another something landed on Paul's stomach, he barely registered it.

It was night and that was the only thing Paul was certain of... Oh, and that he was still alive; he could tell because his leg repeatedly told him so.

"Got to sit up," he said gritting his teeth. He craned his head around, looking for a chair or a couch that he could pull himself up to. "Coffee table will have to do," he said, uttering the words more to shatter the silence and to help him concentrate on anything besides his leg. He first tried to use his hands to pull himself over, but the shards of glass still embedded in them made that an impossible task. He cried out, not in fear, not in frustration, but in futility. His leg, which he thought could not hurt anymore, became ignited with a white phosphorescent flare of immovable pain. He used his shoulders to prop up and see what was going on. A cat had bitten down on his pants where his broken leg was protruding, trying to get at the blood and meat that lay beyond the material. Paul tried to kick it away. The emaciated cat was faster, however, and hissed at him for his troubles.

The burst of adrenaline got him moving, at least, it lasted long enough for him to get his back up against the wooden frame of the table. He cried out again when he placed some weight on it and it slid further back, this time resting up against the couch beyond. Paul looked behind him and up; two cats with swishing tails and hungry looks stared back at him. *I love cats,* Paul thought. He had read the stories growing up about how when an owner had died and was not quickly discovered that his, but usually her, cats would eat their former master. He had believed it to all be propaganda perpetuated by dog owners, who invariably pulled out the article about the dog that had died on top of its master's grave, presumably from a broken heart.

Paul clucked his tongue, trying to establish some sort of repertoire with the feral cats. One hissed and one jumped down by his left side, making sure to stay out of the range of Paul's arm. The third pulled up his front paw and began to lick it; Paul could not help but think it was washing up before it dined.

"I am not food!" he yelled. The paw-licking cat looked up momentarily and then resumed its business. The one that had come down had jumped on Paul's leg, ripping a small piece of denim away. Paul had to bite down on his tongue to keep from passing out again; he knew he would not awaken a second time. He blindly kicked out, finding a great deal of satisfaction when he heard the cat mewling in pain, something in its side, most likely a rib, had cracked.

"Huh! One down, two to go, fuckers!" Paul spat. "Oh no," he said as he looked from the entry to the room he was in and saw two large toms sitting there, eyeing him greedily. "I'm in a cat lady's home," he bemoaned. He realized he could be dealing with dozens of cats and a toddler had more range of motion than he did. The majority of the cats were patient; they were predators, after all. Their meal was wounded, but could still deliver lethal blows. That was made evident by the cat that had been summarily ripped to shreds by the pack when its rib had been broken. The cats were starving and cared little where there next meal came from.

They did not suffer any moral dilemmas with the prospect of cannibalism. The ones that had survived this long were the biggest and baddest of the lot and now all attention was back on Paul with the quick meal made of the one that had attacked him.

Paul looked around the room, star-lit eyes shone at him from every angle. He had never been so close to such a large assemblage of animals. It was unnerving, but still he could not reconcile the fact that they could do him any real harm. Through the haze of pain and the real danger ever present, Paul kept finding his head nodding down every so often, only to be jerked up. On more than one occasion, he noticed a few of the braver, or perhaps hungrier cats, had closed the distance to him. Their tails were wagging back and forth in an aggressive behavior. Paul had seen it many times before from the ones he had owned. They were getting ready to pounce. He felt around looking for anything that could be used as a weapon.

His hands made him wince every time he reached out, but he pulled them up as close to his face as he could. He needed to get out as much of the glass as possible, short of daylight, a pocketknife, a needle and some tweezers, the majority would stay embedded exactly where they were. While he was pulling out a particularly large shard, a gray tabby came within a few inches of his broken leg before Paul instinctually jerked his damaged leg back. The pain was immeasurable. Doctors always ask on a scale of one to ten how severe the pain is, Paul did not think that ten could even begin to describe what he was feeling. The room spiraled out of focus as he fought desperately to stay aware of his surroundings.

At least six cats had come to within a few feet as Paul, degree by degree, dealt with the pain. The smarter, larger toms waited behind for the kill to take place. Then they'd come in and take the lion's share, without any of the risk. The smaller cats had to be more aggressive or they would not get any food whatsoever.

"Mike!" Paul screamed. The cats took notice of the words, like a long, lost vestige of a previous life, but not one moved away; hunger was an all-consuming feeling. They could move no closer to their own self-actualization while the baser of their instincts was not yet sated.

"I will not be eaten. Not by a zombie and certainly not by a bunch of mangy fucking cats," Paul said harshly. "And to think I used to love you more than dogs." Paul pulled himself further up, almost sitting completely perpendicular to the floor. Either shock was setting in or Paul's pain threshold had increased, but his leg was almost a manageable constant at this point.

A small cat, with most of its left ear missing, had had enough and jumped on Paul's chest, all of its claws in the ready and locked position. Sixteen thumbtacks pierced Paul's midsection. Paul grabbed the cat by the neck, squeezing as hard as he could. The cat spat and hissed, bringing its hind legs up to scratch and tear at Paul's wrist and forearm. The pain from the lacerations almost made Paul release his grip. Instead, he slammed the cat down by his right side. The cat was stunned, but not quite dead. He repeated the steps three more times, each bringing a satisfying crunch to the animal that desired to eat his flesh.

"Eat this!" he yelled, throwing the carcass into the fray.

Only a shark feeding frenzy would have been more disturbing. The mewls of pain as cat bit cat in their attempts to get at the meat of their peer was ear-piercingly loud. Fur flew in the air as the smacking of wet, tendon-snapping bites tore through the skinny feline. Paul looked away as one cat tried to escape from the pack with the eyeless head of the carcass. He noted the bloody welts on his shirt as he looked down. They stung, and they could possibly get infected, but right now he had much, much bigger fish to fry. He had to drag himself into a room that did not house any cats so that he could somehow set his leg, find a weapon and get the hell out of this house of horrors.

Paul looked to his left and right, trying his best to figure out a potential layout for a home he had never been in. To his right was some linoleum flooring which generally meant kitchen, the left looked to be his best avenue of escape. The carpeted hallway was less than fifteen feet away, might as well have been a mile with the condition he was in.

"Here goes nothing," Paul said, trying his best to prepare himself. He positioned his hands on the flooring and moved his ass a few inches towards his destination. Then he dragged the rest of him to follow. A couple of the toms, who had not seemed interested in the least with him, now stopped their various inactivities to see what he was doing. Paul repeated the same step until he was at the far edge of the coffee table. The largest cat, a black and white, looked at Paul, then the direction he was heading, and padded silently past him and into the inky blackness of the hallway.

This oughta be fun, Paul thought as he moved again. This time, he would not have the table to rest against. His head swam as his dangling foot caught on the rug for a moment and then released. He nearly bit his tongue in half in an effort to stay coherent. Blood pooled in his mouth and flowed out the sides, mingling with tears rolling from his eyes. For the first time, Paul thought that he might finally succumb to what all of humanity strove to avoid – death. It hung heavy in the air.

He waited long minutes, his tongue searing from the teeth wounds. His hands enduring their own unique form of torture, begging to be raised from their perch. The iron-rich scent of Paul's blood sent the cats into another frenzy. At least three that he could see were advancing. "Fuck you!" he screamed. They halted, but they did not retreat. Paul looked down at his broken leg. He could just make out the problem he was having. The open-ended eyelets on his boot, which were of the fast-lacing design used for speed in cold weather, were now catching on the fabric of the rug. The placement of his foot now ensured that every time he pulled back, they would snag.

He needed to remove the boot or somehow brace his foot in the upright position, although neither idea was something he knew how to accomplish. Going forward was not an option, not like this. Paul scooted back towards the table to catch his breath and re-think his strategy. He noted his boot did not seem so inclined to grab the carpet in that direction. He was not sure if it had to do with the pile of the carpet or if there were more pulled carpet loops heading down the hallway for which he could snag on. But at the moment, the kitchen seemed like the better option, but to what end?

"I can get a knife!" he said aloud. A cat that had been slinking closer tilted its head. *That is, if they have fallen on the floor*, he thought sourly. "At least it will be easier to slide on the linoleum." Paul started his long migration down the coffee table and towards the kitchen. His boot did not seem to be snagging on the rug and he thanked his stars for that small fact. His right hand slipped out from under him as he splashed down onto the linoleum floor and into a puddle of an unidentifiable liquid. His shoulder and most of his lower back became soaked in the foul ammonia-laced smell.

"Cat piss," he said disgustedly. Paul pushed himself back up with a grunt and took a longer survey of the room where he had decided to make his final stand. A small island dominated the larger than expected kitchen. Cat feces and urine covered much of the flooring. There was no clear path to the cabinets where he was headed. The cats lined up at the entryway as he sloshed his way in. Wet, warm piles of shit slogged through his splayed fingers; urine soaked his pants and burned as it came in contact with his bloody hands. As he made his way further in, the cats followed. Some jumped up on the island, others on the counter tops where they had been 'shooed' by their previous master at least a hundred times. That was, until they ate her.

The ones on the counter followed Paul, step for step, as he slid below them. Paul looked up at their watchful, wary, hungry gazes. "I was wrong about you guys. I should have listened to Mike. He always said you were nothing more than rats with a 'c'."

He finally got to the corner he had been heading for. He rested for a moment with his back against the cabinet. He tilted his head back. A cat was no more than six inches from his face, peering down at him. Paul reached up and was able to wrench it down from its high ground advantage by its ear. The cat screamed in terror as he used the momentum to throw it against the island. His grip had not been secure enough to deliver a deathblow, but the supposed weakness was more than enough for the other cats to descend on it and disembowel the cat before it could muster any sort of defense.

"Can't we all get along?" Paul panted, trying to humor himself. It worked badly. For the first time, Paul noticed the blood trail he had left coming into the kitchen. The volume of it alarmed him. "I don't feel woozy," he said aloud. "Better get moving." Paul noticed as he spoke, the cats didn't relent their hunt, but they did sort of hesitate. Their movements were more tentative, like they were being given a reminder of how times were. Paul turned his gaze on the cabinet he was resting against. Traditionally, corner cabinets were the biggest in the whole house and sometimes they did not even have inside walls. If that were the case, he thought he might be able to fit in it. He wasn't sure what he'd do at that point, but it would buy him some time and maybe there was the off chance that a machine gun was in there next to a deluxe first aid kit and a charged cell phone with Mike on speed dial.

With some difficulty, Paul moved to the side a bit and opened the cabinet. He was not disappointed by the size. It could have been bigger, maybe large enough to fit a chaise lounge, but it was at least big enough that he could get in. He wouldn't be in the lap of luxury, but he'd be out of immediate danger as he regrouped. He grabbed boxes of cereal and threw some at the cats as they skittered away.

"Whoa," he told himself just as he was about to toss an unopened box of Trix. "I'm chucking food." And then he saw some stuff that could do some real damage, cans of tuna. The force of throwing the cans pulled on his broken leg, but it was worth it when the third can cracked into the skull of one of the bigger toms that had been waiting, aloof in the background. The cat wasn't dead, but the can had inflicted some heavy damage. The cat had fallen over and its right front and rear paws were twitching violently. It had enough sense to hiss and spit as the other cats turned to look at him and decide if he had just come on the meal plan. The cat tried desperately to pull its damaged skull up off the floor, but it was not to be. It put up a fight and took at least one eye out of the attackers, maybe more, but Paul wasn't completely watching. He was busy pulling out shelves so that he would fit in better. He wished it didn't hurt so much to throw things or he would have tossed the heavy pressboard shelving into the food fight going on at the other side of the kitchen.

Paul wished he had a can opener. He thought he could just about make it to the end of days with the amount of canned food in here. But his hopes of finding anything that would further his ability to escape this house were nixed. Besides a healthy dose of cereal, canned food and Top-Ramen noodles, there were no melee weapons or meds. Paul put his hand into the cabinet and banged the back of his head on the counter top as he placed his ass inside.

"Damn, that hurt!" he said, desperately wanting to rub the spot, but afraid of losing his balance and tipping over. He did not think he could stand another onrush of pain like he had earlier.

His words this time had an undesired effect. The cats were finishing their latest meal and his words pulled their lapsed attention back to him. And they understood escape. Paul was halfway in when five or six cats made a mad dash for him. Hunger outweighed the harm he could inflict. Death by the other cats was merciful in comparison to the hunger that ripped through their stomachs. Two went for his face. Paul picked up a can of corn and caught one of the cats in the chest as it launched at him. The other cat bit down hard on his cheek. Hot needles drilled through his eyes would have been less painful as the cat latched onto his neck with all four sets of claws. Paul was writhing in agony; the thrashing was setting his broken foot flailing about, but even that could not compare to the vermin adhering to his face and neck. He slammed it on the side of the face with the corn. The cat's teeth tore through his cheek, taking a strip of meat as it was pounded away.

Blood from his neck pulsed out. It didn't arc and he hoped the cat hadn't gotten deep enough to do arterial damage. The other cats had gone for Paul's damaged leg while he was distracted. He had not even felt the pressure as they dove on it, ripping at the frayed jeans, trying in desperation to get at the blood and muscle below. Now that the cat had been taken away from his face, his body and mind struggled in an effort to catch up with what was happening. Pain receptors flared to life as cat fangs sank deeply into his flesh. Paul could not even pull his leg away as more and more cats began to pounce. The accumulated weight was too much. Paul struck out with his good leg. As he kicked one away, seemingly two would take its place. They no longer feared taking damage; they had blood in their mouths now and they would not be dissuaded.

Paul's screams filled the night as the cats tore through the denim. Ragged bloody strip after ragged bloody strip of skin, muscle and tendon were torn from his leg. Shock began to shut down nerve centers in his brain, and cognitive thought was becoming increasingly difficult. Paul hardly recognized the lower portion of his leg as two cats tore it from his body and fought viciously for the rights to eat it. Vast amounts of blood poured from the wound; cats became covered in it. Their cries of triumph were the last thing Paul heard as his head slammed back against the far end of the inside cabinet. It was three am in the world of man, but that meant little now.

Chapter Twenty-Three – Mike Journal Entry 13

So ends Journal Number Five. I did not get as much accomplished as I had hoped, yet I paid dearly for it. The world yet spins, but it has become a measurably darker place. Eliza stands on the threshold of victory and I fear that nothing stands in her path to stop her.

Chapter Twenty-Four

"My cat's paws are always cold, I've believe it's due to her walking upon the souls of the dead." Book of Talbotisms #76

"So you're telling me that you and BT both felt Paul?" Gary asked as they walked away from Mary's house. Josh watched them from his bedroom upstairs, eagerly awaiting their return. Deneaux was watching them from the living room window with what appeared to be the exact opposite expression.

"Paul's passing," Mike said. It sounded a lot stranger in daylight like maybe he had imagined it, but it was a pretty powerful feeling this morning.

"I hope you're wrong," Gary said.

"Me too," Mike said in earnest, but his words rang hollow. He might have some doubts about what he felt, but not enough to overcome them.

They walked in silence for a little while longer. Gary, for some reason, just couldn't seem to let the quietness of the day hold. Maybe he also did not want to dwell on the fact that they were more likely heading out on a body recovery than a rescue.

"Sure aren't many zombies for a zombie apocalypse," he said, looking around.

"And that's a problem for you?" Mike asked sarcastically.

"I'm just saying, that you'd think they'd be everywhere. And here we are, just strolling down the middle of the road, like we own the place."

"I for one, am not complaining, brother. I would much rather be strolling than running for my life. You should be thankful, too, because we both know I can run laps around you."

"Not if I tripped you."

"Nice, you tell Tracy when you get back what happened."

"Forget it, I'd rather get eaten." He laughed for a sec.

They had been criss-crossing streets with no real objective. They were just looking for something, anything. Mike thought about calling out or maybe even shooting a round into the air and then he thought a little harder about sounding the dinner bell. Just because there were no zombies here right now, in no way meant that they weren't around in big bunches.

"I don't know about this, Gary."

"About what?"

"I don't know how long we should just keep walking around, aimlessly looking for him."

"Aimlessly?" he asked questioningly. "You mean you're not using your Spidey-sense or something?"

"Spidey-sense?"

"Yeah, don't you have some special powers or something?"

"I wish…maybe we should just get some wheels."

"The noise will attract them."

"I know, but we'll be able to cover more ground, and maybe Paul will hear us."

"I thought you said—"

"I know what I said. I'm trying not to believe what my Spidey-sense is telling me."

"Spidey-sense sucks."

"I agree."

"Whoa! What do we have here?" Gary said, his attention focused ahead of us.

A lone zombie was standing on a small stoop. It did

not, at first, pay them any attention as its gaze was fixated on something small in the side light window to its left.

"That a cat?" Gary asked softly as they got closer. The zombie still not privy to their existence.

"Looks like a small dog. Nope, that's a cat. I can tell by that funky tail-twitching thing they do."

"Someone must be in there," Gary said as we stopped about twenty-five feet from the house. "No way that cat could have survived so long without some help...and it looks pretty fat."

Another cat came up next to the large gray cat; they both seemed to be staring at the men. But this wasn't with imploring, "help us" eyes; this was more like something predatory. "Do they look like they want to eat us?" Mike asked Gary. Their zombie friend finally turned around. Mike would swear its eyes got big as it noticed them.

"I don't know about them, but he sure looks hungry."

"You want the honors?" Mike asked Gary, as the zombie headed towards their location.

"I'll shoot it, but you have to go into the cat house first." Gary blew a hole through the back of the zombie's head before Mike could even utter his response. It wasn't like they had a choice anyway. Zombies would come running. They, however, would not stay out long if they could not find anything worth their while.

The zombie was still twitching as Mike made his way up to the porch. A third cat joined the other two who disturbingly had not moved even after Gary took his shot.

"These cats are freaking me out."

"Get in the house. I swear I hear running feet," Gary said with a wide-eyed expression, doing a quick three sixty of their area.

Mike knocked quickly on the door. "Hi, we're friendly and we'd like to come in. Please don't shoot us."

"That wasn't very convincing."

"I'm all ears if you have something better." They

heard no sound, but a fourth cat was now peering out the side light at them. Mike tried the door handle. "It's unlocked."

"Get in, we'll try our luck in there," Gary said, as he pretty much pushed Mike in. Six cats with tails flicking back and forth were looking up at them cautiously. Gary shut the door behind Mike, nearly stepping on a cat in his haste to peek outside the side light.

"Zombies! I knew I heard them coming. What is that smell?" Gary asked, finally turning around and taking in the view of forty or fifty cats that had now assembled in the room.

"Wow, this sucks," Mike said. The cats weren't advancing, but they also weren't retreating. The ammonia smell of abundant cat urine was prevalent as were the feces that littered everything, but there was also something sinister, some underlying smell that he knew, but was unwilling to identify. Mike would have written down now that it was death, plain and simple, but at that time, his mind struggled to keep away from that realization. Add to the fact that Gary's gagging wasn't helping the situation at all.

Some cats were mostly fixated on Mike, but in Gary's moment of weakness, he saw some of the pests moving in closer. They halted their advance as zombies began to slam into the framework of the house. Gary's head shot up. "Is that blood?" he asked, pointing to the floor a few feet past some of the cats.

The garish, orange-flecked linoleum which Mike imagined led to the kitchen was dotted in reddish brown splotches.

"It looks like it. Is anyone home?" Mike called, hoping to reestablish some normalcy to the situation. The cats seemed to get a little hesitant at the sound of his voice, but they didn't take off and retreat to a safe place. "Come on, man! We're on the second rung of the food ladder, Talbot," Mike said, trying to steel himself for what needed to be done. "Third, if you include sharks."

"Has Tracy been nominated for Sainthood yet?" Gary asked.

"Just watch my back."

"From the zombies or the cats?" he asked.

"The cats, definitely the cats."

"Then I'm coming with you."

They moved a foot forward, the cats yielded half that, seeming to grow bolder as they stepped deeper into the house.

"They've gotten in behind us, Mike. What the hell is going on?"

"I'd say that they're pretty hungry."

Mike's trepidation increased as he got closer to the kitchen opening. The cats seemed very reluctant to yield the ground to their front. They were almost protective, like they had a prize they were unwillingly to share. A cat actually bit his boot as he crossed in, Mike gently kicked it away, not quite willing to add animal cruelty to his list of transgressions. He had never been a huge cat fan, but he'd never had reason to hate them until he walked into that kitchen.

"Oh God," Mike said softly. Gary retched behind him.

A shredded human, bones glistening wetly with the remnants of bodily fluids and cat saliva stared back at them with an eyeless gaze. Its jaw bone was missing as was a portion of its lower leg. All that remained was a shock of hair on top and strips of blue denim. It was the white gold wedding band lying a few feet from the body that brought Mike to the full realization of who lay before him.

Mike whirled, quicker than any of the cats could respond and lashed out with his heavy boot. The crack of ribs as he launched a cat into the far wall was only superseded by his satisfaction as he came down heavily on the spine of another. It wriggled its head uselessly from side to side, its legs now a useless jumble of spare parts.

The cats were mewling and scurrying about, some running, some defending.

"What is going on, Mike?" Gary asked. He was as scared as Mike had ever seen him.

"That's Paul on the floor there and these fucking things did it!" Mike screamed as he lashed out at anything that was foolish enough to get within striking range. Within five minutes, he had killed or wounded at least a dozen of them. The rest had seen the folly of trying to tackle two full grown, healthy, armed and defensive men. Mike had received more than a few razor-sharp claw slashes, but that had only added fuel to the fire that the cats had ignited.

He didn't know if Gary had gone on the offensive at all, but he had protected his back as some of the cats tried to launch themselves at him from varying pieces of furniture. Mewls of pain and rage echoed from around the house. They'd be back, most likely waiting for the cover of darkness.

"Cowards!" Mike screamed. He was shaking with emotions that fluctuated wildly from pain to rage to mourning. Gary grabbed him in a big hug.

"It'll be alright, brother," he kept saying over and over.

But it wouldn't be, now or ever. This was one more hard-stop marker in life that Mike would never be able to step back over. There would be life with his best friend of almost thirty years and then there would be a much dimmer life with him gone after. Mike sobbed into his brother's shoulder to the point where his head ached and a good dry cleaner would never be able to get the snot out of the jacket.

"We need to bury him," Mike finally managed to get out.

"I feel the same way, but I don't really want to stay here long enough for the zombies to leave so that we can do that. Maybe we can head out the backyard and come back."

Gary's idea was valid in almost every way, but Mike

could not leave his friend here with the cats to pick through whatever remained of him.

"The backyard it is, but we're burning this fucker down," Mike said with rage-fueled words.

Mike scoured the house, looking for some sort of accelerant to make sure the house would burn hot enough to rival the depths of hell. The best he could do was a small bottle of isopropyl alcohol. The cats did not come out, but there was not a room in that house that they were not observed by multiple eyes; the only thing that was stopping them – and barely – was the size discrepancy.

"Mike, you should come here," Gary said from the other side of the house, back from the kitchen Mike was doing his best to avoid.

Mike braced myself and did his best to remember his friend as he had been in life, not the carcass that lay on the floor. Mike almost sobbed when he went in. Gary at some point had draped a blanket over Paul. There would never be any way Mike could thank him properly for that.

"What's up, brother?"

He handed Mike Paul's wedding band. "I think you should be the one to give this back to Erin."

Mike would rather hammer nails through his toes than have to give her back her dead husband's ring. She would never forgive him. He lost two friends today. Mike nodded as he took the ring from Gary's palm.

"The stove is gas," he said.

Mike was still staring at the ring now in his hand. Gary's words merely a jumble of mish-mashed sounds.

"Did you hear me?"

Mike nodded only because he heard the uplifting tone of a question and it seemed appropriate. But he hadn't, not in any cognitive way. Mike was shutting down, the accumulated stress of the entire ordeal was beginning to break him. He had always thought those people that claimed they had an emotional breakdown were weak-minded. That was until he began to suffer through his own, and then he pitied each one of them, because if they had been pushed that far to the brink, something had gone horribly wrong in their lives.

"Mike!" Gary said on the verge of a yell.

"I'm here, I'm here," Mike said like a little kid lost in the woods.

"Where the hell else would you be?" Gary asked.

"Sorry, bro, this is just…"

"I know, Mike, I know. We've all lost ones we love, but there isn't time, not yet. You'll have to grieve later. Can you do that for me?"

Mike stared at him through watery eyes. "When did you become the leader type?"

"You like that?" he asked.

"Not bad…and thank you," Mike said. He wasn't better, not by a long shot and maybe not ever, but he was functioning. Mike was still at the abyss; except now it was to his back. He was not sure if this new precarious position was the best place to be, but it gave him a chance to make this fucked-up world pay, starting with the damn cats.

"The stove is gas," Gary repeated. "And I found matches."

The cats were back at the kitchen entrance. Hunger is a powerful motivator, even more so than the need to breed. And how many species killed each other for the right to do that?

"Do you think they know something is up?" Gary asked as he pulled the stove out to get access to the gas line.

"I wouldn't doubt it. I've read that cats have an open gateway to the spirit world and I bet their ancestors are telling them that these shit birds are about to join them in the afterlife. I would imagine that news isn't sitting too well with them."

A large gray tom strode into the kitchen, emboldening the rest of his clan. Dozens of cats were behind him and back out of eyesight, in the living room.

"How's that going?" Mike asked Gary, never taking his gaze from the large gray, and the accumulating throng. He knew if he broke contact with him or them, they would attack. Mike knew they had size on the cats, but the combined weight of the small predators most likely outweighed them both.

"Got it!" Gary said with a grunt as he stood up with one end of the disconnected piping. The noxious gas fumes combined with the ammonia smell almost put Mike on his ass. Something about the hissing of the escaping gas or the smell triggered the cats into action. Mike noted that the gray had not moved as his minions streamed past.

"Gary, get out of there! We've got to go." Mike hoped his voice wasn't approaching falsetto, but he was scared. Gary never did call him on it, so either he had kept it together better than he thought or Gary was too scared to realize Mike's man-code slip-up.

Gary scrambled over the top of the stove and moved to the backdoor before the cats could attempt to cut off their retreat.

"How many are there?" Gary said, fumbling with wooden matches.

"Enough," Mike told him, and he believed it.

The gray began to shimmer in Mike's line of sight as the room filled with dangerous amounts of liquid propane. His tail stilled, and like a military message, the cats as one unit, struck.

Gary had pulled the back door open and Mike was using his rifle as an ineffectual baseball bat. At least three cats had found purchase on Mike's shins and dug in for the long haul. Their curved claws tore through his skin and the muscle that lay underneath. The pain was excruciating, Mike's first instinct was to reach down and squish their necks, but he knew as soon as he bent down, they would attack his neck and face and then it would be game over. Mike gritted his teeth and kept swinging to dissuade anymore cats from weighing him down. Occasionally, he made contact, even Bucky-Fucking-Dent gets lucky sometimes (If you have an old sports book in your safe-house, look it up; if you're a Red Sox or Yankees fan, you already know).

Mike heard the match as it struck against the box. He'd seen enough Hollywood movies to know a giant explosion was about to ensue. He could smell the sulfur as the match lit and then out of the corner of his eye, he caught a giant flare as Gary lit the rest of the matches in the small cardboard box.

Mike knew he was still alive because the cats on his legs were making him painfully aware of that fact. The fireball of matches passed dangerously close to his head as Gary gently tossed it deeper into the kitchen. Mike felt Gary's hand close around his collar as Gary pushed the storm door open and pulled Mike out with him. They were still falling backwards as a flash of ignited gas blew past them. A wave of burnt fur and hair blew by Mike. The fur came from the cats inside, but the hair was his own. Glass shattered as the fire sought air in a need to increase its size. Two of the cats let go of Mike's legs and were running around wildly in the yard, they were on fire. Mike hoped it took them a long time to die. The third cat was trapped between his legs as he pressed them shut more tightly. The cat was ripping wildly at Mike to get away. He grabbed him by the scruff and pulled him up and away. The cat's claws were lashing out. Mike held it up and punched it as hard as he could squarely in the face. He was confident he had crushed its skull with the blow. Mike dropped it to the ground. It had paid the ultimate price for its betrayal to humanity, and now he was done with it.

"Where's my rifle?" Mike asked.

Gary tackled Mike. "Roll, dumb-ass, roll!!" he was screaming. "You're on fire!" He was pushing Mike around on the ground. Mike might have been thick, but he finally figured out what was going on, as the smell of burning hair and skin did not decrease, but rather increased.

Mike rolled around like his life depended on it, which it did. He was finally not actively burning, but smoke was pouring off him; he looked like he had busted a radiator hose.

"Oh fuck, oh fuck," Gary kept muttering, looking down at his brother.

"Pretty bad?" Mike asked. He was in a great deal of pain, but nothing that compared to the look of despair in his brother's eyes. Odds were, Mike had third degree burns and had burned right through the nerve endings. "Help me up," Mike said, extending a blackened hand.

Gary did not reach to grab it; he thought that maybe Mike's skin would slough off if he did. The house roared behind them as the flames began to engulf the structure.

"Zombies are going to be coming, Gary. Help me up."

"Umm," he said and then he took off.

Mike passed in and out of consciousness for the next few moments as the pain began to catch up with him. Blasts of super-heated air roiled over him as the house blazed. He thought he may have seen the large gray staring at him from the back door, but he couldn't be sure. His corneas had been damaged and vision was becoming increasingly difficult. Burning tabbies streamed from some of the blown out windows just in time for the advancing zombies to hunt them down. Mike watched in horror as bulbous blisters began to form on his arms and hands. He may have cried out in pain, but the noise was lost in the destructive thunder of the flames.

Something passed by his immediate field of vision. He stuck his hands up to stop the ensuing bites, either from cat or zombie. Instead, he was hefted up from under his arms and deposited onto the cold, unyielding steel of a wheelbarrow bottom. They, or at least, the person who was pushing it, were now in motion. The heat from the fire hurt his face as the flames came close on the left side as they passed through the gate that led out to the front yard.

Zombies were everywhere. Mike tried to shut his eyes to the horror, but for some damned reason he couldn't, his eyelids had been seared off.

"What's wrong with me?" Mike asked.

"Don't talk, Mike," Gary said with labored breathing. "You're going to be fine, fine."

Mike had watched enough movies to know that line pretty much meant he was a dead man.

"You gonna make it?" Mike asked him. Gary was in pretty good shape, but running for your life pushing a wheelbarrow didn't really sound conducive to a successful escape.

"Maybe, they haven't seen us yet...Dammit! Said it too soon."

"Gary, leave me, I don't think they'll eat me."

"Don't think?" He paused to catch his breath. "Or know?"

He kept running. The wheelbarrow was about as comfortable, Mike imagined, as the old time, horse-drawn buggies of a bygone era, and probably worse because they at least, had some sort of crude, spring shock absorber.

"Mush," Mike told Gary.

His comment did not elicit a remark. Gary was scared and running for both of their lives and Mike didn't think he had the steam in him to make it.

"Gary, get me out of this thing."

Gary didn't say anything or slow down, at least not consciously, but he was flagging.

"Can't...touch...you," he said.

"If you don't, we're both toast," Mike said and Gary winced. It was not the wording he was looking for. "Now, Gary," Mike said with as much force as he could muster. It wasn't much, but it would have to do.

The wheelbarrow almost tipped as he came to a stop. He quickly came around and picked Mike up underneath his arms, Mike was standing on shaking legs. "Run now!" Mike told him.

He looked to Mike and then directly over his shoulder at the zombies rapidly closing the gap.

"Run fucking now!" Mike told him, gingerly placing his smoldering hand on top of Gary's shoulder. Layers of skin stayed behind as he removed my hand.

"No," he said.

"Gary I…I can hold them from eating me, but I cannot protect the both of us, will you make me watch them kill you? Please don't let that happen."

"Are you sure?" he asked desperately. "I can keep pushing the barrow."

"Absolutely," Mike said, although he had no fucking clue.

"I love you, Mike."

"I love you too, Gary. Now, get the fuck out of here!"

He wanted to hug his brother, but thought better of it. He turned and started to run. Mike stood there for a few seconds, contemplating how he was going to get his legs moving, when cats in varying states of disrepair began to stream by. Some had been burnt as badly as Mike he guessed. He'd yet to take a complete inventory. Some had bites taken out of them and at least one or two looked like they might survive the entire ordeal. And then Mike heard their pursuers; zombies were coming up behind him and he didn't have the strength to even turn around and look.

"Time to find a happy place," Mike said aloud. Gary gave one long, woeful look from a few houses down before he turned the corner and was out of sight.

Chapter Twenty-Five
"What do you mean you left him behind!?" BT was asking, clearly agitated.
"You weren't there, BT, he begged me to. I didn't want to," Gary said, finally catching his breath.
"I know, I know how he is. Stupid Talbot and his death wish persona."
Mrs. Deneaux had not said anything from the corner of the room, but secretly she was overjoyed. Surely any questions of her culpability in the death of Brian and Paul's disappearance would die with Michael.
"You ready to go back out and get his ass?"
"You know it."
"You coming?" BT asked Deneaux.
"Not a chance. He got himself into this mess, he will have to get himself out," she replied.
"I would have expected nothing less," BT said flatly. "That's the woman whose words you want to believe," BT said to Mary. "If she had to step two feet out of her way to not step over you, she wouldn't do it. We'll be back."
Josh raced out the door before his mother could stop him.
"Josh! What are you doing?" Mary cried from the front door; she was too afraid to follow him outside.
"I'm the man of the household now and I'm going to help them get Michael Talbot back here," he answered not once raising his voice, just stating a factual matter.
"You will do no such thing!" she screamed, her face turning a bright crimson.
"I am and I will. Let's go," he motioned to BT and

Gary. "I know all the short cuts around here."

"Joshua Hilop! Get back here!" she screamed uselessly. "Do something!" she asked BT desperately.

"He's safer with us than with her," he told Mary, looking back at the hawk-eyed Deneaux.

She grabbed BT's arm, but he shrugged her off. "I don't have time for this little family drama. I have a brother to retrieve. I promise he'll be as safe with us as he would be at your house."

Mary was now beginning to doubt the sanctity of her own home, and looked to be moments away from joining the rescue party. "You hurry up and get back here," she said to Josh. "I love you."

"Mom, you're embarrassing me."

Mary went back into the house, shut the door and watched the small party of three head down the street from the vantage point of her living room window.

"They're probably all going to die," Deneaux said from the chair across the room. She lit a cigarette and took a long slow drag.

"What?" Mary didn't think that Deneaux had just uttered those words, because no one with a soul could have. She chalked up her missed hearing to stress. "There's no smoking in this house."

"Sure there isn't," Mrs. Deneaux said, shaking her ash on the carpet.

Chapter Twenty-Six

Tracy was alternating between sitting at the radio, pretending to read a series of books she couldn't get into and working on the beefed-up fortifications Ron was installing when Henry started barking. A sound that was much closer to a sound a seal might make than any dog.

Tracy crossed the room quickly, trying to follow Henry's line of sight, but since he was looking at a wall, she didn't understand what he was getting all riled up about.

From Ron's front door, you could see the long gravel roadway that was his street and that was where she went. She was slightly hesitant to open the door, lest something previously unimaginable was on the other side. But Henry never turned to look at her as she disengaged the lock and pulled the door open quickly. Kind of like the Band-Aid removal method – do it fast before it can sting.

Ron had come quickly with rifle in hand, almost pushing past Tracy to shield her from whatever Henry was going on about. Henry was all about conservation of movement and energy and would only reveal his true inner-wolf when someone he loved was in danger.

"What's going on?" Ron asked wide-eyed, looking around expectantly for any signs of danger.

"He just started barking, but he keeps looking at that wall," Tracy said, clearly confused.

"Mice maybe?" Ron asked, trying to fill in the knowledge gap.

"Henry? Barking at mice? Not unless they are carrying his cookies away. What's on the other side of that wall?"

"That's south…so about a fifty-foot clearing and then the woods," Ron answered.

"South?" Tracy asked and she began to turn ashen.

"What's the matter?" Ron asked in alarm. "What's south?"

"North Carolina." Tracy was slammed with a heavy dose of vertigo. "I'm…I'm sorry," she said as Ron helped her to a chair.

"Let me get you some water." Ron was back in a few seconds; Tracy felt a little better as she drank. Henry barked a few more times and then yelped once before he walked out of the room with his head down. Tracy's glass shattered to the ground as she passed out.

Chapter Twenty-Seven

"We were about three or four streets over," Gary said.

"By the Fredericks' house?" Josh asked, cutting through some hedges that had looked impenetrable.

"I don't know...how would I know that?" Gary asked.

"Did you see a bright, bright blue house?" Josh said, extending his hands.

Gary couldn't see how stretching your hands equated to brightness, but he went along. He thought for a few moments. He hadn't really been taking in any qualities of the neighborhood. Houses, even garish ones, tend to become less important when one is looking for things that will possibly get them killed. "I don't...wait, I think it was further up the street. I kept thinking that I hoped they got a good deal on the paint because it was pretty ugly."

"Do we know where we're going?" BT asked, clearly agitated.

"Yup." Josh seemed to be reveling in this. He'd probably played this game a hundred times before, hiding from the enemy. It would have never been a real life scenario like it was now, but practice does have a way of making things perfect. Josh pulled two slats from the fence to the side so he could fit his slender form. BT ripped another five off to get through. Josh did not seem pleased, but he pressed on. Within a few minutes, they were assailed with the smell.

"This is the place," Gary said.

"What gave it away?" BT asked, wanting to hold his nose.

Josh opened the gate from the homeowners' backyard

and was heading to the front when BT grabbed him by the collar and lifted him off the ground.

"Hold on. Gary, go check," BT said. "You're the fastest at the moment," he added when Gary passed on by.

"I think that honor goes to Josh, but I'll check."

"Any chance you'll let me down now?" Josh asked, his legs kicking in the air.

"Do not go anywhere, unless it is back to your house," BT said as he gently placed the boy on the ground.

Gary got up close to the side of the house and inched himself around, taking a quick peek. He immediately turned back to where Josh and BT were. "Send him home NOW!" Gary yelled as quietly as he could.

"Now, kid, go home! Do not turn around! Do you understand me!" BT yelled.

Gary had started firing his rifle. BT urged Josh in the opposite direction as he brought his rifle to the ready. He was wholly unprepared for what he witnessed as he turned the corner to stand side by side with Gary.

Michael was completely surrounded by zombies. His skin was the color of burnt hamburger and large curled flaps of skin were peeling away from his singed chest and shoulders. These were being torn off by zombies, struggling to get at the flesh. Michael was screaming as pink, oozing, tender flesh was exposed while the zombies tore off the blackened parts.

At least a dozen zombies were dropped by Gary's and BT's rifles fire before Mike's attackers took any notice. At first, two or three went after the pair and were quickly dispatched, but as Michael went to his knees and then his face, the rest turned and went for the new meat.

Gary was dry firing, screaming in rage as the zombies approached. BT was afraid that Gary was going to go into berserk mode and just start swinging his rifle like a club. BT was getting low on ammo. "Let's go, Gary."

"He's my brother!" Gary yelled, looking up at BT's

face with tears coming from his eyes.

"There's nothing more we can do here."

Gary took one final look back at his brother who had not moved since his head made impact with the pavement. He sobbed as he ran, tears so occluding his vision, he had to be guided by BT.

Chapter Twenty-Eight

"What is the purpose of waiting here, sister? Now is the time to pull back and regroup. Michael is long gone now, yet we have wasted days here."

"We have wasted nothing," Eliza hissed. "While you have been having secret rendezvous' with the enemy, I have been summoning a vast zombie army to destroy everything in our path toward getting Michael, starting with this little town."

With Eliza's human sympathizers out of the way, Tomas had hoped his sister would give up her foolish quest, or at least, postpone it. In the meantime, he had kept tabs on Michael when he could. His former father was getting good at disguising his presence. Mike had delivered a victorious blow, and for the life of him, Tomas could not figure out why the man had not collected his things and gone home. Even with the infection in BT, that should have only delayed him a day at the most. And now his sister was planning on bringing thousands upon thousands of zombies to this town.

"What do you hope to accomplish here?" Tomas asked his sister.

"Either you are still trying to cover for him or you are not as powerful as you imagine yourself to be, but Michael is still around. And even now, he uses his limited powers to save himself. If only he would fully reveal himself to me, I would finish him off myself."

Tomas was taken aback, he had not known his sister realized Michael was still here, but what was more unsettling was he did not know Mike was in distress.

"Don't be so confused, brother. I have blocked you

from him. This is one battle the great and mighty Michael Talbot will need to finish on his own without any outside help." Eliza laughed as Tomas tried desperately to get around whatever she had put in place to hinder his ability to talk to him.

Tomas could feel the psychic push of thousands of zombies as they closed the distance from their original locations to get to where their mistress beckoned as he extended his powers to try and encompass Mike.

"This is insanity, sister, he is gone from here."

Eliza was still for a moment as if she were listening for a pin to drop on a faraway floor. "Perhaps you are right for once, little brother," she said as she turned to walk away.

Tomas was relieved, maybe something could be salvaged out of this after all. Then the barrier that had been erected between Michael and himself crashed to the ground. Tomas nearly fell to his knees as he felt the screams of Michael, and then there was silence, soulless black silence. "What have you done, Eliza!?" Tomas screamed, chasing his sister down.

"I have done nothing, dear brother."

"Why did you let me hear that and then cut it off again?" he demanded.

"I wanted you to hear that, but I most certainly did not cut it off at the end. That was the end. Michael Talbot is no more. He is no longer alive in a dead world!"

Prologue

Blood Stone Part 2

Corporal Tenson could not believe his luck of late and he attributed it all to the blood red stone he had found two weeks previous at the destroyed Lakota village. He had been promoted to sergeant. His commanding officer, whom he could not stand, had swallowed a bullet and he was unimaginably wealthy if he could ever bring himself to sell the stone.

He had been so paranoid about possessing the stone, he had not even showed anyone, not even his best friend Aaron Gentry, a corporal in the same regiment he was in.

"What gives?" Aaron asked. He had been sleeping on his cot when he heard his friend rustling around.

"What are you talking about?" Scott Tenson asked, stashing a small bag quickly into his front pocket.

"I've seen you pull out that bag at least a dozen times and you just stare at it."

"You should just mind your own business," Scott shot back a little testily.

"Sorry, just looking for something to talk about. It's been so boring around here since the old man shot himself. I can't believe he killed himself. I guess I would have too if I came home and my whole family was murdered. Some are saying that it was the shaman from the Lakota tribe we destroyed, seeking revenge."

This had been a favorite topic of conversation within the unit since it had happened. The stories ranged from the mundane: the colonel had come home and discovered his wife was cheating and had murdered his family then killed himself; to the semi-paranormal and favorite among the men: that the medicine man's spirit had done it as revenge; to the completely farfetched: a white witch had taken the colonel's family hostage and forced him to attack the Indians. Not many believed that particular story, but speculation on it made the long nights go by quicker.

Maybe it was the hour of the night, maybe he was sick of hearing the same topic of conversation repeated over and over, but Corporal Tenson did something he never planned on doing.

"Want to see what I picked up at that camp?"

Gentry sat up. "Is that what's in that pouch? Do you have a scalp or something? I thought they'd smell, but I haven't smelled anything."

"It's not a scalp. Check this out," Tenson said, turning the pouch over into his hand. The large red stone dropped into his palm.

Gentry inhaled sharply and then reached out to grab it, Tenson pulled his hand back.

"Sorry," Tenson said, letting his friend grab the stone.

"What is it?" Gentry asked, holding it up to the lantern.

"My ticket out of the cavalry, and into a life of luxury."

"Have you found out how much it's worth?"

"No I haven't told anyone I've got it. I'm too afraid they'll make me turn it over to the captain."

"Nobody knows you have it?"

"Just you now," Tenson said, smiling.

"I've got to show you something then," Gentry said conspiratorially. He handed the stone back to Tenson.

Gentry reached under his cot and pulled something out that caught a glint of light a moment before he plunged it into Tenson's stomach. The long bowie knife ripped through his stomach, spleen and kidney and brushed up against his spinal cord. The pain had been too intense to even formulate a scream. Gentry was not going to give him the opportunity anyway. He clamped his free hand over his friend's mouth and twisted the knife back and forth as more and more pain and shock blazed through Tenson's eyes. Gentry spoke.

"I'm sorry, my friend, I really am. You saved my life

once, and now I'm taking yours. It hardly seems fair. But I fucking hate it here and now I've got a way out and I had to take it, no matter what expense you had to pay for it."

Gentry waited until he was completely sure his friend (although that didn't seem like the right word anymore) was dead before extracting his knife from Tenson's mid-section. He then wiped it off on Tenson's blanket and covered him up with it. He quickly grabbed anything of any value in addition to the stone, which he clutched greedily, and slipped quietly into the night.

***

Eliza had watched the entire battle from her higher vantage point. She was mildly impressed with the Lakota's savagery. Here were a people who had already lost everything dear to them, and still they fought viciously. She hoped the colonel would live, if only to be reunited with his bride, but either way, all that mattered was that the medicine man died.

She waited until the cavalry men departed as she walked amid the smoking ruins of the destroyed village. The Indians lay where they had been struck down. She checked each one of them, yet she could not find the shaman. A little known feeling rose in her breast; it was a sense of unease. She checked the only teepee that was not burning. It was the largest in the village and, by its decoration, she figured it was a ceremonial gathering place.

The shaman was in there, but he was dead. He had been set in a place of honor in the center of the room, enshrouded in soft blankets made of deer and bison hide. Instead of her unease slipping away, it grew.

"This man died before the battle," she said as she walked around him. She ripped the shroud off him, looking for a wound that could have caused his demise. She savagely ripped his clothes off, unsure as to the root of her anger. She kicked his body over onto his stomach when the front did not reveal any damage.

She kicked him again, this time from spite when she could not glean any information. His broken body hit the far side of the large teepee and rolled to a stop as Eliza strode out. Had her anger not burned so brightly, she would have been able to pick up on the faint traces of the information she so desperately sought.

***

Tomas had been one state removed when he began to hear rumors about the cursed cavalry unit. Each story sounded more fantastic than the last. But he had been around the frontier long enough to know that people with too much time on their hands like a fantastic tale. He did not sit up and take notice until some of these tales began to hint about a white witch, her cruelty only rivaled by her beauty.

"Eliza," he muttered, draining his tankard of beer.

"Hey…where you going?" the old grizzled man at the bar asked. "You've already paid for two drinks, I promised you the entire story."

"Buy yourself a third," Tomas said, flipping him a nickel and heading for the door.

The old man continued as if his drinking buddy had remained behind. "So they say that this white witch took the colonel's family for some devilry until the colonel brought her the head of a great Indian chief. And when he came back without it, she had killed his family and then him. And then she cast some kind of spell on the men in the platoon. Seems they started killing each other. I think the witch part is made up. I think it's more the medicine man sent some bad medicine." The old man snorted and laughed at his own word play. "The Indians are some tricky ones. You have to be real careful how you kill them or they can rise up out their grave and get you," he cackled. "Barkeep! Another drink for me and my friend." The old man waved the nickel around.

The bartender shook his head and poured two more glasses. Who was he to judge? A nickel was a nickel.

Tomas bought the best horse he could find in the region and pushed the animal as hard as he dared. After five days of hard riding, and asking anyone he could for information on the battle site, he finally found himself amongst the ruins. Not much was left. It was mostly just pieces of shattered pottery here and there. After nearly a month, any bones of the Indians still left remaining from the scavengers had been picked clean. The village was nearly reclaimed by the land, save one large teepee. Tomas alit from his horse and strode purposefully towards it.

He said a small prayer upon entering. He noted the many footprints of animals that had entered in here previous to him, nearly obscuring the soft prints of the white witch.

"Eliza," he said as he pressed his palm down onto the heel of the depression. He looked over to where the shriveled husk of a man lay. He walked over to him. "Why have the scavengers not taken your sustenance?" Tomas asked. "And more importantly, what did my sister want with you?"

Tomas gently turned the man onto his back. His facial muscles had pulled up and dried into a perpetual smile. Tomas grabbed the blankets that had been strewn around the large teepee, almost shattering an ornate bowl as he grabbed the last one.

He turned the bowl over and over. "This is ceremonial," he said to himself. "That makes you the shaman," he said as he picked the man up and placed him on the blankets he had piled up. "Eliza, what trouble have you gotten yourself into now?" he asked as he left the ghost town with bowl in hand.

Tomas' next destination was Durango, Colorado it was where the Cavalry 3rd Regiment was stationed at Camp Foster. He needed to find out more information and the best place was always the local saloon. Liquor tended to make tongues wag, as did his power of persuasion.

"Who'd you say you were again?" the soldier slurred, trying his best to focus on the person in front of him. "This is some powerful whiskey."

"That doesn't matter," Tomas said pouring the man, boy really, another shot. "You were saying about the curse?" Tomas asked.

"Nuffin's been the same since we attacked that Injun village. Now I don't normally care one way or the other about killing them, but these ones weren't doing anything, they weren't near to any settlement or anything. And there was something about that place." The soldier shuddered just thinking about it. "It was dead there. Does that make sense? I mean before we even got there, you could just sense that something wasn't right. Like the angel of darkness himself had settled upon the place." The young soldier took another gulp of liquid courage.

"It was no angel...and he was a she," Tomas said, pouring the man another shot in his drained glass.

"What?" the man asked looking up from his glass. When Tomas didn't answer right away, the soldier continued. "The Indians put up a good fight, but it almost felt like it was for show. That doesn't even make sense to me." The soldier paused, trying to grasp the correct words. "I...I mean they already seemed dead like they had nothing left to live for. Damndest thing though, we wiped out that whole village and there wasn't a woman or a child among them. I mean normally, your first thought would be, yeah, raiding party, but it was their summer encampment. You could tell by the large gathering tent, that things mean everything to them. They wouldn't take it on raids."

"Could the woman and children have left before you got there?" Tomas asked.

"I asked myself that," he said, wiping the back of his hand across his mouth. "But we hit them so fast and so hard, they couldn't have escaped. And I know we surprised them because most of 'em were coming out of their teepees when we hit. It wasn't like they had any advance warning or anything."

"And this Colonel Broward, he led the charge?" Tomas prodded.

"Yeah, funny thing that."

"How so?"

"The colonel never went out on a mission, ever. And he was hell-bent on getting out to this little fly shit of an Indian village and destroying it. We barely slept, or hardly ate. Eight horses died from being pushed over the edge of exhaustion. Those were some good horses."

"To say nothing of the Indians that died," Tomas added.

"What are you trying to get at, mister?" the soldier said. "I lost four friends out there," he said as he rose up.

"Nothing, I meant nothing by it. Please sit…have another drink," Tomas said, smiling.

"I think maybe I've had enough," the soldier said, about to turn and walk away.

"You'll leave when I say you can," Tomas said forcibly.

The soldier stopped mid-stride and began to size Tomas up. He quickly sat back down. "One more drink for the road sounds good," the soldier said as if he had been thinking that all along.

"You were saying?"

The soldier was smiling as Tomas poured him another drink as if the last few seconds had not happened at all.

"I mean not only did the colonel come with us, he led the charge. He looked like a man possessed. Like the devil himself was on his tail."

"Probably was," Tomas said seriously.

The soldier paused to reflect on Tomas' answer. And then nodded his head in agreement.

"The colonel almost left without even burying our

dead. I think Staff Sergeant Reddings would have shot him. So we buried our men, said a few short prayers and headed back, almost as fast as we had headed out there. Would have, too, if the horses could have taken it."

"Was the colonel looking for anything?"

"Looking? No. Like I said, the colonel couldn't wait to get the hell out of there, like he was late for his own death." The soldier laughed at his own quip. "Which I guess he was, considering he came home to a dead family. Then he killed himself."

"So he didn't kill them?"

"Why would he kill them? There were rumors that he had, but I was the one on the burial detail. I had to help get those bodies out of the house. I've seen a lot of dead. The colonel's brains splattered all over his portrait will be something I can never drink away," he said brandishing his drink. "But the kids and the wife? There was something wrong there; they were all shriveled up like peaches left out in the desert sun. None of them had a drop of blood in them and there wasn't a drop of any spilled anywhere in the house. And I got the same feeling I did at that damned Indian village, something bad had been there, it was like I could feel the evil still lurking in the shadows."

"Did the colonel leave a note or anything?"

The soldier merely shook his head from side to side. "I have fourteen months left on my enlistment. I need to get out of this unit before it gets me," the soldier said desperately.

"Before what gets you?"

"The curse. We're cursed now." The soldier sneered as if to say 'how do you not know?' "I've been hearing that the medicine man of the tribe we killed had cursed the colonel for something and that was why the colonel wanted to kill him, but the curse didn't die with the medicine man. He was able to do some magic that made the colonel's family dry up. And he somehow turned friend against friend."

"How so?" Tomas asked.

"Gentry and Tenson have been friends long before I ever joined the unit. And then one morning, neither one shows for revelry. Of course, it's me that gets to go and check in on their tent. Tenson's still in his rack, but I know he ain't never going anywhere again. His blanket is soaked in his own blood and Gentry is gone. At first, I just can't believe that Gentry did it. They were as close as brothers. But he was gone and so was his stuff. I need to get out of here," the soldier said, placing his head between his hands.

"How long ago was that?" Tomas asked.

"Almost a month," the soldier said, looking up. "You want to see it?"

"See what?"

"The tent, it's still there. The captain is waiting for a magistrate to come out here to witness the crime scene."

"Yes, very much so."

Ten minutes later a swaying Private Bucks was at the tent flap looking around for anyone that might catch them, unwillingly to go in where he would be less noticed. Tomas did as the private asked and did not move or pick up anything. He could sense Eliza's presence here, but in a much more muted form. He could not explain what he felt, just that in some shape, way or form she had been here.

"My sister was here," Tomas said more aloud to taste the tangibility of his question in the open air.

"Your sister?" Bucks asked.

Tomas looked over to the private. "Someone you would be better off never meeting."

"Your sister is the white witch?" Bucks asked as he let go of the tent flap and began to back up.

Tomas moved quickly to halt his retreat. Bucks barely had time to register how strong the boy was.

"What do you know of this 'white witch'?"

"Nothing. I don't know nothing. Let me go. I knew there was something wrong with you," Bucks said, trying his best to release the iron grip around his forearm.

"I will let you go when you tell me what you know," Tomas said as he dragged the wide-eyed private back into the confines of the tent.

"Fine, anything that makes you go away. The night before we rode out against those Indians, I was in the tavern with Gentry and a couple of other guys. And we saw the colonel over at the far end of the place, talking to one of the prettiest women I had…or any of us had ever seen, but there just wasn't something right with her. I wanted to get a closer look at her, but she scared the bejesus out of me. I never did get much closer than about fifteen feet. She looked up at me once, I…I felt like she wanted to kill me. And not that she 'wanted to', but that she could. All that beauty and she was just so cold, so deadly cold." Bucks made a show of wrapping an imaginary jacket around his shoulders to shield himself from the memory.

"And you haven't seen her since that night?"

"No, she's not a face you would forget; but if I did see her, I'd be heading the other way."

Tomas had fragments to this puzzle. Eliza had engineered a cavalry raid on the Indian village, but why? Was she looking for something? Was she afraid of someone? *Impossible,* Tomas thought, answering his own question. He hadn't seen fear in her eyes since the day she bit him. Some five centuries previous. There was no doubt that something powerful that belonged to Eliza had been in this room. *Is that what she was looking for? But why not come back and get it? Why go through all the trouble of setting this thing up and not following through.*

"Did Tenson or Gentry say anything about the day of the raid?"

Bucks looked confused.

"Did they talk about finding anything?"

Bucks had not yet shaken the look off his face. And then a thought he might have never have retrieved, popped to the fore. "I don't think it meant anything, but Tenson was always kind of a glum person. Always the first to bed, griped about everything, even the food, and sometimes that was actually pretty good. But after the raid, even while we were burying our dead, he was smiling from ear to ear. I thought it was strange as hell. But I was tired and we were, like I said, burying our dead. I didn't much pay attention to him."

"How long after you got back did Gentry go missing?"

"About a week. Come to think of it, Tenson started talking about places where he wanted to live and what he'd do when he got out of the cavalry. He even started coming to get drinks with us. He was actually turning into a pretty decent guy before Gentry gutted him like a fish."

"Do you know where Gentry was from?" Tomas asked.

"Pretty sure it's Louisiana. Yeah, New Orleans, because he was always going on and on about the Cajun food and how he misses shrimp."

Private Bucks thought he must have passed out for a few minutes. When he sat up, he realized he was on Gentry's rack and the stranger was gone, if he had ever been there at all. The only thing he could focus on was the mounting headache starting to take root in the base of his skull.

Tomas headed east. Even without getting a location from Bucks, he would have been able to follow whatever Gentry was carrying. It was a faint trail, but it was there if you knew what to look for, and now he did. *Did Eliza?* He pushed his horse harder, but Gentry and possibly Eliza had three weeks on him.

It took Tomas nearly a week to get to Gentry's family home. It was a ramshackle hut built of varying pieces of wood and held together more from force of habit than anything else.

A nearly toothless old woman sat on the front porch. She was strumming a banjo and stooped down every once in a while to pick up a jug with unknown contents. She would drink her fill and then put the container down to begin again on her picking.

Tomas was coming up on her blind side when she spoke. "You from the government?" she asked before turning around. When she did turn to the approaching boy, she spoke again. "No, not the government, you're a powerful one, you are. What do you want with my boy?"

Tomas saw no reason to be obtuse with her. "He has something of mine, of my sister's, actually."

"The stone. That damned blood stone, I knew it was bad, and now it's brought you."

"Better me, old woman, than my sibling. You would not be having this conversation with her."

"I can feel that thing in my house. It itches under my skin, like a tick. It burrows under the skin and spreads." She shivered, even though the outside temperature was hovering around the mid-nineties and the humidity had drenched her clothes. "He won't give it up willingly."

"I can be pretty persuasive."

"I bet you can. Step closer, boy, so I can see what you are."

Tomas did as she asked.

She put her instrument down and grabbed both his hands in a surprisingly firm grip for someone so fragile looking. She spoke as if in a trance. "You walk in both worlds, unable to die and unwilling to live. You have light in your heart, but a darkness where your soul should be. You have seen much pain and misery, yet you try to do as much as you can to prevent it as you go about your journey. You are much, much older than I, yet you look younger than my boy. I do not know who or what you are, but you are the rightful owner of that accursed stone, I can feel it in my bones."

"Is your son home? The sooner I get what belongs to me, the sooner I can get going."

"I think that would be for the best. Gentry!" she yelled, never letting go of Tomas' hands or looking away from him.

Gentry came around the side of the shack and almost started to run when he saw the stranger on his porch.

"Don't be a damned fool," his mother said, not witnessing one nuance on his face as he came up behind her. "This young man," she began and then winked at Tomas. "Says that you have something that belongs to him."

"Ma? I don't know what either of you are talking about."

"You'll kill us both if he won't give up the stone, won't you?" The old woman asked.

"Yes, and still, it will be a better fate than the one my sister would bestow upon you."

"You're the white witch's brother?" Gentry asked, almost collapsing.

Tomas did not need to answer.

"I killed my best friend for that stone and I became a deserter. Both things are punishable by death and still I don't know why I did it. I can't even stand to look at it, yet I carry it with me everywhere I go. It'll be a relief to get rid of it," Gentry said as he reached far down into his pocket and pulled out a stone, which he'd wrapped in a small piece of cloth.

Tomas took a big intake of air as the stone was placed into his hand, now that the old woman had finally yielded it.

"What will you do with me now?" Gentry asked. All the spirit had been drained from him.

"You will go on with your useless life, such as it is, knowing that you killed your friend for a stone that is valuable to no one, save one. I wish that I could feel pity for you, but I don't. Good day," he added for the old woman as he turned to leave.

"What is it? What is the stone?" Gentry asked.

Tomas held it up to the blazing sun. Two occlusions were outlined through the fiery red brilliance. And then like a comet flashing across the sky, the answer came to him. "It is my sister's soul and that of the medicine man that trapped her here."

It was the old woman's turn to breathe deeply.

"Get it off my property! It should have never been here, there are things going on that should never be!"

She was still raving as Tomas found his way down the tree-lined pathway that led away.

This story takes place December, near Christmas 2009, written December 27th 2010.

Excerpt taken from a journal discovered in Vona, Colorado. Its location was a center console in a red Jeep Wrangler. The reader found the story humorous and decided to hold onto it where it was finally paired together with the original writer's works.

Talbot-Sode 1

I've been feeling down as of late. We are on the run from zombies. This has not turned out to be the adventure I had hoped it would be. My hope was that I would make a lasting stand at my household with all my rifles, ammo, food and water. Yet, three weeks after the invasion I had been preparing for almost my entire life, my home has fallen into enemy hands. We're cold, scared, and are draining through hope like a wino through Mad Dog 20/20. My ability to keep my family, friends, and to a lesser extent, our other traveling companions safe weighs heavily on me. My goal with these next lines is just an attempt to bring a smile in a deepening dark that is gathering.

In a time before there were zombies, we lived our lives like the vast amount of Americans in December. We overate, overspent, and waited until the last minute to do our shopping around the holiday. This year was no different. I had just cashed my meager check this morning and my wife felt that we had to get a few more gifts for the kids.

"Go ahead," I told her. Yeah, that went over about as well as you think it did.

"Talbot, get your ass up off that couch," she said. It wasn't loud, it wasn't threatening, but to not act on those words would have been tantamount to suicide. Kind of like the criminally insane do when they point a gun at the cops and then the cops have no option but to open fire. It was the same premise here.

So I got my ass up off the couch and off to the mall we went. Yippeee! The mall at Christmas time. I'd rather go to a drunk dentist for a root canal; it was a lot less painful. The mall was so packed, there was no place to park. They had to plow the snow off a distant field and offer a free shuttle service.

"Recession my ass," I grumbled as I parked the car. The mall was a distant pinpoint of light, off in the distance. "Maybe that's where the baby Jesus lays," I said sarcastically.

"Talbot!" My wife smacked my arm.

We walked up to the sign that said 'Shuttle' just as a white tin can, packed with holiday revelers left.

"It's friggin' cold out here," I said, stamping my feet.

"Maybe if you had worn your heavy coat like I told you to, you wouldn't be so cold," Tracy said, with the all-knowing 'I told you so' lilt.

I opened my mouth to argue the point, but she looked much more ready to do battle than I. So just a little background and you decide if I had a valid point or not, not that Tracy would have agreed anyway.

By '09, Tracy and I had been married somewhere in the neighborhood of twenty-something years. Now, NEVER, ever will I claim to know what makes a woman tick, but I've been around this particular model long enough to know some of its quirks. I might have written this down in one of my earlier journals. but it's worth reiterating; my wife researches and buys her cars on the recommendation of other folks' opinions about how the heater works. So when we go auto shopping, we have to look for heaters that have an extra setting called 'lava', and until molten magma is pouring from the vents, my wife is not happy. I've actually lost the bottoms from more than one pair of sneakers as the glue has melted, and the soles have become un-adhered from the rest of the shoe.

There have been days when the temperature outside is zero or less and I have dressed in shorts and a windbreaker for long car rides, because I know that most likely, my face will, at some point, melt. This trip was no different, but it was a shorter ride so I actually had pants on and a light jacket, not in any way rated for the inclement weather we were in the midst of, but still I was not going to argue the point with her. It would have been a lot colder if I had to walk home.

So I waited, gritting my teeth, feeling my nasal

passages beginning to freeze up. My wife looked fairly toasty in her heavy sweater and full-length jacket, scarf around her neck and leather gloves.

The shuttle showed up seventeen teeth-chattering minutes later. I had to rip my planted feet from the ground. Seems the melted glue had frozen fast to the ice slicked surface. Tracy entered before me and then I came in after. I stepped up on the stoop and looked to the left. Seems the shuttle had stopped to pick up half the state of Wisconsin before it got to our stop. An older gentleman gave up his seat when he saw Tracy approach him and somehow the seat next to her was vacant. I was about to plant my ass in it when it looked like someone had spilled half of an Orange Julius in the plastic bucket seat. At least, I hoped it was an Orange Julius.

Tracy shrugged her shoulders as if to say 'What are you going to do?'

My next option was the large, silver, hand-hold poles that went from floor to ceiling on the shuttle. I was near to placing bare hand on metal when I spotted what looked like the world's largest nose nugget wrapped around the bar twice. The offending brown-green slime was oozing its way down the pole, much like a low rent stripper. I was getting nauseous. Making it through the throng to another pole was out of the question. A kid of about twelve off to my left was sneezing like his mother was shoving pepper up his nose. The friggin' germ factory wasn't even covering his mouth. I felt like I was in a rolling Petri dish. And our shuttle driver must have been a foreigner because he was paying absolutely no heed to state and national laws in regards to load limits.

He kept packing people in like he was getting paid per pound delivered. I was being pressed closer and closer to the pole with the snot snake wrapped around it. I was using what minimal leverage I had trying to keep from pressing up against it. Something or someone was touching my ass. I kept praying that it was some hot Yugoslavian model, but the last time I had turned around, I remember seeing an overweight man who looked like he had just downed a bucket of fried chicken. I noted that his hands had appeared greasy. Now I wasn't so sure what was on his diet and why his hands were greasy, but I was not feeling so good anymore.

I was losing the leverage battle. I pulled my hands up into my jacket so that I would have at least one barrier between the human goop that riddled the pole and me. I gripped it with both jacket-clad hands and moved a foot off to the side. Greasy Hands had two wet fingers shoved in his mouth and was sucking deeply. His other hand was still located where my ass had just been. I felt pretty dirty and violated. He winked at me when he caught me looking. I would have vomited had I the chance to make sure I could get away from it. My luck right now and this bus would break down with the doors unable to open.

Greasy tried to slide over my way, but a small, older woman blocked his path. I would have kissed her except for the thick moustache she sported, well, that and the scowl, well, those two things and the marble-sized mole to the left of her nose, or did she have two noses? I hadn't quite worked that one out yet.

Someone else picked up the sneezing torch as Georgie Germ stopped. I think Fanny Phlegm started hacking up a lung. I could see particulates flying through the air like airborne missiles. I was going for a world record in breath-holding, forty-two seconds and counting. I wondered if anyone would pick me up if I could find enough open space to topple over. Greasy Hands probably would; that was of little comfort. And then I'd be left wondering what was on the floor and if the rest of the shuttle was any indication, then I'd be swimming in a sea of viral stew, with chunks of unidentifiable material.

Six or seven days later, the cross-country journey finally came to an end. Two Nose cut me off as I tried to make a hasty exit. Greasy Hands immediately pulled up to my rear and Georgie Germ heralded our passage with a heavy barrage of wet, viscous germ spewage.

"Tell your kid to cover his mouth," I said loudly to a mother who was too busy playing on her phone to monitor her child. Of course, until I said something about her son, and then she became a Kodiak bear, protecting her cub. Her shrill screams of "Mind your own fucking business" are still etched on my eardrums.

Greasy Hands was making our last few feet out a free for all. As soon as we hit terra firma, I turned and slammed him back into the bus. He licked his lips at me.

I clenched my fists and was about to make him pay for our encounter, when Tracy alit from the shuttle.

"Ah, Talbot, I see you're making friends again. I really can't take you anywhere, can I?" Tracy said, laughing.

Greasy Hands winked one more time and got back on the bus. Obviously, this was something that got his rocks off and it looked like he had been doing it the entire holiday season. Tracy grabbed my tensed shoulder. "Come on, let's go," she said without turning back around to witness what I had.

We had gone a few feet from the bus when I made a great showing of patting my pockets down. "Aw shit, hon! I left my phone on the bus. Go in, I'll meet you there."

"I'll come with you."

"I'll be right there. Go in…get warm."

I had hit the right button; she headed towards the mall entrance.

I jogged back to the bus. Greasy Hands was sitting in the empty bus on the seat that I had previously rejected due to the supposed Orange Julius contents.

"Back for more?" he asked, standing up.

I pulled my fist back somewhere around Detroit and let fly. I caught him flush on the cheek as he attempted to dodge my blow. He sat back down heavily. He would be sleeping for at least the next few bus rides.

"Fuck, that hurt," I said, shaking my hand around.

"You can't do that here! Get out of here!" the bus driver was yelling at me.

"Calm down, I was just getting my phone. And why don't you clean this pit up while you're waiting for people? Starting with Sleeping Beauty over there."

"Get your ass off my bus or I'm calling security! And don't try to get back on, you're not welcome!"

"I'd rather walk on my hands and knees back to the lot than get on this lab gone bad."

Tracy was by the mall directory board when I came in. "Your phone, huh?"

"My what?" I had already forgotten my lying premise.

"Remember? You went back to get your phone."

"Right, right."

"Did you find it?" she asked.

"I had it in my pocket the whole time." I explained, trying to get my most innocent face in place.

"Your knuckles look pretty raw," she said as I jammed my hand into my jacket so she couldn't get a closer look.

"I fell," came stumbling out.

"And you braced yourself with your knuckles?"

"It was a very awkward fall. I was lucky to even get that to stop me or I would have landed square on my chin."

"Oh, and then your new boyfriend would have been so upset."

"He could have at least taken me out to dinner before he started to take liberties with me."

Tracy laughed. "Let's go, we've got a lot of shopping to do."

We hadn't even started and I was already wiped out.

The mall was packed, but fortunately not as bad as the bus, but much more so than my living room, which I so desired to be sitting in. Most folks looked panicked. They were running out of time, and as of yet, not picked out their significant other a proper gift. This led many to go over the top, and at least one jewelry store was the beneficiary of that panic.

There were two competing jewelry stores on either side of an opening that led down to another string of shops. There could not have been fifty feet separating the vendors, yet one was filled to the brim with customers and the other had three people in it, two of which were employees and one who had yet to look up from her split ends she kept pulling up in front of her face.

The packed one was Kay Jewelers, you know the one. I bet you've already sung the jingle without any prompting from me. "Every kiss begins with Kay." Sorry, now you've probably got that stuck in your head. The other was a place I'd never heard of called J.D. Robbins Jewelry. The only difference I could discern in the two stores was that one had a fancy ad campaign with a catchy jingle and the other didn't.

I pointed this out to Tracy, but she didn't seem nearly as intrigued about it as I was.

"I've thought of a jingle that I think would get that store packed!" I told her excitedly.

"I'm sure you have. Do I even want to hear it?"

"Okay, you know the one "every kiss begins with Kay?"

She nodded.

"Now use the same jingle only with these words, Every Jerk-off begins with J! That store would be fucking packed right now!"

Tracy nearly snorted on the cookie we had been sharing, but she quickly recovered. "What is the matter with you? It's Christmas!" She was trying to sound disgusted, but I could tell she was inwardly laughing her ass off.

"I personally couldn't think of a better gift," I said lasciviously.

"Go find your bus buddy!" she laughed as she pushed

me away.

One short year removed from that story, I find myself huddled in the cold with the remnants of humanity. How I wish I was back on that bus, not with Greasy Hands, mind you. I hope he was patient zero, but I'd even take Georgie Germ as long as he was on the far side of the bus. I could maybe do without Two Nose and the bus driver and maybe Georgie's mother, but I think everyone else would be fine. This story has done what I'd hoped it would accomplish. It has brought a smile to an otherwise tired, scared man.

Paul-A-Sode 1

When Paul was on the porch to the cat house this is the memory that flooded his mind, for the briefest of synapses. He remembered a time in college when Mike and he had gotten a particularly difficult Resident Assistant to quit his job. An RA's job is sort of like den mother. It is his or her responsibility to make sure that no parties are held on the floor; or that any huge violations are being broken, (like having an oven in a dorm room). Sometimes they even act as a pseudo counselor when a freshman runs across the familiar homesick blues. Paul and Mike had the unfortunate luck of the draw, with their RA; he took his responsibilities a little too seriously. Most of the RAs were simply in it so that they could break all of the rules in a single; as opposed to the standard, two-to-a-dorm room. Gert (yes, he was a man) was studying to move on to grad school and could absolutely not stand any noise whatsoever on his floor. He had once written a sophomore up because her alarm clock was excessively loud.

Mike and Paul had been written up no less than five times in their first month on the floor. Six meant an automatic meeting with the dean and potential disciplinary actions, up to and including, expulsion. Mike and Paul had on more than one occasion caught Gert outside their door listening to see if he could get that elusive sixth offense.

"Is he there?" Mike asked Paul as Paul had snuck up to the door and quickly opened it, trying to once again catch him.

"No, but he was here recently. I can almost hear the echo of his goosestep as he went down the hallway."

"Good one," Mike had said. "We need to do something about him. We've been good for a few days now, but how much longer do you think we can last?"

"Not long, I'm already itching for another fiesta."

"That's what I'm saying. We need to get rid of the party Nazi."

"Wouldn't it just be easier to wait until next semester and move off this floor?"

"You think we'll make it that far? And then we have to admit that he wins. And that sure doesn't sound like the guy that threw perhaps the largest spitball ever conceived at Mrs. Weinstedder back in the sixth grade."

"You sure do know how to flatter a guy. What's your plan?"

"You think he's in his room?"

"The only time he isn't is either when's he's at class or writing a student advisory slip."

"Alright, we've got to be careful. He's got the other freshmen on this floor so wound tight, they might rat us out if they catch us."

"You sure about all this, Mike?" Paul asked with some concern.

"I'd rather go out in a blaze of glory than skulking into the night."

"I agree," Paul said, feeling himself quite possibly being peer-pressured. *There's something to be said for skulking*, Paul thought.

"Alright, I'm going to need your help with this one."

Paul nodded and noted Mike taking a stack of pennies from their shared coin jar.

"When we get to Hurtie Gert's door, you need to press on the top corner as hard as you can."

"Which corner?" Paul asked.

"Valid question, the one above the doorknob."

"What's that going to do?"

"It's going to give me the room I need to shove these pennies in."

"You know our fingerprints are all over those things."

"So? No way,…do you think he'd get these dusted?"

"Who knows?"

"We don't have our fingerprints on file, do we?"

"I don't think so, but I'd rather not take the chance."

Mike wiped all the coins on his shirt and then put a sock over his hand to grasp the coins.

"That doesn't look suspicious at all."

"Come on, let's get this done."

Mike kept his sock-clad hand in his pocket to allay any prying questions, should they arise. The twenty-five-foot walk to Gert's door was uneventful. The only noise was when some unlucky student had dropped his chemistry book on his foot and cried out in alarm and pain. Paul and Mike had frozen, thinking Gert would come busting out of his door to quiet the offending student. He didn't do that, but he had yelled for the clumsy scholar to shut up.

"He's a very caring individual," Mike had said, turning back towards Paul.

The door had groaned slightly as Paul pressed on the top corner.

"Harder," Mike had intoned, looking at the gap being formed from the pressure.

The gap had finally widened to a liking for Mike as he pulled the pennies from his pocket and placed about seven of them in a stack against the bowed door and the frame.

"Let go," Mike said.

"There was a brief second where the corner of Mike's sock got pinched in the door. Paul thought it had been Mike's finger and was waiting for the resultant scream that would most assuredly get them kicked out of school. Mike quickly pulled the sock out and bolted for their room, Paul hurriedly followed. They had no sooner shut their door when someone down the hallway had opened theirs.

"That was fucking close," Mike laughed.

"Now what?" Paul asked, not sure what was going to happen. All he could think was that Gert might be mildly surprised with the clatter of change and would be seven cents richer for their effort.

"We wait."

"This seemed funnier when we were talking about

what we were going to do."

"Wait, buddy, it gets better."

As it turned out, it wasn't too long of a wait before Gert decided it was time to go to the cafeteria and get some food. At first, there was nothing and then came the struggles of someone beating on their door. If it had been anybody else besides Gert, they would have received a violation. Nearly every door on the floor opened to see who had the balls to make that much noise.

Gert was beating on his door with closed fists, swearing in his native tongue of German.

"I always wondered how to say that," said a pretty little brunette named Debbie, who Paul remembered was taking German as her language of choice. "Interesting."

"Someone needs to call the fire department! I am locked in my room!"

"He can't get out?" Paul asked, turning back to a laughing Mike.

"No, man! The pennies wedge the lock up against the slide; he can't even turn the handle."

"That's brilliant, man."

The ranting, cussing, and general screams of fear continued for a full two minutes longer until a junior who had seen the prank before recognized it for what it was. He told Gert to move from the door. He then pressed against the corner of the door, and the pennies fell to the floor.

"What the hell is going on!?" Gert screamed as he came through the door.

Most of the meek freshman retreated back into their rooms.

"Was this you?" Gert asked the junior who had helped.

"Screw you, man, I just helped you. I should have left you in there." And then he walked away.

The hallway was clear, save a few students, who decided this might be a good time to go get some food. Gert honed in on Paul and Mike like an eagle to a mouse.

Mike quickly pulled Paul in and shut the door.

"Do you think he knows?" Paul asked, smiling.

"I'm sure we're on a short list."

"Kind of like Spindler?" He was the boys' old high school principal, who followed them around relentlessly, at least until his car mysteriously burst into flames.

"Kind of like that, but by the time we're done, we'll make all that look like child's play."

For two weeks, Mike and Paul had harassed Gert to no end. On a particularly eventful evening, Paul gained illegal entry into Gert's dorm room via a credit card and some precision maneuvering. Paul had hooked up Gert's Bose stereo system to a timer set to go off in the wee hours of the morning. At precisely three-thirty-eight am on the morning of Tuesday the eleventh of October, *Runnin' with the Devil* by Van Halen ripped through the night like a fire truck through a sleepy village.

"Fitting song," Mike told Paul as they sat at their doorway. They were careful to only open their door when they heard the rest of the floor doing the same.

The music and Gert's resultant cursing had been heard on the floor below and above. Despite Gert's protestations, he had received his first written warning since he had started school four years previous.

"How much more of this do you think he can take?" Paul asked Mike after they had seen a hangdog expression on Gert as he exited the student lounge.

"I guess we'll see," Mike had answered. "The good thing is he's been too paranoid to write anybody up."

"He doesn't look like he's slept in days," Paul said. "I'd almost feel bad if he wasn't such a prick."

"If who wasn't such a dick?" Debbie asked. She was working the counter at the snack shop.

Mike looked up guiltily. "What did you hear?"

"That Gert's a dick," she said, flashing a smile.

Mike and Paul quickly rewound through their conversation trying to see how much they had given away.

"We never said Gert," Paul said. Mike was inclined to believe him, but they had just shared a particularly large joint and Mike wasn't entirely too sure what they had said. He had been so fixated on the large, frosted, chocolate chip brownie, he hadn't even noticed Debbie working the counter.

"I saw you working on Gert's door two days ago," she said to Paul.

"Shit," Paul answered her. "But that was two days ago, if you knew…and we're still at school."

"Relax! I can't stand him either. He asked me on a date on the first day of school and when I told him no, he wrote me up the next day for having a candle in my room. Didn't matter to him that it wasn't even lit." Debbie handed Mike two brownies.

"I don't have enough for two," Mike told her, brushing the dust off his wallet.

"They're on me," she said, flashing another smile.

"Sweet, thanks," Mike told her, doing his best to smile back, but the munchies had taken a serious hold on his social skills and all he could do was concentrate on the treat.

"What do you want?" Paul asked cautiously.

"Nothing much," Debbie answered coquettishly.

"Huh?" Mike asked, looking up, half a brownie in his mouth, chocolate on his cheek.

"You don't get out much," Debbie said, smiling. She wiped his cheek with a wet towel she had behind the counter.

"She wants in," Paul said.

"In what?" Mike asked.

"Dude, get your face out of the brownie."

"Sorry, man, I'm pretty hungry."

"We just had dinner."

"Yeah, but that was before."

"Before what?" Debbie asked.

"Uh…nothing," Paul told her evasively. "Mike,

Debbie here thinks we are up to something with Gert."

"No," Mike said, looking around. "I don't know what you're talking about."

"I don't want to play hardball, but I saw Paul trying to get into Gert's room the night we all listened to a very loud rendition of *Running with the Devil*."

"It's runnin'," Mike corrected her.

"So you know what I'm talking about?" Debbie asked him.

"All I said was that it is a common misconception that the title is 'Running' when there is actually no 'g'."

"It's your word against ours," Paul told her.

"Do you think Gert's going to need much more than that to get you two kicked out?"

Mike was busy finishing off his second brownie when Paul agreed to let Debbie in on the next prank.

"When?" Debbie asked, joining them at a small table tucked away in the shadows of the small shop.

Mike could not get over the feeling that they were spies in German occupied France during WWII as they discussed their plan. Some was due to the subject matter they were studying, but a larger portion revolved around the magic bud they had enjoyed fifteen minutes ago.

"We have to lay low for a couple of days. He's so high-strung right now that whenever someone's door opens, he yanks his open. It's pretty friggin' funny," Mike said, having a hard time not snorting.

"He scared the shit out me the other morning," Paul said. "I was going down to take a shower, I don't even know how he heard me, but I was right next to his door when he jumped out and told me he 'Got me.' Dropped my shampoo and everything. I know he's close to losing it because he actually apologized."

"Don't you feel bad?" Deb asked us.

"A little, but it's him or us, and I'd rather it was him," Mike said, and Paul nodded. "I don't want him to go all Hara

Kari on himself or Texas library roof, I just want him to relinquish his job as dorm douche. Oops! Sorry."

"Don't worry about it," Deb laughed. "Both of my parents were in the Navy."

They had left it at that point and promised to reconvene their clandestine meeting two days hence. Either that was too long or Deb was too amped up, but she decided to take matters into her own hands.

"What's going on?" Paul asked Deb as he came up to the dorm room after his Sociology class.

The entire population of the dorm's occupants were milling around outside.

"Hey, buddy," Mike said, tossing a football in the air. "I was sleeping and someone pulled the damn fire alarm."

"Didn't you have English Lit?" Paul asked.

"Was that today?" Mike asked, throwing the ball back up in the air.

"I know it was you!" a soaking wet, towel-clad Gert yelled at Mike as he dropped the ball from the distraction. "I can't prove it, but I will. You super-glued my lock and I couldn't get in after my shower!"

"Whoa! Hold on there, boss! I didn't even think you European types showered," Mike said.

"You think this is funny? You freshman turd! I'm freezing my ass off in a towel."

"I actually think it's hilarious, but I still don't know what the hell you're talking about, Jert," Mike said.

"It is Gert, Gert Hans. And I promise you that I will have you and your roommate thrown out of this school."

"Listen, Hansel, I was sleeping. I was having this weird-ass dream about huge Pop-Tarts. I have no idea why you are out here soaking wet and in a towel. And why do you not have flip-flops on? Oh, please don't tell me that you go into a public shower without footwear? That is just disgusting. That's how people get foot fungus. Man, you've been in school long enough! Haven't you learned anything?"

Gert was so sure that he had nailed Mike that he was completely put off by Mike going on the offensive.

"I know you did it," he said weakly. "I know you did everything."

"I'm a little sick of your accusations. You've written us up five times for puissant violations and now our academic careers hang in the balance because you're a control freak. My roomie and I have walked the straight and narrow for almost three weeks. I was hoping for some congratulations, but instead, you accuse us of even more trouble-making. I'm sure the list of folks who loathe you is a relatively long one. Maybe you should go back and rethink who else would do this to you."

Gert stood there, anger flaring, his skin tone changing hues, from blistering blue to raging red. Paul was certain Gert was about to go ballistic.

"Um…" Debbie interjected into the testosterone fray.

"What?!" Gert spat.

"Umm, you've got a little something hanging out," she said, pointing down.

Gert was so lost in his anger, he did not know what she was talking about.

Mike looked down and then made his pinkie finger fold and unfold. "The lady said you have a little something showing," Mike laughed.

Paul almost went to his knees, tears running from his eyes as Gert's red rage turned to a fevered flush when he realized he had just exposed himself to a girl.

"You know, I'd say you could get in a lot of trouble for that if we had actually been able to see anything," Mike yelled to Gert's retreating back.

"What did you do?" Paul asked Mike.

"Dude, I'm serious. I was snoozing hard," Mike answered his friend.

Paul turned to Deb who was now wearing a wicked smile. "What did you do?"

"Pretty much everything he said Mike did. I waited until I saw him head for the shower, then I went and shoved half a tube of super glue into his door lock. Next, I waited until I was pretty sure he had just lathered up his head in shampoo, then I pulled the fire alarm."

"That's kind of risky. What if someone had seen you?" Mike asked her.

"I went to the third floor lounge and did it. No one ever goes there unless it's to study and nobody does that at three on a Friday afternoon."

"I thought we agreed to wait a couple of days?" Paul asked her.

"I did, but I changed my mind."

"Nice." Mike said, shaking his head in disbelief. "He looks like he's about to cry."

Gert was over by the fire truck, yelling at whoever would listen that someone had pulled the alarm on purpose and that they just wanted him to come out into the cold weather in merely a towel. The fireman was hardly even acknowledging his existence as he checked on the truck equipment.

"I need to get back inside before I catch pneumonia!" Gert was screaming now.

"Listen, kid," the fire captain was saying, "we'll let everyone, including you, in when we are convinced it's not a real alarm."

"I'm telling you it was not. It was pulled specifically while I was in the shower so that I would have to come out here like this. I even tried to go back to my room, but I could not get back in."

"Dankins," the chief yelled over to one of his subordinates. "Could you please get this kid a jacket and shut him up? I've got better things to do than play babysitter with him." And he walked away.

Gert looked like a war refugee, all wrapped up in an oversized fireman jacket, huddled up on the stoop of the truck. Paul and Mike didn't know if Gert's winning charm had won the captain over, but it seemed to them to be one of the longest fire alarm resets that they had ever been through.

"Man, he is never going to take a shower again," Paul said as the three of them sat in Debbie's dorm room.

"I wasn't kidding when I called him on the whole taking a shower thing anyway," Mike said. "He always smells like ripe sauerkraut."

"That's so gross," Deb said, holding her nose.

"Great prank by the way," Mike told her, and she blushed slightly.

"Thank you," she said, doing a small curtsy that did not go unnoticed by Gert.

He did not know for what reason she had performed the small bow, but that she was flaunting her body to those two good-for-nothings infuriated him.

The trio laid off Gert for close to two weeks. The guy was wound so tight, he wouldn't even go out anymore to get food. He had delivery come two weeks straight.

"I don't think he's even been to class," Paul said to Mike as they watched the Chinese food deliveryman leave the building.

"Was that for Gert?" Deb asked, catching up to the two boys and pointing back towards the driver who had gotten in his car and was getting ready to leave.

"Yeah, that's the third order of Chinese this week," Mike said.

"I almost feel kind of sorry for him," Deb said.

"You should. You're the one that gave him the flu," Paul said.

"He should have gotten a shot like the rest of us," Mike said, absently rubbing his arm where the vaccine had been administered a month prior.

"Are you going to keep messing with him?" Deb asked.

"Hey, you're the one that brought it to a whole new

level," Mike told her.

"Maybe we should stop, maybe he's finally figured out that he can't just do whatever he wants around here because he has a clipboard," Paul said.

"That's two warnings!" They could hear Gert yelling from the hallway. "One for keeping an excess of garbage in your room and the other for not making your bed!"

"Not making your bed? What the hell is he talking about?" Paul said as the three went over to the door and looked out.

Residents up and down the hallway were looking to the fuss, Gert was walking into rooms and going ballistic, writing students up for infractions that he seemed to be making up as he wrote.

Most students got the message and began to close their doors, hoping to escape the wrath of Gert Gone Mad. Paul was one of them.

"Leave it open," Mike said.

"What are you doing, Mike? Look at him, he'll write you up for your shirt," Paul nearly whined.

"What's wrong with Ozzy Osbourne?" Mike asked.

"Fine. I'm going to start packing my things."

Gert was making a beeline for the only door still open. Mike stepped in his way just as Gert was about to enter.

"Whoa there, pardner," Mike said with a Southern drawl. "Where you going in such a hurry?"

"Mandatory room inspection!" Gert was nearly frothing at the mouth, his pen was already making contact with the clipboard.

"On whose authority, Gert?" Mike asked him.

"What?! You dare to stop me!? On my own damn authority!" Gert raged, and then made a motion to push past Mike.

"Listen, asshole," Mike said, pushing Gert across the hallway to the far wall, "I'm going to say this real soft so that you can't subpoena any witnesses, so pay attention." Mike got right up to his ear. "You ever try to enter my room without my permission, I will beat you to within 2.58 centimeters of your worthless existence."

The rage in Gert's eyes cleared for a moment as he looked into Mike's eyes, trying to ascertain if this were an idle threat and whether he should continue with his mission as planned. The tension in Gert's bunched muscles eased as he realized this might not be the best time to make his last stand.

"This isn't done, Talbot, all I need is one more infraction and you and your halfwit friend are out of here. And I've got a feeling that neither of you idiots will make it another week."

Mike released Gert from his grip and left him to weasel away to another unsuspecting victim.

"What happened?" Paul asked, pulling Mike in the room and closing the door.

"We've got to keep pressing his buttons," Mike said. "One of us is close to leaving and we need to make sure it's him. That dude is a whole suit short of a standard deck."

"Looks like all you get when you stretch an asshole to its limits is just a bigger asshole," Deb said.

Mike stopped what he was thinking about. He looked over at Deb before he busted out laughing.

"What?" Debbie said, blushing, not sure exactly what she said to elicit such a response.

Paul had joined in with Mike and once tears started to flow, Deb joined in, not even sure what for.

It was the seemingly least innocuous prank that finally pushed Gert to his limit and the trio had nothing to do with it. The local chapter of Iota Gamma Upsilon sorority (or more commonly known by the call letters of their house as I Go Upstairs, a reference that many had found to be a truism much to the delight of all the party goers) saw to that. As an initiation right to their pledges, they had given each one a giant container of Vaseline and told them to use it around campus in any manner they saw fitting, but to not come back until the tub was empty.

Randi Betcher had used the container in a way that half the basketball team and part of the track team would not soon forget, but that is a tale for a much different kind of book. Wendy Treadman had decided that spreading the sticky gel on the door handles at every residence at the James House dormitory was just absolutely the funniest thing since just about ever!

She had just finished up and was heading out the door when Gert had hit her shoulder, nearly knocking the plastic jar to the ground.

"Watch it!" Gert had sneered at her.

She was going to call him a big fat jerk, but she told her best friend, Jenny, that he had crazy eyes and she just wanted to get away from there.

Gert had just received his first grade of C in his entire academic career and could not even begin to process the information. He had nearly needed to be tossed from the class when he got loud with the professor, arguing that he could not come to class because there were people out to get him.

Professor Garrity had told him that he needed to get some help and that maybe he should just go home and get some rest.

Gert had mumbled to himself the entire walk from the far side of campus. He had wanted to hit the little Humpty Dumpty girl that had gotten in his way as he walked into his dorm. When he made it to his room and his hand came down and made contact with the Vaseline on his door handle, something inside of Gert quite literally snapped. Had anyone been close enough to listen, they might have been able to hear it.

He didn't scream – his normal and usual venting mechanism – this time he internalized it. Gert tossed his book bag, smashing his floor lamp which landed on top of his illegal toaster oven, something he had purchased since the attacks so he would not have to leave for dinner. Gert leaned up against the door, his ear pressed firmly against the cool metal, the first person that walked by his room was the guilty party; he was convinced of it.

Soft footsteps padded down the hallway. "Gotcha, mother fucker," he breathed out softly. He waited until he was sure the guilty party was outside his doorway doing all sorts of unspeakable things against him again.

Gert ripped the door open. "I know what you did," he said calmly enough, but the red-rimmed eyes and clenched fists belied his demeanor.

Debbie stared back at him in shock and a growing sense of foreboding. *How could he know? I'm going to get thrown out of school for this.*

Gert was somewhat taken aback when he saw Debbie standing there. He knew that she secretly had a crush on Mike Talbot, that asshole, but could she be in on the pranks with him? *Of course! It all makes sense that she would be, probably trying to impress him, I'll fucking show her.*

"I need you to come in here so that we can discuss this." His words were calm enough, but emotions swirled like a whirlwind inside.

Debbie felt trapped, but maybe she could mitigate the damage. She stepped into his room, Gert looked up and down the hallway for any witnesses, then quickly shut the door.

"Please sit," Gert said motioning to his desk chair.

Debbie noticed the tossed book bag and shattered lamp, and for the first time since seeing Gert at the doorway, she took a long at the Resident Assistant. He looked bad, in fact, worse than bad. His eyes were streaked with thick heavy lines of red, his sockets were sunken and his features were even pale for a man of European descent.

"I need to go," Debbie said, just realizing that she was in the den of the enemy.

Gert slapped her so hard she thought she could hear her fillings rattle. *Should have taken better care of my teeth* was her only thought as she sat hard in the chair, the momentum of her fall sending the chair rolling for a couple of feet until the rollers came in contact with Gert's throw rug and then her neck snapped back.

Gert was on her before she could defend herself. His heavy blows rained down on her. She wanted to scream, but Gert had delivered a shot to her stomach and she found herself devoid of sufficient air to produce sound.

Gert pushed Debbie off the chair and onto his bed. "Now I will show you how I discipline bad people the correct way," he said as he began to pull his belt off.

"Please, no," Deb said, weakly holding her hands up to defend herself.

Mike had left class early. He had been having another major disagreement with, his what? What was she truly to him? He didn't know. They dated, they had fun and they were intimate, but she was in a committed, long-term relationship with a football player from a distant college. *Oh man, I'm the OTHER guy in this relationship,* he moaned.

He could think of worse ways to be used, but even though he was a guy, he wanted more out of the relationship. They were going to a concert next week, maybe he would give her an ultimatum then. *Or not,* he thought sourly because he would rather take a piece than nothing at all.

It was these thoughts he was thinking as he got his key out to enter into his room, but the key ring caught on his pocket and fell to the ground. "Fucker," Mike said as he bent down to pick them up.

He heard a loud 'thwack' as he stood back up. He was staring straight at Gert's door. *What is that crazy bastard doing?* Another thwack, this one immediately followed by a low groan of a female.

What the fuck? Mike thought in alarm. *Maybe if Gert had got laid once in a while he wouldn't be such a butt dart.*

But this didn't sound like any kind of lovemaking Mike had ever heard of. Mike was moments away from saying that this was none of his business. He was afraid he was going to go down the hallway and open that door and a leather-clad Gert would be holding a whip. Then, after he found out this was part of Gert's sexual escapades, Gert would do the unthinkable and turn around to expose his assless chaps. That would be something Mike would never be able to burn out of his cortex no matter how many bowls of weed he smoked.

Another thwack. Mike jumped back startled, but the barely audible "Please stop," galvanized his resolve.

He almost squinted when he opened the door in the belief that if he was about to see something he didn't want to, his eyes would be closer to being completely drawn and he might be able to salvage the ability to eat the next week. Mike was completely caught off guard when he cautiously opened the door and saw Gert standing by his bed, hand raised high with a belt ready to deliver another blow.

"Umm…hi, Gert, um your door was open and I…"

Gert turned around, his face pulled back in a mask of rage.

Holy shit! Mike thought. He was scared. He felt like his balls had just been dipped in ice water independent of the rest of his body.

A swollen-faced Debbie peered from around Gert's frame, her hand came up pleadingly. "He's insane, help me," she muttered.

Mike became enraged as recognition of what was happening here rapidly dawned on him. The time for words was over. Mike charged Gert, every muscle, every tendon, every spurt of adrenaline surged in the reflex to protect Debbie. Gert was slow to change the course of his force and only half turned by the time Mike had crossed the distance of the room, slamming into the side of him at a full sprint.

Gert's right leg caught on the rug as the force of Mike's dive nailed him in the side and the two fell onto the bed next to Debbie. Gert's lower leg was pinned against the oak side rail. The resultant snap did little to stop Mike as he mashed his fist repeatedly into Gert's bloodied face.

"I will fucking kill you!" Mike raged, his knuckles bleeding and scraped to the bone from making so many connecting hits.

It was Paul that pulled his friend from the now passed-out form of Gert, saving his friend from a manslaughter charge. Gert's attorneys did try to charge Mike with assault, but the judge threw it out. Gert got expelled from college. Once his leg healed sufficiently, Gert had to do a mandatory thirty-day psych eval that ended up being a one hundred and eighty-day stay at a sanitarium and five years of probation.

After that, they never did find out what happened to Gert, but like all things in life, they thought he might be back someday. Debbie went home for a couple of weeks and Mike was fearful that his plan to get rid of Gert would also get rid of his new friend. Mike couldn't believe his happiness when Deb finally did come back; so much so, that he was happy he had given his 'sort of girlfriend' the ultimatum that he had. The girl had said she wouldn't break up with her boyfriend, so Mike broke it off with her. They missed the concert, but how big of a deal was that anyway? Now he was free to pursue whomever he desired and he gave Deb a huge hug when she got out of the passenger seat of her mother's car.

"Good to see you!" He had been so thrilled, he accidentally/on purpose kissed her lips. Both of them had blushed when they realized Debbie's mother was watching.

"Um, Mom? This is the boy that saved me."

Mrs. Branch's face quickly turned warm as she came over to give Mike a hug. "Thank you for helping my daughter."

"You're welcome," Mike said, slightly embarrassed.

And that had been the start of a particularly warm and loving relationship for Mike.

Talbot-Sode 2

Real life has a way of interceding on some of the things we would like to do from time to time. Paul and I lived in the same state, Colorado and we were actually only one town away from each other. I had not seen my best friend of close to thirty years in nearly six months. There was just always something to do, one of the kids would be having a birthday party, athletic event, just plain sick, or the car would need work, or a bathroom needed retiling. It's just the way things work. We would have the best of intentions to get together and drink a beer or seven, but even when I would finally have a weekend night free, he would find himself in his own 'real life stigma' and we would once again, promise to try to do something soon.

I missed my friend. We had literally grown up together, and shared some of the funniest times with each other, and not all of them were even drug-induced. Oh, to be sure, quite a few were, but not all. I'm sure in some of my other journals I have noted Paul's fear of commitment; and that extended even to extracting a day in which we could get together. When I realized that my favorite group on the planet, Widespread Panic, was playing a two-day concert down in Telluride, my mind was set. I was going, and I was going to do everything in my power to nail Paul down to a promise. Might as well have grasped a Vaseline-soaked eel in my butter-slicked hand. But every once in a while, you just get lucky. I shut my eyes and swung. Paul agreed to go. Now he might be difficult to get that promise from, but once delivered, he would never pull it back. Maybe that was why he was so fearful about giving it in the first place.

I enticed another friend that I had also grown up with on the east coast and who now lived an hour away in Colorado Springs to join us for the event. Dennis was a good friend of mine, even if he was a Yankees fan. Not everyone can be perfect. I want everyone to realize I am in no way condoning the events that unfolded that weekend. I'm just trying to relate a story, so I'm covering my ass under the protection of the author umbrella. I had my Jeep Wrangler, (oh how I miss that car. I've actually thought a few times about going back and getting her as she sits in Vona, alone…sigh) stuffed with enough beer and booze you would have thought three times the number of people were going to this show.

Dennis sat in the shotgun seat and was in charge of the radio, Paul sat in the backseat and was responsible for the drinks. (Go back to the part where I said, I'm not condoning anything!) The show was at seven pm that night and the ride into Telluride took seven and a half hours from Denver. (Side note: I did not tell Paul or Dennis this small fact because I thought they might opt out.) We left at ten that Friday morning so that we could get down into Telluride, check in at our rental house, maybe get some food, and go to the show.

So it was before noon and we started off slow. That first Red Stripe was delicious. Now listen, I know it's completely wrong, but I'd be lying if I didn't say that a 'driving beer' wasn't fucking awesome. I don't know what it is: the loud tunes on the radio, the air blowing past your face, the illegality of it, maybe everything combined. So we started with a beer, and then a second, and then Mix Master Paul set up shop in the back seat. He literally started creating mixed drinks. Some grape, cranberry, vodka concoction was damn near perfect. By the time we hit the halfway mark, I was fairly lit. We stopped for a much needed bladder release and some grub and then hit the road again.

For the entire drive, we drank, and I don't know if anyone reading this has ever had the true fortune of visiting Telluride, but it is a lot like the Alps right here in the States (so they tell me) with the winding mountainous roads and all. It was coming up on five-thirty by the time we sloshed our way into town. We were so hammered we drew straws to see who would have to go check us in. Dennis pulled the short straw. Paul and I sat in the Jeep and smoked one of those funny left-handed cigarettes – like we needed it.

I was thrilled to learn that the concert venue, a huge open field, was within walking distance of our temporary abode. I'd pushed Slush, the patron saint of dipshit drunk drivers, as far as I dared. For those of you that have gone to a concert, I'm sure you've come across your share of the paraphernalia police that will search every nook and cranny of your being for a roach. Most won't even take you out for dinner beforehand. Well this was nothing like that. At the opening to the field, which was about ten feet wide, there was one staff member. This I could tell because he had on a bright yellow shirt that said "Staff" on the back. He was busy talking to a group of girls that were heading in.

I had a liter of vodka shoved down the front of my pants. I guess I was drunk enough to think that nobody would guess that I was anything but well-endowed in the nether regions. Between my bowlegged walk, and the extreme bulge in my pants, I shouldn't have made it. I pulled the bottle out the moment I crossed the threshold into the park, and if anyone saw, they didn't comment. I think we could have carried a keg in and nobody would have given a shit. I would remember that for tomorrow's show.

Widespread came on maybe an hour later, I couldn't tell, anything resembling timekeeping in my head had been eradicated for the evening. So there we are in this field that is more like a bowl surrounded by jagged peaks, pretty special place to see a show, when black, ominous clouds began to roll in. They were the kind that screamed 'storm'. I'd occasionally steal a glance at them as they rolled over the tops of the mountains because they were that cool looking, right up until the rain started. Widespread was on the third song of the night when the heavens split open. This is no exaggeration. Are you a kid? Whether grown up or not? Or do you have a kid? Have you ever gotten a super soaker for any of the aforementioned people? Yes? Then you will know what I'm about to say. The rain was coming down in such a deluge that it was like being repeatedly nailed with a full spray from a Super Soaker.

Now for those of you who don't know what a Super Soaker is, it is in NO way comparable to a squirt gun from the days of my youth or possibly yours. Unless you lined up about four hundred of them and just started spraying the hell out of one individual. That is the power of a Super Soaker. I think you could drain a pool with one in half an hour in a particularly intense water fight. So I'm roughly four to maybe five sheets to the wind, I wouldn't have cared if it was hailing, but apparently the band had issues when the lightning began to crack overhead. They finished their third song and headed to safer parts. The crowd, my friends and I waited another hour or so. It was actually pretty cool. Some of the concert goers had the foresight to bring tarps and I found myself traveling from makeshift party tent to makeshift party tent. If you know anything about Widespread, it is, for the most part, a very laid back, Havin'-a-Good-Time type of crowd. There was not one tent where I was not offered some sort of smoke or drink for my travels, and more times than not, I partook.

The rain did not relent, and they finally called the show for the night. The mass exodus of wet, cold, hungry, wasted people began. At some point, I had taken my sneakers off and lost my socks, but the mud squishing through my toes was magical. (Hey, I'm easily entertained when I'm drunk). We more or less followed the crowd as they headed out, a fair portion over-taxing the local pizza joint, us included. Two hours later, we left with our two pizzas back to our rental. We ate like drunk people do, noisily and then divvied up the sleeping arrangements and headed off to bed. All in all, it was a pretty nice day. But the real fun was to begin on the morrow.

I awoke. One eye would not focus, no matter how much I tried, my mouth was shoved full of cotton, my head had become a blacksmith's anvil and he was busy making horseshoes. My stomach was a churning whirlwind of undercooked pizza and a cocktail of differing brews. I had broken my own cardinal sin of mixing alcohols and was now paying the price. The one good eye squinted against the harsh sunlight that poured through the window. I rolled out of my bed and onto a wet pair of socks, I would have stopped in amazement to try and figure out how those had gotten there, but I smelled the cure-all of many a hangover. Bacon! Bacon! Bacon!

Paul was in the kitchen making scrambled eggs and bacon, and it smelled wonderful. I think if it hadn't violated so many man-code rules, I would have kissed him. Dennis was on the couch, holding his head with one hand and a glass of what I figured to be juice in the other.

"Grab your drink on the table." Paul said, motioning with his spatula.

"Drink? What kind of drink?" I asked, my stomach protesting at just the mere mention.

"No drink, no bacon," he told me.

"What do you have, Dennis?" I asked.

"He told me the same thing," Dennis wept. "And I really want some," he finished pathetically.

"Come on, man! Food first, then whatever this devil's brew is," I begged Paul.

"Oh my God! This bacon is fantastic!" Paul said, tearing into a big strip.

"Ass," I told him as I grabbed the glass off the table. I sat next to Dennis so that we could commiserate. Dennis just kept staring at his drink like he hoped it would evaporate. I've never been one to think before I act. "Here goes nothing," I said to Dennis. I was trying for a wicked grin, but I'm sure that it was more of a sickly smile. I tipped the glass up and just started gulping. The cold fluid washed the cotton from my mouth and put out the fire caused from heartburn in my throat and stomach. (Don't let anyone ever tell you getting old doesn't suck). I don't know if he had Alka-Seltzer in the drink also, but the roiling immediately stopped as did the hammer-smacking anvil in my skull, and immediate warmth passed through my extremities as a familiar buzz washed over me.

"Holy fuck!" I said aloud, holding up the empty glass, looking for an after trace of whatever magical ingredients had been present.

"Pretty neat trick, huh?" Paul said as he put a portion of food down on my plate and his.

"Are you kidding?" Dennis asked.

"Not at all, man," I said. I had instantly transformed from one of the walking dead back to a fully-fledged participant in the human race.

"Really?" Dennis queried, holding up his glass like I had mere moments before.

I was already heading for the table and the food, and if he didn't hurry up I was going to eat his portion too. Dennis must have realized this because he downed his much like I had. It was pretty fun to watch his transformation as it happened.

"What the hell was in that thing?" Dennis said as he nearly launched himself from the couch.

"You'd really be better off not knowing," Paul said around a mouthful of toast.

"Man, you should market that stuff," I told Paul, as I mowed through my eggs.

"Nope, because then I'd have to disclose the ingredients."

I looked at Paul like maybe I would beg him for the info, and then I thought better of it. Sometimes ignorance is bliss.

We ate our meal, cleaned up some and then decided to take a small tour of the town we were in. The day was phenomenal with not a hint of the rent-open skies from the night before. We went to the local liquor and grocery stores to replenish our supplies. We must have bought eight or nine pounds of deli meat so that we could make sandwiches when we got home from the show tonight and not have to wait for a pizza. The thought of those cold pepperonis from the previous night threatened to break through Paul's elixir, but it held fast. We toured around the town, hung out with a bunch of our neighbors who were also concertgoers and played a bunch of cards. Every couple of hours, we were required to keep dosing with Paul's medicine; and not once did I feel an after effect from the previous evening.

Our plan this fine night as the concert got closer was to stick with one type of alcohol--vodka; but like all the best of intentions, it quickly went out the window. Partied a bit beforehand, but nothing like our marathon session the day before. By the time we headed out for the show, I had a pleasant base buzz from which to build upon. If it were possible, the security this night was even more lax. They didn't even check for our tickets. We could have driven a beer truck in. How fucking awesome would that have been!? Paul immediately went to the concession stand and bought a half dozen sodas to mix our vodka with. In retrospect, I sit here wondering why we didn't just bring in our own cups and a couple of two liter bottles.

So there we are, Dennis, Paul, and me. The sky was lit up a brilliant blue, the temperature hovering in the eighties, we were surrounded by majestic peaks on all sides. Throngs of people danced to the music in their heads (the show had not started yet) or played Frisbee or hacky sack, or just sat and talked. It was a festival and I was soaking it all in. The buzz was starting to build as we drank more and smoked some community joints. I somehow had the ability to suspend my germ phobias whilst drinking because if I'd been straight, I would never put a joint to my lips after passing anyone else's, especially some of the wookies that were passing them around. (Wookies are unkempt hippies that generally tour with the band. Something I would have been had I not had a family.)

There we three sat, laughing, and talking on our small blanket when this younger guy came across our path.

"Mushrooms?" he asked.

"Naw, man, we don't have any," I told him.

He looked at us a little funny, and then must have realized we started partying a few hours ago. "No, I've got some," he said.

I looked over at Paul. This had not been on the agenda at all. I turned to Dennis, who had no clue what was happening. He appeared to be checking out a sweet, little honey twirling around in a yellow sundress.

"Sure," Paul said.

And then I thought something went wrong with the whole conversation, because the guy pulled out two Cadbury Easter Eggs from his knapsack.

My ever tactical self spoke up. "What the hell are those things?"

Paul paid him twenty dollars.

Dennis turned just as Paul got the eggs in hand. "Awesome man, I'm starving!" Dennis grabbed one from Paul's hand and shoved the whole thing in his mouth. Paul started laughing. I was still confused.

"Hey, ris rastes funky," Dennis said, still chewing.

"Here, wash it down with this," Paul said, handing him a fresh drink.

Dennis gulped it down. "Where'd you get those? I think they were old or something."

"Dude, you just dosed," Paul said, still laughing.

"What?" I asked before Dennis could.

"The guy cooked up the mushrooms into the chocolate," Paul explained.

"I just ate mushrooms?" Dennis asked, taking a large gulp of his drink and then turning back to watch the yellow sundress twirl.

"Shall we?" Paul asked, splitting the remaining egg in half.

"Why not?" I said shoving my piece into my mouth.
"Down the rabbit hole," Paul said.

Twenty minutes later, there was very little that did not completely mesmerize me. Blades of grass became primordial jungles. The mountains were the great mountain barrier of the north that protected us from the hordes of orcs that waited on the other side. The occasional cloud that drifted over became a message from the gods themselves. Dennis, at some point, had started to twirl with Yellow Sundress. It was funny trying to figure out which of them was further out there. By this time, stagehands had started some music through the PA system. I found myself encapsulated in the eclectic blend of music they played. Paul and I laughed at times so hard that tears would stream from our faces. I knew at least I was having a hard time keeping my equilibrium,

The sun, as if on cue, hid behind the tallest peak just as Widespread came onto the stage. Again, in retrospect, I'm sure the timing had more to do with the band than the sun, maybe. Yellow Sundress had at some point twirled away, possibly upwards. Dennis came back to share our small blanket as we grooved like only three middle-aged, white men can--horribly. But we didn't care and nobody else did for that matter. We were havin' a good time and that was what it was all about. At some point, the band or possibly a concert-goer told us that Widespread was going to play an extended show because the previous night had been cut short. That was fine with me. Anything that extended the magic of the night was A-okay!

We had not gotten as close to the stage as we would have liked, but we did at least try to get in as strategically placed an area as possible. We were immediately to the left of the soundstage. I did that on purpose so that we would have a point of reference to come back to. We were in a field with thousands of other people with no formal seating and we were wasted. Finding a particular person in that kind of environment is not the easiest thing to accomplish. Think Walmart at Christmas time times ten.

After the first set break, there was the mass exodus to the portable toilets and the various food and beverage vendors. The johns were about a hundred and fifty yards straight back from us, and the vendors were maybe two hundred yards back and to the left as we turned to look at them. Might as well have been five miles in the state we were in. Dennis volunteered to lay claim on the blanket while Paul and I made our way out to the head. I think he wanted to stay back because the task looked entirely too daunting when you looked over the sea of heads. I can't say I blamed him. If I'd had the foresight to wear Depends and just go in my adult diapers, I would have. Don't scoff at me!

There were lines, but they weren't horrible. The worst part was tripping your trees off and then going into the small confines of a blue, plastic shell that smelled of piss and chemicals and shit, yeah, that was the bad part. At one point, I thought I might be trapped by my bladder. If I had a watch, I think I might have set a world record for longest piss. I got so tired of standing, I leaned against the side. I will neither confirm nor deny that at some point, I might have missed the little side toilet. Give me a break! The thing is the size of a kidney, and I was swaying like I was in gale-force winds. At least, I didn't get any on the ceiling to drip down on the next person.

I thankfully stumbled out from the head, now feeling like I had been reborn. Paul was nowhere in sight. I could tell I was still smiling from ear to ear because my cheeks were burning from the muscle contraction.

"You done, man?" someone asked, trying to get past me and into the toilet.

"What?" I said trying to focus on his/her face, I'm pretty sure it was a guy. That would be good because he'd understand about not being able to aim correctly. I still got out of there though before he maybe called me on it.

Even over the PA, I heard him. "Why is there piss all over the place? Am I stepping in piss?" he yelled, as I evacuated the area.

I gleefully headed over to the beer tent, because that sounded like just about the best thing on the planet. Still no Paul, but I was keeping myself some really good company.

"I would like three nectars of the gods," I told the woman running the counter.

"You have ID?" she asked blandly, probably sick of listening to all the messed up people.

"I have three kids," I told her. "Don't you see all this white in my goatee? That's from them."

"I don't care if you have three elephants, if I don't see ID, you don't get three beers."

"Now three elephants would be pretty cool," I told her as I gingerly went to the pocket that housed my wallet. At the best of times, when I am as sober as a newborn, I fear about losing my wallet or dropping contents out of it. So when I go out and know I'm going to be drinking, I keep it in a zippered or buttoned-up pocket and my OCD makes me touch that spot a good twenty times an hour to make sure that it hasn't found a way out on its own. I will usually keep a twenty in my front right pants pocket for easy access with the added bonus of not having to take my wallet out.

"Do I really look nineteen?" I asked, trying to flirt my way out of getting my wallet out. I showed her the twenty.

She completely shut me down. "No, you don't look nineteen at all, but I have to see everyone's ID."

"Your mellowing my high," I mumbled as I grabbed my wallet.

"Just think how mellow it will be if you don't get these beers," she responded.

"You must have been a nun in another life," I told her, trying my best to keep an eye on any errant articles from falling out of my wallet as I fished my driver's license out.

"What makes you think it was a previous life?" she

asked, grabbing my ID. Bitch didn't even look at it as she handed it back. "Was that so hard?" she asked as she waited impatiently for me to put all the contents of my wallet back together and then try to find the twenty I had put back in a different pocket.

"You have no idea," I told her as I briefly panicked until I located the wadded up bill.

Nineteen fifty for three beers. She took her time with the change, I guess expecting me to tell her to keep it. I waited patiently and she begrudgingly handed it over. I'll be damned if I was giving her a nickel for making me go through that while I was in my altered state. I don't think I won the particular encounter, but I didn't lose either. Now I had to try and figure out how to get back. Easier said than done, but I figured at the absolute worst, I would be alone with three beers.

I found the sound stage just as Widespread came back on. I circled around a bit until I saw Dennis. He was once again twirling around with Yellow Sundress; she must have landed nearby. I looked up in the sky, I guess looking for her falling vapor trail. I tapped him on the shoulder. The relief slash joy that flooded across his features as he saw me was, in a word, awesome, and then compound that with his added joy when he saw what I was carrying was just plain cool as hell.

"Wasn't sure I'd see either of you two again tonight," Dennis said joyously as he took the proffered beverage.

"I knew you'd be thirsty, my friend," I said, putting my arm around his shoulder.

"How's Yellow?" I asked.

"Who?"

"The girl you're dancing with."

"I'm dancing with someone?" he asked in earnest, looking around for his mythical partner. "You seen Paul?" he asked when he figured I was messing with him.

"Naw, I hoped he made his way back here by now."

"Maybe he'll bring some beers too. That'd be great!"
And I nodded an enthusiastic agreement.

Widespread played an inspired second set. Dennis and I had finished our beers, and out of a toast for our missing friend, we split the third beer evenly and drank it down. Paul was still nowhere in sight. By this time, I think Dennis' eyes were turning yellow. I could see a hint of panic in them as he tried to gauge his success rate at holding it or making it to and from the john.

Yellow saved the day. She was walking by without a care in the world, semi twirling as she moved past.

"Hi!" I yelled to her louder than I needed to. I imagined my face to be a washed out version of itself from the hard partying I was in the midst of.

She looked over, her smile never wavering. "Hi yourself!" she said.

"Are you heading to the bathroom?" I asked (yup that's me! Always the smooth one.)

This time, her smile slipped for a second, like 'What the hell was my problem?'

I wasn't so messed up, (okay, yes I was) that I couldn't see her confusion. "My buddy, here," I said, pulling Dennis over to my side. He had not the slightest idea that I had been talking to his dance partner.

"Do I know you?" he asked. I wasn't sure if he was asking her or me.

"We're fabulous friends," she said, her smile returning. "We might even be married."

That was news to me, although I'd met Dennis' ex and this girl blew her away, both looks-wise and personality. He could have done a lot worse, like going back to the miserable thing he'd divorced.

"Umm, okay, since you two are potentially married, your husband is in some desperate need of (I swear I almost said relief, but that would have sounded way to sexual) help. We're a little on the other side of normal, and I don't think he'll be able to find his way to the restrooms and back."

She laughed a warm, mirthful laugh and put her hand out for Dennis.

He grabbed it, and then asked who she was again.

I had my doubts I'd see him again tonight. By now, I was wondering if I would be able to find my way back to our temporary accommodations. The odds weren't stacked in my favor. I was constantly scanning the crowd for Paul. He had been missing a long time. Sometimes I would call out his name, thinking that maybe I had seen him close by. But always the person was walking away, threading through the crowd to parts unknown.

If you've read all my journals up to this far, first off congrats for getting through my ramblings. But you should have a good idea that I do not like big crowds and I do not function well within them. However, there I was thriving. The collective consciousness of that crowd was uplifting. My soul was bobbing up and down on the strong electric current. I know it sounds corny and maybe a little too hokey, but I was having a blast and who's to deny what I was feeling, no matter how cheesy?

Twenty minutes later, half hour, seventy-eight parsecs? I don't know. I saw the bright rays of Yellow Sundress gleaming through the crowd, and like a heralding angel, she was leading a beer-laden Dennis.

"I hope you two are married!" I told her.

She was still smiling, but I think she forgot she had ever said that.

"I come bearing gifts!" Dennis yelled. "And I'm not ever doing that again!"

I hoped he hadn't meant peeing because eventually you'd just blow up.

Yellow handed Dennis a piece of paper with her phone number on it. "Enjoy the show," she told him as she gently stroked his face and went twirling away into the crowd.

"Who the hell is that?" he asked me, handing me a beer.

I picked up the napkin that he had dropped. Her name and phone number were on it. I think her name was Susan, but I won't attest to that. I stuck the piece of paper in Dennis' rear pant pocket.

"Paul?" he asked, sipping his beer.

I shrugged my shoulders. "Did you get the beer Nazi?"

"No ID, no beer!" he said, smiling.

It was another few, maybe ten minutes and the lights dimmed down, the third set was starting.

"DUDE!" I heard from behind me.

It honestly took me a few moments for my reeling brain to put the image before me and match it up with Paul's.

"BUDDY! Where the hell have you been?" I responded.

"I'm not really sure. I remember going to the bathroom with you and when I came out, I couldn't find you. Then I realized I was starving, so I went over and got some beef teriyaki."

"They have beef teriyaki?" Dennis asked as he turned to join the conversation. "Paulie! Hey, buddy!"

"So I ate, and then I was thirsty as hell. I went and tried to get some beer, but I didn't bring any ID."

Dennis and I gave knowing glances to each other and started laughing.

"I was floating around trying to get some brew, and I ran into this guy that had brought a cooler in and was selling them for like two bucks a piece."

"Two bucks? Damn!"

"So I bought like a six-pack."

I looked down into his hands, bummed that I didn't see any of them hanging there by the plastic holder.

"By the time I got the beer, I was all turned around and I had no idea which way to go. So I started playing

Frisbee with this group and then I might have done some
hula hooping. I was thinking that maybe I'd remember where
we were by then."

"Didn't work so much?" I asked.

"No, so when the music started, I hopped on
someone's blanket and drank and danced."

"So how'd you find us?" Dennis asked, still looking
at Paul's hands like beer might magically appear. That night
it might have actually happened.

"I saw the girl in the yellow sundress and I seem to
remember her being around us."

"You saw Dennis' wife!"

"What?" they asked in unison.

"Long story!" I yelled, wanting to get back into the
groove of the music.

The music was playing again, my buds were back, I
placed my arms over both their shoulders and we enjoyed the
remainder of the show. I would have bet money that Dennis
was the most effed-up one of us all, but I kept repeating over
and over at how amazed I was that he knew the way home.

Nothing we passed looked even vaguely familiar to
me. Other revelers walked around us, our footfalls echoing
on the tree lined roadways as we trekked our way home. I
caught snippets of meaningless conversations… "Jenny
wasn't even seeing him…."
"Which way to the universe?" (I could relate) "Is that a
barracuda?" Even I couldn't piece that one together.

A few homeowners turned their lights on to make
sure no one decided to make their front lawns a resting spot. I
saw more men and women openly pissing in the street than I
will ever care to admit. I might have seen a couple having
sex, or it was a lawnmower – I can't be sure. More than once,
Paul's hand would reach out and prevent me from toppling
over as I tried to scale the massive curb when the occasional
car ventured forth.

Now I'm not so dramatic that I felt I was Bilbo

Baggins on a quest for the ring that ruled them all, but by the time we got to our condo, I felt like it. Relief flooded through me as I took in my now favorite, intensely red couch and butcher-block kitchen table.

"MEAT!" Dennis shouted, heading for the fridge. He started slapping packet after packet of various Deli Delightables on the counter top. Dagwood had nothing on us after we piled different animals onto our Kaiser rolls. It wasn't twenty minutes later that I found myself deep in the throes of a food coma. Somehow, I had passed out and slept on the table. The next morning did not bode well for my back as I cantilevered off. Sometime during the night, my head had been cleaved in two. I could not focus on anything. I felt threadbare, like I had wrung my soul through a cheese grater. My cohorts weren't in much better shape, although Dennis got to sleep his happy-ass in the back seat the entire seven-hour ride back home.

Paul was up intermittently to keep me company, but he just couldn't stave off the effects of the night before and none of us was having anything to do with his secret elixir. Paul said that he didn't even think that he could handle the smell of the ingredients anyway.

I relate this story because although it happened nearly eight years ago, it was truly one of the last times that the three of us as best friends that had shared so many life experiences, journeys, quests and adventures, got together. Dennis, just two years later, would die from a series of strokes and heart attacks. Unbeknownst to us, he had been diagnosed with type-two diabetes. I guess he figured that if he ignored it, the disease would go away. It didn't.

And like so many friendships as we grow older, there just isn't the time available to devote to them. This Telluride trip would be, for the most part, mine and Paul's swan song. Sure, we saw each other a few times over the remaining years, most notably Dennis' funeral, but nothing like the days of yore. I don't want to count our days of running from zombies. That is not a chapter I wish to include in our long and storied past. I will miss you, Paul, those days we played football, our experimentation with beer, and bongs. Our voyages to Indian Hill, to our college days and beyond. You were the best friend, damn near brother, that any man could ask for in life. I feel honored and privileged to have known you. A piece of my heart will always be missing with your passing. Rest in Peace, Paul 1966-2011.

Post Script – If you have asked yourself the meaning of the picture that heads each of Michael's journal entries, it is a simple and powerful explanation at the same time – it is his path home.

I hope you enjoyed the book. If you did please consider leaving a review.

For more in The Zombie Fallout Series by Mark Tufo:

Zombie Fallout 1

Zombie Fallout 2 A Plague Upon Your Family

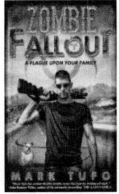

Zombie Fallout 3 The End....

Zombie Fallout 3.5 Dr. Hugh Mann

Zombie Fallout 4 The End Has Come And Gone

Zombie Fallout 5 Alive In A Dead World

Zombie Fallout 6 Til Death Do Us Part

Zombie Fallout 7 For The Fallen

The newest Post Apocalyptic Horror by Mark Tufo:

Lycan Fallout Rise of the Werewolf

Fun with zombies in The Book of Riley Series by Mark Tufo

The Book Of Riley A Zombie Tale pt 1

The Book Of Riley A Zombie Tale pt 2

The Book Of Riley A Zombie Tale pt 3

The Book Of Riley A Zombie Tale pt 4

Or all in one neat package:

The Book Of Riley A Zombie Tale Boxed set plus a bonus short

Dark Zombie Fiction can be found in The Timothy Series by Mark Tufo

Timothy

Tim2

Michael Talbot is at it again in this Post Apocalyptic Alternative History series Indian Hill by Mark Tufo

Indian Hill 1 Encounters:
Coming soon from Permuted Press

Indian Hill 2 Reckoning
Coming Soon from Permuted Press

Indian Hill 3 Conquest

Indian Hill 4 From The Ashes

Writing as M.R. Tufo

Dystance Winter's Rising

The Spirit Clearing

Callis Rose

I love hearing from readers, you can reach me at:

email
mark@marktufo.com

website
www.marktufo.com

Facebook
https://www.facebook.com/pages/Mark-
Tufo/133954330009843?ref=hl

Twitter
@zombiefallout

**All books are available in audio version at Audible.com
or itunes.**

**All books are available in print at Amazon.com or Barnes
and Noble.com**

CONTEST

Back in September of 2011 I had written on Facebook my desire to put out a book that was completely written by fans based on the *Zombie Fallout* world, and whereas I did get some great submissions it was not near the volume I needed to make a full size tome. In the meantime, Tammie Holloway the Director ROP/CTE of the Napa County Office of Education contacted me and said that she had a great idea in regards to getting their student population excited about reading.

What she proposed was that the high school students create art based on the series and submit it for submission into the book. I said "Sure they can create the art, but I'm not judging it." (Chicken – I know, but I didn't want to have that much responsibility!) So they had a competition on their end with about 300 kids getting involved, I told her to send me the top dozen (she sent me thirteen, not sure what that says about the California educational system, but I'll let that go, I didn't want to have to tell any of the kids they were cut, she had to tell 287 of them.)

Below are the finalists in the competition, if you could do some applause for each one, I know they would greatly appreciate it!

A huge thank you to all the students that participated I greatly appreciate it!

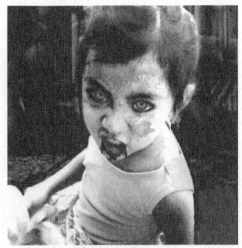

Algamae Ramos

Gabriela Pizano-Euseblo

Mark Tufo

Lenora Oakes

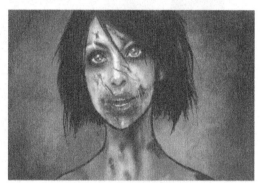

Michelle Sciambra

Alejandro Tamayo

Alise Huddleston

Hannah Cline

Morgan Heying

Alyssa Oram

Cameron Harrison

Dakota Hernandez

Roger Abarca-Talavera

Juan Hernandez

To those that signed up to be mentioned here, good luck in finding your name! (So just remember I typed as CAREFULLY AS I COULD no editor went over these, if I misspelled your name please let me know!) – *Martin Munro and his pups Skye (West Highland Terrier) Keila and Belle (both Border Terriers),* Stacie Shular, *Michael Martin,* Matty O'Shields, *Matt Heaps,* Adeline Becker & Ray Westerman, (Kids) Wyatt, Adeline Grace, Damien, Claire (Dog) Tara, *Cindy & Steve Snitily and Noah Bingham,* Tammie Holloway, *Tiffany Barnes,* Mike Markham, and his Border Collie children Sassy and Sammy, *Jennifer Honemann Carroll (she loves pop-tarts),* Elizabeth Briscoe or Liz (but not Eliza!), *Jimmy Phillips and his 9 month old daughter (future zombie lover) Kensley Grace Phillips,* Hillare Lafond, and her Jumping Jack Russell Jenna, her big goofy Boxer Zoe and an old Mamma Lab Sushi (stay sane!), *Allen Gurganus,* Gloria Bean, *Adam James McKissock (Love the Scots!),* Duncan Sheedy (doesn't want in, but really does), *Christopher Scott Caldwell and Lisa Marie Williams (he's my pusher!...of books),* Jen, Jerry, Damien and Taylor Turpin (he's teaching his kids young about zombies…good call!), *Jesus Echevarria & Rosie Lorenz, and their faithful war dog Gunner,* Christy Peery, *Vix Kirkpatrick (fluffyredfox),* Hunter, Bobbie & Scott Warren and in remembrance of Maggie their deceased English Bulldog, *Jerome Lim (that's an English Jerome and not a French one!),* Kat Stone Olsen, *Joleen Gerardo,* Chris Blackburn, *Susan Cornwall,* Jason Lifsey, *Marty Boren,* Cindy Sawyer, in memory of her boxer Make-a (thank you for telling your friends!), *Gareth John (good luck on your book!),* Elaine Byrne, and her dogs Bailey & Buzz, *Natasha Pena and her Westie Ezio (good luck to you also on your book),* Marty Boren, *Matthew Clark,* Wes Harding and a shout out to his Beagle Demon dog Karma…she's a bitch!, *Peter Mckeirnon,* Jason Waugaman and he thinks his mom Cheryl Graff wants in too!, *Rob Cook,* Rob Caddell & Megan Waggoner and Fatty the old English

Bulldog! (I love that name), *Lorna & Randy Rankin and their wonder mutt April, Rottweiler and Weimeriner mix,* Zadik, Zane, Jason, Roseann and Chelsea Thorne and their beautiful boxer Astro, *Jacci Hatton,* Carol Brereton in memory of their beloved dogs Finn & Sheena, *Gordon Fellis (GGIHHTPTT),* Becci Barlow (now prepared for the zombie apocalypse!), *Linda Bouyea,* Paul White, *Ashleigh Riddlestone,* Samantha Swetman Cato, *Emma Hinks*, Crystal Drumheller (pre 5/20/12) Crystal Scattareggia (after! Congrats!), *Jamie Gledhill from Scotland!,* Ronnie Srdchiko Pacheco in loving memory of Kiko his dog, *Martyn McNeil,* Andrea Piper, *Jackie Davis,* Carolann Carlile and Shivers, *Tim Root and his 12 month old daughter Alexis Root,* Donna Powell, and Poppy the dog, *Chuck Stultz,* Nick Reed, *Michelle Harper and Mr. H.,* Paula Best, *Suzanne Meaney,* Damon Boyle, *Gavin & Debs Tor, and Zowie the Zombie Hunting Hound!,* Daz Hull, *James Fenwick and Dan Wybrow,* Joe Hallett, *Elaine Moyies,* Mark 'Yammers' Powell, *Paul Gosling and his daughters Milayna and Lorien,* Rob Horowitz, *Wanda Ivette Guzman,* Tamalyn Roberts, *Robert 'Galv' Galvin,* Grant Tillie, Zombie Slaying Scotsman!, *Don 'DShizzel' Shelman,* Renee N. Moore, *June Brown,* June Wells and her goldendoodle Bella, who may be spastic but is the sweetest thing ever!, *Dean & Janice Window and their beloved H,* Doug and April Ward, *Edward Gemmell (I had to look up ailurophiles-and they most certainly do not rule!),* Suzy, Corrin & Katie Anderson (Mini Zombie Hunters in training!), *Kathryn Fiel,* Charles Pittaluga, *Ray OConnor and Nandi the Bulldog,* Kalon Barrett Carnahan (Ka-Bar), *Melissa Beck,* Jill Smith, *Melissa Buker,* Danielle & Andy Farnham and Saffi the Labrador, *Debbie Dangos,* Paul & Claire-Louise Harpham, *Wanda Martin,* Christian Wallner (from Austria…awesome!), *Charleigh Deane,* Kristi Winston, *Matt Disney,* Colleen Bendzlowicz, *Isabella Roxby and Dottie the Dalmatian! (get it?),* Paula Baca and her dog Dogo Argintino, Ignacio. (Her 100lb pup!), *Shannon Durkin-*

Wade, Joyce Lewis Irwin, *Pauline Milbourn,* Ernie Hembree the humble magnificent, *Micki Basile,* Stephen Deese, and Ug (I love that name too!), *Tori Kurtz and Ash,* Robin Mahaffey and Duchess the Dalmatian may she rest in peace, *Kelly Green,* Dawn McDonald, *Jordan Morgan,* J.H. Wood and her daughter Delaney Wood, *Margaret Sands,* Andrew Collier, *ClaireBear McCauley,* Joseph Leonard, *Benjamine Fisher and his son Zane Fisher,* Brandon & Roxy Dog Strickland, *Mark Brenner,* Kayla Sylskar (your name is in print!), *Pat & Susanne McLaughlin,* Angel Kirby, *Louise Saddington & Trevor Dog Saddington,* Guy Reynolds & Amaya Myoko the Akita, *Catherin Wallen & her dogs Pickles and Grimus,* Lawrence Challen and his dog Ziggy, *Kyle Lally and his dogs Maggie and Merlin,* Andy & Brianna Lovelace and their 3 lil' ones Calysta, Brayden and Kade, *Audra Spencer,* Greg Lose, *Jennifer Reiman Paul,* Talea Fields (zombie hunter) and yes they WILL be jealous!, *Sandy and Nick Colella,* David Monsour, *Darcie Genetti,* Cat Cimino, *Chris Crinigan-Friedly,* Cayler Friedly, *Bill Fortner and Darian Fortner,* Angie & David Malmin, *Tim Clark,* James Agbey, *SPC Mike Taggart,* Andrew C. Laufer – Civil Rights Lawyer for the Undead, *John Planker,* Shawn Breen, *Harvey!,* Elina Menendez-Kelley, *John Harrington,* Diana Johnson, *Jessie Rideout-Murillo,* Thomas Alex Brown, *Gina DiPaolo,* John Timothy Harrington, *Kyle Sell,* Michelle Olson Post, *Luke Whiteman,* Jennifer Iuliano Haskins, *Debby Zeman,* Edward R. Ladner, *Joe Carman,* Daniel Delanis, *Lena Ann Balambao (actress wannabe),* Lisa Williams aka Darkangel (she's got my back!), *Brian and Katt Wamsley,* Michael Turner and his dog Jack who he lost in April after 15 years, *Sandy Young,* Eureka Delanis, *Michelle Thelwell,* Jeffrey Hoffman and his dogs Toby and Darian, *Clare Espley,* Ann M Gentile, *Jen Gustwiller,* Scott Gordon, *Commodore Mann,* Jason Cookes, *Brenda Tate,* Shawna Schmidt, I think you'd be just fine in a zombie apocalypse!, *SPC Michael Mason,* Katie Splain and Dexter the Lab, *Jim*

King, William Franco, *Bryan J Miley,* Joshua Smith, *Hope York and Lucy (The zombie killing weinie dog),* Wendy Weidman and her son Joey Mannion, *Susan McSherry,* Stephen Hirt, *Aisha and lil' zombie Bell Blevins,* Marcus, Rebecca, Mya and Gavyn Fontenot, *Susan Campbell Lee,* Finlay Grant, *Jeremiah and Angela Huffer,* Jennifer Locascio, *Gerald Hughes Jr.,* Bobbie Ayala and her dogs Bella and Rosie Ayala, *Stephen Wright and his dog Whisky,* Dwight L. Smith and his dog Thora!, *Ben Owen-Raymond and his Black Lab Scooby,* Steven Morecroft and Bruce the German Shepherd, *Lisa Draughn,* Scott McConnell, *Darlene Thompson of NY in loving memory of Buster their dog of 12 years,* Harriett Gibson and her demon cat Sammy (who may just be misunderstood), *Joy Buchanan (I ate all the cake!),* John Jarsma, *Joey Perez and his dawg Skittles,* Shawnda Picraux (fellow author), *Mike Giardina and Wynnie,* Steven Conte, *Patty (or Party!) Quinn,* Reine Ivie, *Nicholas Blomgren,* Rebecca Wilson and her dog Kato (who can't read), *Lisa Corsi,* Chad Hendren and his dog Cash, *Joey Kemp,* Brian Parks, *Wy Bowman,* Chris Labelle and Gordy the coolest Boston Terrier he ever met., *Yazzamatazz and Sadie dawg,* Stephanie Geballe, *Joanne Dixon and her 18 year old dog Gizmo,* Therese Morin, *Kathy King and her dogs Rose and Sammy,* Chris Nelson, *Scott Walker,* Gareth Moase – King of Wales (your highness!), *Rachel Hart,* Maria Bigar, *Bobbie Winding,* Kimberly Bickford Welsh, *Sean Ward,* Shannon Whitehead and her Corgi Winston, *Martin 'Red' Whitehead,* Jacob Whitehead, *Ethan Whitehead,* Kendall Benavides, *Scott Walker and his daughter Aimee Walker (she's 3 and apparently MENTAL and will appreciate this when she gets older!),* Joshua Sankey and his fiancée Lauren Doan, *Perla Tirado,* Greg and Christie Lose and their daughters Aubrie and Claire, *Sarah Martakies from England,* Sandra Byrd, *Sonnet Ozowski,* Jerry Duncan from Gadsden, AL, *Shawn Groves from the Backwoods of WV,* Lorraine DiLorenzo, ~~Chris Baines,~~ Greg Schmidt, *Thea Hollis,* Chris and Lili Cutler (she got her hubby into the ZF series), *Jessica Goldoni,* Heather Renea Eckles and Bama Jewel Eckles "Our beloved Boxer", *Sean Marsh,* Melissa Kendrick and Princess the Cat, *Mieko with his little hedge hogs,* Jason Wilkinson, *Cassie Ways and her pitty Ares,* Nancy Tripp, *Wade Newman,* Sonja Flanigan and her beautiful golden Seamus Flanigan (who barks at everyone), *Kristin Adams,* Chris Reid, *Eric A. Shelman,* Joshua Kolak, *Cathy Harris,* Brian Battaglia, *Courtney Beam,* Ken Vervoorn and his bearded dragon Eddie, *Mark Hassman,* Steve Carlisle, *Brandy Stangland and her dog Rambo a husky, shar pei mix,* Gloria Marin and her dogs Maddie and Molly, boxer/lab mix and a boston terrier, *Jerry Whitt,* John Salinas, *Simone Dover and her son Quentin Moore, who may be my youngest fan at 6!,* Amber Allaman and her soon to be hubby's pit mix Mocha, who would need to get past Riley to have a fling with Henry, *Tina McLeod,* Mike Yuhas, *Vernon Gainey Jr. and Winston the bulldog,* Felicia Kilbane, *Richard Nelson (yes I love the Army, but as a former Marine I also must dog every other service!),* Donna & Aaron Macdonald who hail from Port Moody BC Canada with their kids, Asha (13) and Kael (10), *Aidy Fellows (from Australia!),* Doug Waterfield (who wants in with some bacon smothered brains, is it wrong if I think that sounds good?), *Sarah Ayala,* Michael Reed, *Gem Preater UK,* Bob Mains, *Debbie Watkin,* Brandy Collins, *Frank Sherman,* Katherine Coynor and Chelsea Coynor the courageous dachshund that has never met a fight she couldn't run away from!, *Andy Swanton,* Tina Hargrow, *Chef Jim Zipko,* Mo Patching and her faithful mutts Poppy, Schmoo, Scamper and Katiepup, *Vikki Hammond,* Thad Putnicki, *Brian Barakis Kielbasa,* Jim King, *Deb Yarborough (avid fan!),* Kat Stone Olsen, *Tim Kareckas,* Amber Sudduth and her precious Italian Greyhound/Jack Terrier mix Kalee!, *Faith Grogan & Brandon Grogan,* Bobbi Bradshaw

CPSIA information can be obtained
at www.ICGtesting.com
Printed in the USA
LVOW04s1620070316

478101LV00018B/1156/P